BEST FOOT FORWARD

LAND MYSTERIES

CELIA LAKE

BEST FOOT FORWARD & INTIMACIES OF THE SEASONS

Best Foot Forward takes place in the spring of 1935 in Albion, Austria, and Germany.

Intimacies of the Seasons is an epilogue novella of 20K words following Alexander Landry, Geoffrey Carillon, and various others through the following summer of 1936.

The author's notes for both follow *Intimacies of the Seasons*.

The enemy of my enemy is not my friend.

Carillon wants to do the impossible.

He needs to get an imprisoned alchemist doing key research out of Germany before the world gets even worse. Carillon's cover as a slightly daffy aristocrat will get him where he needs to be, but he can't do this mission alone. He has many magical skills, but not the ones he needs to free his friend.

Alexander is a stranger in his own land.

A skilled and powerful member of the Council, Alexander is responsible for tending the land magic of Albion. However, the Council uses him as their enforcer, adeptly doing terrible and necessary work from the shadows. When Carillon proposes the expedition into Austria and Germany, can Alexander carry off the subterfuge and still keep his hands clean and his inner self barricaded in enemy territory?

Any two professionals can tolerate each other in service of a goal.

That's true even if Carillon has excellent reason to distrust the Council, and Alexander has just as much reason to keep everyone at arm's length. When matters move from possible blackmail into a sought after invitation to a remote Schloss, Carillon and Alexander find their lives entangled in ways neither of them had ever dreamed of.

Best Foot Forward takes place in 1935 in the magical communities of Great Britain, Vienna, and Berlin. It is an enemies to "it's complicated" M/M romance full of espionage, magic, extreme competence under pressure, music, and healing from the traumas of the Great War.

BEST FOOT
FORWARD

CHAPTER I
TRELLECH OPERA HOUSE ON FEBRUARY
9TH, 1935

Alexander leaned on the balustrade, looking down into the foyer of the opera house. The performance had ended half an hour ago, and the dancing had not yet started. They'd finally got through the winter holidays and all the obligations of his position there, and now they were launching into galas, balls, and charity performances. He was used to the rhythm now, how the formal rituals and social whirl of the Winter Solstice gave way to the more public events, before everything tumbled into the springtime gatherings and workings.

This one of the interminable string of events that dotted this part of the year at least had a decent purpose: roof repairs for the main library. It was certainly a cause Alexander could support without comment or controversy. He might just have given his usual generous donation, but there had been a handful of pieces from Berlioz's *Les Troyens* on the program. Alexander hadn't heard it sung since the first full performance, in Germany, when he had been much younger, and the world had been far simpler. That had been 1890, while he was on what was effectively a Grand Tour.

The world had been much simpler indeed. This month, one headache after another had come to rest at his feet. Cyrus had always offered his assigned headaches with a cordial "Can you spare the time, Alexander?", but none of them had actually been requests he could refuse, and they both knew it. Alexander had been back and forth between Trellech, the Council Keep in northern Wales, the middle of nowhere in Yorkshire, and a particular house in Skegness. He resented the last one most, since it had a nosy neighbour he needed to avoid.

He'd hoped the music tonight would transport him, for at least a little. The tenor singing Aeneas wasn't bad, and his youth brought a certain intensity and earnestness to the role that rather suited, especially early in the piece. The mezzo singing Cassandre, though - he couldn't help but give it the French form in his head - was nothing on Luise Reuss-Belce. He wished her a joyful and well-earned retirement. Someone should get to have one. Alexander looked down, trying to decide whether to hurl himself back into the social fray again. He ought to, he knew that. He should go down and be charming and witty. Alexander should remind people he was worth knowing, whether it was because they wanted the ear of the Council, or because he could help with some particular question of ritual magic or translation, or a dozen other things he did well. Being needed, in a particular way, was the control he had and the value he offered. He'd have to make another show of it sometime, and now was as good and as bad a time as any.

It wasn't even as though his particular friends were down there, such as they were. Isembard and Thesan were deep in the throes of the Vestal Term at Schola. Whatever friendship he'd had with Cyrus had shivered into a strange edged shape when Cyrus took over as Head of the Council three years ago. Besides, if he went down to join Cyrus and Mabyn, it would be an instantly political conversation. All eyes would be watching to see what might come of it. Two of the Council who were near enough married could pass through without it being a matter of particular speculation, but a third would make ripples, even if he only wanted to put on the veneer of sociability.

Everyone else down there posed nearly as much of a challenge, socially speaking. He'd have to thread between the expectations and the implications, and make it look good while he did so. And he was tired and worn out from that dance.

No, he'd stay up here with his drink a bit longer. Looking broodily attentive went well with his overall mode, anyway. For all he'd lived in Albion his whole life, he was foreign and different and never entirely trusted. He knew well how that game was played, and he'd learned to use it to his benefit. Observing from afar did wonders for his reputation in all the right ways.

That was the plan, until he heard a cough to the right, about ten feet back. Alexander pushed himself off the balustrade, stepping back on his heel into an automatic defensive position. Isembard would mock him for not being ready for anything. Isembard would be annoyingly correct.

It was only Lord Carillon. Everything Alexander had heard about the man suggested he was largely harmless. He was an aristocrat of the old school, interested in early books, horses, and falconry, not necessarily in that order. Alexander had heard nothing meaningful against the man, not since he'd inherited, but he knew Carillon's lands were doing well, and the land magic was strong. Whatever foibles the man might have privately, he was quietly competent at those matters the Council might care about.

Carillon had moved to lean on the balustrade himself, a glass in his hand full of some pale liquid, looking entirely at ease. Alexander hesitated, not sure how to cover for his jumpiness, and then leaned back himself. "Lord Carillon. Good evening."

"Pardon, shouldn't have startled you. It's not kind. Council Member." Lord Carillon nodded back at him. "An interesting combination of pieces tonight, wasn't it?"

"I didn't care much for the Reticelle - not one of my favourites of the Illusionist school of music. And I thought the tempo a bit plodding, it does better with a sparkle. I came for the Berlioz. I heard the original full production, back in my youth."

"Germany, wasn't that? I noticed the program notes didn't go into the history. Not my period of choice, as a rule, but I enjoyed it. The tenor, particularly. Well-trained, and also a more natural performance than some. I don't mind artifice in my theatrical outings, but one can take it entirely too far."

It was an entirely pleasant, reasonable, and artistically sensible analysis on all fronts. It also made Alexander rather suspicious. Of course, one couldn't ask flat out why another man had turned up. That wasn't how the game was played. Even if he was not entirely sure what Lord Carillon was doing, or, for that matter, why he might be doing it at all. Certainly, he was not the sort of Lord who sought to curry favour with the Council.

To his surprise, the other man lifted his drink in a slight salute. "May I call on you in the next few days? I gather we have some interests in common."

Alexander blinked. "Call on me?" Oh, now he sounded like a first year at Schola, startled to be singled out in class. That was no good at all. Tonight was Saturday. Naturally, he'd promised to go out to Schola for the bohort match tomorrow, and hopefully for drinks after supper with Isembard and Thesan. It would depend how long the match ran, though. "Monday afternoon. Did you have a location in mind?"

"Your home, if you don't mind. The townhome, I mean. You're at the end of Fulton Lane, aren't you, by the turn onto Agnetian Way?" Carillon's voice had an easy drawl, as if he were arranging a minor social outing.

Alexander allowed as how he was, with a nod. "The bright blue door," he agreed. Now, he was curious, and he didn't entirely know what to do with that. "Half-two? I have an evening obligation." It would give him time to gather himself in the morning, no matter how late he got back from Schola.

"Half-two. My actual question won't take terribly long, but it may well provoke some others." With that, Lord Carillon lifted his glass and glanced down. "I see my wife and I'm sure we should make a show of the dancing. Monday, then." He waited for Alexander's nod and disappeared, fading into the shadows near the stairs as quietly as he'd arrived. That showed rather more skill at stealth than Alexander would have guessed from the man's reputation. Neither falconry nor pavo called for it.

It left Alexander to stare down to the main floor and watch as Lord Carillon crossed the room a minute later. He'd abandoned the glass on the way, so he could offer his arm to his wife. Lady Carillon was not exactly a beautiful woman, but she was striking. More interestingly, they seemed fond of each other, which was somewhat unusual in these circles. He could see it in the way she held out her hand to her husband, the same inviting curve to the wrist Thesan had with Isembard. He watched them for another couple of minutes before he went downstairs, handing his glass to a passing waiter as he swept through on his way out the door.

The next afternoon was pleasant enough weather, thankfully. He'd seen entirely too many bohort matches in weather that foiled even his best cloak. Supper, afterwards, had given him plenty to chat about. His end of Schola's staff table had got into a long debate about a recent article on healing advances.

It wasn't until Thesan was putting the children to bed that he had a chance to talk to Isembard. Alexander couldn't tell if she'd figured out he wanted a private word, or whether she was favouring her husband's bad knee. The match hadn't been too long, only about ninety minutes, but Isembard had had to fish players out of magical snares three times, and the last one had been muddy and chaotic. "You go to dinner with the Carillons sometimes, I know."

Isembard had stretched out in his chosen place on the sofa in their quarters, feet up on a footstool, with a bottle of his preferred cider in his hand. "A couple of times a year. Never privately, always a supper party with two or three other couples. They're pleasant, intelligent. They both appreciate Thesan. And astronomy." Which explained why they kept going. Isembard was unsubtle about snubbing people who didn't respect his wife's work, and Alexander thought it was charming.

"He asked to speak to me tomorrow. I don't know him well at all. Any idea what it might be about?"

Isembard frowned, half-closing his eyes. "Council business, or something else?"

"He's not going through the proper forms, if it is Council business," Alexander pointed out. They both knew people often didn't, for all sorts of reasons. But in that case they were usually hoping to lean on a personal connection, and there was none of that here. "And he struck me as a man who appreciates tradition."

"Oh, that, certainly. What he's known for are incunabula, pavo ponies, falconry, being fond of his wife, and - mmm. That's about the limit." The training of mounts for pavo, the mounted form of bohort, suggested a certain amount of competence, however, beyond what the health of the land magic indicated.

"He was the younger son, wasn't he?" Alexander tried to remember. "Couple of years before I came back." He'd spent the years after the War dealing with various diplomatic needs elsewhere, always on the Council's behalf. Some sorts of needs had to be underlined with ritual magic, or sealed, or with various of the negotiation rituals in play, or needed the hand of the Council directly. Not that he hadn't had other tasks as well, and now Alexander wondered if one of those might be catching up with him somehow.

"Not a year I remember much of. Twenty-two? Before I dug myself out of a hole and a bottle and started teaching." Isembard grimaced. "Younger son, though he's done well by Ytene. It's a flourishing estate, now. You must know that as well. Not much farming, but it's forest, you don't expect that. Excellent stables, he's supported some crafting in the area. Prize-winning pigs, as well as the ponies."

"And his wife?" That one, he at least somewhat remembered. "They got married, what was it?"

"The autumn Thesan and I were betrothed." Isembard lifted his glass, amused. "We went to the wedding, which was more or less what you'd expect, but we weren't on good enough terms then for any of the smaller dos. And of course, she had obligations to her Guild and we were planning our own nuptials and arranging for this space to be set up properly." A trifle busy, yes. "Three children. Their oldest, Edmund, is a year or so older than Ursula. The youngest, Rosalba, she's six months older than Leo, and there's Meraud in the middle. " Thesan and Isembard's two children, currently seven and almost three.

That at least helped Alexander place it. A decade ago, then, with Lady Carillon being nearly of an age with Isembard. "And her father and uncle, they were the explorers. Disappeared, no trace, sometime in the early 20s?"

"Still a mystery." Thesan came back into the room. She'd given up on making her hair stay up, and had pulled the pins out of her bun. Her long blonde hair cascaded down her back.

"How long have you been listening?" Isembard made a move to stand, and Thesan shooed him back into place with her hand.

"I can get my own drink, thank you." Definitely Isembard's knee, then. Or some other injury. It had all started catching up to Alexander in his forties, and he was sure Isembard was learning the same lessons about the relentless progression of time. Thesan came back with her glass and settled into her spot on the sofa. "Is there a reason you're asking about the Carillons? I missed that part."

"I hadn't said." He would with them, though. "He turned up and asked if we could speak, tomorrow. No idea about what." Alexander shrugged. "I said yes."

"You are bored." Isembard could tell. And Isembard could tease, at least to a certain point. Alexander lifted his own glass, in both acknowledgement and to signal his former student not to press too hard. Not tonight.

"That is not a cue to ask me if I miss teaching. I miss the good parts of teaching, but not the marking, the patrols, or the hauling students out of their idiocy on the regular. On the other hand, you both, I am sure, have stories. What on earth happened in the match, for one thing?"

It was a deflection, and they all knew it, but it was a comfortable one, all the same.

CHAPTER 2

ALEXANDER'S HOME IN TRELLECH ON
MONDAY, FEBRUARY 11TH

Alexander was as ready as he was going to be. There was tea set out in the library, the best warded space bar his workroom in a house full of warding and protections. He had chosen the larger library, of course, not the smaller private library with the more delicate and vengeful books.

He'd arranged to be alone in the house. The married couple who saw to his needs had retreated to their mews flat at the far end of the garden, and would stay there until he rang again. Whatever it was Lord Carillon had in mind, Alexander suspected it was better not overheard.

Precisely at half two, Alexander felt the slight disturbance in the warding on the front steps that indicated someone was near the house. Then he heard the bell. He peered through the window and then parted the wards and opened the door. He found Lord Carillon dressed in an ordinary afternoon suit of medium grey. His blond hair was bound back at the nape of his neck, and a darker grey Homberg and cloak capped off the outfit.

Alexander had considered this point carefully, since he

got home last night. "Be welcome in my home if you come in amity." He had thought it best to offer a particular sort of guarded welcome, and of course there was a traditional one for this sort of situation.

Lord Carillon's mouth quirked, just once, and he bowed. "I come for conversation about your skills and knowledge. I mean you no ill, I promise. Do you need my oath on it?"

Not the ritual response, but a prompt and carefully worded specific one. The fact Lord Carillon offered his oath suggested that asking for it would not improve anything. And if Alexander couldn't protect himself at home, with all the enchantments built into the place in play, well, he deserved what he got. He shook his head. "Do you need mine?"

That got him a snort. "I invited myself, Council Member. I have some idea what I just walked into."

"This way, then. I thought you'd prefer the library." It was ten steps down the hall.

Lord Carillon's eyes lit up. "I've heard a few things about your collection. I shan't be so rude as to go look at titles, of course, but I do love a book." For all it was a light comment, there was something deep there. Alexander had a sense of musical overtones and echoes, the way a single note reverberated up and down if allowed to ring.

"You have a particular interest in incunabula, I know. Other books as well, then?"

"Oh, yes. The early printed books, illuminated manu-scripts, of course. All sorts of books. I've even been known to read recent novels. But for me, the gift of a book is partly the object itself, and partly what it contains, what it brings you toward." That was also a fascinating way to put it.

"Not, however, what you came to discuss today."

Alexander was fairly sure of that point. He showed Lord Carillon through the door on the left that led to the library, and delighted in the reaction. The room itself was a deep faience blue, highlighted by touches of bright coral red. The shelves were a deep black, setting off the leather of the bound volumes like gems. "Take the chair on the right, there." Two brown leather chairs were waiting in front of the fireplace, the tea on a table between them.

Lord Carillon took one more glance around, and then settled himself in the chair, deliberately taking a more casual pose. It was one from which it would be difficult to move quickly. It was one more thing that upended Alexander's impressions of the man, that he did not seem on the defense at all. Alexander had to wonder if that was deliberate. He didn't rush anything, as Alexander took his time pouring tea and sitting, himself. He took just lemon with it, which was easy enough. Alexander added a splash of cream to his, and waited.

The silence drew out for half a minute, and then Lord Carillon spoke. He didn't hurry, he didn't try to fill the space, as if he were utterly sure of how to pace his approach. "May I lay out a situation for you, before we discuss why I approached you in specific?" His voice was even.

Alexander nodded. It was certainly a reasonable approach. "A hypothetical situation?" Or one that he was supposed to treat that way, even if they both knew it was anything but.

"A real one. The question is in the reaction to it. Who reacts, when they react, how they react. The conjugation of reaction." He waved his hand. "Ready?"

They would not make progress without that, and Alexander had to admit he was curious. "Go on, then."

"I know you're well up on the current political climate, at home and abroad." Lord Carillon said it as if he were saying, 'I know you know that water is wet'. He was right. A good three to four hours of Alexander's usual day went to keeping up with the news in various forms. "Posit a man, currently in Germany, who has information, knowledge, and skill related to munitions development. Alchemical and chemical warfare, specifically."

"There are certainly a number of such men." Alexander agreed. "And more active than desired."

"Quite." That was dry, sharp, and Alexander was suddenly certain there was something deeply personal in this for Lord Carillon. There hadn't been anything obvious in his public service record when he'd checked that this morning. "The question is where and how one acts."

Alexander raised an eyebrow. "Why are you presenting this to me?" He gestured. "I am obligated to the Council and the land magics. We both know that."

"Yes." Lord Carillon considered. "But I have gathered you are a man of wide-ranging vision, about future risks. Unlike many of your peers, you fought directly. You saw." He let that hang there for a moment, then went on, his voice still that even, insistent metre. "You are measured about how you approach them. And perhaps most importantly, you have a skill I need."

There was the pivot, wrapped up with a surprisingly tidy set of compliments. They weren't the shallow ones; they were the ones that kept Alexander awake at night, wondering if he'd done well enough. He let that sit and asked, "What skill?"

"Name magics. The researcher in question, he's been bound by his name. Not dissimilar to some of the oaths on the Silence, but a different construction. Getting access to him will be a trick in the first place, though I have some ideas on that front. Getting him free - that's the goal. And near impossible without an expert on hand, ready at that moment."

"And if you can't get him free?" Alexander gestured. "What then?"

Lord Carillon shrugged. "Get his information, first and foremost. Which is the easier part, by far. If possible, get him out alive, with his wits intact." Then, his voice clear, "He's said he'd rather die than be left." Alexander considered that, the attitude he was used to hearing from others on the Council, but rarely outside it. People got squeamish. That Lord Carillon wasn't suggested further layers that Alexander would have to consider.

"Do you have an idea what sort of munitions work?"

"Gasses." Lord Carillon near hissed the word. "We both know better than to say they're forbidden."

Alexander nodded. "I've no love for them either. Particularly the magical ones. We were entirely too lucky, last time, that none of them were as effective as desired, in the way that was hoped for." They both clearly felt that the Great War would not be the last, as everyone had hoped, not that either of them had said it right out.

Lord Carillon acknowledged that with a nod, and then he settled back and waited. He hadn't yet asked for Alexander's help, nor had he given further context.

"Tell me," Alexander took a sip of his tea, pacing out his own response. "Why are you the one approaching me? Why not go to the Council as a whole? Something like this is rarely the action of a single man."

"Three questions." Lord Carillon lifted his cup and tipped it in a small salute. "Why not the Council? I have my reasons." It was flat, absolute, and that made Alexander exceedingly eager to figure out why. "Why you? You know, of course, that Professor Fortier and Professor Wain have been guests at Ytene for years. Charming, both of them, and Lizzie enjoys Professor Wain's conversation quite a bit. They speak well of you." There was a moment there, a flash of that same obvious affection for his wife. And the use of the nickname, where he kept carefully to titles for regular guests on good terms.

"I do. Saw them yesterday, in fact." Alexander waved a hand. "The bohort match and supper and drinks afterwards. Isembard was a student of mine, back when we were all much younger, and Thesan is indeed charming." He didn't expand on that, because doing so would show his hand. "They've enjoyed their visits. That much was clear."

Again, that brief flash of pleasure showed, just a gleam in blue eyes. Then, deliberately, Lord Carillon set down his teacup. "As to why I am approaching you, I did my time in the trenches before getting pulled out for the Intelligence Corps. I've kept up the connection since, taking on an occasional task here and there. I travelled widely, before I inherited, and we still travel regularly, though it's tricky with young children. Lizzie's a member of the Explorer's Club in her own right, of course, and has been since she was eighteen." There was a decided note of pride there.

"Our Ministry, or theirs?" The question first, to cover the shock of the new information, which explained a great deal about Carillon's methods so far. Alexander considered the options. Magical and non-magical.

"Both, in this case, though theirs obviously doesn't know the full scope. I've been promised access to suitable resources."

"And you feel your skills are up to it?" Alexander posed the question almost casually. "After all, this isn't pavo, nor a book-dealer." The Intelligence Corps certainly implied things, as well as explaining that knack for stealth, but he wanted to know what the nudge would bring out.

That brought out a sharper flash, before Carillon let out a laugh, a rather honest one. "You, of all people, must know the mask and what it hides fit together, but are not at all the same."

Alexander spread his hands. He was, in fact, quite curious, and more so with every sentence. "You must have some plan, for getting access." he said. "How long do you expect this to take? What role do you see me taking in that?" He lifted a hand. "It's been a long time since I followed another man's command." Alexander had fought and clawed his way to a place where the orders were at least made as requests, and only a handful of people dared that much.

That got Carillon raising a finger, and then relaxing his hand, as if he'd had a thought he would not share. "You speak German, yes?" It was checking for confirmation, and Alexander nodded. "You have a minor reputation in art history among the non-magical. You've written a monograph or two."

Alexander blinked, but nodded. Not something he advertised. Carillon went on, his voice even. "I thought we might pose as collectors, buying up art for my estate, and perhaps for museums. There's quite a lot of it on sale, at the moment, and more to come. I'm the money, of course." Isembard had suggested the estates were flourishing, and his tone implied that the exigencies of the global economic depression had touched the Carillon finances lightly.

The Germans had been declaring an increasing number of artists, composers, and writers to be degenerate, and the list seemed to grow every time Alexander turned around. "And I am what, in this script?"

"An advisor. My man for art. If I am expanding my holdings. I can manage my own expertise with incunabula, and a range of other forms. Admittedly, not so likely to be marked as degenerate just yet, on average. Possibly some Egyptian and classical art, if you're up for that. The German collections are quite good."

That was a nod to Alexander's heritage, his mother's side of the family. He inclined his head. "I can muddle along there. How long?"

Lord Carillon considered. "A few months in total, most likely. We'll need to establish ourselves first, and then to get invitations to where we need to be. There's a remote Schloss or two, and the munitions work is nearby. An easy walk or ride once we're there, but getting ourselves invited will take some careful positioning. Some back and forth to Albion, but intermittent. I'll need to be back for the land rites, at least. I'd love to get it done in two trips, but chances are good it will be three or perhaps four."

Alexander was sure there were a dozen complications Lord Carillon wasn't mentioning here, at least. For one, there was the serious problem of how quickly and unpredictably things were changing in Germany. On the other hand, that sort of complication had been Alexander's bread and butter for decades. He considered. "I'll need to discuss being gone for that long with my colleagues. I may, I assume, mention what you've told me here?"

There was a brief sharp stillness in Lord Carillon's face, but then he nodded, as if he'd known that was coming. "What I've told you today, yes, if in your judgement it should be shared." Curious, and more curious, that.

Alexander nodded. "We've talked about how we would

like more information about matters on the Continent. I expect we'll come to an agreement, but it may take a week or two." He tried to remember everything that was already on the agenda for Wednesday. Cyrus preferred to discuss rather more than Hesperidon had as head, which had some virtues but made for lengthy meetings.

He wasn't entirely sure what the rest of the Council would make of the request, or for that matter, that he'd be making it. He refused, as a matter of principle, to make other people's arguments for them. This, though, intrigued, and on several levels. Likewise, if anyone were to go into Germany, he was the likely choice for half a dozen reasons. He was, however, not well-known there, and trading on Lord Carillon's presumed contacts would open doors he would find difficult to move on his own. Most of his work on behalf of the Council had been in the Commonwealth countries.

Lord Carillon simply inclined his head. "Planning is such a help, don't you think? No need to dash headlong. Move along promptly, yes, but better to do the thing right. I thought to leave in a month, do an initial foray, be back for equinox, and then set off again. Better weather, anyway. And we'd need to shore up the background research." Then he brushed his hands off. "If you'd show me out, I'll leave you to your consideration of the proposal."

It was sharply and neatly done. Alexander also knew when he'd been out-manoeuvred. "Of course. I'll be in touch."

CHAPTER 3
YTENE IN THE NEW FOREST, THAT AFTERNOON

Carillon came up the stairs, ducking into Lizzie's day room after the briefest of knocks. As usual, she was at her desk, facing the large window, her reading glasses perched on her nose. From the look of things, she'd been deep in sorting out some of the recent gossip columns, an essential and annoying task in this household. She had her journal propped up on the stand, and four different sets of newspapers out. Of course, her sheaf of notes was under her hand.

"Any comments about Saturday?" he said, coming over and leaning down to kiss her cheek.

She twisted in the chair to tug him closer and make it a proper kiss, before gesturing at the sofa under the window. "Nothing out of the ordinary. I was just finishing up. Pour me a drink, and one for yourself. How did it go?"

Carillon took a moment to soak her in the way she was. He'd thought, many times since they met, that she flowed like water. She was steady and certain, following her own rhythms. Today, she was dressed informally, in a simple housedress of deep green, her hair in a braid pinned like a

21

crown around her head. It was one of the ways he liked her best, honestly, the sort of best that grew deeper every time they had space to be with each other.

He went to the drinks cabinet in the corner, under the 1732 map that hung there. His eyes landed on what would eventually be Germany and rested there a moment, before he poured a glass for her, and one for himself. Then he shed his jacket. He'd have to remember to tell Wallace where he'd left it.

By the time he turned back to the sofa, she had removed the reading glasses and left them on her desk, and settled herself on one end. Handing her glass over, he set his aside for the moment, and moved to lean against her. She patted her leg. "You know you want to, my dear subtlety."

"I am feeling I need to soak it up. Being with you." There were a number of pieces of this plot he did not care for. Being away from Lizzie for the better part of several months was one of the ones that weighed most on him. He'd miss the children, he knew they would miss him. He did not know how they'd explain to Rosie, just turned three and too young to understand. All the same, he slid down to rest his head in her lap. He let his eyes close, feeling her hand slide to the back of his head and loosen the ribbon that bound his hair back.

No, the part that troubled him most was losing the space she made for him. His life was infinitely better for moments like these, quiet at the heart of everything. It didn't matter whether it was a nightmare in the middle of the night, or a moment like this, snatched out of the chaos and perpetual movement of their days. Something about her - many things about her - made it better. They sat there for a good two minutes before she asked again, "How did it go?"

In anyone else, it might have been nagging. From her, it felt like redirection. It was a pencil line on the page guiding the perfection of the letters or the unerring sense of direction a compass offered. "He's discussing with the Council. Said it might take a week or two. I think he wasn't sure if there'd be time on their agenda for this week. I could see the pause while he thought about it."

"We expected that." Her fingers played along his temple, drawing the hair looser so she could stroke and touch and reassure him she was right there. "Is his house like you thought?"

Carillon snorted at that. "Oh, and then some. Warded to the teeth, of course, we knew it would be. He's a clever man, even if we've been putting him off-balance. Bearding him in his lair was the only option, and I'm even more sure of that now. Layers of protections, a fair few I don't even know the feel for." It wasn't his particular area of expertise, except insofar as the protection of his land was very much his business. He knew what most of the preferred forms felt like and the townhouse had those, but also something beyond them. To say he'd stepped into a pentatonic piece, like Debussy, would be the wrong mode, but it was something like that, where all the harmonies worked differently than he was used to. "Very tidy, though. Not sterile, but more like a temple or a workroom, everything useful in its place."

Lizzie nodded. "Well, that only makes sense. And the house itself?"

"Oh, the library." Carillon let out a sigh. "I can't imagine I'll ever get a proper look at it, mind. Very Egyptian, rather than French, interesting which sides of his background he plays up, and when." Being English, back to the Conquest and before, that was a dance Carillon didn't know how to do. Lizzie was the same, though of different stock on her father's side, back to ancient Cornwall. "Black shelves. They must be ebony. It made the books really rather striking, with that glowing blue, and some bits of red, and he'd clearly had things bound to match in many cases. Not at all English, but why should it be?"

Lizzie nodded. She let her hand continue to drift over and through his hair. "No redoing the library this spring, not when you'll be gone." That was teasing. "What did he ask about?" They'd known Alexander would ask questions. It was just a matter of which ones came now, and which ones later.

"I'm sure he hadn't had a chance to do much research about us. Though he mentioned he'd seen Thesan and Isembard yesterday." Carillon waved his hand, then let it rest on his chest again. "Let me come back to that. He asked three things, fundamentally. If I had an idea what sort of munitions work. Why I was the one approaching him. Why not go to the Council as a whole."

"Did he ask how you knew?" That had been one point that had kept them up late, discussing. Carillon had a number of sources, besides the naked request for help from an old friend. But even the supporting sources were delicate these days.

"No, but everyone with sense knows they are throwing resource after resource into munitions development. I'm sure he'll ask more when he gets his feet under him." Carillon could handle that, really.

"And the approach?" Lizzie's hand shifted, the backs of her fingers resting against his cheek. Carillon peered up at her, thinking about how to go through this, watching her reactions.

Carillon shivered once. "I couldn't tell him the truth."

The truth was that Carillon could bear to approach him because of all the Council at the time, Alexander Landry was the one he was sure hadn't had a direct hand in killing Temple. That Landry hadn't been the reason Carillon's life had changed in an instant, when all the land obligations had landed squarely on his shoulders at the death of his older brother. That four years ago, he wouldn't even have dared this much of an approach, not with Hesperidon Warren having been head of the Council for decades. Hesperidon Warren had been at the house party that sealed his brother's end.

Lizzie knew that. He didn't have to spell it out for her. "I just said I had my reasons. Now we get to see how he explores it, what he asks them about." Them, the unnamed ones. There had been changes on the Council since then. A third of the people were different, but that didn't help with this particular maths problem.

"No sign that he'd sorted out - well." Lizzie swallowed. "Before we married?"

"Benton did a search, again to check, last month. You have to know there's a court case about Madam A to find anything about it. The notice in the papers just mentions me being called as a witness." Carillon had done a rather effective bit of bribing. Or rather, Benton had, as a particularly exemplary service. "I'm sure he'll find it before we talk again."

"And as to why him, it was getting to know Isembard and Thesan better. Which you could say."

"I admit, that has helped. Though really, it would have to be him. I don't know of anyone else who'd both have the skills to do the ritual work quickly and on the fly, and who'd be up for an extended trip. And who I could possibly trust to do the work." Whatever else he thought about Council

Member Landry, the man exuded competence, and always had. In those records they'd been able to find, he had a consistency about popping up, doing what was needed, and fading into the background again. Carillon knew exactly what kind of skill that took.

Lizzie went back to petting his hair and Carillon let his eyes close again. They sat there in quiet for another minute, unrushed, before Carillon spoke again. "Talk me through it again, domina?"

Her hand shifted, the breadth of her palm cupping the curve of his head. "You never think you've done enough." She shifted her shoulders, settling into a more comfortable position. "It was the right choice, then. Madam A had attacked both of us. You, in particular, but she didn't care who she hurt. It made every sort of sense to step back. To play up being - well. The you who wears a monocle and a few carefully chosen obsessions that can't remotely be dangerous. Not even terribly magical, other than the pavo, and you don't play that in public anymore."

"No." Carillon sighed. His shoulder wouldn't permit the vaults and stretches of his youth. The scar tissue had stiffened up more in the past decade, even with several useful ideas from the Healers. "And there are the children."

"There are." Lizzie agreed with that. "They're out with Nanny. They went down to the village in the pony cart. I'm sure they'll tell you all about it when everyone's back. We've got another half hour of peace and quiet."

That was a particular protection, being here. The New Forest around them wasn't entirely safe. There were bogs and a few magical creatures that could be dangerous, but they were only about a mile and a half from True Eyeworth, the nearest magical village. Everyone knew them there. And everyone looked out for the little ones, whatever they thought about Carillon and Lizzie themselves. Even that was, on the whole, quite good. He tended his lands attentively. The land magic had responded generously over the past decade and benefited everyone.

A decade ago, they'd come back from their honeymoon with Lizzie sure she was expecting. The Healers had confirmed it shortly after. Everything had changed again, and Carillon had been willing to do anything to keep his children safe. And Lizzie, for all Lizzie was clear she'd take her own risks here and there.

Now, though, doing so meant changing again. Like a leopard changing his spots, or a snake shedding a skin. Perhaps like a caterpillar becoming a butterfly. He closed his eyes, remembering the snow leopard years ago, high on a mountain. She'd been willing to do anything to protect her little ones, even risk what a stranger might do.

For all the time since, he'd kept his head down, let all the parts that didn't threaten anyone show. The work he'd done as an investigator had been quiet. He'd hand over the information to the Guard or the Penelopes or the courts and they would deal with the matter without bringing him into it, even as a witness.

The same had been true for the occasional outing for the Intelligence services. Lap Manse, his handler of many years, had a gift for finding subtle things Carillon could do well that still made a difference. Since he'd settled into marriage and parenthood, that had been mostly courier work.

He and Lizzie would use their social status to get a thing from one place to another. It meant doing things the slow way, the invisible way, but Carillon had got rather good at that. He prided himself on the subtlety he could bring to threading the needle between several complex pieces until the thread caught them all together.

Now, though, protecting his children, protecting everyone's children, protecting the land, meant taking risks again. He wasn't sure he'd have been able to, except that he knew far too well how damaging the gases had been. How much more so they could be, if there were some new great conflagration.

All that he'd heard, all the careful inquiries he'd made, made him more and more sure that something awful was coming. And so Carillon would drag himself out of his safer places, his homes, his family, and he would go forth once more. Rather like Parsifal, really, the endless, uncertain quest.

Lizzie just let him be with his thoughts, though as they sat there, with the light beginning to fade outside, she murmured, "You come back to me. Do what's needed and come back."

"Domina." It was, of course, the most sensible order, and he would give his all to obey it.

CHAPTER 4
VERITAS IN KENT ON SUNDAY, FEBRUARY 24TH

Carillon stretched slightly, feeling his shoulder stiffen. Beside him, Lizzie caught the movement. They'd been talking with the Edgartons for a solid hour now, working through the logistics of Carillon's plans now that Alexander Landry had agreed.

"And we've sorted the cryptography - take a copy of the book for the key, there's a list of the code phrases in case of emergency in the front. Remove before travel." Giles finished up the commentary with a wave at the books. "Lizzie and Kate finished up the marginalia last night." Madeline, his recently acquired guide dog, peered up at him to see if she needed to do something. When he dropped his hand back in his lap, she settled her brown and black head on the ground again.

The code itself was ingenious. A book cypher relied on matching copies of the text, but could be broken if you had a match. Here, Carillon had leaned on Giles and his brilliance with cryptography for something that could not shatter under brute force.

The text of whatever he wrote, whether by journal or by

telegram or by letter, would indicate the page. The marginalia would point to another location, and they would decipher from there. The trick was identifying the same words in the book, but pointing to them from different places. If his copy fell into the wrong hands, they couldn't use it to break the code without knowing the trick of identifying the pointers.

As to the list of phrases, they were the sorts of things that would naturally come up in art sales and the related small talk. But they were not things Carillon would be likely to write about in the normal course of events. References to obscure Dutch portrait artists, frescos from Siena, and grand historical tableaux of events in Carpathian history were easy to avoid unless he meant to use them.

Richard Edgarton was about to say something else when his wife tapped his hand. "You're distracted, Carillon. Out with it." Alysoun was, in that way, rather like his beloved Lizzie. Outwardly, they both were exemplars of the perfect lady of the age. Impeccably turned out for the occasion. Charming, intelligent, but not demanding. Carillon knew there was much more to them both. As did Richard. Giles snorted and settled back.

"It's rehashing the same ground. You know it. Why bore you?" Carillon spread his hands out, and Lizzie took one of them before he could fold them back in his lap.

"You keep coming around to it, therefore it is still important." Alysoun pointed out.

Giles coughed. "You've been dancing around it with me, for one. Perhaps saying it straight out would be a help. Either in the saying - I know that's Kate's line, but that just means she's right." His wife had been unexpectedly called out on duty this afternoon. "Or we might spot something else. You never know."

"If anyone would, I suppose it might be one of you." Carillon let out a small sigh. He didn't enjoy talking about this. He didn't enjoy thinking about it, even, and he'd had to do a tremendous amount of that. "Where do I start, then?"

Giles and Alysoun spoke at the same time, and Alysoun promptly ceded it to Giles, "Go on, Giles, dear."

"Talk to me about the personal and the professional. And specifically, your quite reasonable concerns, the ones I share, about authority and life and death decisions." Giles had been thinking about this. It was the voice he used when he'd been chewing on something in private for a good while, working out all the permutations of information that might be relevant.

Carillon grimaced. He knew they agreed on that point. The War and its catastrophic decisions had left Giles blind, Carillon injured, and an entire generation battered and bruised at best. Many of those who had come home did so with their magic damaged, lives uprooted, and everything tangled up. The Council had not been responsible for that, but they had put their thumb on the scales over and over again, in ways Carillon could not countenance.

"I do not trust any of them." There, he'd said it, in a bare seven words. "I haven't since Temple died." Technically, about two weeks after Temple had almost certainly been murdered, for all he had no undeniable proof. Even if he'd had proof, nobody could have made charges stick. The Council had the authority of a king, in Albion's lands, and over Albion's people, the sort of king that could make choices about who lived and who died, at least in certain circumstances.

"And now you must make common cause. What do you think of Landry, then? As a person, before we get into his oaths and obligations and fealty." Alysoun picked up the thread smoothly.

"Of all of them who were Council then, I know Landry wasn't directly involved. He was an ocean away, throughout. They might have consulted him, I don't know." There was far too much they didn't know about how the Council actually worked.

Once upon a time, a dozen years ago, Richard had considered seeing if someone in their sphere might challenge for a seat. They'd wondered if someone could learn and change the Council from within or at least share a bit of information. But Richard and Alysoun's son Gabe had refused. Carillon would have nothing to do with the idea. Kate had been entirely busy with her own obligations to the Guard and besides which, came from entirely the wrong sort of family. People did sometimes die in the challenges, and no one knew why, either. Too much risk, too much distrust, too much unknown for any of them to want to move forward in that particular way.

Now it left them scrambling for information and context again. Carillon did not know if the Council had a procedure for approving murder. It was a betrayal of hospitality that would have called down the curses of the Greeks on all their houses. Perhaps only some of them had to agree, and Carillon couldn't decide if that was better or worse. He couldn't even make plans out of the fragments of information they had.

"And he's never been particularly prominent." Alysoun tapped her fingers.

Richard shook his head. "I know the public biography. We all do, but it doesn't reveal much. French father who died before he was born, Egyptian mother and older brother who came to Albion rather than stay in France, which suggests some sort of problem there. Some sort of family connection on the father's side to the Fortiers and a few other families. And both the mother and brother died around the time he was done with Schola." Quite an age gap between children. "She was terrifying, for the record, though I was still a boy when she died."

Richard added after a moment. "He was in Fox House, two years ahead of me. But he kept to himself, mostly, or a small number of others. Again, some of the Fortier connections, and that continued. Very controlled, even at that age, though, and absolutely refusing to be baited by anything."

Carillon nodded. "The relationship Isembard has with him is more like an apprentice master. Though I've got the impression Isembard's not actually as close to his own apprentice master. It was an informal arrangement with Alexander, additional training in his school years, before they served together in the War." They'd talked through that, actions unspecified, the sort of thing people got medals for that had no details attached. "A little touchy, I've thought several times, because of that. Affectionate, trusting, but there's space there, too."

Alysoun considered that. "And Landry didn't come back to Albion until, what, 1924?"

"Again, no details on why, but he spent two years teaching at Schola. Thesan likes him. I've seen her with him at a few social events besides her comments."

Lizzie nodded. "At the Solstice events we've attended, they're friendly and relaxed. She'll partner him for the ritual dances, tease him. I've seen him smiling at something, or pointing something out to her. He doesn't seem to think she's lesser, for all her background's not up to snuff in that set."

Giles tilted his head. "Not so much as Kate, though?"

Carillon laughed. "No, differently so. Thesan - well. It would tip my hand to have her and Kate at the same parties. But Thesan will be the first to say she's two genera-tions out of good yeoman farming stock, Fourth Families, nothing at all fancy. Her parents went to Alethorpe and Dunwich, and she and her siblings all went to Schola." Which was in the grand scheme of things a meteoric rise. "And now she's married to a Fortier, and he's likely to inherit, or their son will."

"Garin and Livia Fortier clearly not having children. Nor inclined to adopt." Alysoun tsked over that. "For all they fuss about custom and obligations. It's the hypocrisy I can't stand, honestly."

Alysoun had the same ruddy sense of generational obligation that Carillon held to, that one should do the best they could to maintain the land magics. And she had every right to be satisfied. She had delightful grandchildren already. The Council was supposed to be focused on that longevity of magic as well. Carillon did not know what it meant when two of the Council, Lord and Lady of their lands, married to each other, had not had children of their own. Nor had they adopted in someone from a cadet line decades ago.

"Landry doesn't have any direct land obligations, of course. And he's never married." Giles was still teasing out the details.

Lizzie spoke up at that. "Not only never married, never associated with anyone as a partner."

"Not even gossip. And I think I'd have heard hints if it had to do with men, even if I never heard who." Carillon could be open enough about it here, how his aesthetic pref-erences ran to quick-witted tenors as freely as it did to his wife. Not that he'd done anything about that for an age and a half. Lizzie had been quite reasonable about it, the twice it had become remotely relevant, so long as she knew what was up. He squeezed her hand again, and she squeezed back, quite aware what he must be thinking.

"I suppose he could be entirely private about the whole thing. Some people are." Richard offered that, a little diffidently.

"I've seen near every kind of scandal and secret go by, Richard, my love, and you've seen even more. This isn't even ripples on a pond. Just - nothing. You'd think the man has no personal life at all." Alysoun pointed that out with some bemusement.

"He dines out, but always with the same people, in public. He spends most of his time on Council matters or educational ones." Lizzie ticked that off. "Though I will say he's been a willing ally when it comes to broadening the qualifying exams for Schola."

"I've never known what to make of that." Carillon admitted. "Does he want more people for his own reasons, from a wider range of perspectives? Does he have something else in mind for the ones who no longer make the cut - whose families are good, but where their skills are not up to the work? Does the man like making enemies?" Some people had that as a hobby, as he well knew. But even when it came to enemies, the man was an enigma.

"So. No close relationships, other than Isembard, Thesan, and some few of the Council. Work with a small group during the war, Isembard and three others. Peredur Judson was killed in 1917. The other two made it through, but Landry went off on his own after that, near as we can tell." Giles summed up efficiently.

Richard picked up smoothly. "On the less personal side, he was out of the country for more than a decade. Who knows what connections he's kept up there. Landry's known as a talented ritualist, but that doesn't even tell you much. It's not as if you can question people about that sort of thing. Nothing I heard suggests he's been seen doing anything other than the public rituals for the Council and a few other such things."

"And you must still figure out in which ways you can trust him. You're going to need to." Trust Alysoun to get to the heart of it.

Carillon spread his hands again. "Exactly. That's part of why I proposed this initial outing. A fortnight in Vienna or so, laying the groundwork, seeing what connections we can pick up. Come home for the equinox, then see what we do from there. It should be enough to help us get the measure of each other. And if we have a fumble, it will leave Berlin clear."

The one satisfaction Carillon had at this point was that he must be nearly as much of a mystery to Landry as Landry was to them. His public reputation was pleasant, amiable, happily married, a tad obsessive about his interests, well-educated but perhaps not particularly sharp-witted. Nothing remotely out of the ordinary for someone of his background. The question would be what Landry would make of it. He'd made it clear there was more to him, as he was sure there was more to Landry.

"Right. Then let's go through the packing list one more time and see if we're missing anything." Alysoun remained ever-practical. Carillon was sure between them, she and Lizzie had something for most occasions, but one more review wouldn't hurt a thing.

CHAPTER 5

IN THE SALLE AT SCHOLA ON SATURDAY, MARCH 2ND

A lexander made another pass, sending off one charm after another. It was not enough to stop Isembard, but he hadn't expected that it would. It was, however, enough to make Alexander put up his hand after another exchange. "Hold?" He was getting old, he could feel it.

"Hold." Isembard agreed immediately and put up both of his own hands. That at least suggested Alexander wasn't doing too badly, keeping up his side of things. They knew each other too well, in many ways. It made their duels an act of stamina, each of them using charms and counter-charms to keep going, longer and longer.

Alexander made the appropriate formal little bow. He waited for Isembard to do the same before he turned to fetch their flasks of water from the bench at the side of the salle. It wasn't yet half eight on Saturday morning, and most of the students weren't up and about yet, or if they were, they were at breakfast. They'd closed and warded the salle doors, of course, but Alexander twitched his chin. "Your office?"

Isembard nodded, drinking from his flask. "Tea? Don't have your favourite down here."

"I'll make do." The usual standard was fine. Honestly, Alexander didn't need to make a fuss about it. It took them a couple of minutes to arrange themselves with the tea. He had claimed one of the cracked leather easy chairs that had seen better days. Isembard made one more check of his privacy wards and settled down in the other, stretching out his long legs.

"So. What brings you here now? Clearly, you don't want to run into Thesan." Trust Isembard to lead with that. It had an amused bluntness to it. His wife taught late on Friday evenings, with her fifth years, and their nanny always took the children on Saturday morning.

"Sorry for taking you from her. And your bed." Alexander didn't see the point of such things himself, he never had. But he knew he'd interrupted one of the few relaxed times they had together in the average week.

He also knew, though they'd never been rude about it, that Isembard and Thesan still enjoyed each other's company tremendously in a wide range of ways. Including in bed. Startlingly often, still, even after two children, given Isembard's previous wandering playboy reputation. On the other hand, Alexander could be sure she'd be asleep for another couple of hours, or at least not wandering about interrupting them.

Isembard shrugged. "You know you've earned it. Mind, I'm glad you don't ask too often." He looked Alexander up and down. "You're not worried you'll need your duelling skills, are you?"

"What's your professional opinion, then?" As the Protective Magics professor at Schola, Isembard had a wide range of experience, and these days, he was much more in practice for formal duelling than Alexander was.

"You'd do better in a pitched fight than in a socially approved one. But then, you always have." Isembard propped his elbows on his knees and peered at Alexander. "Do you think either's likely? You haven't said a great deal about these plans."

"That is because we do not exactly have plans. More like a sketch and a compass heading. A bit like, what was it? The thing in Belgium in '16." Which had been a long and tedious slog, more in dust than in mud for a change, ending with a flurry of lethality. Alexander did not object to lethality, he was not that kind of hypocrite. But it made his bones ache these days. And the rest of him.

"That ended well. For us." Isembard offered it a bit diffidently. "Though it makes it hard to keep up a cover story."

Alexander grimaced. "Don't remind me. Why I've got to be the expert, presumably a paid lackey, I don't know. His man for art." Alexander pitched the phrase to echo Carillon's easy drawl.

"Because Carillon's the money. And the title." Isembard leaned back again. "You're the one who agreed to do this."

Isembard was right, and that was the especially annoying part. "I did. The Council thought it a grand idea, and that doesn't make me feel any better about it. At all." He would have to dance around some of the reasoning, when Isembard asked. And Isembard would ask. Almost no one else would, mind. Thesan, if she could figure out the constellations to inquire about. Not many others.

"Start there, then. You took them the proposal, they accepted. You told me that part a fortnight ago. But we didn't get into the details." There had been bohort matches and Alexander helping with a particular class as a favour, all of which were fine things but didn't leave time for private conversation.

"What have you got from Garin?" That was a place to start. Isembard's brother and sister-in-law were both on the Council, but there was no point asking what Livia had mentioned. She wouldn't have shared much with Isembard, she never did with anyone. Bad at sharing. That was Livia all over.

Isembard shrugged, picking up his mug of tea. "Livia's nervous. Not that she said why, of course. Not to me, and I'm sure not to Garin. But she's been even sharper recently. With the kids, too." Ursula and Leo were both old enough to have shown some magic, but far too young to know much more than that about whatever potential they held. "More, I don't know. Attentive to her legacy. If I didn't know better, I'd say she'd had a premonition."

Alexander considered that and the undercurrent it implied. "And Garin?"

"Alchemists talk. Across countries, still. He's not happy with what he's not hearing from Germany, though. A number went silent, or - well. About anything he's interested in." Garin was not one for social chit-chat. Isembard was the socially gregarious one, the brother you went to for charm and ease, not that he wasn't also very skilled in his own ways.

Alexander nodded. "The Council wants a better sense of the landscape. Who's active, who's not, who's visible, who's disappeared. Who's nervous. We're spending much of our time, at least on this trip, on the non-magical side of things." That much was all entirely reasonable, in fact. He flicked his fingers. "Can you get me a list of who Garin isn't hearing from? I can keep my ears open."

"Sure. Not something you can write about, though?"

Alexander shook his head. "But I've got a memory." He did, too, complete with a memory palace, painstakingly built over decades of work, a shimmering temple that helped him place each piece of information into proper context. "I assume Carillon's got some way to manage it. He mentioned he knew a cryptographer. Does he share the cryptographer? No."

"Now you sound like Leo wanting someone else's toy." Isembard smiled at that, then lifted his hand. "Not that you shouldn't have your own cryptographer, I suppose. I'll add it to your list of possible presents."

That made Alexander snort. Only Isembard would put it like that. Well, Isembard and Thesan. Thesan had opinions about presents, and they had rubbed off over the years. Though presumably, she didn't have a cryptographer to share either. She wouldn't have much need for one. "I'm not used to working with someone I don't know. Relying on their resources."

"Which are sizeable, in this case." Isembard agreed. "And also subtle. We've had supper there, oh, several times a year for a decade, and if I had to suggest one of them did Intelligence work, it would have been Lizzie. They'd have made a good cover, the two of them."

"I asked that, our second meeting. Neither of them wanted to have both of them gone from their children as long as this might take. And there are obligations to the tenants and all that. Someone needs to be handy." Which did not, he realised, clarify what Lizzie's role had been previously. "And he needs me for a piece of it, a skill she doesn't have."

Alexander did not have that trouble with obligations. He had no ties to the land magics, not that way. He'd hoped for it once. Alexander just had the Council ways, which were quite enough, thank you. "I never paid him any attention before this. Something of a dandy, always well-dressed, but all about the books and the pavo and the horses." What Alexander had always rather filed as the indulgences of the aristocracy, at least those last two. Books, he understood.

"I saw him play bohort once." Isembard was looking away, now, at the back corner of the room, as if searching his memory. "Just the once, while I was in the league. He almost never played bohort in public, just pavo. It was an odd match. The puzzles spoke to cleverness, to wit, rather than sheer power or bloodymindedness."

"What did he play like?" This, Isembard would know better than almost anyone else. He'd spent several years playing on one of the league teams.

"Sharp, for all it was Richmond rules, not Westbury. He played Defender. Not out in front, taking all the risks, but very clear where everyone was on the field, what was going on. In pavo, on horseback, there's a bit of that, but it's less obvious. The horses obfuscate."

Alexander sat back and considered that, and what it meant if Carillon went so far to avoid playing in public to keep his true level of skill hidden. "And you don't know more about what he's up to, when he's not wearing his genial lord face."

"No. Plenty of pleasant dinner parties, an occasional outing in their garden, seeing each other at the usual round of social expectations. But we're not in their inner circle. Nor are they in ours. Though Thesan likes them, especially Lizzie. Proper appreciation for astronomy, both of them." Which didn't hurt, of course. "I like them too, honestly, as far as that goes. I'm aware they've plenty they keep private. But they're generous outside of that. I've got more than a few book recommendations from them both. A few introductions to families we've more in common with than it looked like."

"Huh." Alexander considered. "I have looked up his records. Apprenticed in ritual, though not with anyone I knew well." The cloistered walls of the ritualists based in Oxford were not for the likes of him. "But an interest in Materia, as well. He spent some time travelling, before the War, he said as much, on the Continent. And elsewhere, after. What's the art at Ytene like?"

He probably ought to arrange a visit out there, to see what he was consulting on. But Carillon hadn't offered, and Alexander couldn't ask. It was bad manners to ask, if it wasn't wanted, and Alexander had built his reputation by avoiding courting that kind of snub. It wasn't entirely necessary, anyway, to keep up appearances.

"A lot of it's family pieces. It makes it harder to get a sense for their own taste. Some ancient tapestries, rather stunningly revived, actually, about the Bisterne dragon. That's a local New Forest tale. Various familial portraits, though they're all exiled to their own gallery. A fondness for the late Renaissance, the sort of thing that's about fables and tales, not religion. I'm fairly sure they keep to the Britanno-Roman sort of rites, but I've never asked."

Alexander raised an eyebrow. "That's informative, for not having much to go on. Anything about his travel?"

"I've heard a few stories, but fewer than I'd have thought." Isembard considered that. "Likely he had other goals on those trips. I know he was angling for Materia on them. Plants, animals, that sort of thing, not stones, I think, or wood. Bringing samples back, or rootstock. I don't think growing them is his gift, mind. The gardens at Ytene are lovely, but unsurprising. Possibly information as well, especially as he went back and forth."

"Fairly sure we're not going to wander into unusual plants this time, at least. We're starting in Vienna." Alexander nodded, though, thinking it through. "So be prepared for the unexpected. Both in terms of his level of skill, and where that takes us."

Isembard shrugged, amused. "That's good advice, anyway. Just - take care of yourself, all right?" That last had a queer note to it.

Alexander raised an eyebrow. "You're not worried, are you?"

"Oh, no. I know you can take care of yourself, old man. When you choose to." That, there, was a bit of teasing Isembard would never have dared a decade ago. "And age and experience go a long way. Just - no one with sense likes what we're hearing out of Germany right now. At the very least, it's unstable."

"Quite." Alexander stretched. "Do you think Thesan would cook us breakfast in a bit?" Suddenly, he wanted something uncomplicated for just an hour. Someone else glad to see him, without expectations.

"I suspect so. Come on up, you can have first go in the bath. I think we've got a spare set of your clothes freshly laundered." He stayed over just often enough they probably did.

CHAPTER 6
VIENNA ON FRIDAY, MARCH 15TH

T he plan was proceeding slowly, but Carillon felt as if they'd finally got solid ground under their feet. They'd spent the past ten days migrating from art gallery to museum to studio, round and round. Of course, they made regular pauses for church art, coffee, and cafes. The cafes were works of art here, as well as a place to see and be seen. Which meant one selected the cafe of the moment with a precision more suitable to a spot of safe-cracking than afternoon refreshments usually required.

It was a bit like going round and round the Ringstraße that circled the core of the city, really. It would have been vastly easier if they could have just progressed around it in a stately promenade, moving ever sunward. But of course, it was not nearly so easy. They went back and forth, crossing the city dozens of times by various means, fuelled by admittedly excellent coffee and pastry.

Over the past ten days, they had made some headway. Being seen was a help. They'd an outing to the opera, a perfectly reasonable production of *Der Rosenkavelier*. It had the advantage of being recent, first performed in 1911, so of course he'd not seen it on his extended stay in the city on his nominal Grand Tour in 1908. He had fond memories of the opera then, and of Anna, the glorious soprano whose company he'd enjoyed for a time, but he was in no mood to make any of that obvious.

They had also been seen at the Philharmonic concert on Sunday, enjoying Maestro Bruno Walter's conducting. Carillon had enjoyed the Mozart more than the Bruckner, as he expected. That had led to an equally energetic conversation with Landry over supper, the first time they'd broken out of their cautious and somewhat stilted interactions.

Carillon had actually felt transported by the grandness of the Menuetto. Mozart often broke through his cynicism, certainly more reliably than a number of other composers, and the skill of both musicians and conductor had shone through. Landry had preferred the somewhat mercurial quality of the opening of the Bruckner, a headlong rush. Walter leaned into the momentary dissonances of the dense harmonies rather than trying to make them disappear.

Carillon also rather thought he preferred the style of the orchestra. They overall had a brighter tone than many, and far less use of vibrato. It was rather in contrast to the stereotypes of Continental concert halls, where the music directors often seemed to want to fill the space with quivers and quavers. The uniform bowing of the strings also gave a more precise and cleaner sound, something Carillon wasn't sure how to interpret at times, and that Landry was also uncertain about. This, though, was why he travelled, to take in novel approaches, and see which he might wish to spend more time with in the future.

What they did not discuss, certainly not where they might be overheard, was the note of disquiet that ran through it. Walter was Jewish, and such a man had no place of prominence in German civic life, not under the current regime, with Germany looming over Austria as it currently did.

Landry was careful to play his part well, and that did not involve offering political commentary of any form. Seeing as how he was visibly non-Aryan in appearance, that was the only way forward. And Carillon, of course, was aware they were certainly being observed and weighed. He simply hoped they could thread the needle here and now, and even more so if they made it into Germany.

People nodded at them, now, when they entered a gallery, as if the concert outing had made them visible in the city. A visit to a museum on Tuesday led to a conversation. That conversation turned into an invitation to a private gallery show over cocktails. And there, when Carillon mentioned he'd not been able to get hold of anyone about an auction on the Friday, the heavens smiled.

His host simply turned, beckoning to a smartly dressed young man with thoroughly pomaded hair, who turned out to work for the auction house. Once Carillon presented his bonafides the next morning, the man welcomed them into the inner sanctum. He walked through the catalogue for the week's sale, giving several recommendations for things they simply must see.

Landry gave no sign of annoyance or discomfort, simply consulting here or there on a piece of art and taking precise notes. He had rolled into being Carillon's man for art with exceptional skill. He didn't attempt to elbow in when it came to incunabula. But he had a good eye for some of the early printed books, and even more so for 19th century engravings.

Landry suggested a couple of pieces of Egyptiana,

smaller and more portable statuary. He focused on the sort that looked impressive no matter where you put it, reading and translating the inscriptions fluently. Then he'd turned his hand to commenting on a bit of Roman pottery before moving on to a rather ornate French painting. He managed to put them in context, framing the information as one would for a collector looking to expand the offerings of a museum. Agreeable, informative, laying out his resources for Carillon's selections.

The auction itself, now, that had been delightfully promising. Carillon had set out a budget. They had discussed it over lunch that afternoon at a restaurant. It was exactly the sort of information Carillon wouldn't mind someone overhearing. He went on, amiably, about the fact that a few of the pieces were interesting, but not quite what he was looking for. There was no way to cue Landry about some of this, not beyond what they'd discussed while still back in Trellech. Carillon was sure they were being over-heard in the hotel by now and he did not wish to tip his hand there.

In short, Carillon was angling for what the German government was beginning to refer to as degenerate art, and for two reasons. The one that was less directly related to this mission was getting it somewhere safer, out of Germany. Certainly, a number of the galleries and museums with strong holdings of the Impressionists, the Fauvists, the Surrealists, and others were looking at ways to sell them off. It gave him a wide range of names to drop.

Landry, bless the man's wits, had picked up on it read-ily. And more to the point, prepared well. They were milling about after the auction finished, waiting for a few trivial pieces to be wrapped up. They were deep in a discussion about artists they were interested in. Carillon made a point of expressing his interest in picking up art of Britain, but also possibly some other pieces.

They had been speaking in English, adding a comment in German or occasionally French when the occasion called for it. Being visibly polyglot wouldn't do them any harm here. Landry's French was better than Carillon's, but Carillon had expected that. His own German was more idiomatic, though admittedly, it had a bit of the Austrian accent, which was all the good here.

Landry's was more German in accent, though Carillon noticed he kept a precision about his noun cases that wasn't always the case in some dialects. In Berlin, where they were aiming, it would mark them as foreign, but their looks did that as well. Landry's skin, for one, but Carillon's clothing was deliberately English rather than leaning into more Continental and ambiguous styles.

At any rate, he kept chatting on to Landry about their plans. About how it would be grand if they could find someone looking to sell, a Matisse, a Chagall, or perhaps come across a Sterling-Wise. Landry was about to make some comment as they looked obligingly at an undistinguished minor work on the wall. Some German artist Carillon did not know.

"Grüß Gott," the man began, before switching into English. "You are English, yes? A good evening to you both. I hope you are finding your stay in our city to be enjoyable?"

Carillon nodded. "Lord Geoffrey Carillon. Certainly English, don't you know? My man for art, Monsieur Alexander Landry." It was not a wrong title for him, though certainly not one that anyone used often about Landry. Carillon made sure to give the little French roll to the rs in the name. "Most enjoyable, yes, though I am afraid we cannot linger too long. Business at home, but we're hoping to return. Perhaps back here, perhaps Germany."

"You are buying, then, rather than selling?" The man nodded. "I am a seller of art, a gallery, you understand? But I have colleagues in other places. Perhaps you will call before you leave our city, and I might offer letters of introduction?"

Carillon knew perfectly well how this game was played. "Charmed, old man. I would be delighted to see your gallery. Perhaps something there will catch my eye, mmm?"

The man nodded, extending his hand. "Frederick Karl Huber." He bowed slightly as Carillon shook his hand. "And you are seeking?"

"Artwork, both for my estate, and possibly for a donation or loan to one of our museums. Or perhaps my alma mater, my old school." Carillon let the chatter flow along, bubbling like a brook. Amiable, chatty, harmless Englishman here, nothing to pay attention to. "My parents always favoured books, mind, and I like a good book. I've a fondness for the early ones, the incunabula, but I've some walls could use something new on them, you know how it is."

Huber looked him up and down thoughtfully. "And you do not mind, pardon, mein Herr, art that is more modern? It is falling out of fashion."

Carillon shrugged amiably. "Well, that may mean I might get a bit more, mmm?" He gestured. "Monsieur Landry tells me some of it might be worth keeping around. The techniques, what was it you were saying, Landry, the implications of the light, no, was that the word?"

"Just so." Landry spoke up, just as smoothly, and with a particular note of deference that Carillon had not expected he'd manage. Not that Carillon would presume on it, of course. He wasn't a fool, whatever he looked like at the moment. "Herr Huber, my employer appreciates quality, of course. None of this experimental varnish that ages horribly. Lord Carillon thinks about the art as it will be seen by his children and grandchildren. As a man of his long lineage does."

"Ah!" That apparently put it into context for Huber. "You are a gentleman of ancient nobility, then. I did not place the name."

"A minor estate, not well known outside my particular circles." Carillon said, amiably. "But Monsieur Landry is quite right. I've little ones in the nursery now, and it would be a treat to tell them about spotting something interesting in my travels. The story's as much a thing as the art, don't you know?"

That made Huber nod along, amiably. "I have a few things you might like, Herr Carillon." He hesitated. "May I ask, is there a Dame Carillon?" He gave the honorific the two-syllable pronunciation, as one did in German.

"Lady Carillon is at home with our children. Our youngest is still quite so, and she did not wish to be away for so long." Carillon shrugged. "I have wandering feet, and she indulges me." He could not bring himself to lie, not even here. But he added, "And if I get up to a few things while I am away, with lovely lithe and sleek..." He did not add a gender to that, deliberately, but let his voice trail off, hoping Huber would read it as an interest in men as well as women. English was most helpfully ambiguous that way, compared to German or French. He'd chosen his words carefully, though. Lithe might suggest men, rather than willowy women.

"Ah, indeed. I am wishing her well, of course, and perhaps we can suggest some small thing that will please her eye? A bauble of jewellery as well. I can recommend such a place." Herr Huber bowed again. "And perhaps I might introduce you to a few places you might enjoy, on your journeys." That was promising. This was an exceedingly delicate dance. Austria was not Germany, but Germany had taken a sharp turn, quashing those places where men who preferred men might find each other. Women who preferred women, as well, though Carillon knew less about that.

He did not glance at Landry to see what he made of it. That would give the show away. Carillon had not been explicit about this piece of it, not exactly. He had implied that the crowd he wanted to insert himself into was rather bohemian, as London standards would have it. He was angling at the generation of men and women who'd come of age since the Great War. He was on the old side for it at forty-five, Landry, at nearer sixty, was incredibly staid.

From there, the conversation turned to more general matters, a comment on a painting here, a question about a sculpture there. Huber was feeling out Carillon's professed preferences - in art and in figure - rather deftly. Carillon appreciated someone who knew how the dance was done. He made it clear that he was just as interested in images of men as of women, in all their forms of beauty.

CHAPTER 7
SATURDAY

The day after the auction, Alexander waited to see what Carillon would do. The man was an enigma, wrapped in a mystery, topped off by a puzzle. Also, he was damnably good at what he was doing. It made it rather difficult to be angry with him, or even peeved. Carillon had a plan, it was working, and it was Alexander's job not to get in the way.

For all that annoyance, it had also been a remarkably productive trip for Alexander's purposes. He'd had more than enough opportunity between the pauses for coffee and pastry, the art galleries, and going back and forth in the city to overhear quite a lot.

He'd taken advantage of being sent on tasks for Lord Carillon to ask a few more questions. Quite a few of the more established magical researchers had been removing themselves to the remote countryside, ducking away from public notice. Several seemed to have actually disappeared, a project he couldn't pursue at the moment. He made note of the names, and who he'd heard it from, and there would be quite a lot for the Council to discuss when he returned.

Alexander couldn't even complain that Carillon hadn't told him the details of his own plot. The man had started with a map, and Alexander was clear he was improvising in a number of places. He was laying out opportunities and seeing which bore fruit.

It made Alexander wonder, suddenly, about how Carillon ran his stables. There was an element of luck in breeding horses or dogs or cats. Or people, like the scions of the First Families often did, whether or not they actually admitted it. But there was a larger element of excessive preparation.

And it wasn't as if the man could stop and explain in the midst. That was not how subterfuge and espionage worked. Explanations were for the detective at the end of a country house mystery novel. Something made with everyone gathered in the library or the drawing room, decorously avoiding commenting on the bloodstains on the rug.

What Carillon did, after an early afternoon visit to Huber's gallery, was turn to Alexander and say, "I've a fancy for the Prater. Coming?"

As if Alexander could refuse. They caught a taxi across the city, to the massive park. Alexander had skimmed through various descriptions of it, in guides to the city. A former hunting park, now with a variety of attractions. The massive Ferris Wheel loomed over the rest of it, rising well above the trees. Carillon made a beeline for that, of all things.

It was an afternoon in March, so it was not terribly crowded. Once they got to the head of the line, Carillon counted out coins, speaking charmingly in a German that made the ticket seller smile, and getting six tickets in return.

Alexander waited until they were inside the sizable compartment, all to themselves, to say, "Six tickets?"

"Three times round, each. Take our time, have a bit of a breather from all the dashing around being sociable. We've somewhere between half an hour and forty-five minutes to take in the scenery." Carillon gestured. "Have a seat?" There wasn't much to choose from, just a broad wooden bench. The place seemed reasonably clean, at least, and Alexander took a place, facing outwards, as the great wheel began to move slowly and smoothly.

It wasn't until they were a quarter of the way up that Carillon pulled out a small book from his inner jacket pocket. The jacket had been made with more than a touch of magic, given that the book hadn't marred the line of his coat at all. He flipped it open, not bothering to hide what he was doing from Alexander.

Which meant Alexander could not bring himself to lean and peer. Carillon might not be hiding this, but he wasn't inviting curiosity either. The man placed three fingers on spots on an illustrated page, something with a man in Roman robes and ravens, and then murmured something quietly.

"No one's overhearing us, nothing to record. If you wish to make your own checks? We'll need to pause the conversation when we get halfway round. Other topics, from, mmm. Seven to five, by the clock?" Carillon's voice was brisk now, as if he had shrugged out of his formalwear and into whatever he wore to do proper work.

Alexander nodded once, and countered, "Eight to four, to be on the safe side." Carillon nodded agreeably, not arguing, while Alexander rummaged in his own inner pocket. He pulled out the amulet he kept for such things, hooking the cord loop around his thumb and tucking the rest back in the fabric roll he kept them stored in. Carillon, he noticed, did not lean over to peer either.

The amulet glowed once briefly to show it was active and then dimmed again. He kept it out, cupped in his hand like a worry stone. It would be useful to know if people were trying to overhear them when they drew close to the base again.

The precautions in place, Alexander glanced over. "A randomly selected carriage, across the city from anywhere we've been since we got here." He had to admire the dedication to craft apparent in this plan.

"Exactly." Carillon grinned, almost boyish for a moment. "Also, I do like a Ferris wheel. Built by English-men, even. The view really is worth the ride, even if the park is a tad out of its glory." They moved up again, before pausing, presumably to let someone on below. "I owe you an explanation and a map." "I would appreciate it, yes. What on earth were you up to last night? Do you have a death wish, insinuating?" Alexander had not exactly been shocked. Carillon had managed the implications deftly. He had said nothing at all compromising. But doorways had been left open.

Today, Carillon had bought a painting, three prints, and a small and rather tacky sculpture he claimed one of his distant relatives should have. There had been no direct offer of anything that might be illegal when it came to personal preferences. But Carillon had come away with a half-dozen letters of introduction, labelled in tiny precise letters on the outside, and sealed with sealing wax in different colours.

"I mentioned that our route would be, of necessity, somewhat bohemian. The letters, today, are to a handful of art dealers in Berlin, at least two of whom are in the same set as our targets."

Alexander wished to lean back and close his eyes, but a backless bench high above the park did not permit such things. He was not afraid of heights, precisely, but this was rather higher than he preferred to be. He permitted himself to rub the bridge of his nose. "And the plan?"

Carillon considered. "We are playing, here, on certain of my known preferences. Largely before I met my wife, mind, it is older gossip and only in certain places. I do, however, still know the ways that one signals such interest, even if I am not precisely up on the latest approaches amongst the younger set." He shrugs. "I am older, but I have money. I can signal I might treat someone reasonably well, that my tastes are, mmm. Not dangerous, on the whole."

Alexander shrugged, irritably. "And my part in this?" He was feeling boxed into something, and he could not label it properly. It did not fit into the forms of writing he knew.

"I do not expect you to take part in such things. Or to watch, or to - have anything other to do with it. It is fine if you are uncomfortable with it, even. So long as you keep the cover story intact." An employee could show discomfort, of course, but not disapproval. "And honestly, I would prefer not to need to act on it myself. For a variety of reasons."

"Your wife?" It was the obvious answer.

Carillon shrugged. "She and I have agreements about a number of things. We will sort that out privately as needed." Which was a pretty set of words that said nothing at all informative. Alexander admired the use of language, while still being annoyed that Carillon was so deft with it. Then Carillon went on, as if wishing to bestow a small token of interest. "More that there's a decent chance whoever made an offer to me would be a spy or in someone's pay, or easily bribed. And that is so terribly tiring, isn't it?"

It made Alexander snort. He'd had people try that a number of times, and yes, it was. The delicate dance of declining such interest without betraying your actual goal. It was never the same dance twice, either. There was always some new factor to consider.

And if one turned down that offer, as he always had, one then had to find some other place to appear to give. Somewhere someone might wedge themselves in to take advantage. It didn't do to provide an impenetrable wall. Such walls were inherently suspicious. The trick was making the visible weak spots something you didn't care about. Alexander's own devotion to self-control permitted nothing else, but it made trouble at times.

By this point, they were coming back round toward the base. Carillon picked up with a cheerful commentary on the landscape of Vienna. He chattered on about a trip before the War when he'd heard a tremendous concert at one of the palaces. Alexander's amulet glowed slightly in his hand as they hit the seven o'clock mark. Alexander himself made agreeable noises, asking a question here and there, drawing Carillon off into a discussion of other favoured composers, beyond where their conversations had gone so far.

Carillon had more fondness for a fugue than Alexander had patience for, though he preferred Buxtehude and Scarlatti to Bach in this case. But they both agreed that Dufay's *Nuper rosarum flores* was a gem of a work. Alexander suddenly wondered what Carillon made of it in terms of ritual magic, written as it was for the consecration of the duomo of Firenze. Alexander had visited Florence only briefly, but he gathered Carillon had spent more time there.

Then they were back up high enough in the air, and Carillon picked up again, without missing a beat. "At any rate, we are angling for an invitation to a Schloss outside of

Berlin, an old hunting palace. There is a certain set, on the edges of the political sphere, who spend time there, and they include a range of people who might be found through such channels. I am on the older side for this, mind, so I must first make it clear I am not so stodgy as all that."

"Because I am hopelessly so?" Alexander couldn't resist prodding.

It made Carillon snort and chuckle. "Because I will not ask a man to do what I will not do myself. Because I do not know your preferences in such matters. And because we must keep you available for the name magic when we have a chance to do that. I, perforce, may need to create a distraction." He held up a hand and went on. "A modest walk from that Schloss is a small compound, the word might be, that holds our scientist and his laboratory."

Alexander had to admit it was a reasonable plan, inasmuch as it was a plan at all. "Do you have maps or anything else?"

Carillon shook his head. "Closely kept. That's why we need a personal invitation. A dash of inspiration may be called for. Now that I'm sure I know where we're aiming, there will be a full dossier of what we do know waiting for you when we return to Albion for the equinox."

Alexander inclined his head. Not something they wanted to have found in their belongings here, no. "And how did you know I would go along with this? Seeing as you didn't ask in advance?" Alexander wanted, very much, to hear the reasoning behind that. Not that he disagreed. It was as solid a plan as one might want at this stage.

There was a long pause, as if Carillon were deciding exactly what to say here. "Fundamentally, I have been trusting to your experience of the world." He frowned. "That is not adequate."

No, it was not. Alexander merely inclined his head and waited.

"We need your skill with name magic for this to work. Similarly, I had to bring you in now, so that you would be included in whatever invitations were issued. But I also needed to see how you would react if I did not explain myself."

Alexander frowned, contemplating. "Because you do not trust me."

"I do not trust the Council. By logical expansion, I do not trust you. And so I will not give you secrets that might jeopardise our goals."

"While, at the same time, needing to tell me certain things in due course."

"Exactly so." Carillon shrugged, and then stood, going to look out the broad windows. "We do not know each other, Landry. But I respect your skill and knowledge." Carillon was clearly unsure about respecting him as a person. Which was entirely fair, even leaving aside whatever issues the man had with the Council. Alexander was often not actually respectable, if in rather different directions than they'd been discussing.

When Carillon turned around, Alexander simply nodded. "So we make a good impression, return to Albion, and then go on to Berlin." He made it a statement, not a question. "I'm in. Though I do appreciate whatever information you feel you can share. It would help with my packing list for the next trip."

There was a moment of utter blankness on Carillon's face, and then he broke into a smile. "And we can't under pack for an important engagement, can we?" Then he brushed his hands together, as if ritually closing the conversation. "I thought perhaps supper out tonight, a concert tomorrow, and then we could make our way home on Monday. Let me know if there is anything further you would like to see before we do."

Alexander nodded. "There's an exhibition I wanted a look at. Both some recent art, and some classical. It might do for conversation starters, if nothing else." He named the gallery and Carillon nodded.

"I'll make arrangements to go home on Tuesday, then. Another round, to enjoy the sights?"

Alexander glanced out the window, and then nodded. Another round would let him file away what they had discussed, tucking it into hidden corners of his mind. They went round again in silence, as if Carillon knew he could use the space to sort out his impressions.

CHAPTER 8

AN ALCHEMICAL LABORATORY IN
TRELLECH ON SATURDAY, MARCH 23RD

Carillon perched on a stool at the workbench. He watched Cephus bustle around, pulling things from the elegantly labelled apothecary jars at the far end of the room. He then glanced over at Lizzie, who seemed entirely at ease with the entire process. Though, granted, she was more likely to be the one here needing some bit of analysis or another than he was, at least these days.

"Sedative, you said. Fast-acting? Slower? Deep sleep? Something else?" Cephus moved his hand to the right, then frowned, and came back to the centre.

"You might lay out the entire range, Geoffrey." Lizzie said, amused. She had been in a particularly glorious mood since the equinox rites yesterday. It had been grand for him to come back, to be swung up into the lives of his children, his wife, his stables, all the simpler pleasures he'd come to depend on.

Cephus turned around. "That would help. You said the fewest number of containers, concealable within your clothing. And you're not taking a valet?"

Carillon shook his head. "I won't risk it. Too complicated if we have to get out fast." He would not leave one of his own behind. Landry could presumably take care of himself, and whatever else happened they'd likely be fleeing together. Getting someone out of the servants' quarters in a castle he'd never been in, deep in the German woods - that was an entirely different sort of problem. Honestly, it would have been easier to manage in rural Africa. Tents and huts at least didn't produce a maze of twisting passages full of possible discovery.

"And how many hours have you had to argue with Benton, then?" Cephus waved a hand. "I know he's your steward now, has been for an age, but I'd have thought you'd bring him."

Carillon settled back as much as one could on a well-proportioned stool. "Benton is honest and forthright as the day is long. We've done a number of spots of subterfuge, mind, though it is a trial for him at times. But anything that requires, mmm, decadence, is not really in his remit. And Wallace, my current valet, has a delicate hand with a lock. But he doesn't have any German, only French, and this came up too fast to get him adequately fluent for eavesdropping purposes."

"In other words, I shouldn't teach my grandmother to suck eggs. Right." Cephus frowned again at his shelves. "Who are you going with?"

Lizzie, thankfully, held her tongue. Carillon shrugged. "Competent in his own way, he's seeing to his own resources. He's got access to a skilled alchemist or three, but I don't know if he'll ask them."

Cephus snorted and doffed an imaginary hat. "No one at all like me, though. As we all know. All right. Are you likely to need to bring samples back?"

Carillon considered that particular problem. "Possibly, but I don't think a large sample." Granted, he was sure that Garin Fortier wasn't remotely in Cephus's class when it came to genius and innovation. No one was.

"What are you after, then?" Cephus braced a leg on one footrest of the stool at the tall lab table, peering at the piles of paper on which he'd scribbled notes. "Gas research, you said."

"Gas research. And that would be pellets, wouldn't it? Even if there are gas canisters, I can't imagine we can plan to bring them back. I don't know if they've actually got that far, though."

Cephus tapped his fingers. "So a couple of sealed containers. You remember the trick with the beeswax?"

"And the charm, and the incantation, yes." Carillon didn't mind Cephus checking. It was absolutely critical in his line of work. Both of their lines of work.

Lizzie added, "Already packed the candle kit." Fortunately, your average remote German hunting lodge still didn't have reliable electricity or even gas lights. Packing your own spare candles was just sensible and would not attract much attention.

"Right." Then there was a flurry of scribbling, the sort of thing that produced a chain of linked boxes with arrows between them. "Sedative, varying forms. We can get a fair bit of that with pastilles. Perhaps more like homœopathic sugar pills. Choose the dose you want. Memory?"

"If I need something that blanks someone's memory and don't have it, it's going to be awful." Carillon hated using the things, but there were times when it was exceedingly helpful to insert a couple of hours of amiable vacancy in someone's head. "Got something better than last time? The bitterness is hard to hide."

"You're going to be in Germany. Surely they appreciate bitter?" Cephus waved his hand. "No, no, I see the point. I had one more revision, need to find someone to test it on, which is going to be tricky in what, a week?"

"A week before we leave. I need to be back for May Day, of course, so we've got about a month."

"All in one fell swoop, then, or do you need another trip?"

Carillon flicked his fingers. "Hoping to do it all in April. I don't like how things are going in Germany one bit, and neither does our scientist."

"Do you trust him?" Cephus stood, standing and peering at a row of amber jars, lined up in tiny, accurate rows.

"I do." Carillon hadn't seen him for, what, a dozen years now, but he trusted him.

"And you say he'd rather die than be left there? I can do something about that. Easy enough to plant somewhere he can get to it. But if it's found on him, it might be - identifying. Or if he handed it over for analysis, willingly or otherwise. Capsule, not liquid, so no residue if he takes it."

Carillon nodded. "I'll only give it to him if he's got that much choice about it." He felt, on the whole, that letting a man choose the manner of his death was sometimes the only gift you could offer. And Berthold had been very clear about his preference there.

"Just so." Cephus pulled out several of the wax-stoppered vials and turned to put them on the lab bench in a small rack. "I'll have something in three days for that. Usual in terms of protective powders, warnings, and all that?"

"Please, yes." Cephus had come up with a fascinating powder that could be sprinkled on one's food to identify harmful agents, broadly defined. It was most handy - and readily applied using an antique poison ring. He'd have to check with Landry about his own accoutrements on that front.

"Anything else?" Cephus would be deep in his work inside half an hour. Carillon knew the expression.

He cleared his throat. He'd already mentioned this to Lizzie, of course, and so she was sitting there beside him, just waiting. "Something that mimics the goldwasser, if you would. As closely as possible, without causing problems for the dragons or for anyone exposed."

"Euphoric, hallucinogenic, a touch of muscle relaxant. I don't know that I'll be able to get the travel fixation in there, but I might have an idea. Or you'll have to do it by suggestion. Do you care about the colour?"

"If you can get the glow of it, that would be quite handy. It doesn't need to be gold, but it would mean I didn't have to come up with a new name. Something that would take a charm for long enough would be fine. A couple of hours." Carillon waved a hand. "I can handle the suggestion if needed. Something to make that easier would be welcome, of course."

Cephus came back to the lab table and scribbled several things. "Magical household? How much? A bottle? A case? Do you expect other folks to search your room?"

"Non-magical household to start, probably, but don't assume we're the only ones who are. And we should end up somewhere magical, depending how things fall out. At least four bottles, if we're treating it like wine, a minimum of two if you can get a liqueur. Easier to travel with, that. And I'd be surprised if they don't." Carillon replied just as promptly.

Lizzie said, "We are sending him with only the best underthings, nothing mended." Her tone was so pleasant that it took both men a moment to realise what she'd said, and Carillon snorted.

"Well, can't let the image slip. Even if he's not taking a man." Cephus nodded. "Right. Got what I need. Go away now. Three days for most of it, may need a couple more for the sedatives. Tricky to tier the dosing right. I'll let you know about the memory potion, but if I can't do it in time, you'll just have to add some sugar or something."

Carillon stood and offered his arm to Lizzie. "Anything you want before we go home?" Still such glorious words, to have a home to go to. She shook her head. "Cephus, I'll have some more for you, analysis, when Geoffrey's gone again."

"You may make free with my diary, m'lady." Cephus half-doffed the imaginary hat again, and then bent over the lab bench, ignoring them immediately.

Getting back to Ytene was simple, and for once no one urgently needed his input on any decision. It was a Saturday, so while there were stable hands around - the care of the horses was unending - there was no active training in progress. Rufus would be in his house, with his own children, enjoying the afternoon. Or perhaps out in the Forest, enjoying the spring.

Lizzie tugged him along to her office, nudging the door closed with her hip. "No surprises there, my dear subtlety."

"Even about giving a man a deadly poison in case he's trapped?" Carillon had been a little unsure of how she would take that one.

"You are kinder than you admit to, Geoffrey." She leaned to kiss his nose, then took his hands to bring him with her to the chaise under the window. He let her sit, admiring how she moved. Her high-waisted skirt flattered the length of her legs, and the blouse brought attention to her face. He let it soak in, knowing he would have to steel himself for weeks away from her. She caught that shift in mood and nudged him with a foot. "Sit, love." He sat, of course. He tried not to be an idiot.

"I will miss you. For all the obvious reasons, Lizzie, but for your sense. I don't—" Carillon hesitated.

"You don't know Landry. You certainly don't trust him. And he's decidedly neither me, nor is he Benton. I'd feel better if we were going, but I'd need an entirely new wardrobe, the sort that takes weeks to work up. And you're right that Benton would manage much of it admirably and stumble over his honesty." Lizzie considered. "We haven't really got into it. How was he?"

"Landry?" Carillon sighed, and shifted, settling his head in Lizzie's lap, her hand automatically settling on his head. "Competent. Sharp. Didn't jog my elbow at all, and yes, that's a compliment and a mark in his favour. Very good on art, even with little direct preparation. I don't disagree with nearly as many of his opinions about music as I thought I might." He shrugged. "And I'm sure he got a fair bit of the news he was aiming for. We certainly heard plenty of fragments of gossip."

"So," Lizzie agreed, amused, "You might manage to make this work. At least when it comes to your part and his."

"I am more hopeful than I was. And I really can't think of anyone else who could pull off the naming magic. It's a finicky slippery eel of a rite." Carillon had done his fair share of tricksy ritual workings. More than his share, truly. But what Berthold had got out, in a complex and limited code, had clarified that they needed someone with a particular knack. And moreover, the ability to do the work on the fly and adapt at need.

Not someone Carillon otherwise had on tap. Nor had

the Edgartons or the Leftons or Cephus, or any of the others they had consulted. Which meant there were very few in Albion with the skill.

"Have you heard anything from him?" Lizzie asked, almost casually, but he grinned up at her.

"He appreciated your dossier exceedingly much, not that I told him it was your work, of course. He noted that I appear to know how to be actually informative. I do believe I made him cranky. Though, to be fair, twenty minutes of partial information on a Ferris wheel is in fact rather low, for a week's effort."

"You would also be cranky in that situation." Lizzie brushed her fingers over his cheek. "I am glad he approves of my work, then. And you have time to discuss it with him before you go back to Germany."

"Mm-hmm." Carillon let out a long, slow breath. "He's staying with the Fortiers. Isembard and Thesan, I mean, in Essex. Not out at Arundel."

Lizzie wrinkled her nose. "Well, I should hope so." She did not care for Garin or Livia Fortier, neither of whom appreciated travel. Among their other failings. "Are you meeting him there, or is he coming here?"

"He asked for his townhouse. Trellech on Tuesday. If you have any little errands?"

"I may send you with a list." Lizzie agreed. "For the moment, though, we have an hour or two before the children demand teatime amusements. I am sure we can find some suitable way to spend it. Books, bed, or both?"

"Both, domina. Both."

CHAPTER 9
ISEMBARD AND THESAN'S HOME IN ESSEX
ON SUNDAY, MARCH 24TH

Alexander flicked over the page of the book he wasn't reading. And then the next one. He knew he was out of sorts, and he was fairly sure it showed. Now that the distractions of the equinox rituals were over, he had fallen into an irritable funk, the sort that meant he'd been unsettled for three days.

He heard Isembard's steps before anything else. Alexander was tucked into the leftmost of the three chairs by the library windows. He'd seen glimpses of Thesan, Isembard, and their children go by out the window for the past hour. Well, mostly Ursula, who at seven was old enough to stay on her own little dappled grey pony more of the time than not. Leo had his few moments balanced in the saddle, but at three was not remotely riding by himself. The pony was a delight with children and a terror with anyone else, which just made Alexander think of Carillon and grimace.

"It can't be the book." Isembard paused by the drinks cabinet. "Drink?" He peered at the glass on the table by Alexander's hand. "Refill?"

"It's just tonic water. I could use something if you're pouring. Something sharp."

"Moment." Alexander could hear the burble of liquid, the hiss of the tonic syphon, the clink of ice. "Thesan will be down in a minute. She wanted to change. Unless you want me to tell her to give us a bit?"

That made Alexander peer over his shoulder. "Not you, too? No. It's fine. Or at least, it doesn't make a difference if she's here or not. It is your library, and I know she has notes spread out." He had at least settled back quickly into the routine of holidays with them, as they had established over the past decade. It was usually a pleasure to spend the time in a comfortable and compatible sprawl of books, conversations, a spot of duelling. Perhaps he'd add a ride or walk every day, along with wide-ranging conversations, and quite good food.

"Not me too, what?" Isembard came over, a glass in each hand. Alexander took the one Isembard offered. He drank, feeling the bitterness balance something out. Perhaps also the alcohol. Isembard set the other down on the table between the two empty chairs and went back to collect his own.

Alexander considered. He could discuss this knot in his head. He could avoid discussing it. But this was Isembard, who had already seen and remarked on his discontent. And Thesan would be along shortly, and she worried. More at the moment, for all she didn't expect him to actually tell her what he was up to.

But of all the people in the world, this was the place that felt most like people wanted him around. Made space for him. It was also uneasy. He and Isembard had so much history together, both good and bad. They were grown men. They'd sorted enough of it out. But they had once been teacher and student, back when Isembard was barely at Schola, and that kept changing things under his feet. And then he'd been responsible for Isembard's life, for four lives, as their commanding officer, and that changed things too.

Even leaving aside Perry, and he knew that Perry's death had shattered Isembard too. Differently, but no less thoroughly. Alexander was sure Isembard blamed himself, and blamed Alexander, and he was never sure of the balance of those two things in any given moment.

It made him think, though. Carillon wasn't that much older than Isembard, a decade older than Thesan. And yet, Alexander had no difficulty treating him as a peer in experience, in every sense of the word. Although he barely knew the man. He had been so frustratingly in control of every interaction from his approach at the opera forward. Alexander grunted again and drank a bit more of his gin and tonic.

"I'm fairly sure you'll bite my head off if I ask what has you in such a mood." Isembard settled in the further chair, leaving the middle one for Thesan. Who was, admittedly, at somewhat less risk of Alexander's temper.

"Carillon." Alexander rolled the name around in his head. "Lord Geoffrey Ambrosius Ardington Carillon." A moment later, he heard Thesan's steps. She had changed into a relaxed day dress in green.

"You make him sound like a stubborn five-year-old. Alternately, a young man of seventeen, sure he can rule the world." Thesan settled down and smiled sunnily at her husband. "Why?"

"Because he is being annoyingly competent. And I do not understand."

He didn't miss the glance they exchanged. It was the problem with them, really. They'd been married nearly a decade, and unlike many couples of their social standing and influence, they actually thrived on each other's company. Good thing too, seeing how closely they worked together during term time, and how much they saw of each other, in all sorts of moods and seasons. He leaned back and waited to see what they'd actually ask. And who would take the risk.

A moment later, Thesan shifted. "What can you tell us about the sky in your head, then?" She could be trusted to go for the astronomical metaphor, of course, that was her field and her joy.

"I am rather having the..." He considered. "Posit a planet we had no idea about, having influence over the sky in ways we know must have been there for millennia. If not, perhaps, at all obviously."

"So, Pluto, then." Thesan grinned at him, utterly unrepentant. She knew he knew the theory there, for that still recently discovered planet. And they'd wrangled amiably about all the theories about Planet X before that.

It drove Alexander to a long string of Arabic, the best of his languages for swearing by far. Even if he knew Thesan would follow a fair bit of it. She leaned back and waited him out. "Pluto doesn't have much influence, does it?"

"It depends on how you define influence, don't you think?" Thesan pointed out. "Which might well apply in this case. You've been complaining that you weren't sure what to expect from him." She lifted her glass. "Who else are you going to talk to about it, if not us?"

"You continue to be annoyingly right." But Alexander nodded. "He has been undeniably in control of this particular dance from the beginning. Even his approach. I have no idea how he knew he might find me at the opera that night."

Thesan considered. "Lizzie is on the committee that chose the music. Though I don't know how much influence she had on the choices."

Alexander filed it away. More things he might never know. "At any rate, he has been entirely in charge of all of it. He is frustratingly good, too. It would be one thing if he were stepping wrong, but he's not. Other than not telling me things I would, if pressed, admit I do not need to know. Yet. That it would be a risk for me to know."

Isembard leaned forward. "You mean he outmanoeuvred you." He tilted his head. "I don't think I've ever seen that last long before. Rellington's Fifth or Hellephont's Third?" There was a mingled note of uncertainty there, like the great fallen statues in the Egyptian desert, with Isembard's fascination with the idea.

"Hellephont's Third." It was a manoeuvre, ironically enough, that he had taught Isembard, ages ago. And which Isembard had once used to save Alexander's life. Or that they'd used to save each other's lives. It was one of those things where you had to trust the other person to move exactly as expected.

"Well, no wonder you're as cranky as Leo when he hasn't had a nap." Isembard did not actually duck after he said it, but he realised he'd pressed a tad too far. "Pax?"

"I am cranky." It felt better to say. "The man's an Owl. All about his decorous academic interests. Incunabula. A spot of music. Even pavo. Nothing notable in the past decade. A few comments from people before that, and I do not know what he might have got up to in his travels. I'm beginning to wonder."

"No useful contacts in those halls?" Isembard leaned back, using all the small tricks they both knew to show he would not press further.

"For a long time, I was those halls, you. Or near enough. And I never came across him, or signs of his presence that I can recall. Though, to be fair, I spent a lot of the time he was wandering the globe in America and Canada." Among other places.

Thesan cleared her throat, and Alexander glanced over at her. "You know we've talked about Houses. Endlessly." She flicked her fingers. "And how you might have been better suited in Owl. We certainly know how you feel about having been sorted into Fox." Fox, with all its social manipulations and ambitions, its reaching for power in many forms. Alexander had risen to that challenge, and well. But it had bent and woven him into a particular shape. Near broke him, even if he could only admit that to himself in the darkest private bits of his soul.

Before Alexander could reply, Isembard followed up, as if they'd planned it, with "And you know how everyone assumes that someone of that sort of background must be Fox. Where else would a decent person be?"

It hit him then that Carillon was a mirror, showing what Alexander's life might have been if people hadn't shoved him into a box that had never fit. What that flexible curiosity of mind could do, if it was turned to something other than power and ambition and manipulation. Mercury's quickness in counterpoint against Jupiter's expansion without restraint. He would not bring that up. He did not care to get a half-hour lecture on the limitations of the system, even if he agreed with Thesan on all points in this case.

He stood abruptly, almost hurling the glass to the floor as he set it down too hard and it skittered across the table. Alexander stalked over to the far corner of the library to get a grip on his temper. Neither of them followed him, neither spoke. He stood there, breathing as hard as if he'd been duelling for half an hour, his hands clenching against his legs.

It took him a good ten minutes to get himself to a point that would not explode in his face as soon as anyone spoke, including him. Behind him, neither Isembard nor Thesan moved, though they, at least, had experience with student fits of the kind. Finally, he came back and settled himself precisely in the chair. "What I might have been in a different life, then."

It cut like a wound to his heart. Seeing it. Knowing it was possible for someone to be that sure of himself, that confident in his skills. He wanted, desperately, to be around that, to see if it rubbed off. And he wanted nothing to do with it, with the way it scraped him raw. The man was, what, a dozen years younger. How did he have a confidence Alexander had never had?

Thesan hesitated for a moment, and she didn't look at Isembard. "Not what Perry would have been. But what you wanted for him, in his own way."

Perry, his chosen heir. Isembard's best friend from their first year at school. Perry who had died. Whose body they had barely got back. Perry, whose grave he couldn't visit, because his parents blamed Alexander, rightfully, for the whole mess. Perry, who had had all that glorious certainty, but who had been a Fox through and through, from the very beginning.

Alexander hated it, but it was true. And the work of his life, as much as he had one, demanded that honesty, brutal as it was. He nodded once. He couldn't manage more than that. His throat was a lump, he could barely take a breath.

Again, they gave him time. The horrible and necessary gift of time, not hurrying him. He was an excellent teacher in the classroom, as they were. But they had long surpassed him - both of them, Isembard, as well - in this symphony of comment and silences. The quiet carried even more meaning than the sound, the questions, the words.

Finally, he coughed, feeling like he'd run a race, as if his body would catch him up with aches and pains and agony as soon as he paused. "You have a gramophone? Records? Symphonies. Mozart, by preference. Bruckner. Or, mm. Buxtehude. Scarlatti."

"Of course." Isembard leaned forward again. "Down in the music room, but we can bring it somewhere else. Here?"

"My rooms, please. I may not be down for supper." Alexander stood up. "I'm not angry at you. Either of you. I'm angry at the world."

Thesan spread her hands. "You have a lot of reason to be. Take the time you need. You know how to find us." They didn't fuss at him, as he stalked out to find his own suite of rooms. Behind him, he could hear Isembard ring for one of the staff.

CHAPTER 10
BERLIN IN EARLY APRIL

T he first three weeks of April were an endless chain of putting on the right face to go with the right hat and the expected monocle. Berlin was not Vienna, not in a thousand ways. The cultural community was unsettled by the recent political changes, and that was only a flicker of far deeper uncertainties.

They were both tracking the gossip, Carillon was sure of that. This person who had gone unexpectedly to the country. That person had been given a promotion. They weren't in deep enough to hear some of it, to make sense of it, but they could file the details they heard away. They could certainly read between the lines in the newspapers.

The first fortnight of the trip played out much as Vienna had. Landry was scrupulously attentive, professionally speaking. But there was an underlying edge of something primally complicated there now. That was new since Vienna. Carillon had had the strong sense, several times, of Landry scrutinising him. Far more so than Vienna, which was saying something. Being attuned, in the way he'd felt a few times, most recently with Lizzie.

It wasn't that Landry had developed some mad passion for him, Carillon was sure of that. Whatever Landry was thinking had nothing of that flavour. It was more like being sized up as a duelling partner, and Landry not being entirely sure what to make of him. Whatever signals or reactions Landry was looking for, Carillon was fairly sure he was not obliging.

At least they were suitably professional with each other. Whatever was pricking at Landry, he didn't let it get in the way of his work. Carillon appreciated that no end. Carillon wasn't trying to be difficult in this matter, at least not on purpose, but he also couldn't simply ask the man.

For one thing, they had next to no privacy. The staff at the hotel were exceedingly attentive, and Carillon had become quite certain that there was some method of eavesdropping on them. Perhaps even peepholes. He'd checked a few times with his illuminated book. Every time he'd spotted listeners or the gleam of a wing that indicated some sort of interference in the charm. When they were out and about, there were always people around.

Worse, it had been horrible weather for any extended period outside. Carillon was, after all, English. A bit of rain didn't bother him on average, and it kept other people inside. And he'd been through every climate imaginable on various expeditions. But he did rather dislike the sort of chilly drizzle that got into everything, especially when it came with bursts of hail. Being out in it would also have looked entirely odd, which was rather more of a problem.

That was before taking into consideration the electrical wires. On the one hand, very efficient in ringing for a maid. And in the right circumstances, the wiring could be helpful in warding. On the other hand, it interfered with a number of charms and protections, and it left Carillon slightly on edge.

Fortunately, their hotel was near to the Zoological Garden and the Tiergarten. Finally, on the 15th, the weather was clear, and they had no other obligations to be at. They strolled up to the zoo from their hotel, and then took their time inside. There were signs up about a special exhibit, a "human zoo". Mutually, without consultation, they circled out in other directions.

They were over by the bear house when Carillon said conversationally, "Someone gave Henry III a polar bear, did you know? Twelve hundred something. Kept at the Tower of London. They'd take it down to fish in the Thames on a lead."

Landry looked at him. "You're pulling my leg."

To be fair, Carillon was trying to provoke him into some reaction beyond the tense absolute correctness he'd been showing for the fortnight. Not that tense correctness was the wrong mode, not here and now. It fit right in with everyone else. He spread his hands. "Truth. Swear on my mother."

Landry grunted, and looked off toward the bear, who was paddling amiably about in the bit of water available to him. "Brave man, whoever did that."

They were sufficiently on their own to permit Carillon to draw out his book. He checked to see there was no one overhearing, and murmured, "If you'd confirm?" The children at the zoo were off watching some demonstration or other. It seemed to be feeding time up in one of the pools. The walrus, perhaps, those were remarkably deep bellows. That was near enough they could see and hear the commotion, far enough away to be no concern.

Landry pulled out his talisman, whatever it was, but

nodded. "As good as we're likely to get," he agreed. They looked out at the bear, the picture of two men visiting the sights.

Carillon considered where to begin. They didn't have long, though they might stretch out the conversation over a couple of stops at points around the zoo. Antelope were not vastly popular, for example, as he understood it, though they were scenic enough in a field. "You're angry. May I ask if it is something I did that I might mend?"

As he'd thought, that hit home, and hard. Landry shook his head and took a breath before he answered. "It is nothing you have done to me. Or even, I admit, at me." He had a precision of speech that Carillon greatly appreciated. "I had certain things pointed out while we were back home. I am considering what they mean. You are, you are an example of the thing. Not the problem itself."

"Ah." Carillon nodded. "Anything that will affect our visit?"

"No." It came out curt and clipped. "I will see about amending my attitude." Landry let out a long breath. "Where are we?"

Honestly, this conversation, even if someone overheard it, would not be terribly informative, except perhaps about the zoological habits of monarchs. It was, honestly, a delight working with a fellow competent professional. It had been a long time since Carillon had done that with anyone other than Lizzie, who was not quite in the same category.

"The galleries have been promising. We have tickets to the Philharmonic on the twenty-fifth, assuming we're still in town."

Furtwängler was conducting on the twenty-fifth, an all-Beethoven program, though of course affairs might take them in a different direction. It was clear the whole concert was a political move in six directions. It might turn out that being there would open some door, or at least allow them to sort out the parties more effectively. Certainly it had been all the gossip at several smaller chamber concerts they'd attended, and every art gallery but two.

Landry was thinking along the same lines. "A good place to make some connections, perhaps. We might inquire if any of the galleries know of others who might wish to dine together that night?"

"Excellent thought, Landry," Carillon agreed. "Perhaps you might take the morning tomorrow and go round and make some inquiries?" There was no reason they needed to be joined at the hip. "I had that invitation to look at some books, and I got the impression Herr Becker was hoping I'd come alone." And Herr Becker was one of the people they thought might be a line to their actual target.

"Herr Becker or Frau Becker?" Landry's grin turned a little wicked. "Perhaps you would do better with a chaperone?"

Frau Becker had quite the reputation, apparently, even if Carillon didn't know all the details. He knew the sketch of it. She was the sort of woman who delighted in snaring and discarding interesting men as a hobby, as one changed frocks or hairstyles. "Ah, we are far from home, and many things might happen, I suppose." He shrugged, agreeably. "And her husband has an excellent library, I gather."

"As you wish." Landry nodded. "I can do a circuit of the galleries, see about who else might be available. A chamber concert perhaps, or some exhibit?"

"I trust your judgement on what might be of interest. You know my tastes."

Landry made a small bow. "Do you think we will be in Berlin for long?"

"The way things are going - well. There's some fine art, but not quite what I was hoping for, in terms of the range. We may have to go travel for my obligations at the end of the month and come back." Much as May Day had become a highlight of his year, both the more private rituals and the more public ones, down in the village, he hated having to pause.

"It might give people time to decide on what they're willing to sell. I've heard a few rumours of people wanting to free up some capital. More options. Investments and so on."

Investments, fleeing the country, bribery of all kinds. It covered quite a range of wanting your money in easily transportable coins or bills or jewels, rather than delicate artwork. At that point, a group of blonde and plaited school girls came up to the fence. They were calling out excitedly about the bear. The two of them nodded and moved on. They didn't get another sure enough chance the rest of the day, and retreated to the hotel.

Frau Becker was indeed rather taken with him. She made inquiries about his wife, she knew how to play the game. And certainly how to avoid embarrassment at a sloppy proposition. Carillon made an agreeable noise here and there, implying that he'd been known to wander from time to time. But also, he made it clear he was not inclined to tumble into bed with just anyone. And of course, refer-ring to the fact he expected to have to go home in a week or so.

It was after the third visit - all properly made to both Herr Becker and his wife - that they extended an invitation. Perhaps Lord Carillon might join them at their nearer country home, a Schloss just west of Berlin. A glorious library, a party of two dozen or so for a few days, getting away from the dreariness of the city. And he could bring his art man. They had plenty of space. And quite a lot of art, not that they were interested in selling. But perhaps they might furnish an introduction to others, depending on how things went.

It would not be the first time Carillon had bedded someone for access to contacts, but he rather hoped it wouldn't come to it this time. For one thing, it had been a good while since he had had to do so, and all his instincts now were for Lizzie. For another, for all he and Lizzie had discussed the possibility, it would bruise her, and he would rather not do that, even in an excellent cause. He would, if he needed to, she had told him to. But he would rather not.

Carillon beamed and accepted promptly. That led, of course, to a handful of other invitations, inquiries about what to pack for the gathering, and a bit more about the guest list. None of their direct targets, but four different couples who could move them forward. Exceedingly promising, that.

The concert on the twenty-fifth was something of a lull. The Beethoven was splendid, of course, though there had been some changes in the orchestra. Carillon rather thought none of them exactly trusted each other as they had. It altered the music, and not in an interesting way. It made all the spaces between the notes have the wrong weight. That was how he might put it.

On the other hand, the audience seemed most delighted to welcome Furtwängler back to the stage, calling him back no less than seventeen times. Carillon could catch some of the undercurrents, but he suspected he was missing more than a few. Not the sort of thing anyone would tell a stranger.

On the morning of the twenty-sixth, they set off with the Beckers in a private automobile, motoring along out of the city through a light rain and mist. It made the city look rather nostalgic, honestly, and Carillon commented on it. Landry made a small noise, and when the others looked at him, he cleared his throat. "Lord Carillon has a fondness for England, these days, and I believe the rain reminds him of home."

It was an interesting statement. True, mind, but with a weight to it that suggested hidden implications. He didn't dwell on it, simply got Frau Becker to share a summary of who would be there, for Landry's benefit. He, of course, had done a bit of additional reading and research about them. A mix of up-and-coming couples, rising in political and cultural influence, mostly mature rather than younger. The Becker's children, mind, were off at the family estate rather further away, suggesting this was far more pleasure than familial enjoyment.

Carillon did not wish for an interesting event, precisely. He was far too old to find interesting the desirable adjective. But he hoped it would get them unstuck from the mud they'd foundered in, and move them forward, by whatever means.

CHAPTER 11
A COUNTRY SCHLOSS ON SATURDAY, APRIL 27TH

By the Saturday, Alexander had settled into the background of the gathering. He made up a quartet for cards twice, and played a sustained but undistinguished few rounds of chess. Enough to make it clear he had brains, not remotely well enough to be any kind of worry.

He'd perfected that line over his years in America and Canada. This was not the time to be threatening, or even permit a hint to come through in someone's unexamined emotions. Far too many people had unexamined emotions. It made them easy to manipulate, but annoyingly imprecise to anticipate. Alexander prided himself on his utter control, not letting himself be played. Forced to action at times, by oath and obligation, but not played.

The gossip had been excellent, at least. Most of these couples were well in the midst of the political changes, looking to see how they could benefit. He could see why Carillon had been angling this direction, and it was paying off. Not the way Alexander would have gone at it, but he'd never been in a position to play the game of confident lordling.

Carillon was doing the thing properly, given the stated goals. Alexander admired competence and discipline, and Carillon showed both. He was easy to talk to, but not at all milquetoast about it. He had opinions and drew people in with them. All the while, he'd kept carefully away from politics, here. He charmed his way along the party, starting with Frau Becker, but continuing with every other woman present and most of the men.

Alexander was certain that particular lady had expected Carillon's presence last night, or perhaps snuck into his room. He wondered, suddenly, what sort of precautions Carillon took about that sort of thing. The man had fought in the War, as Alexander had, surely he took steps against being surprised. As Alexander did.

Whatever had happened, Frau Becker was all smiles and delight, but also favouring another man with her attentions. It had a touch of the coquette about it, drawing the eye of her husband, certainly. But she was also making a point of displaying her charm to the others in the party.

Alexander himself was glad that no one was going to look at him that way, not on this mission. Normally, he relied on people's terror of upsetting one of the Council to sidestep that kind of uncomfortable assumption. Here, he would have to make do with the stigma of the paid employee instead.

He'd paid attention to the rest of the party over the meals and various amusements so far. Chatting between pieces in a small concert last night, he'd gathered most of the others were nearer Carillon's age - and the Beckers - than his own. They were younger sons and daughters of the aristocratic class, with a bit of decorous business dealings in the midst to keep things interesting. None of them particularly shone, intellectually, but they - like Alexander himself, and, he irritably acknowledged, like Carillon - might be hiding that aspect.

The conversation had wandered in a few interesting directions, however. One of the guests had expressed an interest in returning to some of the older land customs. He wasn't magic, Alexander was sure of that, but there was a rise in that sort of interest in Germany as a whole. It was something Council wanted to learn more about. Alexander had asked a few questions, couching it in references to art and literature. Goethe and Schiller, Schubert and various of the other lieder gave him plenty of opportunities.

The artwork had, at least, been worth seeing. Herr Becker had given them a tour of the collection that afternoon, after everyone had returned from improving walks in the extensive grounds. There were quite a few pieces of the sort that Carillon wanted, and Alexander had done his best to back that up. Not recommending or disapproving, precisely, but talking about how the pieces would fit with other pieces they had looked at, or other items known to be in Carillon's collection. Despite their earlier demurrals, the Beckers were clearly willing to consider a sale or six.

This Dutch portrait was a later work by an artist whose earlier work had been in the Carillon family since near the time it was painted. That statue was a thematic pair to a piece of Egyptiana they'd seen at a Berlin gallery. It was one Alexander suspected might be worth more than was under discussion, especially if you took the magical considerations into account. He'd have to research it further. This one was modernist, not in mode in Germany now, but the English were so dissolute, one more painting wouldn't hurt anything.

Saturday evening offered a chamber concert, clearly an excuse for everyone to retire reasonably early and prepare for another night of vigorous bed-hopping. Alexander took his leave of Carillon at the younger man's door. Carillon had been granted a room with pride of place, conveniently near to Frau Becker's rooms. His own room was down at the far end of the Schloss, the next floor up, small and uninspired. He'd stayed in far worse, and at least the place was clean and lacking in obvious rodents.

He took his time undressing, writing notes in his own particular shorthand and code before charming it to look entirely innocent. Well, so long as one read Demotic script, which most people did not. If one did not know the charm, it was a simple diary entry. If one did, the lines were interleaved with his actual text. Thus, he was still in his shirt sleeves, about to undo his cufflinks, when there was a soft knock at his door.

He waved a hand to loosen the wards and protections. It was likely a maid checking if he'd needed anything. One of them had come by last night.

"Come?"

Not a maid. The woman who came in was well-dressed, in a fashionable silk gown of a deep purple that dipped rather lower than most women would wear it. She had been quietly at the back of the group during the concert, someone who had arrived this afternoon. She'd been an addition to the party with several other women who had chatted agreeably over supper and cocktails with the unattached men in the group. Or at least those men whose wives were not present at the moment. Her blonde hair hung in a single perfect corkscrew over one shoulder, as if she had just unpinned it. Her makeup was the height of precision, her lips still startlingly red.

"Herr Landry, may I join you?"

His every sense went on alert, but he nodded. Whatever her intentions - and he could guess at them - doing this in the hallway would be worse. His charmwork muffled sounds, at least. She came in, closing the door quietly behind her. "Frau Becker bade me see to your comfort." She spoke in clear German, as if she were not entirely sure of his level of fluency. A local accent and manner of speech, Alexander noted.

Alexander turned to face her, bowing slightly, retreating to the fussy little manners he had employed all along. "Frau Becker is a considerate hostess." Now, there was the question. Whether he played dumb here, or whether he came up with some excuse that would be believable. A headache, a bit of neuralgia, or some old War injury might do, for example.

"At the concert, I noticed you, so alone. And Frau Becker, she says to me, such a man might like a touch of something, to end the night." She raised an eyebrow and repeated, "May I join you?" This time, she used the informal 'you', making the intention obvious to anyone who'd studied German for a matter of minutes.

She punctuated it by resting her fingers on her collarbone, highlighting painted fingernails, a sparkling ring on one finger, and the dip of her dress against her breasts. Aesthetically speaking, he appreciated the display. This kind of proposition was, above all else, a particular and intimate theatre. It did not arouse him; he wanted nothing to do with touching that skin. But he could appreciate the art form, as readily as he appreciated opera or oil painting or poetry.

She was good at what she was doing. And he did respect competence. But that competence made things rather more tricky. "Pardon, but may I ask your name? I do not believe we were introduced." One could scarcely ask if she were a lady of the horizontal profession, as the German put it, but he could at least get a name.

"Gisela, mein Herr." Now she was more comfortable, taking a step toward him. "So glad to be here, this evening, with such a charming guest." By which he suspected she meant that he was not so distasteful as all that. He bathed regularly, he had not got his hands all over her in the first ten seconds.

He would need a direct refusal here. Was she here to distract him from whatever was planned for Carillon? He could logically assume she might report back to someone, perhaps Frau Becker, perhaps Herr Becker, perhaps some other party. He permitted himself a glance off toward Carillon's rooms. Carillon had hinted at his wide-ranging preferences during this gathering. The sort of language that those with ears to hear it would place without being crass.

"Ah, Fräulein..." He hesitated, and she nodded minutely at the title. "I regret, but I am unable to enjoy your kindness." Doing this in German, of all languages, annoyed him. It was difficult to apply appropriate sexual innuendo in his sixth language, even if he were generally fluent in it. It made him file away the thought that Carillon must have had some previous practice in the matter, to be so deft with it now.

She raised an eyebrow. "We are quite private, mein Herr. Is there some concern that you have? Some gentlemen are concerned with health or such."

"Ah, no, Fräulein. It has nothing to do with you. I am, I am." Some wild impulse took hold of him. It was the kind of instant decision that he would chew over indefinitely later, but must trust in the moment. "The truth is, dear lady, I have eyes for another, and I am one who does not rise to attention with women." That was, he hoped, clear without being coarse.

Not that he rose to attention in that manner with anyone, but that wouldn't do to mention here. He must keep up the mask of a slightly anxious employee, eager to please, certainly unwilling to anger Lord Carillon. And what he said about having eyes for another was true enough, if not remotely in the way she'd take it.

Gisela glanced down his body, a long slow gaze that certainly would have made any attraction more obvious. Nothing changed, he knew that. She looked back up, meeting his eyes, then she hesitated for only a second. She brightened. "Ah, then, mein Herr, you will wish to go to him. He is alone tonight, I am sure of it." Which meant he hadn't been last night. "There is a hidden passage within the walls, if you will come with me?" She looked him up and down again. "Perhaps in your carpet slippers and robe?"

Alexander nodded once. "So kind, Fräulein, to be under-standing." He paused to undo his cufflinks. They were the sort of thing that a lesser man might forget about and leave in the wrong place, and he removed his tie for the same reason. Taking off his shoes, he left them neatly by the door, and stepped into the slippers. Finally, he rumpled the bed and half-pulled back the sheets, before shrugging into his dressing gown.

She looked him up and down, knowingly. Good, he'd at least made the proper show of a man who snuck into other people's bedrooms late at night. "You will remember the way back, yes? And you should lock your door." Alexander did that, risking the last little moment that anchored the wards again. They'd seal when the hidden passage door closed, he hoped. All of his more personal possessions were on his person or tucked away in the hidden compartment of his trunk, held in a blood lock. There was no one on earth who could break that, now. Not without being woven into the bindings. No one of a close enough family connection.

She waited for him to join her in a corner of the room, then pressed at a particular point on the wall. A door panel opened, leading into a small passage that left just enough space for entrance from the room next door, with stairs leading down to a low hallway. Eyeing it, Alexander thought it six and a half feet, enough he did not need to duck, but only barely.

Gisela led him through a branching set of passages, pausing once or twice to gesture at a marking to find his way back. The route was actually straightforward enough, a path that cut below the main hallway of the floor. Then it turned left, and came down one last set of tight spiral stairs to a little landing. There was just enough space there for someone to stand, and sturdy stone walls that would not betray a sound. This was an old part of the house.

He caught just a glimmer of light, enough to suggest some sort of peephole, before she pressed a latch beside the door. "Herr Carillon? I bring you your friend. He missed your company." German was opaque on this matter, one signalled the intimacy by the possessive and the gender. Carillon, Alexander noted, got the formal 'you', and a notable degree of deference.

Carillon had settled in bed already, wearing silk pyjamas. He looked a tad like a startled rabbit, the perfect British lord surprised at leisure. Then he smiled broadly. "Alexander." He let the last r roll, in the French manner, rather than the flipped German. "You are a gem, Gisela, isn't it?" Of course he knew her name and got it right. "So kind. Come, come, right here." He patted the bed beside him, reaching to set his book on the opposite night table.

Alexander had no choice. The room looked different at night, with some moonlight coming through broad windows. It had a rather tremendous four-poster bed, with curtains at the corners. He took a step forward, then another, as Gisela hung back. She murmured, "The maid comes at half-six to light the fire." Then she disappeared back through the hidden door.

Carillon looked up at him, now letting most of the mask drop, before he said, quiet and clear. "Do come here." It wasn't until Alexander settled on the bed that he could hear the catch in Carillon's voice, the way his heart must be pounding still.

CHAPTER 12
THAT EVENING

Carillon swallowed hard. He had to get himself under control, had to set aside the way his too-tense nerves were jangled by the unexpected knock. He'd assumed it was Frau Becker, and that would have been quite complicated to navigate a second time.

Instead, it was Landry, who presented an entirely different sort of challenge. But panic, even reactive response, wouldn't serve here at all. Carillon knew he had to take this slowly and delicately. Always bearing in mind the potential audience.

He had to assume someone was observing, listening. And then there was Landry, who looked very much as if someone had asked him to get into bed with a viper. Good thing he was facing away from the doors, and toward the window. The light from the lamp put his face into sharp relief, with far too complex an expression for anyone who expected pleasure in the evening.

He mouthed, "Moment" and drew his personal book out, a sleight of hand that made it appear it was more or less the book he'd been reading. He flipped pages, brushing past Mercury and his ravens for a dozen sheets or so, to an illustration of Jupiter. The great figure was sweeping a great veil of a cloak up and around his head, hiding his secrets from everyone but Juno.

He traced the line of the cloak with one finger. Carillon took pleasure as he always did in the small shifts of colour and delicate ink work that laid out hints of what those secrets might be. Lizzie had helped him design this, and work through the illustration. He felt the brief flare of magic that drove the charm into being and then the way it fell over them, like a comforting blanket. Or at least comforting to him, Landry flinched.

Once that was done, he flicked back to the ravens, and pressed his fingers against the three that triggered the charm. Good. If they spoke quietly, others would hear the murmuring, but nothing detailed. "Please." He gestured at the bed and then dropped his voice as quiet as he could. "I give you my word, on whatever you like, whatever we say quietly here, cannot be heard. But we will need to make a show of the thing. Do you trust me?"

There was a flash in Landry's eyes, something that did not bode anyone well. Carillon had no idea what had brought the man here, and in such a mood. Landry held utterly still, for a second, and said, his voice as quiet, "You will have to guide me." It had a grudging quality to it, a resistance to being in this place at this time.

Carillon pitched his voice a little louder. "I did not expect to see you here, not like this." He could play this as a relatively new thing. It would explain Landry's nerves and twitches. "I know you didn't want to presume."

That got him a glare, but it seemed a more honest sort of reaction. "Gisela is lovely, but not for me." Landry kept his voice to the same pitch. There, that would be enough for someone to hear. "And I - you know what I feel."

The man had a gift for ambiguous language, as befit any master of the ritual arts. Or mistress, not that that was relevant at the moment. "I have some idea. But here you are, now. Will you join me? To talk a little, first, we've scarcely had time." He couldn't ask Landry to make a show of it. He wasn't even sure he was up for doing so by himself, with that imposing glare focused on him. Some things rather deflated a man's ardours.

It worked, at least. Landry settled on the bed, then hesitated, and removed his slippers and his dressing gown, leaving him in shirtsleeves and trousers. He glanced up at the curtains, and raised an eyebrow, where only Carillon could see it. Carillon nodded. "Draw the curtain if you like. There's a touch of a chill, isn't there? Especially if, mmmm, I can get some more of your clothes off of you."

Another glare, enough to deter a lesser man, but Landry nodded. Carillon shifted to tuck his book under his pillow, and blow out the lamp at the bedside. It left them with just the moonlight from the window at the end of the bed. Enough to see shapes, but not so much as to see that glare, unless Landry caught the light just right. Carillon pulled on the curtain on the other side, so the sounds would match, but only halfway, before opening it fully again.

He did not want Landry to feel caged in. He was walking a delicate line here, pressing without going too far. Worse, he did not know what too far might be. He did not know whether Landry might be up for a spot of shared deception. Nor did he know whether the man could not bear to be touched at all, or whether sex disgusted him entirely. It was, honestly, easier with someone where you knew something of their history with others, to have a guess what might be acceptable.

Once that was arranged, Landry cautiously settled on the bed above the blankets, leaning on one arm like a Roman senator. He kept his voice quiet. "There's a peep-hole. I agree about the curtain."

Carillon nodded. "I assumed. Good to know where it is." Though his room met the corridor on the other side, there were limited places to put one. He considered his options. "How may I make this easier for you? I won't touch you without permission." He flicked his fingers. "The assumed roles give me the power here." He was the lord, he was the employer, he was the money. Three out of four - every virtue of power save age - would tend toward certain assumptions about whose pleasure mattered in this presumed whatever this was.

Landry swallowed hard. "You will if you need to." It came out as near enough an order, and Carillon lit up at that, laughing enough that it would carry. That wouldn't hurt anything. Suddenly, he wanted to know what would bring this man to wanting it. If anything could make the man willing for any intimacy whatsoever. For all, at the same time, he had not forgotten who and what Landry was.

"Oh, yes, I will. You know I will." He let that carry as well, before shifting quieter. "We may need to make some show of it. Though honestly, this is enough to blackmail me with. And possibly open a few doors. Whatever possessed you?"

Landry hesitated, the first time Carillon had seen that kind of uncertainty from him, a place where there was a chink in his carefully constructed armour. "I couldn't have, not with her." He hesitated. "I am not inclined. And I did not think claiming a headache would do, not here and now."

Carillon tilted his head. "Not with anyone?" Immediately, he added, "Pardon, that is a terrible question, and certainly not one you should feel you must answer."

"Not part of our agreements, my lord." Landry put a little heat into the title, not quite mocking, but certainly anything but servile. It wasn't the way Benton said it, not the way Lizzie said it when she teased, not the way the household staff did. In his mouth, it was something full of distance and distrust. Carillon wondered who on earth made him like that. It was the mirror of Carillon's own distrust of the Council and their power, but that didn't explain why Landry felt so strongly about it.

"No." Carillon wanted to smooth that over, to ease it. He did not know what to do with this prickly, discontented man in his bed. They would have to make some sort of play of it, for an hour or two, at least, before Alexander snuck back to his own room. Any less time, and that would be worth comment and tangle things up more.

Landry hesitated, as if he almost wanted to say something. "You know where my promises are. That is as much answer as you need." Now, that was a puzzle that would keep Carillon up at night. Landry's oaths were woven securely into the Council, not to any piece of land. And Carillon did not know what that could possibly mean, not in this context.

It was also, in a way, a compliment. That Landry thought it was any sort of answer at all. If he was speaking honestly now. Carillon knew Landry could lay out a distraction as cleverly as Carillon could himself. There was still an edge he didn't much like, the way Landry's breath was shallow and tense. It was a good thing their observers weren't closer, or that much might show.

"I've seen you eyeing my book." It was a good distraction, at least. "A family habit. Remind me to show you sometime, when we've more leisure and better light." He could at least offer that small intimacy, and he'd pulled it out often enough that Landry had seen a few of the charms anchored in its pages. There were a few he was unlikely to ever explain to someone other than his wife or children. But several others might well be useful to Landry, and they weren't unique to the family.

Landry nodded, and then reached into his shirt, pulling out the amulet on a long chain, and cupping it in his hands, confirming what Carillon already knew. And what Landry had known in his heart, or he'd have checked rather sooner. "Effective." This was less grudging. "What do we do now?"

"We occupy each other for the while. Two hours, three might be better. We are neither of us young men. They'll expect it might take a while." Carillon could lay out how to do this. He'd certainly used those calculations in the past. He knew how to weight what degree of dissipation and decadence would attract the least attention in the circumstances.

"Something you find yourself doing often?" Landry asked. He settled a little on the bed, a titch more comfortably.

"It is surprisingly handy." Carillon agreed. He considered. "If I do fall asleep, apologies in advance if I kick. Or what have you."

Landry wrinkled his nose. "Do you expect that to be relevant?" There, that was a man who never slept with anyone, even platonically. Carillon had with Benton, for warmth and protection, never mind his various partners over the years for other things. With men in the trenches and on expeditions, all crammed in together. And of course, the last glorious decade, with Lizzie. He missed her very much, right now, not least because she would help him settle and figure out what was swirling in his head.

"It seems kinder to warn you. And it has been a long day. If you are insufficiently interesting, I might nod off." Carillon offered it a little diffidently, to see what Landry did with the idea.

Landry snorted at that, more amused now. "I am accused of being long-winded, perfectionistic, picky, and a number of other things. But insufficiently interesting is not something I hear from anyone able to keep up with me."

Another compliment. Carillon smiled at it, let it show. He needed Landry's skills, but the more time they spent together, the more he wanted to understand this man, how he was coiled about with roses. No, not roses. That was a very English motif, and it both fit and jarred. More like acacia, perhaps. Yes, that would do well until he had a better metaphor.

"So we talk a little, and then give some sort of show. Movement, at least, perhaps some more noticeable sounds. Something to make the activity clear. We could play it that you are recently come round to the idea of a man's touch, or of showing another man pleasure. Where do they think you were educated?"

"Does that matter?" Landry was leaning into the challenge now.

"British schools do have a certain reputation, you realise. What young men of good breeding get up to in the dormitory. What inclinations certain experiences might give a man once he's grown." A taste for the cane, or for a man's mouth rather than a woman's. Or discourses on what all those classical vases of wrestling led to, the pictures on other ruder and more explicit pottery. Reading certain texts in the unexpurgated Latin might give a man quite a few ideas.

"I have not said straight out. But my English is good, the sort I learned early, the idiom."

Carillon nodded. "Not your first tongue, certainly, but as a child." He could tell the difference, certainly. "They can take their guesses, then."

CHAPTER 13
LATER THAT EVENING

Alexander held still, not sure what to do with this. He discarded the first dozen thoughts that flashed through his head. He could not let annoyance or anger or uncertainty show beyond this space, and he absolutely did not trust Carillon with the last one.

"How do we make a show, then?"

Carillon stretched easily and sensually, as if he did this sort of thing every day. "Do you have a mode of thinking of the act at all? One might contemplate it as a conversation, a ritual, a dance, a contest, a dozen other things."

Alexander hesitated, then shook his head slightly. "I had given little time to it." Making that admission felt as if he had failed at a test he had not known he was taking.

Carillon's face shifted. It was hard to describe it in the dim light, but there was a new interest, somehow, an avidness that Alexander couldn't comment on. Doing so would make it real. More real.

Fortunately, Carillon went on. "Tonight, oh, let us use the model of a symphony. I prefer four movements here over three, one of the later Classical composers or a Romantic. Beethoven, Bruckner, and so on." His head tilted. "I suspect Beethoven's fifth suits your mood more tonight than the sixth." They'd heard both on Thursday. Of course, those are the ones that would come to mind.

Alexander managed to unclench his jaw enough to reply. "I am decidedly not feeling pastoral." Stormy and tempestuous, on the other hand, he had in spades. "And taking about as long as a symphony? That seems - inconsistent with some things I have overheard from unhappy women."

That made Carillon laugh, loudly enough, Alexander expected, to carry through the charms. It would probably do them no harm. He dropped his voice, still chuckling. "My wife has no complaints on the matter. But it is the buildup that carries the length, you understand, before the final explosive movement."

"Must we have the wordplay?" Alexander closed his eyes for a bare moment before opening them again. He needed every scrap of information he could get.

Carillon waved a hand. "The wordplay is what I have to work with. Let us say we have moved from the knock at the door, the early intimations, through the first movement. Theme, development, recapitulation. Yes, we are entirely in the fifth here, with its stops and starts." He stretches. "Now we move into the andante con moto. My thought here is to get a few things from my trunk, the way I would if I were to get my hands on you."

"Give me strength. You're actually enjoying this." Again, as he made himself look, there was that flash of something complex. It was the kind of layered nuance that made Alexander want to sort it out, find out what was going on.

Carillon shrugged, undaunted, despite Alexander's responses. "Sex should be enjoyed. I see a way to make the show without asking you to do anything you do not choose. But I will not slight that divine lady by making a mockery of her gifts." He added. "I'm going to get up. You move to the far side of the bed. Or even off it, if you think it won't be seen." He considered. "Would it bother you if I pleasured myself? It would be far more, mmm, realistic. You needn't watch, if you can get to the floor."

Alexander sighed. "And my part in it?" He'd have to listen, though, to be ready to respond.

"To keep quiet, mostly. We will play this that you are pleasuring me, at my instruction. That we are still quite new to each other, I am introducing you to the pleasures a man might offer. A few gasps here or there, a hint of nerves and uncertainty, if you can manage it, but you need not attempt a moan. We will settle ourselves, take our time in the andante con moto with some exploration, and then dance and fling ourselves into a frenzy. Let me do all the work."

It wasn't as if he had a better plan. Blast Carillon for being that quick to come up with one, and willing to do it, besides. He was making it as easy for Alexander as he could, and Alexander did not care to carry this debt along with so many others. But they had little choice but to give the watchers and listeners something satisfactory. "As you wish."

He waited for Carillon to lever up on one arm, saying more clearly. "Let me fetch a few things from my trunk. You make yourself comfortable." As soon as that lordly self was up and moving - very lordly, in the way he owned the room. As if he had no worries in the world.

Alexander rolled over to the far edge of the bed, and then off the far side. He didn't risk sitting up, where it might more likely be seen through the curtain by some trick of the light. That, at least, he could do with a modicum of skill and silence. He braced his shoulders against the bed, pulling up a knee and contemplating how he might best get through the next stretch of time.

Carillon chattered along, coming back as he undid a button or two on his pyjamas one-handed, carrying something in the other. "Here we are, found just the thing. You remember that oil I tried last time, beginning to show you what we might work round to. Nothing like that tonight." There was a brief hesitation, as if he'd contemplated some endearment or pet name, but hadn't dared go so far. "Yes, like that, so you can curl up behind me, get your hand on me properly."

Alexander glanced up and over his shoulder, seeing Carillon kneel on the bed. Then the man took his own place on his side, settling nearer the doorway and the curtain and facing them. Carillon arranged a pillow so he could lean back on it a little. He had tidy movements, a ritualist's touch with placement, and Alexander couldn't help appreciating that skill and attention to detail.

Carillon had spared one brief glance for Alexander's position, and he did in fact have a bottle in his hand as well as a handkerchief. Alexander supposed that might add a touch of verisimilitude, a few fallen spots of oil or of other liquids. He'd curse Carillon for thinking of even those tiny details, but it would mean cursing competence. Alexander couldn't bring himself to that, even as the shadow play began in earnest.

It was not quick. He sat there, leaning back in the dark, his eyes closed and his ears straining for any sound from the building. He heard all the small murmurs, the way Carillon offered encouragement. "Try this, here, now." and "Curve your hand like that, your thumb, oh, yes." that trailed off into a louder moan. Not so loud it would carry beyond the room. The man was remarkably adept at that.

Eventually, the words dropped away into eager breathy sounds. The moans edged more into countertenor range, but with an urgent bass driving grunt between the pitches, as if he were giving himself over entirely to the pleasure and sensuality. For a fleeting instant, Alexander wondered what he was thinking of in this moment. Then he shoved that thought and any remotely related one to the back closets of his mind. He used every inch of training and willpower he could marshall and threw away the key. He could not lose control, not of his thoughts. They were all he had, all he ever had.

Finally, there was a quiet, agreeable. "Ah, yes." It held a hundred implications, and Alexander could not decipher what most of them were. "You are well?"

That was his cue. "Quite." It came out clipped, uneven. "I - pardon." He also pitched his voice so it would carry. There, he could at least sound shy, unsure what to do with doing this thing in someone else's home, all the inclinations of man new to this sort of decadence.

"Go wash up, if you want? There's a pitcher on the dresser. But do come back." That was not an order, exactly, but it was an expectation. He supposed they needed to spend some time in the aftermath or some such. He levered himself to appear like he was getting off the bed, before walking stiffly to the dresser, washing his hands fastidiously. Once he was back on the bed, he found Carillon on his back, eyes sharp, but the rest of his face rather more relaxed. The rest of him, too.

In the dim light, Alexander almost didn't spot it as he leaned on one elbow. Then he caught the edge of a ridge of scar tissue, right in the left shoulder joint, where it had come uncovered by the pyjamas.

Carillon caught where he was looking. "A long time ago." That was quiet and unyielding. Not the time and place for questions about it, certainly, since it had every sign of having been a German sniper. And especially given what he had been able to find about Carillon's War service. He nodded once.

Then the other man's face shifted into pure amusement. "I enjoyed the symphonic metaphor. Goodness." It had a thread of not just pleasure, but outright perkiness, entirely out of sorts with Alexander's mood or the situation.

"How can you be so bloody cheerful?" Alexander kept his voice to a low rumble.

Carillon's smile got bigger. "First, you gifted me with a problem I could solve promptly. Second, you have kept me from needing to drug our hostess again. And third, mmm. Turns out I enjoy a bit of honest subterfuge in my sex life."

Before Alexander could stop himself, he let out a little barking laugh, loud enough it would definitely carry to their watcher. He had to figure out, as quick as a duel, how to follow through. "Is that what you think, then?" It had a note of incredulity to it, even a challenge, but Carillon just grinned.

Blast the man. Alexander had assumed Carillon had bedded Frau Becker last night, but clearly not, even if he couldn't ask about it here and now. He wouldn't know what to do with the answers, anyway. The first point was fair enough. Alexander knew he had the same desire, sometimes, for the problem that could be solved in the moment and the satisfaction it brought. The third, though, there was a gleam in Carillon's dancing eyes that made him wonder again what the man had thought of while he stroked himself. Unruly thoughts.

All of it should have made Alexander more cautious, but somehow it didn't. This man had been fair with him. Carillon had not asked Alexander to do anything Carillon wouldn't do himself. Hadn't done himself. Rather less, in fact, as soon as he realised Alexander's limitations in this area. What he was beginning to realise were rather notable limitations, at least in terms of application to spycraft.

"And now?" He settled down on his arm. "Do you sleep?"

"Not just yet. I do try not to be rude." Carillon shrugged. "Also, I enjoy talking to my wife, and most particularly when we have found our pleasure together. Not at all fashionable, but sometimes the only point in a day when no one else is demanding our attention."

Alexander let out a breath, a slow one. "And you would have - with me."

Carillon tilted his head, as if considering several possible answers. There was still that sense of control, which had slipped only momentarily in the heat of the moment. Perhaps not even then. It wasn't as if Alexander had been observing every expression. "Ask me when we're back in Albion."

Then he turned all to business again. "Linger here a while. Half an hour or so, and then you might reasonably fuss about finding your slippers and gown. Give our watcher time to retreat before you go back to your own room. In the morning, we'll deal with whatever innuendo comes. You may stutter or blush, if you think it helpful tomorrow, or simply look to me, and I will manage things."

"You take the idea of blackmail so calmly." Alexander was not at all sure what to do with that, with a man who could hand that kind of power to someone else and not fear it.

Carillon's mouth quirked up again. "I didn't expect this, no. But." That shoulder, the half-bare one, shrugged. "Make do, want not."

They lay in silence, then, until Carillon coughed some time later. Alexander had not been able to think of anything sensible to say, and his mind was whirling. He made the appropriate fuss over sneaking back out of bed, and finding his slippers and his gown. Only then could he disappear back through the hidden tunnels, to find his own room still locked and undisturbed. His dreams were uneven, shards of glass with faces and expressions from the evening that he could not mend, no matter what charm he used.

CHAPTER 14

YTENE, EARLY AFTERNOON ON MONDAY, APRIL 29TH

"Domina?" Carillon had written ahead, but he had not expected Lizzie to be waiting for him on the bench by the portal, book in hand. Of course, she closed it as soon as the portal flickered close behind him, and held out her arms.

He went to meet her, gladly and quickly, burying his face in her hair and inhaling the scent of her perfume. Delicately adventurous, built from the places they had been together and those she'd travelled to long before he met her. Today, he got the strongest whiff of spices.

They stood like that for breaths, before she lightly patted his good shoulder with the book. "The children are out. We have the afternoon."

"Queen among women." He kissed her cheek as he drew back. He hadn't known how to ask for that, what to arrange, and of course she had.

She snorted. "You are predictable in a number of ways, my dear subtlety." Then she took her own step back, looking him up and down. "You didn't write much the last day." Sunday, they had travelled back to their hotel, and then taken the portal near the train station this morning.

Carillon grimaced. "Our code book was a tad inadequate, it turns out."

Lizzie just raised an eyebrow. "Well. Come on, then. There's tea and sandwiches in our rooms, and whatever else you might need."

He took her hand, lacing his fingers through hers, as if he'd drown without the contact now. "You. I need you." That need carried them upstairs, out of their clothing, and into bed. This time, the symphony was triumphant, exuberant, and above all about their mutual joy. Mozart, rather than Beethoven, he rather thought. There was a thought there, just as Lizzie came apart in pleasure and he found his own, but it danced away before he could put words to it.

It wasn't until they were nestled in the aftermath that either of them spoke again. He had wriggled around to get his head in her lap, the way he most loved. She leaned back against the voluminous pillows against the headboard with a light peignoir of rich blue draping loose over her chest and pooling to the sides. She looked like a queen, secure in her own power, with her hair coming down in loose curling wisps out of its braid.

"To begin." He cleared his throat, and she nodded once. "You might come across some gossip out of Germany. That I have - shown affection for another, a man. With sufficient evidence for blackmail."

"Not just the implication, then? My, Geoffrey, you have been busy. You'd only intended to aim for innuendo." She let her fingers linger on his cheek. He could feel the slight tension there. He knew the way any hint of secrecy in this sort of matter brought up the old wounds from the man who had betrayed her, now long ago. Some things scarred and were never the same again. They both knew that perfectly well.

"Landry." It was not a name you could make crisp and curt, it wasn't shaped for that. Curious that it was such a counterpoint to the man himself and all his thorns.

Her fingers stopped for an impossibly long time, and he couldn't breathe until they started up again in a gentle stroke. "Decidedly outside your plans. Tell me, love. Talk it through." She was withholding judgement, he knew that. Not out of anger - she would have rightfully been angry if he kept this from her. As it was, it changed a number of their shared calculations, and she needed to know what he'd learned.

He explained the whole tangled mess of it. He had been delighted in Cephus's new sedative concoction. It had worked perfectly. The suggestions he'd charmed into Frau Becker's ear had sent her prowling off in other directions. They'd made several useful connections to other art collections. Only then Landry had knocked on his door.

"I would not have thought him to be such an innocent in such matters. Whatever his inclinations, I'd have thought he could make the expected show of it." Lizzie contemplated the situation, watching his face. She saw something there, something Carillon couldn't have hidden if he'd wanted to, but he did not know what. She tapped his cheek once and said, "Go on. Tell me the rest of it first."

He wanted to ask her what she knew, what she'd discovered in watching him, but he would obey her, of course. He went through the charade, the way he'd set it up so that Landry had the least to do with it.

"And did you do the thing properly, Geoffrey?" Her fingers had gone back to stroking, like she'd pet one of their cats. It was gentle and steady and all about enjoying the sheer pleasure of touching and being together.

"Every skill at my disposal." He let out a long breath. "Thinking of the music helped. I did with you earlier, too, until I couldn't think." He hummed a few bars, in this case, of the piece he'd had most in mind, Mozart's Jupiter symphony, with its lighthearted dancing quality and expansive fortunes.

"And after?" She leaned back a bit, relaxing for some reason he couldn't sort out yet.

"We waited a suitable amount of time. I pointed out that he could play it as shyness or uncertainty around others. He took that, being that much more deferential the next day, even though..." He frowned, remembering that vicious 'my lord' from earlier in the conversation. "He reminds me of Hippolyta FitzRanulf, her utter distrust of anyone with a title, and with a solidly good reason."

Lizzie tilted her head. "Huh. No particular cause you could tell?"

"He does not care to defer. Or take orders. I certainly did not want to give him any."

She hesitated, deciding between two paths. He certainly knew her well enough to spot that, and it wasn't as if she were attempting to hide it. "To the degree you can leave aside his Council commitments and affiliations, what do you think of him? I know that is asking a great deal."

Carillon swallowed and let his eyes close to focus his thoughts. Lizzie was lovely, and also exceedingly distracting when she set her whole mind to something. "Competent. Quick. Widely read. Idiomatic. Wisely opinionated about music and a number of other topics. He's made himself into my man for art with skill and expertise, without complaint. Committed to doing the thing right, whatever the cost. He doesn't give the simple answer. I want to provoke him, sometimes. To see how he will react. He must be the devil's own to duel."

"Tenor or baritone?"

His eyes flew open, and he read her expression as easily as any book. "Tenor." He swallowed. "Bloody hell." Then he grunted, shoving all the emotion elsewhere. "He doesn't want anything like that, certainly not with me." It was useless wanting anything in return.

"You said he said he's had no inclination at all. With anyone. Some people are like that." She shrugged. She was certainly not one of their company, but they'd met a handful of others in their life together. "That does not determine your heart. Just what you do about it."

Carillon half-whimpered, and immediately she cupped his cheek with her hand. "My dearest subtlety, you are dreadfully out of the habit of noticing you fancy other people than me." She followed it, more gently, with a "And of course, the fact that he's Council, has been near all his adult life, that would muddle it all up."

He spluttered and she let him, just giving him space to thrash around in his own head with the idea. It took him a while, enough that the light out the window changed as the sun travelled. "Are you sure?"

"You could go explain it to Alysoun. Though I'm certain she'd say the same thing." One didn't ask this kind of question of Richard, he'd just blink until he'd had an extended think about it. Alysoun, though, would cut through all the deadwood promptly.

"Thank you, no." Carillon tried to gather his dignity. That was admittedly rather a challenge in his present position, both physically and emotionally. "It would be like talking to my mother. What do we do about it?"

The pronoun choice made her smile. "Bitte," she said, using the German deliberately. "Invite him to come out for tea and dinner. A proper visit. I would like to get a good look at him, in private. On our home ground."

Carillon winced. "How on earth do I do that?"

Lizzie shrugged. "Not today, not Tuesday, certainly not Wednesday." He had come home for the May Day rites, and he wanted and needed to fling himself into those. At least they should settle things out for him magically. He always floated in the aftermath for days, feeling like he was young again and could do anything. "Thursday would do. Or Friday. Write in the journals, you know he has one. Suggest that you might more efficiently plan here and that I have some notes to share with him."

"Tipping your hand, domina?" They had obscured that Lizzie was the one who had prepared the full dossier for this trip, as she had for others before. And likely would again, the world being what it was.

"Would it bring him?" Her question cut to the heart of it.

Carillon considered. "Probably. He appreciated the last set. Complimentary, as I told you." He frowned. "And I suppose if he saw our art, he could better discuss additions."

"Two reasons to share. Excellent." That satisfied her, at least on that matter. When she spoke again, it was to veer in a new direction. "I have more questions, love. Or properly, a question and a comment."

"You generally do." Now they were on steadier footing, at least.

"The comment, then. You said he near enough gave you an order. What did you feel when he did?"

Carillon grimaced then half turned his face away. "I liked it."

Before he could pull further from her, Lizzie's hand was right there. He set himself to sturdily resisting that knot of guilt and all the ways a man like him was supposed to give orders rather than take them. "You do like it when someone else can be decisive. When you can set that down for a little while." That promised she would do a fair bit of it between now and Thursday. Something in Carillon's shoulders finally gave way, the tension releasing like a bow, flinging an arrow at a target.

He let her hear the sigh as well as feel it. "And?"

"You felt something in the - what do we call this? The encounter."

That, there, was the thought he'd lost. Carillon's breath caught. "I felt like a cur. Selfish. For finding my own pleasure while ignoring his."

Lizzie nodded once as he carefully looked up at her. "If you want to find anything that matters with him, beyond this plot of yours, you will have to offer him pleasures he will take from your hand. Think of your falconry, my love. No two birds the same."

"Nor two horses." Carillon exhaled sharply. "There's no small challenge to take on." She was right, though, and he knew it as well as she did. "And for now?"

"For now, we invite him to supper. Let him see us at home, what that changes. You can spend the next few days deciding what you're willing to show him, and what you keep hidden."

Carillon snorted. That was a puzzle box that would keep him busy between their other obligations. "How long before the children are back?"

Lizzie glanced at the clock on the bedside table. "Ninety

minutes. Perhaps two hours, but I suspect not. Hand me my book, please. You need more sleep."

He did, too. He'd slept more and more uneasily the longer he'd been gone. Carillon didn't argue, he had more sense. Instead, he stretched to reach for her book on the side table. He handed it to her, and twisted to curl up against her legs, letting her use his head and shoulders to rest the book. She would wake him in good time.

CHAPTER 15
THE SCHOLA LIBRARY ON LATE MONDAY AFTERNOON

"I appreciate the time." Alexander set the last of the books they'd pulled for reference on the table. He and Ibis had claimed a small room at the end of the Schola library for this afternoon's project.

"You bring me the most interesting questions, Alexander." Ibis glanced up from where he was flicking through a few pages. "You mentioned several pieces?" He ran his hand through his dark curly hair, though he'd at least shrugged out of the academic robe for the moment. They caught on books annoyingly sometimes.

"Two similar statuettes, a foot high each, and we came across a few other items. A stele, a scarab that might be a talisman, but I couldn't get close enough. A bit of tomb painting that I felt sorry for, but it needs a bit more than that to buy it."

"A more personal connection, perhaps?" Ibis had, in the past decade, learned how far he could push. He'd grown into himself, since he'd become the Materia professor here at Schola. And more recently, head of Seal House, since

Richart Hase had retired from that role nearly two years ago.

At the moment, it was his Egyptology skills Alexander wanted more than the others. Ibis spent a fair bit of his research time on the inscriptions and magical implications of items taken by archaeological excavations of their shared ancestral home. He had expertise and knowledge Alexander had never been able to make time for.

He considered that question. "It's not impossible that it came from Memphis. Where my mother's family are from. Who was it, the University of Pennsylvania, before the War? And Petrie, of course, getting his hands into everything."

Ibis snorted. "Did you ever meet the man? I've lurked in the back corner quite a few times and been cordially ignored. Doesn't have a scrap of sense of the numinous, but to be honest, it probably makes him a better archaeologist, considering."

That made Alexander consider asking a question he'd been contemplating since they got back from Germany yesterday. Before he could frame it, he heard a chime from his journal. "Beg pardon." he said. "Do you mind?"

Ibis waved his hand. "It will take me a minute or two to bookmark the references I expect to want."

Alexander flipped the pages open, then blinked several times. It was from Carillon. Who suggested that their next round of travel might be made easier if Alexander had a sense of the existing art at Ytene. And of course, since Alexander had hosted previously, the Carillons would be delighted to return the favour. He was invited to tea and supper on either Thursday or Friday, as suited his preference, and apparently Lizzie was looking forward to meeting him and discussing some additional notes.

He could not imagine what Carillon might have told

her. Could have told her. He swallowed hard, then glanced at Ibis, this time more thoughtfully.

"I'm not one of your students. And if you annoy me too much, I won't share my knowledge without further bribing." Ibis had decidedly grown into himself, yes. He knew Alexander wouldn't actually threaten him with anything meaningfully dangerous, for all sorts of reasons. Not here and now, or to Ibis in particular.

"You've been to supper at Ytene more often than Isembard and Thesan, yes? Because of Pross." Ibis's wife had shared a house common room with Carillon for several years. But she'd also lived in the village nearest the Carillon landed estate. Until she'd moved to join Ibis here at Schola and taken over the bookshop in the village a decade ago.

"Regularly still. Though not in term time, of course. And he was busy in March." Ibis tilted his head. "She requires entirely different bribes, you realise." Again entirely conversational and holding his ground.

"He's invited me to supper. Related to this project I'm assisting with. The art."

Ibis raised an eyebrow. "Not just art, of course, though I know neither of you is going to tell me what you're up to, and quite proper, too." He leaned back against the wall, leaving one book propped open. Alexander smiled, a little shallowly. Ibis had done Intelligence work in Cairo during the War, and it would be foolish to underestimate him.

"Just so," he agreed. There was no reason to be unduly difficult, not when he was now asking for a handful of favours.

"This week?" When Alexander nodded, Ibis grinned. "Just after May Day is delightful, for the record. Ytene is a very responsive bit of land these days. I don't begin to know the details, but you'd have to be denser than Petrie in that regard not to notice." He nodded at Alexander. "Which, naturally, you're not."

Alexander smiled at the compliment. "And Ytene?"

"Respectably old estate, even by our standards." Given that they were more used to measuring age in millennia than centuries. "Established by the Domesday Book, but with all the usual conveniences for guests. Excellent libraries." Plural, very specifically.

Ibis went on. "Simple but lovely gardens. I gather it's not Lizzie's particular interest. I've never seen the ritual workroom, though I know there is one. Nothing particularly grand architecturally other than the great hall, which has some excellent tapestries and woodwork, the sort that looks impressively vibrant even before you know more about the history. But a lot of smaller and more intimate architectural details."

Not unlike its lord, then, who was not precisely showy, but who had layer built on layer. Frustratingly and annoyingly, at the moment, but it made Alexander curious about seeing him in his native land. More curious. "And what are they like at home? How fancy should I expect things to be?"

"What's the invitation for? You by yourself? This week?" Alexander nodded. "Fairly relaxed, I expect. Their cook is excellent, but English, not French. If you have any particular preferences or requirements, let them know, she's quite used to accommodating. We're often there with the Leventhals, Pross loves a chance to talk shop with them."

Alexander nodded. He enjoyed the Leventhals and their expertise with books too, and he knew they kept to kosher food. Ibis continued, helpfully. "Bring a good bottle of wine or some such, if you need a hosting gift. They'll be delighted with books, but that's hard to do without seeing their library. Apply to Pross if you want to make the attempt."

"I'll stop in on my way to the portal and see if she has any recommendations that could be managed this week." Alexander believed in trusting the competence of experts. And in this case, Pross would be far more sure of a welcome literary gift.

"Anything else? No? Let's start with the statues." Alexander shook his head and drew out the notes he'd tucked into his journal.

"Here are the sketches. That's Sekhmet, of course. I've seen dozens, if not hundreds. I have a catalogue for the one on sale from the gallery, too, though the photograph is only passable." The lion head - male, not female - was rather striking.

Ibis took the pages, frowning at them for a long moment, then peering. "And the inscriptions, do you have those?"

"I didn't get a chance to write everything down." Alexander passed those over, with his neat hieroglyphs to the side, and a rough translation. "More on the Becker's. They let me get a good look."

Ibis tapped the sketch. "That's a Sekhmet. As you say, lovely, but not that uncommon. Tutelary mother of Memphis, among her many other roles." He then turned his attention to the second sketch, holding out his hand for the photograph as Alexander flipped to the proper page in the catalogue.

Almost immediately, Ibis looked up. "Get these. Please. Get these." There was a burning intensity there all of a sudden. "By all that's holy, in all the sacred places, get these."

Alexander held up his empty hands. "I'll do my best. Why? Are they a risk?"

"Magical." Ibis took a deep breath, as if calming himself. "That is Sekhmet." He tapped the Becker's statue. "That is not. That is Nefertem." Sekhmet's son, one of the classic triads of Egyptian myth.

Alexander saw what Ibis had already realised. "Two of the three. Where's Ptah?" Memphis's third, god of craftsmen, often also seen as the father of Imhotep, the land's greatest sage. He took a step or two back to lean against the wall. "Is there..."

"Not that I know of. No surviving triad. If there's a third piece, we could use the two to find it. Get them. Please. Whatever it takes. Get them." His fingers kept tracing the images, then the words.

Alexander nodded, just once. He knew that kind of furious need, coursing through veins and thoughts. "We'll do what we can. They were both willing to sell, and - the statues are fine, but not splendid. The trick will not be tipping our hand. Fortunately, Carillon already made some comments about how they'd look lovely on plinths in his library, on either side of the fireplace or some such." He lifted his hand before Ibis could protest. "Just an excuse for buying them both. We could tell there was something unusual when we saw the second one."

"I expect there's some sort of magical connection, as well. It's hard to tell, from the text here, but this, here, and there. That suggests some sort of link, from point to point. Warding or protection or blessing, something of the kind. I can't possibly say more without them in front of me. Perhaps something in the bases. You didn't handle them, did you?"

"Under vitrines." He nodded. "It will give us somewhere

to start when we return to Berlin. No promises, but I'm quite hopeful."

Ibis let out a long, slow breath. "Good." He let himself sink into a chair. "Pardon, need a moment."

"Great discoveries often do." Alexander took a chance to find a seat as well. After a minute or two had passed and Ibis had gathered himself, Alexander spoke again. "May I ask you a more personal question? Not about this, not directly."

Ibis glanced up, then shrugged. "Ask, I'll see about answering?"

"We've talked, before, about your experiences under the keep, your first year here." When Isembard and Thesan, Ibis and Pross had gone on something of a restorative quest to the lady who smiled on this particular isle and her chosen lord. "How does that feel, compared to Ytene? Or any of the other landed estates."

"You must have been to a number, surely?" Ibis ran his hand through his hair. "Far more than I have."

"But I do not have that particular experience to compare it with." He had been excluded from that invitation, as an honoured guest in Schola's halls, no longer one of her teachers. And certainly not young enough to shoulder the burden of protection Isembard had thrown himself into after that solstice. It had cut and burned, even as he was so happy that a place that he loved was better than it had been, in the most ancient and magical of ways.

Ibis might have guessed something, in the years since, because when he spoke again, his voice was rather gentler. The way he spoke to an upset student, not a challenge. "When the land, the place, the deity of the place, is happy, everything smiles. You can feel it, in the ground and the air and the water and the light. I don't think it's ever the same twice, that river of potential, but there's a song to it when it's flowing as it should. It's not about the formal rituals, or the proper words, though those don't hurt. It's about the heart. Turning toward the heart, not going astray."

"In our sense of the heart?" The place that held all the good and bad in a life, the soul, the centre of being. Alexander knew, without a doubt, that his evil deeds far outweighed the good ones. He'd known it would since he'd walked out of the Council rooms, his first full meeting as one of their number.

Ibis nodded. "There are times when I paint the hiero-glyph - henna, usually, sometimes a magical ink - on my wrist. To help me turn there always."

Alexander contemplated that. "Thank you. It won't do in the moment." Too much chance someone would spot it. Carillon, for one, and that was not something Alexander could begin to explain, even if he'd wanted to. "But that's a fine idea." It was, too. Ibis had sound instincts for the connections that magic made, which only made sense, given his focus on Sympathetic magic as well as the Materia used to give enchantments physical shape. "The other pieces we were looking at aren't nearly as interesting, but I'd still appreciate your insight."

Working through the details took them an hour until Ibis had to take himself off to make sure none of his students had got in the wrong sort of trouble. Alexander did not reply to the invitation until he had acquired a suit-able book from Pross and a bottle of wine from his own cellar, setting them to be ready. Thursday would do well. He wanted to see Carillon closer to the land rites rather than later.

CHAPTER 16
YTENE ON THURSDAY, MAY 2ND

By early afternoon, the weather had settled out into something pleasant enough. It was brisk enough that Carillon was wearing a half cloak over his sweater and trousers, but warm enough that the children were happily enjoying the chance to play in the courtyard, supervised by their nanny.

Lizzie leaned her hand on his thigh. "Ready, Geoffrey?"

Carillon nodded. They'd talked out the logic of it, in the last days of April, to give his mind something to keep busy with. When he'd woken up on May Day before dawn, he'd trusted his instincts, and he'd become more and more sure during the day. By the time he and Lizzie had fallen asleep, well-sated, he had the beginnings of a plan to put into play. It wouldn't survive more than a few minutes with Alexander, even the best plans wouldn't. But he had that thread to guide him.

The portal flared open, precisely on time. Carillon stood, offering a hand to Lizzie. Landry stepped through. He wore a suit and cloak, and he had a leather satchel over his shoulder. Carillon could see the brief evaluation in

Landry's eyes, taking in not just the immediate space and any threat, but the larger domain and what it offered. Both challenge and support, in this case.

Carillon waited. He could feel the ground under his feet, the drums from the May Day song yesterday still pounding with his pulse, and the vibration of the coming summer. The world near him was glowing. It was loved and tended and made of magic.

Landry nodded once, almost to himself, before he made a formal bow. "Lord Carillon. Lady Carillon."

There were formalities to be observed, and Carillon had contemplated which bit of language to choose here. He had almost settled on the ordinary, the phrase that did not presume anything about the visitor beyond the routine bounds of hospitality. Instead, he chose the formal phrases that made it clear he knew the guest had potent magic and possibly arms at his disposal. And that these things were seen, recognised, and permitted. "Be welcome to Ytene and my demesne."

Landry's eyebrow went up for a moment, and Carillon caught the quirk of a smile. Good. He'd given Landry plenty to think about when he returned home tonight. "A pleasure to see an estate I've heard quite a bit about, one way and another." He added with a slight wave of his hand. "I do have a token of my esteem, but better done inside. Lady Carillon, a delight to be your guest."

Which did not say anything about Carillon himself, and everyone knew it. Ordinary etiquette did not precisely cover this situation.

"You are very welcome here. We thought a bit of time in our library and tea. Perhaps a quick tour of the gardens and a look at the horses if the weather holds, and then supper." Lizzie waited a moment, a measured beat, before she added, "Our more personal guests normally call me Lizzie or Elspeth, and you are welcome to do the same. Do you prefer Council Member or Magister or Professor?"

That last one cut close to something, in a way neither Carillon nor Lizzie had expected it to, and Landry had another of those quick-hidden mysterious reactions. Then he considered. "We are working closely together for the next weeks."

Carillon spread his hands. "I am Carillon to nearly everyone, including inside my own head. That's not much help. Lizzie, of course, has her own pet names, but that is rather a different category."

"Alexander, then. We are colleagues, that is what my colleagues call me. Though play it as you see fit when we return to Germany?"

"The informality would be indicative, wouldn't it? Well, technically, nominative, but if I continue along that line of puns, Lizzie will frown, and we can't have that." It was partly the land rites, but he could feel himself bubbling over and he suspected Alexander would disapprove and not in a useful way. "This way, through the courtyard - the children were out playing, but they'll be off to their own tea shortly."

The children had, in fact, paused in whatever game they'd been up to as soon as they heard the portal. Something approximating a bohort puzzle, given the hoops and balls and various other found items scattered across the cobblestones. Edmund was keeping an eye on his younger sisters, but he straightened quickly and came over. "Papa?"

"Our guest, Council Member Alexander Landry. This is Edmund, our eldest." And going to be his heir, almost certainly, when he turned twelve in three years time.

Edmund came over, offering a hand that Nanny had obviously recently cleaned, with a slight bow. "Council

Member, Papa has spoken highly of your competence, and a bit wistfully of your library. Please, be welcome to Ytene." It was tidily done, and Carillon didn't bother to hide his pride at all.

Alexander was not sure what to do with this, exactly, but he bowed back. "Pleased to make your acquaintance. And are these your sisters?"

Edmund encouraged them forward. Lizzie took over. Merry managed a quite competent curtsy. "This is Meraud, Alexander, and our youngest is Rosalba." Rosie was a tad shy, and hid behind her mother's skirts as soon as Edmund let go of her hand.

"Please don't let me keep you from your games, but I am glad to have met you." It was cordial, exactly the sort of thing he would expect from someone who had little experience with younger children.

"This way, we'll settle in the library. Edmund's quite right, of course. I'm very curious about yours, and also quite aware my curiosity will go unsated." Carillon was trying not to be too much, but it was a difficult line to walk at the moment, with the land magic still soaring through him.

Once in the library, they settled into more expected pleasantries. Alexander presented a bottle of wine - quite a good one, a comet year, insisting they not serve it with dinner, but enjoy it themselves at some later date. And a book, which clearly had Pross's hand in it. Carillon glanced up after looking at the title page. "One thing I have come to respect about you, Alexander," He used the name for the first time deliberately, "Is your willingness to consult."

"I admit that if you have been curious about my library, I have been curious about your cryptographer, and I suspect your alchemist." He glanced from Carillon to Lizzie. "May I be specific?"

"I tell Lizzie everything not otherwise sworn, and try to do precious little of that. So yes, she knows about Frau Becker. And also about the titch of blackmail that might come more my way than yours." Carillon leaned back, visibly showing his ease with it, while Lizzie snorted, letting Alexander read her amusement and comfort.

"In that case, I am quite curious about that sedative. And what else you might have up your sleeve that would be relevant."

Carillon nodded. "Some of it we should certainly discuss. In other cases, I prefer the value of surprise - it will go better if you don't know what I might pull out, still." He had lines he would not cross. And there was a delicate balance here, given their ultimate target. "Let me think about it, and see what I'm willing to share when we get to the after-dinner drinks."

Lizzie snorted at that. "To make up for it, we both know you want to browse the shelves. Feel free, for a bit? And then we'll sort out the tour. We were planning a relatively simple meal tonight. Cream of asparagus soup, roast venison from last season, properly kept up in stasis, of course, mushrooms, new potatoes. Syllabub to finish, Mrs Mudthon does a tremendous one. And wine, of course, Geoffrey's following the family tradition of an excellent cellar. But if there's anything you don't eat, there's still time to make adjustments."

Alexander nodded. "Quite delightful. My compliments to your cook in advance. And..." Carillon caught the little spark of something there. Alexander's eyes had lit up, with actual honest interest, something Carillon hadn't expected. He wouldn't have noticed it, certainly not the same way, except for what Lizzie had named just a few days earlier. It made Carillon lean into every observation, tiny though it might be, because she was, in fact, correct. He wanted something more with this prickly man than professional competence. "I am intrigued by your library, of course."

"Not everything is here, naturally. Lizzie has her own books upstairs, and there are a few under appropriate protections elsewhere. But the bulk of it is in the room." Carillon considered. "I trust your handling, the incunabula are largely on the glassed in shelves." With all their additional protections against humidity and pests and thieves and fire. They had, of course, removed a good dozen or two books to the workroom's library this morning. But the bulk of the collection in the library was intended to be appreciated.

That agreeably took up the next forty minutes. Alexander made periodic comments about this volume or that, exclaiming over a detail of a particular edition. He knew his books, as well as Geoffrey had expected. It certainly helped settle him a bit, to have time to learn more without expectation.

The sun came out as they were doing a brief circle of the garden. Not at her best, of course, not this early in May, but the elder trees were coming into bloom nicely. They wandered by the pasture - Alexander was agreeable about horses, but more in a practical sense. He asked several good questions about the breeding goals and the benefits of adding the local ponies into the mix. Intelligent ones, but Carillon wouldn't have assumed anything else.

It was when they got round to the mews that Lizzie had her bit of fun. They had checked on Carillon's current merlin, Hildegard, a bird of four who'd replaced Helena two years ago. They had two others he flew regularly, as well as Lizzie's current peregrine falcon, Artemisia.

"Why a merlin?" Alexander had taken more of an interest in the birds. "A lady's bird, many would make it."

Carillon grinned toothily. There were implications to the choice, besides the much smaller size of the merlin, and he enjoyed seeing what people made of that. "That injury. I used to fly an Eurasian eagle-owl, Theodora. Trained her myself before the War. She's still thriving, they're long-lived birds, but she is up in Cumbria."

There was a beat before Alexander turned and blinked at him. "You mean, you kept walking into gathering after gathering, carrying an owl? When near everyone keeps forgetting your House and your inclinations? Including myself." He then almost collapsed into laughter and had to take himself outside the mews to avoid startling the birds too much.

It wasn't until they were all gathered again, nearer the paddock that Lizzie offered, in the tone that meant she expected it to trigger even more laughter. "There are a number of reasons I refer to him as my dear subtlety. Because he is, and he isn't. Often in the same paragraph. Periodically, the same sentence."

That indeed got Alexander into another round of laughter, and there was again something honest about it, in a way that made Carillon want to step closer. He didn't, of course.

"And now you fly a merlin." Alexander considered. "According to Juliana Berners, that makes you a lady - or an emperor, by some." He shook his head, still chuckling, and Carillon let himself grin freely. "Not in your library?"

"Alas, no. I've only seen rather abused copies of the first printing, and the facsimile is less interesting to me in that case. There's a copy of the 1881 printing at Hawk's Breath, in Cumbria. Father found it amusing." Carillon tilted his head. "I'm intrigued you know of it."

The Boke of Saint Albans was thought to have been written by a nun in the immediate aftermath of the Pact and the Tudor rise to power. It made the first edition quite of interest to him, but the actual material in it was rather more spotty. "I admit, I find the palaeography dubious when it comes to the emperor, though I defer to your expertise. I make it more like melowne, rather than merlyn, and there is a difference. Whatever a melowne is, which is a different debate entirely."

"Not my particular area of interest, but I've had to turn my hand to all manner of documents from the period." Carillon supposed that would be true for the Council. Many of their oldest documents would come from then, the ones that built the foundation for what they became over the centuries. "Should you ever get a chance at a clean copy, I'm glad to take a look."

If they came out of this still talking to each other, that was, and there were still half a dozen reasons Alexander might regret that offer and the assistance it suggested. Carillon smiled, hiding his own uncertainty under a new question. "Do you believe Juliana Berners was magical? I read quite an interesting article about the history of the family. I have a copy somewhere." That topic amiably occupied them as they strolled back to the house to wash up. Lizzie needed a few minutes to change into a frock suitable for an informal supper.

CHAPTER 17
THAT EVENING

Alexander felt like his attention was being dragged everywhere and yet thoroughly grounded in the moment. It was, he realised, rather like standing in the centre of the Temple of Healing, looking up at the stained glass and the central dais. There were a million details lining up to make shapes and patterns, but they all held together at the core. Once he named it, it was easier to thread his way through the conversation.

The Carillons were charming and remarkably relaxed hosts. It was just the three of them at supper, though from both the seating and various comments, others on the estate often joined them. Lizzie - he was still struggling to use the informal nickname - had mentioned their steward, long in service to Carillon, as well as their head of the stables and his wife. That was unusual, certainly. Garin and Livia Fortier would never have done such a thing, nor would Garin's parents. Which might honestly be a recommendation.

The supper was also exceptional. Alexander had dined

all over the world and had people attempt to bribe him with meals in some of the best restaurants. This food was neither fancy nor fussily presented, but it was solidly its best self. Everything had flavour, everything had been treated with proper attention. It was a vast difference from many meals he'd eaten as a guest where the food had come cool to the table - or sometimes half-melted. That sort of food had nothing to commend it except the decoration, and that made a painfully scant meal.

When the meal ended, Lizzie murmured, "I know you have plenty to talk about, and I promised I'd read to the children. Geoffrey?"

He smiled at her, and Alexander saw how readily he lit up for her. "I'll let you know, of course." Know what, he did not explain. Carillon did not explain things, and Alexander could not complain too much. Alexander himself was known for not explaining.

Once they were settled in the library, port in hand, Carillon spread out his free hand. "You are the guest. Where would you like to begin?"

There were a considerable number of options. Was this bribery, for example, or an apology for high-handedness in Berlin? Was it going to lead to a great deal more information, or only a few threads? All right, chances were good it was nearer to the latter. Why on earth had Carillon arranged it this way, of all the options he had at his disposal?

In the end, he went for a feint, to see what it got him. "I did not expect to meet your children." Among aristocratic circles, they were kept out of adult view, certainly when complicated guests were around.

That got a broad smile, that hint of tipsiness Alexander

had noted a dozen times today. He did not trust his interpretation of it at all, especially since Carillon had been
drinking quite modestly at supper. "And?"

Alexander considered how to answer. "Rather younger
than the age where I do best with students, but not so
different from Isembard's and Thesan's in years. Your
younger two, anyway." He then offered the gift he knew it
was. "Your Edmund has a great deal of poise for his age.
And attention to detail. You must be proud of him."

"Oh, I am." That had a glowing warmth to it, and
Alexander suddenly wondered what it was like to grow up
with a father like that. A father at all, he'd only known his
much older brother, and neither he nor Alexander's mother
could be reliably described as warm. Carillon went on. "I
was very curious about your library. I still am, of course."
Carillon lifted his glass and took a sip. "And we are a family
who loves books in their many forms."

It was something of a non sequitur, and Alexander
couldn't decide if it were deliberate or on account of the
wine. It did allow a change in topic, though. "You read to
your children? You and your wife?" It was not an assumption he'd make in most households like theirs, though he
was quickly becoming sure they were not at all what most
would assume. Carillon nodded, as if any other answer
would be wrong. "What do you read?"

"At the moment? Some of Richard Halliburton's works.
Somewhat annotated with commentary around safety
precautions for mountain climbing, ocean voyages, and all
that." Another shrug. "Along with the usual mix of mythol-
ogy, fantastical stories, and, oh, Merry and Rosie are all over
that set of Nesbit novels right now. Endless play about it."

Alexander blinked. "You must know Haliburton's reputation." Bohemian was the kindest way people put that, that he preferred the company of men, and also took unfathomable risks for the sake of adventure.

Carillon shrugged. "I do try not to be a hypocrite, especially in the nursery. It seems a quick road to self-hatred all round. We don't get into that, of course, though they know people in a variety of personal situations. As to the adventuring, I mentioned Lizzie's membership in the Explorer's Club in her own right, and I had my own by the time I was twenty-four. We'd honestly prefer they have good sense and examples of what they need to know well-established before their wandering feet catch up with them."

Alexander took a sip of his port, as much to give himself time to think as anything else. "You're not like Garin after the land rites." It came out of his mouth before he could quite stop it. It was correct, any fool knew that, but it revealed so much in the asking.

Carillon blinked, then laughed long and loud, setting down his glass to avoid spilling. "By Mercury, I should hope not." He shook his head. "I gather Arundel is properly tended, mind. They are attentive to their commitments. But, I suspect, a very different mode."

"If I didn't know better, if I hadn't seen you all afternoon, I would assume you were drunk." Alexander nodded and tipped his own glass minutely. "I was thinking, earlier, it is all of a piece. You lead the eye, you swear by Mercury, who for all his other gifts is also god of thieves and tricksters. The owl, in plain sight." Carillon beamed at that. "And yet, you lay out your truths like pillars of stone, unalterable and inarguable."

"And you do not remotely know what to do with it, do you?" Carillon's voice had turned softer. The way he spoke to his wife when he teased. It was as if he was holding out a hand with that glow, ready to share something of its magic.

Faced with it, Alexander could not refuse, not and continue in their task. He did not know how to accept it. He had known once. His Council trial had been like that, a moment when he knew, down to his deepest heart, where he was and what he was good for. And then he'd turned from his heart, or been forced away, never quite finding that light again except in glimpses through shadows and riverbank reeds.

When he looked at Carillon again, something had changed. Other men would have pulled back that gift, shut away everything. There would be another door barred against him, another table at which he could sit only conditionally, so long as he made himself useful. This, though, was an expert ritualist making an offering, finding it was not the right time, and stepping back in respect to see what might be welcome instead.

Carillon spoke again, gently. "I have been pressing you. In Vienna, in Berlin - especially that night - and again today. You know all the reasons why, of course. The ones we've talked about, and others as well." He took a breath again, the careful ritualist choosing his words with precision, knowing they'd make the intangible real. "I find I respect you. Even when I resist all you stand for, all your oaths obligate you to."

That, at least, gave them a way forward. Alexander nodded, taking his time to gather himself, to meet that gesture somewhere in the middle. Despite all his inclination to curl inward and let thorns and sharp magic do their work. "Why are you so wary of the Council? There's nothing in the records since you became Lord."

He saw a reaction, a spark of something that made him want to chase that fleeing comet. There was something there, something his research so far hadn't turned up. It was horrendously tricky to go back before that, with how often Carillon had been away from Albion. How often Alexander himself had been away.

"It is the ambiguous unknown magics, done without checks and balances. Any sensible person would be wary." His tone had the hallmarks of a true answer that was still not the most important truth.

"To be fair, you are clearly in favour of the ambiguous and unknown magics when it comes to you and the land rites." The retort leapt from his mouth, and he saw it hit, before Carillon laughed again.

"Fair, fair. At least in terms of debate." He took a breath, cocking his head. "I came to you because I was almost certain you were not involved with my most particular reason for caution and concern. Besides, of course, the fact that none of them can match your skill with naming magics. Cyrus Smythe-Clive is a fine sort when it comes to ritual, but not at all in that mode."

Alexander caught that particular offering and accepted it for what it was. He would not get an answer today. The gift was in knowing the shape of the questions to come. "No, he is not. And he cannot take months to dally around Germany, even without the possible risk." That was true. As head of the Council, Cyrus was a fine target for ransom or worse, even if he hadn't needed to be available in Albion at short notice.

Alexander went on, posing another question. "Your own training, mind, keeps surprising me. The more since I set foot on your lands."

That got Carillon beaming, the way most men would

beam at some compliment of their appearance or the beauty of their wives or the abundance of their wealth. "Wide-ranging training to start, and then I picked up more on my travels. My apprenticeship was with Mistress Alworthy, largely, though I also spent time with a number of others who had the gift of her training."

"At Oxford, the Academy?" The magical college, entangled with Oxford's others.

"I read history at Exeter, with the Academy for my magical studies." That involved threading a fine needle. Though Exeter had a reputation for men who got their academic work done well enough and spent their time on other activities. Sneaking off for magical rituals and enchantments rather than being out on the cricket pitch or punting on the river would be easier than amongst a bunch of diligent swots. Not that Alexander had anything against diligent swots, being one himself. And balancing two sets of studies, well, that must have suited the Owl that Carillon was to the heavens.

"And then, in your travels, the same mix of magic and otherwise?" It explained a lot, if Carillon had lived much of his life that way.

"Exactly so. You've done a fair bit of the same, I suspect? Though, to be fair, it's hard to tell from the public records available."

Alexander snorted. "We are both equally defeated by the lack of information, then. Beyond what we choose to share with each other." He nodded once. "But yes. That is why our current plans are working so well, I expect. We are both used to those negotiations. Honestly, I've found it most challenging walking as if I am non-magical, while still needing to keep a weather eye out for magic. I think how we've gone at it has been valuable." He preferred the challenge, and he was becoming more sure Carillon did as well.

"And I did promise to show you my book." Carillon beamed. "Along with some other necessary discussions. As you say, my cryptographer, my alchemist, my provider of dossiers. Also, perhaps, some plans."

CHAPTER 18
THAT EVENING

Carillon settled in his chair. This was the part where he had to trust his magic even more than his history. Especially today, of all days. If he could not see truly with the land magic still glittering in his blood, on his own lands, in the heart of his home, then he should not risk any of this. But it had to be a dialogue, a discussion, mutually carried forward.

It was why he'd let it show that whatever cautions he had about the Council, the largest of them was before he became Lord of Ytene. And that they'd been at a time when Alexander was away. It remained to be seen what Alexander did with that.

Alexander took a long breath and let it out slowly. "All those things, and especially the plans. I do not assume, of course, that you will tell me everything. I cannot return the favour, for one thing."

"I would not expect you to." Carillon shrugged. "I do understand about oaths and commitments, even when they are inconvenient to my desires." The phrasing got a snort out of Alexander. Good. Carillon wanted him to continue to be relaxed. This would be much easier if they could manage that. "And as I said, I certainly have not laid out the full situation. May I?"

Alexander leaned forward. "Oh, yes." There he was, ready to go on the hunt, and Carillon found that distractingly attractive. Not a thing he could indulge in, not remotely. The next sentences might change a great deal, though.

"Alchemist, remote estate, gasses." Carillon said, by way of a brief reminder of what they both knew. "Once upon a time, Berthold Hoffman and I were lovers. I was on my Grand Tour. He was spending a season or three with an alchemist in Florence. Various of our people would like his information, but he will only trust me to get him out." He waited to see what Alexander did with that.

As Carillon had expected, there were flickers of thoughts and complications. It had been unfair to keep this detail back. But he hadn't been sure Alexander would continue if he'd known it. Some would say that was more reason to share. Carillon's experience - and he was sure Alexander's, when he thought about it - made it clear that timing was all in such things.

They sat in silence for a good two minutes. Carillon was entirely willing to wait. They were here in his library. He could wait forever. Finally, Alexander stood and circled the room before coming back to sit down. "Were you originally intending to tell me?"

"I hadn't decided when we began. Truth. And then, well. The Beckers. Which we will come back to, as we must." Alexander grimaced as Carillon mentioned that, but he nodded. "Would you like to know more?"

"Yes. The answer to knowing is yes, with me." Alexander picked up his glass and waited expectantly. "What's the man like? Reliable?"

"I haven't seen him more than fleetingly since 1908, but we've kept up a steady correspondence. A few times we've been in the same place since then at some conference or event. Near thirty years is a long time, though, to be in someone's life. About my height, but much more slightly built. He's pale with wavy black hair, usually in chaos." Carillon smiled as he said it. "Very pale. An alchemy lab is no place for the sun." As he thought about it, Berthold was not unlike Alexander himself, except in the skin tone. Though Alexander had a more aristocratic nose. "Ferociously intelligent and creative, but not worldly. Which is why he's where he is now."

"Lured in by offers of a lab and supplies and funding?" Alexander coughed. "It is not quite so old a story as being betrayed by a woman, but near enough." He tapped his fingers on the stem of the glass twice. "You have kept in touch?"

"Oh, yes. We've got quite a mutual code, actually. It is not as comprehensive as we'd like, being largely referential to art, opera, literature, and all that. He's implied strongly the letters are being read. But also that cutting off all correspondence would be noticed by a variety of people. As has happened with others."

He shrugged. "I have the gist, in any case. He's being asked to make gasses and weapons he wants no part of. He has no one else to turn to, and if he can't get out, he'd rather die than continue. It's not just the perversion of his art, mind, he also - he fears for what they'd do if he refused. He'd die, but it would be far worse." There were in fact awful things that could be done with a death and magic. No one was sure how much of that might actually be going on at any given point, especially now.

Alexander nodded. "You have a new dossier, then?"

Carillon grinned. "Lizzie will bring it down when we're ready." He let that piece fall into place, watching Alexander's eyes widen. "It is part of why she wanted to meet you."

"You play close to your chest." Alexander patted his own, flat palmed, in punctuation. "Deft. And again, I can't exactly argue. I've done the same in the past, and for far less reason." He considered. "You've done this sort of work with her, then?"

"Mostly courier duty, these days. The children - a brief trip, a week or two, is one thing. Or some excursion when we travel as a family. She keeps her hand in far more with analysis." He didn't say where, or for whom. Alexander could probably guess at most of it if he thought about it for a bit. "But we make an elegant couple to invite to all manner of things, and she has a knack for getting people talking. More easily outside of Albion."

Alexander inclined his head, slowly. "My compliments. She does far better work than the usual run of notes I get, even given how much you were both obscuring. She wished to meet me for a number of reasons?" It wasn't entirely a question.

Now, it got to the delicate point. It wasn't as if Carillon could admit what she'd seen in his face, that he wanted something far more than a temporary collaboration with Alexander. He couldn't name most of his wants, either. Just more of the challenge and competence and whatever it was that Alexander had shoved so far away it was barely visible.

And, of course, to pick his brain about ritual magic and charms, and dozens of other topics.

"I mentioned she'd been betrayed in the past. The man's long dead." It came out with a sharpness Carillon had not entirely intended. "The War, not by my doing. Or hers. Leander Sibley. He made every sign of courting her, making much of her. Then she turned up somewhere he didn't expect, only to find he was within days of a betrothal to another woman."

Alexander tsked, thinking back. "No, I heard about that. His death, I mean. We were nearby at the time. Foolhardy, sure magic would save him, got a dozen others killed where a better man would have brought his people through safely. Also, the Sibley men tend to inconstancy." He waved a hand. "Clearly, you both are very happy with each other."

Carillon noted that, how he was not grudging about it. Many would be, presented with something that did not seem on offer to them. Even if they didn't particularly seem to want it. "Oh, yes." He let the delight into his voice, all the ways of using tone and pitch in ritual he'd learned, for making the true thing more solid. "I told her, as I said, about Frau Becker. And about what you and I had done."

"Should I make an apology to her? Some sort of amends?" For a moment, Alexander seemed entirely earnest. Carillon suspected, suddenly, that Thesan got that tone out of him from time to time. In her case, likely through force of sheer human decency and entirely different familial expectations. And also, a great deal of experience with young men and women who didn't yet know all the ways they could put their feet in their mouths.

Carillon waved it off. "Lizzie is not at all upset with you. Or with me. But she felt we should invite you for supper. And she is wise in this, as in many other things. The question she set me, though, is to decide how we play it going forward. The shape of it - again, we are back to music, the form of the composition - is that you had come into my employ. I had made advances, you had not declined, but these things are entirely new to you. Perhaps an abuse of my power, perhaps my animal mesmerism." He made that last a joke.

Alexander, thankfully, half-laughed. "You do not have the sheer weight of presentation of that walrus at the zoo, but you explained the form well enough, I suppose. And you think it would ease our invitations further?"

Carillon nodded. "The estate where Berthold is kept is held by one of the notable magical families in Brandenburg. Much as we have a townhouse in Trellech, and the estates, they keep a house in Berlin, and an estate in the forest, an hour or two's travel by automobile."

Alexander nodded, slowly. "So distant, but not too remote."

"Quite. Though the country house is surrounded by forest." Carillon continued. "The older generation are in Munich this month, making themselves known and liked. The next generation are a hair younger than I am, down to their mid-twenties. Though there's a daughter who married into the Howards living here in Albion with some children. Her brothers are very, mmm. Dissipated. What we want, in short, is access to the estate while Mummy and Daddy and others who might be more wary are away."

"And you said, before, that you knew how to signal that appropriately." Alexander frowned. "Don't I put a spoke in that plan?"

"Yes and no. If we are known to be, mmm. Entangled, it makes sense we might be more willing to take a risk or three for a space that won't be raided. As others there should be in the current environment. We don't dare be more public than a drink in a certain kind of club. The place where people make private arrangements for later, slip a man a key, not the sort where scantily clad men and women make their pleasures known directly."

Alexander blinked. "I have been to a few such places. Surely they're not much to your taste?"

"Oh, but they're so useful for the spy." Carillon lifted his drink. "I am no musician, but that sort of thing is my pipe organ, given a chance." He waited for the awful punning to hit and then grinned broadly when Alexander groaned.

"All right." He swallowed. "She has more notes. We might wait for her for those details, such as we know them at the moment. I assume you have some maps or something of the kind?"

"Thankfully, yes, or this would be a great deal harder. Also, a few carefully transferred hairs and a few scraps of paper with drops of blood. We've been at the conversation a long time. He knew what he could get out." Though that had been another place the code book had been scant. Berthold had resorted to a reference to the Scottish play, drawing attention to a particular line of text with an apparently random splotch of ink. He'd had to trust that Carillon would read between the lines and find the smaller red spots of blood doing their best to imitate a semicolon.

"Your cryptographer? Your alchemist? Your book?" Alexander shook his head. "You are rich in resources, and beyond the obvious."

Carillon tsked. "You've all the Council's behind you, theoretically. Are they reasonably satisfied with what news you've got out, by the by?"

"None of it good, but far more information than we'd had? Yes. I have some specific people to hunt up this trip, if we can manage it. I suspect so, they all have some useful connections. All Berlin, still?"

"Yes. Too much moving around would attract notice, and I don't want to get caught out by rapidly changing events. But we might see about some social gatherings with people who have recently been to other places. Give us your lists, as much as you can. Lizzie will see about how to make some connections between the people we might talk to and those you want to know about. Harder, in Germany, of course, but she has a few tricks." And she and Lap Manse had been collaborating heavily. Carillon tapped his fingers. "My cryptographer permits me to mention his name. Giles Lefton."

That got a glorious reaction, bafflement and a certain thread of envy. "He only works for the Ministry. He won't have anything to do with the Council. Not, I think, that they've asked since the War."

"A number of your peers have regrettable assumptions about injury, did you know?" Carillon kept his tone mild, but he was certain Alexander was reading his grinding fury. The Council had refused to offer work to Giles. As had the Ministry, until Richard had dragged the Guard through the necessity.

To be frank, Giles was doing far more creative work than he had before he became blind, in half a dozen ways. He said he made fewer assumptions, now; he took the thing as it was, from all angles. And he'd found collaboration - necessary, for some of the manipulation of the material - also improved his work, and not just when it was with his wife.

Alexander grimaced. "I can't argue with that charge. And won't. Please convey my appreciation, and if he's at all willing, I am curious about his current work."

"Before you leave tonight, I have a book for you. It's a complex code structure, partly reference, partly replacement. Not hard to do, but slow to work with."

Alexander nodded. "Far more than I deserve." he agreed. "And your alchemist?"

"My alchemist is more dubious about trusting you, but he has been willing to share more of what he made for me, by and large. The sedative, quite handy, obviously, and designed for a range of dosing. One for memory. I used that as well, just enough to cause a pleasant blank for a couple of hours." Alexanders' face went still for a moment, then he raised one eyebrow, inquisitively.

Carillon considered how to put this. "I then whispered in Frau Becker's ear that we'd had a delightful time, with a few choice examples. I suggested she might have a romp with Herr Weber when the opportunity presented. Much tidier than - mmm. More intimate engagements, though as I said, Lizzie and I have agreements about that when engaged in a spot of espionage."

"And otherwise?" Alexander's question wasn't what Carillon had remotely expected. In any other man, it would have been flirting.

"And otherwise, though the terms are, of course, different." Carillon smiled a little. They had, mind, discussed the outline of what Lizzie required should Alexander be willing for certain things, and they'd do so again later tonight. Carillon had rather more to share about a number of details there.

"And the book?" Alexander flicked his fingers at where Carillon's sat in its hidden pocket. "I'm sure it's on you."

"A family tradition. Magic sewn into the binding, then anchored in the illumination. We make the books and inks ourselves, do all the artwork except perhaps the initial sketch. A host of ritual work to enliven the whole thing. I won't show you all of it, but of course. You've seen my Mercury and his ravens. That's for whether anyone's listening." That could and would occupy them until Lizzie was ready to come down again.

CHAPTER 19
A BERLIN NIGHTCLUB ON THURSDAY, MAY 9TH

Alexander settled uncomfortably into the broad-benched corner booth. Or rather, not precisely a corner. They were tucked into the curve of the room. It was something like an opera house in miniature, with a balcony ringing the floor below, and a stage and musicians at the front. At least it meant no one could sneak up behind him. Here, though, the music was pervasively modern, a mix of jazz and a singer who would have been quite at home in a number of Paris clubs.

Carillon leaned back beside him, sipping a cocktail made of blue and sparkles and smoke, as if he did that sort of thing every day. His tie and pocket square were of a bright red, contrasting against a charcoal grey suit, his hat at an unusually jaunty angle. Not his usual understated mode at all.

"I should have anticipated you'd want to find a club for our sort of background." Alexander lifted his own glass, a more sedate wine. "Magical, in this case, I mean." He coughed to cover his nerves. They had to assume people were listening, and magically, this time. Which meant they'd know if either he or Carillon used any kind of protective charm.

The truth was, this was ferociously dangerous, and they both knew it. They'd discussed it in their planning for this latest trip. After the crackdowns on gay bars and cabarets and theatres, this was taking a specific sort of risk, and out in public. It was one thing to give someone material for blackmail, in private, with no direct evidence besides testimony. It was another to be out in public. Carillon, however, had been insistent that this was the surest way to get the invitation they wanted.

Carillon inclined his head. "I thought you should get a chance to see how the other half lives, mmm?" he offered. "Free-flowing drinks, beauty all around, the charms of Berlin at her brightest and best." He seemed entirely in control. He lifted his drink and smiled across the room at a rather glowingly blond man in his late twenties or early thirties. The man smiled back before turning back to his companion, a slightly younger dark-haired man.

"And who is that?" Alexander frowned.

"A talented young artist. I met him a few years ago. I was hoping to catch him here. Rather nice oils, switched over to watercolours recently." When Alexander blinked, confused, Carillon added, "For the kind of art that would get him in trouble these days. Watercolours don't leave the scent of turpentine in the air." Whether the man was painting erotic art, political caricature, or something else was apparently an exercise for Alexander to sort out.

"Also faster to dry..." He offered after a moment. "Easier to pack away."

"Just so." Carillon beamed at him, as if delighted and pleased that he had seen it so quickly. Alexander had even less idea of what to do with that. The praise was as baffling as the gentle welcome he kept offering in subtle small ways. He was a grown man, nearly fifteen years older than Carillon. He should not need that praise or even want it.

The pause, even, made Carillon grin more broadly. "If you learn nothing else tonight," he said, then added a purring, "Alexander." It made the hairs on Alexander's neck stand up, and not exactly in a warning. "It is a chance to look again at the roles society makes us take." He nodded slightly. "A powerful man, a lightly built one, a very masculine one, one who is more feminine. There are expectations, there. As there are for women. And between men and women." Even if, clearly, that was not particularly the topic now.

The room was, in fact, at least two-thirds men. And he suspected some of those in frocks were men at other times, though sorting that out by dress or manner or style of walk was not his particular forte. It was not as if he understood those mysteries in women. Bar, perhaps, where she might have hidden a talisman or wand or some other magical device in a gown that showed every line and arch of the body.

"And we sit here and - look?" Alexander was not at all sure of the customs, now they were in the middle of it. Carillon had carefully briefed him. Thoroughly, finally. They were just to look, not to do anything that might be seen as intimate in public. The club was magical, which meant it had some protections. But there were magical folk among the rising political figures, more than a few of them, and the same with those enforcing the laws and limitations. Just attending the club, though a risk, was a manageable one.

And Alexander's nerves would be understood in this context, as someone new to the environment, sure his eyes or mouth would give him away. At the moment, he wasn't sure whether to look at the singer, or where. He was scantily dressed, shaking his body with a degree of an unsubtle show that Alexander didn't know what to do with.

"It is no more ridiculous than most opera." Carillon was nearly purring. "And you like that well enough. Also, most people are here to be looked at."

"You're enjoying yourself." Alexander had to swallow to get his jaw to relax.

"Well, yes. No reason I shouldn't." The singer finished, to be followed by a dark-haired tenor, with a piano for backing. This relied much more on musical skill than the previous show. That, Alexander noticed, made Carillon shut up and enjoy the song, one finger tapping the beat as if he couldn't stop himself from some slight movement. One foot, perhaps, too, since Alexander could feel it moving, bare inches from his own, the beat of the toe slightly vibrating the table.

Carillon losing himself in the pleasure, Alexander noticed, was the sort of thing some people made art of. He was still the somewhat daft lordling, the persona he put on like his coat and hat when away from home. But there was something honest in his enjoyment that Alexander found charming despite himself.

When the song finished, the artist from across the way had approached. As soon as Carillon smiled at him, he came over. "May I join, mein Herren?"

Carillon beamed. "Friedrich." He nodded. "My friend, Alexander." He added a word there that puzzled Alexander, 'dear' friend. He could take the meaning well enough, what in English might be an emphasis on "particular friend".

Friedrich caught the implication immediately. "Such a

companion is most fortunate." He said it with a simper at Alexander that was about two parts amusement and one part envy. "I did not believe my ears when I heard you were in our city. Tell, tell, what brings you. Oh, and Antonio is in Cologne for the month. He will be sorry to have missed you."

"Oh, I do hope he is well. I wish him all the best." Carillon seemed entirely in earnest. Then he picked up the conversation masterfully, traipsing through the steps of a complex dance like it was a walk on a well-paved straight path. He explained their interest in art, made an agreeable reference to the Beckers, and laughed when Friedrich commented on Frau Becker's known tastes.

Friedrich offered an interesting point or two about who was interested in selling art right now. Carillon mentioned they had appointments at several galleries in the next few days, as well as the Beckers. He was at least making a solid effort to get those Egyptian statues, without tipping their hand too far. They were part of a longer list of items that were, honestly, less use to them and far poorer art.

The conversation wandered back and forth from there. After a number of exchanges, Friedrich said, as if the idea had just occurred to him, "You know, you really must see about an invitation to the Heinrichs. You remember Constanza and Gerhard, of course?"

"Oh, yes." Carillon made a slight face. "But I had heard they were in Munich this month? And also." He shrugged. "They would not approve of Alexander, no?"

Friedrich looked Alexander up and down. "Very set on proper German custom, mein Herr. And focused on Germany's people and magics." He sounded apologetic about it, which was as much as Alexander could expect in the circumstances, really. "Herr Carillon is as, mmm. Much pressing their bounds as they are interested in."

Carillon grinned suddenly, almost boyishly. He added in English. "Sticks in the mud, as we'd say." He switched back to fluent German. "Why the Heinrichs, then?"

Friedrich laughed. "Oh, you are both rather to Sepp's taste these days. Possibly also Annaliese's. His wife." He added that. "Though they have a very, is the word permissive? Marriage." He considered and addressed Alexander a bit more cautiously. "Do you know, erm, Dita Howard, I think it is?"

Alexander nodded. "Married to Reginald, a good old family." Well, it depended a bit on what quality 'good' was describing, but old and powerful, though not generally angling for power through the Council. "I do not know her well, I am afraid?"

"The middle daughter." Carillon took a sip from his glass. "Now with a child at Schola, and one starting this year, if I have my numbers right. Is Quirin around? The younger son." He added the last for Alexander's benefit. "Well. They do take hospitality seriously, the Heinrichs."

"Oh, yes." Friedrich giggled, outright giggled. "They're having people out, the end of next week. A big party, friendly." He shrugged, taking in the room. "To people who might want a bit of privacy. Or a bit of a party. Both, ideally. Do say you'll come? Where are you staying? I'm seeing Sepp for supper tomorrow. I must have him send a note round. Might get Quirin. He's been in and out, no idea what he's up to."

Carillon gave the address of the hotel, in a steady voice. Alexander could feel his barely suppressed hum of pleasure as if it were a counterpoint to the music still going below them. "Do, please. We are, well. Strangers in the land, and cautious. Being among like minds, that would be grand. A few days, you think? So we know what to arrange."

"Oh, mein Herr, I will make sure it is a good long delightful time. Five days or a week, perhaps? So many amusements." Friedrich lit up. "You will not have to leave for other business? It is a little distance."

Carillon assured him they would have finished most of that by then, or at least be able to take a hiatus in their endeavours. It was all amused and amusing chatter, smoothing over. Finally, Friedrich smiled and gestured. "My friend waits. Look for a letter, do, and if you do not hear, you may find me at my studio." He fumbled in his tight-fitting jacket to bring out a small printed card. "Soon, mein Herren."

Once they were alone again, Alexander chose his words carefully. "A particular friend, him? And the Heinrichs?"

"Once upon a time. I know the senior Heinrichs better, related to art and music." It had a hint of something complex that Carillon certainly would not discuss here and now. "Friedrich is pleasant enough, isn't he? He chatters, but he is charming. And I do enjoy enthusiasms, both public and private." That was made of innuendo enough to fill the room. "Not quite my usual type, though, and he knows it." He nodded at the singer. "I prefer quick-witted tenors for certain amusements, to be honest."

Alexander bit his tongue, not quite meaning to. That description could, he knew, fit him as correctly as others. Surely, Carillon had not meant it that way. Or if he did, it was only making a show of it, for whatever listeners there might be. "And you think we will be finished with the art business by then?"

"The Heinrichs have quite a good collection, actually. Though any negotiation would be with Constanza and

Gerhard, naturally. Sepp is..." He considered. "He enjoys a good time, very much, preferably with other people around and Anneliese - his wife, mind - enjoys watching other people have a good time." That implied that at least some of the entertainment might be something like an orgy. Especially with that particular clarification.

"And Antonio?"

"Friedrich's - mmm. Not quite an uncle. A family connection of like mind. A friend from my Grand Tour, and a fine tenor. Growing into his voice, last I heard him, which is not always how that goes." Alexander thought he heard a more personal pleasure there. More to his tastes, then. Carillon offered the tidbits about his apparent former lovers without much shame or discomfort. It was a fascinating contrast, given how he had previously been so close with any details.

Alexander did not know what else he might ask here and now, so he merely nodded, and let his own gaze slide over the people around them. It was not solely checking for threats or risks. He wanted to try to understand who Carillon was watching, and why.

CHAPTER 20
A ROWBOAT ON A BERLIN CANAL, SUNDAY, MAY 12TH

Two days later, they were out on a small rowboat on the canals of Neu Venedig, well away from anyone else. They'd taken the train down mid-morning. It was easier to make sure of privacy in the middle of the water. They'd already checked there was no device in the boat itself that might cause any problems. Alexander sat in the stern facing him and looking somewhat uncertain about his situation. The distrustful way he'd looked at the narrower canoes had made the rowboat the obvious choice of the two.

"Not usually out on a rowboat?" Carillon considered their position and angled them in toward a rudimentary dock. They were well away from any houses or other people, a good place to stop and chat and snack. "Check that we're private, mmm?" That would keep Alexander occupied while Carillon manoeuvred.

"I'm a good swimmer, but I prefer my boats larger. Steamships, ferries." Alexander hesitated. "Though I suppose that must be..." He made an apologetic moue, the way you did when you realised mid-sentence that your companion's parents had died on a ferry.

Carillon shrugged. "We are unlikely to be torpedoed by a U-boat in a German canal," he pointed out. "For about six reasons. So on the whole, the smaller boat seems safer at the moment, whatever might be true at other times."

Alexander ducked his head, while Carillon wedged them sufficiently into a curve of the river that should hold them in place but allow them to get out when they wanted. "We're clear of anyone around. You've been saving this, haven't you?"

"We can only go boating so many times, it is true. Especially the way you eye small boats. You should have said something." Carillon settled back on the bench a bit, then twisted to grab the picnic basket they'd brought with them. "Meat pie? Pastry? Something to drink?"

Alexander opened his mouth, closed it, and then nodded at the offer of the drink. Carillon poured out some tea. Alexander cupped his hands around it. "My preferences in such matters aren't important. Just getting the job done."

It was, on the whole, a remarkably revealing sentence, and it had dozens of implications for the work at hand. Carillon set some of that aside for the moment, it wouldn't do to swoop on it too quickly and startle Alexander further. "Mmm," he agreed. "Where shall we start with the plans?"

"You seem very calm about this." It was not precisely where Carillon had expected to start, but it was a fair question. "Not the boating. Clearly, another of your unmentioned skills."

"I did spend a little time on punts while at Oxford. It's near enough obligatory," Carillon pointed out. "And various lakes, here and there, while visiting people. A rowboat isn't complicated, though I'd not want to fight the current much." As it was, his shoulder was going to ache tonight from his showing off, but that was what salves and magic were for. And a strong drink before bed. "As to the rest of it, I have a decent idea of the landscape. I'm used to a lurking threat. Nothing new."

Alexander blinked at him. "Are you?" Goodness, the man hadn't discovered the trial, had he? Though, to be fair, Carillon had been keeping Alexander rather busy with more obvious lines of inquiry when they were in Albion. It meant he should choose his words carefully.

"Do you have a nemesis? Mine is apparently in New York this season, or was a week ago." Under an assumed name, and trying to get her brought back to Albion for trial had been deemed not worth the bother some time ago. Too much strain on international relations for not enough benefit, someone in the Ministry had decided.

Obligingly, Alexander leaned forward. "A number of professional enemies, but none I'd consider so personal as a nemesis. May I inquire? Is he relevant to the present situation?"

"Other than that it involves alchemy, no. You remember Wallington Aylett, surely? Died in the early 20s. No one's actually entirely sure when, it turns out. His wife. Medea Aylett. She tried to kill me - or Lizzie, she didn't care which. Probably still doesn't."

That got delightful jaw-dropping bafflement, all of Alexander's masks failing for an instant before he pulled himself together. "And she's still alive?"

That, mind, was a compliment. "Her co-conspirators were tried and punished, she got away from Albion in the middle of the night. She rocketed around various distant points for a while, and then settled in California apparently. People invent whole new histories there regularly, I gather."

He considered how to put the next bit. "Lizzie and I were a few months from our wedding, and by the time we came back from our honeymoon trip to Italy, we knew she was expecting. Which changed the foundation entirely, really. I went from being a more visible investigator about town to keeping it entirely sub rosa."

Alexander hesitated at something in that but then nodded. "Of course you'd protect your children. And your wife. Though I am sure she is more capable of her own protection than others might guess."

Another fine compliment, and Carillon lifted his own tea in a silent toast. "I am glad you appreciate her excellence." He shrugged. "This is not the same situation, but I have been living with that measured analysis of risk every day since then. And before then, too. I never really set it down after the War, like so many others. Frankly, someone impersonally trying to kill me because I happen to be in the wrong place is almost relaxing, comparatively."

"Long before the War for me." That was what he'd expected from Alexander, if Alexander said anything at all. "And so now we should discuss the particular risks here. You said that Sepp and Anneliese wished to meet us for dinner tomorrow?"

"Mmhmm." Carillon gestured. "We'll come around to how to play it in a moment. I think that's the longer discussion. Other questions, first?"

"The most obvious. Let's start there." Alexander offered it, almost teasing. "You do have an unexpected taste for the obvious from time to time."

Carillon beamed at that. It was a tiny step forward, but that the man could tease, even about something where they were working together, an obvious question. That was promising. "Yes?"

"Is this a trap?" Oh, that was a pure delight. He wasn't sure if it was an examination question or a judiciously blunt inquiry, but either way, it wasn't hedged around with thorns. It was fair and sensible and a fine beginning.

"If Constanza and Gerhard were present, I would be more concerned. As it is, we will need to be careful in the house, and a fair part of the grounds, but the sort of precautions we'd have been inclined to, anyway. Take your average aged Council home, and work from there. They will, however, expect a certain amount of protective warding on our personal items and rooms."

"Tell me about them." Alexander settled a little more comfortably on his bench. "And a bit of the food, perhaps. We will be here a while?"

"I will give you plenty of warning of any further potential upsets." It was a sincere promise, especially since Carillon hoped to discuss all the major forthcoming ones in the next few minutes. He passed over a meat pie and a pastry. "The land magic is different here, you know. No Pact of course, no formal agreement like that. Not the same way, certainly. Though there are now customs around how magic is and is not discussed."

"Mostly not, as I have observed." Alexander nodded. "Where the Pact explicitly placed the tending land magic in the Council - for Albion herself - and in the landed Lords and Ladies. Germany places it in her people at large. Whether they have magic or not."

"Quite. There is a sense of tending the land, of noblesse oblige, of the folk customs and traditions mattering. Things being of a place. And of course, the old divisions still matter. Germany, as a united country, is still so terribly young." Sixty-four years was, well, Alexander's lifetime, give or take a few months. No time at all.

"People will say they are from Bavaria or Munich or whatever place they are connected with, before they speak of being German as a whole. Even since the Great War." Which had, honestly, solidified the 'like us or not like us' nature rather a lot. The political situation since had simply accelerated and hardened it.

"And the Heinrichs?"

"Long established on their estate, going back four or five hundred years. Deeply aware of the customs and places. They have their own portal, if that gives you a sense of the thing." It was not at all common on the Continent, where they were solely in the gift of the Fatae. Carillon considered. "I met them in a magical context, as it happens. My Grand Tour, someone Mistress Alworthy thought I should become acquainted with was in their circle."

"What sort of magic?" There were, mind, quite a number of options.

"Constanza has a certain gift for incantation, as we'd count it. Also, a fair bit of tending the magic of the land like a garden, though that's a poor metaphor. Gerhard is more fond of formal ritual, though very much in the more local forms. He'll tolerate some of the initiatory branches, or something Roman. But he rather dismisses most such things out of Albion, and certainly anything from your mother's side of things. Foolish, but there you are."

Alexander grimaced. "On the one hand, I do hate the hospitality of bigots. On the other hand, it does leave some potentially useful gaps. Are they the best choice for your alchemist to get out?"

"There were three possible estates. As far as we can tell, the compound is a manageable distance from all three, a few miles at most. But the Heinrichs were the most promising, both for location and for, mmm. The likely circumstances."

"And you don't think the invitation, if we get one, is a trap." Alexander, of course, came back to that.

"Dangerous, yes. A trap, no. Sepp prefers men, Anneliese prefers women. Especially in the current circumstances. They've been inclined to host like-minded friends wherever his parents aren't, in order to make sure the club they're in won't be raided. If you'd not put it together, Sepp also likes a dollop of exhibitionism, and Anneliese enjoys watching other people's. I know less about their magical skills. Neither of them makes much of it, but assume competent training."

Alexander contemplated that, opened his mouth, then shook his head. "Let me think on my questions about that a few more minutes. What sort of protections on the house, no, Schloss, isn't it? Have you been there before?"

"Yes, but not since before the War." Carillon considered. "They'll know we're magical. They're familiar with my more public skills, and a bit beyond that, unfortunately. If you keep to things I might reasonably know, it will probably go without comment. Constanza and Gerhard might realise you're Council, but they might not. They have not been overly political until, well, recently." Carillon couldn't even blame them for that. Any sensible person would know the politics would catch up to them, and it would be better to have a workable reputation in place when that happened.

"And Sepp and his magic?"

"I rather get the impression Anneliese is more attentive to it, but that might be show. I do not know them well enough to be sure, but I think anything that would pass with their parents would go unremarked with them as well."

Alexander considered the implications. "What will they think of the invitation?"

"If they hear about it? It's not as if Sepp will entirely advertise he's inviting us for an orgy or what have you. They disapprove, both in principle and of hearing any of the details."

"Not unreasonable, in parents." Alexander pointed out. "I suppose I have a common enough name, considering. It might not stand out. And I've spent very little time in Germany, mostly in transit. That's been to my advantage before."

Carillon considered him. The shade of his skin was striking, especially here, but that might simply be a good tan. The dark hair, the same thing, there were other explanations. "And we've not played up the Egyptian connection in our travels, other than our interest in a wide range of art. And your ability to read hieroglyphs. Which could come from a number of places. Let's keep it that way, shall we?"

Alexander spread his hands and nodded. "My plan is not to draw too much attention to myself, to be honest. You do much better being the centre of things."

The way he'd phrased that made Carillon tilt his head. "When you've had business outside of Albion, how do you usually play it?"

"If I'm directly representing the Council, all that formality, of course." He waved a hand, dismissing the pomp and fuss. "But far more often, as a businessman, a magician of private means, a book collector. All of which are true enough, except for the business."

Alexander paused, as if deciding what he might reasonably share here. Carillon thought he made the choice to be more informative, rather than less. "That's managed by one of the Council, a cover for whatever we need. Imports and exports, largely, but some specialised woods and other materials. An excuse to be anywhere in the world, honestly, bar the Arctic and Antarctic. He has an excellent man of business who does a precis of a proper story as needed."

"So this is nothing new, then. And your name isn't widely known. That's a help." It had been what Carillon and Lizzie had gathered over their research, but it was good to have confirmation.

CHAPTER 21
IN A ROWBOAT

Alexander nodded. So far, this conversation was informative and pragmatic. It was, frankly, a pleasure to sort through the details efficiently with someone whose competence was a match for his own. Carillon thought about the same issues, and while they might weigh some of them rather differently, they had quite a similar approach as such things went.

It made Alexander wonder what sort of investigations Carillon had got up to in the past. And what, by all the named gods, he'd done to draw that kind of blatant attack. Not something he was going to ask about now. If they made it back to Albion safely with Hoffman, perhaps it might be a topic for drinks after the debriefing.

The magical considerations were, really, also what he expected. They had a range of potions and enchantments made up to look like ordinary sleeping pills and other minor medical aids. Carillon's pet alchemist really quite good, and unlike Garin, willing to hide his skill behind unthreatening labels that did not articulate his brilliance.

"That brings us, I suppose, to the other topic. How do we handle the, ahem. Personal side?"

"Ah." Carillon settled back, now watching carefully. As he would, Alexander supposed. This was delicate on all fronts. "Do you have particular concerns here? Or rather, pardon. Which of your concerns are upmost at the moment?"

Alexander permitted himself a twitch of a shoulder. "To be honest, I am worried I will give the whole thing away. Recoiling at the wrong point, showing some sign, easily read by others, that I am a fraud in this." It was a matter of pride to handle his part properly, as well as, frankly, essential to both their safety.

Carillon didn't rush him. And he didn't dismiss the concern. It was a real one, and they should both have the sense to know it. Instead, after a moment, he steepled his fingers. "There are options for how we approach it. We have arranged things that you are new to a man's touch. Do you think you can manage startled, unsettled, surprised, at interactions, rather than disgust?"

"What I feel is - pardon, it is not a topic I am used to articulating at all, to anyone. It is not disgust. It is that it has been utterly irrelevant to me, except as a topic of social amusement, teasing others about their escapades. I know the language of it well enough, I suppose, but it does not connect to much I have done. A bit like cooking, really. I can manage field conditions when I must, but no one would look to me for anything beyond that. Or this boat. You see, yes?" Suddenly, it mattered that Carillon understood that whatever Alexander felt, it wasn't disgust or shame or something else poisonous.

Again, that quiet nod, taking his time. "On the physical level, I hope very much we can avoid more explicit intimacies, bared skin, a public touch in private areas. Even if the touch were something you welcomed, I am not terribly inclined to make a show in front of others that way. Innuendo, yes. Brash exhibitionism, no."

Carillon hesitated, took a sip of his tea. "We may be in the room when others indulge. I suspect it is the sort of party where that will happen, at least as people get deeper in their cups. But how are you with me leaning in? A hand on your thigh, or around your shoulder or waist? Being a bit unsure, nervous, stiff, that is fine. But I do not wish to offend, or press beyond whatever limit you wish to set." There was something in that last that was suddenly earnest.

Alexander spread his hands. "As I said earlier, my preferences do not matter. Simply the task at hand."

"Now, that is not something I would tolerate in bed. Will, if I have any say in it. Though, as you say, circumstances may require things we do not choose. That is why I would like to know your preferences now. And if they change, in the midst. It would not be unreasonable for us, say, to have a lover's tiff. High feelings, drinking, drugs, all good reasons for that, as well. A bit of drama might even play well to the audience, come to that."

"I would prefer not to argue with you." That slipped out of Alexander's mouth in a moment of truth that was very like Carillon and not at all like Alexander's usual mode. "Fight, I mean. I - I would not know how to take it, how to play it."

It was a feeble excuse, though it was also accurate enough. More, that if they fought, he did not know how to recover from it. He had no clue what to do with those gestures of warmth, of inclusion and welcome, that Carillon kept making, but he did not want to lose them. At least not until he understood them better and why they kept catching at him like burrs.

"Then let us do our best to avoid it. Unless it is strategically relevant. Storming off for a long walk might be handy at some point. That, though, I suspect we could fake simply enough." Carillon nodded, as if counting off points in his head. "Leaning? My hands?"

"Both of those are fine, so long as I may be stiff about it. Is there - is there sitting in laps, or something of the kind?" He tried to think of what else he'd seen. "Presumably not naked wrestling, but close dancing, or ..." He thought about a few of the people in the club, two nights ago. He didn't entirely have language for the way they made one body out of two, coiling against each other so tightly no air showed between them.

"Oh, probably." Carillon said it breezily, then furrowed his eyebrows. "Ah. We should talk about that, in particular. I mentioned there are roles, assumptions, in sex."

"And that even though I am older, in all the other ways, they will assume that I am, erm. The passive partner, as it goes." Alexander was not sure what to make of that. The assumptions, what they meant, the apparent rigidity of the thing.

"Just so. And in this case, that is to our advantage. If I am the more active partner, it is expected I would guide you, show you what I wanted, what I expected. It would also be mine, under some customs, to make sure you were not frightened or hurt by others. Though again, you're a grown man, not a stripling boy new to the world."

Alexander nodded along at that, but he caught some echo here, something he wasn't sure how to interpret. "May I ask about your general preferences in the matter, or experience?"

That, for some reason, made Carillon's back straighten up, as if he'd run smack into a wall of expectations that did not quite fit. Alexander had seen that in dozens of men over time. "My experience is almost entirely as the active partner. Certainly, the past two decades or so." Which implied there had been times it had not been.

"That does not entirely answer the question." Alexander ventured it carefully, taking a narrow road between pointing out the obvious and giving offence.

"No." Carillon let out a puff of breath. "It is not a conversation I'm willing to have here and now. It does not bear on our plans. No one there will have known me to be anything other than the one in control, no matter what rumours they've heard. Can you manage that?"

Alexander would not push. There was no point in it. For all that, it had been a fairly gentle refusal. No blaming him for asking. He held up his hands palm up, in silent agreement.

A moment later, Carillon went on, as if he were talking about something entirely ordinary. "When we are done with this, I am glad to engage in a larger discussion of the topic of what men do with men, if you wish. I have quite a collection of pillow books in my library, as they're called, with a range of illustrations to please many tastes. And there is quite an extensive body of magic to bring pleasure. Which, now I think of it, may I use that on you? Sensation, warmth, pleasure, perhaps a touch of prickling."

"Do people really find that pleasing? The last one?" Alexander wriggled his fingers. "Pins and needles, you mean?"

"Some do. What people like when it comes to sex and their bodies is an exceedingly wide map, honestly. For any given taste you can think of, no matter how outre, someone probably shares it. The trick is finding that person, without having to wade through a hundred people who will shame you for it or worse."

Alexander nods. "All right. And we are playing it that we are new to this. We might have engaged, um, in the most climactic act in private, but my nerves will not permit it around others?"

"Just so. That you have learned to touch me in ways that please. That I have been showing you how to take a man and enjoy it, but it is still new and fragile. Perhaps I might imply things about your talented mouth." That got a hint of a purr to it, though Carillon immediately pulled back on it, at some expression he caught. "I hope not to be too specific, at least not in your earshot. I'll let you know what I've bragged about in private conversations if it comes up."

"And should I expect others to make an overture? Will you, with anyone else?"

"Likely, yes, but you can defer to my preferences. And particularly my insistence on training you to my particular pleasures. There are people who would love to spoil that, but I think none is likely to be in this set. It is a particular kind of power play, and we are distant enough from that kind of politicking to be safe this time. As to whether I'll bed anyone else? Again, I hope not, but I will take that choice rather than risk pressing you."

"You also have a right to say no, do you not?" Alexander thought that this was, at least, fair. He was not used to being permitted limits, but if he was, surely everyone else also was. That was just logics.

Carillon's mouth quirked up. "As you say, no limits on what is needed for the work at hand." He brushed his hands off, making it clear he would not be argued with here. "Anything else?"

"Not directly about that. I am..." Alexander considered his word choice now. "I appreciate you laying it out so clearly, and I will do my best to follow your lead. As much as I can manage. I also appreciate your, your. That you asked my preferences, even if they may not serve." It had been a long time since anyone had thought that his preferences in more than minor choices of food or drink mattered.

Again, Carillon inclined his head. "Of course." As if he would not permit himself to offer anything less. "That implies another question."

"You'd explained the charms in your book at Ytene. But I had a passing thought today. Why the image of Jupiter and Juno, for the muffling sound? It seems curiously specific."

That made Carillon relax into an open smile. "It hinges on a particular detail. Namely, that Juno pulled back the cloak from Jupiter. It works only so long as I am honest and open with Lizzie. She helped me design it, her blood is in the paint, same as mine. Delicate and fiddly work. Since, of course, there are times we cannot tell each other a thing, or we have some surprise we're keeping. A gift, an entertainment, a fantasy to share later that requires some planning." He shrugged, as if those were all ordinary things in his life, both to give and receive. "But in such cases, we are honest we have something of the kind in mind."

That was far more foreign to Alexander than the sex, the implications of intimacy flowing freely. He'd seen a glimpse of it with Isembard and Thesan. But they both were inclined not to wave the details in front of him. He saw flickers, not the whole thing. One star, not the constellation. He gathered his thoughts. "Did she require that of you?"

"She finds it reassuring, certainly. But no, I offered. First, it is a particular challenge, the ritual that set it, and I do like to tackle the unfathomable. But also because I wanted to be honest with myself. If I am doing something I would not tell her about, there is something wrong. In that matter, at least. Best to mend it quickly." He turned his hand palm up. "We had an incident when we first were getting to know each other, where we misunderstood that, and I do not wish to dwell in that place again."

There was something darker there, clouds across the sun. Something that ran deep, chiseled on him like the scar was, even if just as frequently hidden. Alexander nodded. "Thank you." For the details of the charm, and for letting him see that hint, both. He trusted Carillon would understand. "Should we think about getting back? I would offer to row, but we'd be in the water."

"I can manage. You just keep an eye out and tell me what's coming up. Or if there's any interesting birds. Might as well enjoy the outing while we can."

CHAPTER 22
AN EXCLUSIVE BERLIN RESTAURANT ON MONDAY, MAY 13TH

Monday evening, Carillon smiled as he and Alexander were shown into an alcove in one of Berlin's most exclusive restaurants. Set on a street among other magical businesses, he could see the flashes and sparks of charms. There were drinks bubbling over in entirely unnatural colours, and of course, all the glittering decorations. Sepp half-rose as they entered, offering his hand. "Herr Carillon."

Carillon beamed at him. "Carillon, Sepp, everyone calls me that. No need for formality, yes? A delight to see you, it's been forever." He turned to bow over Anneliese's hand. "And Anneliese, you are even more brilliant than last I saw you." He was playing up the informality quickly, using the informal you as well.

Sepp was dressed sharply, a beautifully fitted suit and deep golden yellow tie, but Anneliese might have walked out of a film set. Brilliant red lipstick, a sapphire blue dress, and bright pins in her golden bobbed hair shimmering like feathers. They might have started as feathers, for all he knew. They had a crispness to them that seemed unlikely to be purely metalwork. "My friend, also assisting me with a bit of art dealing, Alexander Landry. His German is excellent, of course."

"Herr Landry." Sepp settled back in his chair, while Carillon stepped to his own chair to give Alexander space to make his own greetings. Once they were all seated, Alexander was on his left, Anneliese on his right. They had their backs to the entrance, which was going to make Carillon at least, all nerves. More than he already was.

Though of course, Sepp had fought too, or at least been in the Army. They had, naturally, never quite discussed that, nor had Sepp's parents brought it up. Sweeping the War under the rug was something some people could do, even if Carillon had never been able to follow suit.

"A charming place." Carillon glanced around, and then settled in to make small talk while the staff brought drinks, inquired about their orders, and all the other fripperies of such an outing. When the waiter withdrew, Carillon raised an eyebrow. "How much discretion do you prefer?"

"We are modestly private." Which was no help at all, but Sepp was not made for helpfulness, he was made for other things. He was, at the moment, eyeing Alexander up and down, thoughtfully. "I had not thought you to prefer older men, Carillon. But, oh, I do see why Friedrich thought we should have supper."

That, at least, gave some sense of the privacy. Right. Politics, likely to be reported. Not that Carillon intended to go anywhere near that. Sex, on the other hand, at least somewhat permissible.

Carillon smiled, one of the smiles Lizzie referred to as owl-like, deceptively simple. He shifted his left hand, resting it lightly on the centre of Alexander's forearm. He felt the tension immediately under his fingertips, and cocked his head with just a hint of possessiveness. When he glanced sideways, Alexander's face had a half-smile, the perfect amount of uncertainty and newness. His face held no sign of the tension Carillon's fingers felt, and he left his hand where it was. "Sometimes, life brings us gifts." That let him give a little half-smile at Alexander.

Anneliese was languid, but with an edge to her expression that made Carillon wonder if both she and Sepp were employing glamours. Given the world, it seemed likely, and also their expressions were a little forward, a hair too perfect. "You know we're having a party, Thursday to Sunday or Monday. Quite a few people, while Sepp's parents are in Munich. Lashings of drinks, Carillon." She flipped the r prettily. "Should we invite you? It's no fun if you two hole up in a room by yourselves, mind. All our sort, with magic, mind, you needn't hide that." She paused, just a fraction of a second. "You know about Carillon's reputation, Herr Landry? A most excellent one, when it comes to intimate amusements, private and public." Her eyes gleamed on the last word. "People still talk about his skills with, what was that charm, the one that trails pleasure like fireworks?"

Ah, there it was, the challenge. They weren't going to just roll over and do what Carillon wanted or needed. Carillon shrugged. "I am still, how shall we say, encouraging Alexander to enjoy himself fully. He is not a man made for easy relaxation, but I do enjoy a challenge."

That made Sepp laugh. "You always have, yes? My parents, most complimentary about your wits. Even if you are English." Which was unfortunate, actually. This would be much easier if people thought him a bit dim.

But the last time he'd been at one of their other homes, there had been a problem with a deranged bull, which had been sent wild by eating something magical that had not agreed with him. Given the choice between being seen as competent and lethal horns aimed at him - and worse, at innocents - he'd take the competence showing every time.

Carillon simply inclined his head, murmuring, "Thank you." Then he returned to the point. "I enjoy a spot of watching. And of course, Alexander understands that I do have needs. If he is not willing to oblige in the moment, I might look elsewhere." He let his finger tap once, then withdrew his hand.

It was aided by the waiter coming in with their first course. The ensuing bustle was a natural break in the conversation and the obligatory "Guten Appetit!" from Anneliese as the hostess. She picked at her food with her fork. "How do you find Berlin, Herr Landry? Or may I presume?"

"Alexander, please." He cleared his throat, took a sip of wine, unhurried. Carillon admired the grace under pressure, though of course it was there. The man lived in an eternal state of pressure without relief, as far as Carillon was beginning to realise. The rare pause, but never a release. "A fascinating city. Rich in art and beauty. My father was French, I know Paris well, and I spent a number of years in the Commonwealth countries and America."

"But you speak German quite sufficiently!" Anneliese made it sound like that was a surprise.

Alexander half-smiled at her, tipping his glass. "You are most kind. It is one of the languages of knowledge and science, of course. I have been to Cologne and Munich briefly. It is a pleasure to see the charm of Berlin." He favoured her with another smile. "And to meet such a lady, a shining jewel among the stars of the realm."

It was entirely over the top. Everyone at the table knew

it, but Anneliese laughed. "Oh, flattery! Indeed, a great gift. I do not generally favour men, mein Herr, but every woman does like to be told she's beautiful."

Carillon lifted his own glass, a tiny gesture of amusement, before he took a sip. As he set it down, Sepp nodded. It was one of those silent conversations, though they were not so subtle at it as Carillon and Lizzie prided themselves on. "Do say you'll come. We'll have several cars going up Thursday morning, back Monday afternoon. Perhaps Sunday, if there are pressures from the larger world. The portal here in Berlin was so convenient, but reserved for government business now."

Anneliese flicked her fingers. "In between, drinking, dancing, more than a few other treats." Potions and drugs, then, as Carillon had expected. "And of course, a grand time between the sheets. Or on top of them. Or not near any sheets as well. We've some acrobats coming in on the Saturday, a decadent feast."

"Of course we'll come. So generous, so hospitable. A warm place. And I've told Alexander how beautiful the forest is. Haunting, but beautiful." He added to Alexander, "Not at all like the New Forest, mind. My home." That was to Anneliese and Sepp.

Alexander coughed. "Very generous, thank you." He seemed unsure what to say here, or whether to let Carillon make all the arrangements.

Carillon went on smoothly. "Just one thing, if it isn't a bother. A quiet bedroom, perhaps, though, to recover? I am a tad jumpy if woken in my sleep. The War, you know." Carillon expected Alexander might be even more so, honestly. He'd had a decade to set down some of those habits, even if being away from Lizzie made them jerk to life again.

Anneliese waved a hand. "I have just the room in mind, and of course, our maids are trained not to interrupt."

"Just so. Anyone else invited I might know of?" Carillon eased the way into the question he wanted answered before they arrived.

Anneliese picked up smoothly. "You might not. Our age and younger." She mentioned a few names, ones Carillon only knew of through Lizzie's research. She concluded with, "Oh, and Quirin, possibly, you surely remember Sepp's brother. And Dita wrote about something she saw you at. An event in, oh, Trellech. In February?"

"The opera gala, of course." Carillon half-smiled. Where he'd baited Alexander, not that he could let that show. "A wonderful concert, yes. My wife and I were there. Doing our bit for the arts, you know."

He could feel Alexander beside him, a sense of the energy roiling, but when he glanced over, still the possessive love, Alexander seemed outwardly well enough. "Have you done much previous work with art, Alexander?" Sepp shrugged one rugged shoulder. "My parents have quite a collection."

"A lifelong interest. I have done a bit of research, various projects for those who need a willing scribe or someone to go hither and yon, sparing them the travel." Which was a fascinating way to describe himself, Carillon thought. But of course, he could scarcely bring out that he was on the Council, or that he was master of several magical arts, at one time a professor at Schola. Sepp and Annaliese might know that, but if they didn't, better not to hint at it. "This has been most intriguing."

There was a momentary hesitation, as if he were considering what name to use. "Carillon has quite an eye for fine art. We'll be wrapping up our purchasing by Wednesday. Lunch with the Beckers, tomorrow."

Anneliese giggled. "I gather Frau Becker had a lovely time. She didn't quite come out and say so, darling, but it was clear who she meant. Well-bred Englishmen having more surprises than she'd anticipated. It put me in mind of your reputation, of course, all to the good."

Carillon spread out his hand and gestured at a bow. "I do endeavour to give satisfaction when I take to the field. And if it left her inclined to consider our other offers, then we have all benefited, yes?"

The next course was brought in, then. Finally the conversation shifted a bit. Alexander kept his comments pleasant and mild, the sign of a man who knew he was the one with the least influence in the room, by a long shot. Once they were well into the meal, Carillon turned the topic to more magical subjects. "I have been trying to explain to Alexander how things are different here. Rather more of the local folk magics."

"Mutti has made quite a study," Sepp agreed, amiably. "And of course, they take tending. You have customs around May Eve, but they are different, I remember? Walpurgisnacht, it is coming back into some fashion. Costumes, pranks, wildness." His eyes glittered. "Witchcraft. There is a growing tradition to take that out amongst the people. Scare some of them into doing as proper Germans should."

Carillon firmly repressed a shudder at the implication. It likely meant tormenting some poor farmer or a licence to harm whoever had the least power. "Not our traditions, no. With us, there is a fire at dawn, seeing the sun back. I have customs, as the lord, of course, they take much of the day." Including enthusiastically bedding Lizzie, not that they needed a particular day to encourage that, on the whole. But it was a blessing on the land that he would not skimp on.

"Carillon attended Oxford University. There is a tradition of singing there, gathering around a bell tower. A particular song, if I recall?" Alexander slipped the comment in smoothly.

Carillon picked up from there, grateful for the space to expand. "A hymn, in Latin, written in the 17th century, yes."

"Ah, that is a shame. We are beginning to see a return to what was before Christianity. Very ornate, churches, but not always the power one would like." Anneliese dismissed well over a millennia of power with a flip of her hand. Carillon was no Christian, but he thought the world was better with more ways to find comfort and beauty and compassion rather than fewer. Even if, as Alexander had noted, he tended to the Mercurial himself.

However, that let them ask a few questions about those changes, which gods were getting more attention now, at least among the magical of Germany. Carillon did not entirely like the sound of what he heard, but it would be useful information if it came to any sort of greater challenge.

It was not the gods themselves that bothered him. All cultures had gods of conflict and victory, just as they all had gods of peace and civilisation. He rather thought people needed both. The world was not a static place. It was the tone, though, that ran through Anneliese's comments and even more through Sepp's. A chance to avenge themselves on the world. That boded no good for anyone at all.

As the supper finished, Sepp drew Carillon aside and murmured. "A most handsome man. Do see if you can loosen his nerves. Or if we can provide something that will?" They'd have to be careful of drugs and potions in the food at the Schloss. A bother, but nothing they hadn't done before. And nothing they weren't prepared for, really, thanks to Cephus.

Carillon merely smiled and raised an eyebrow. "We will see. I intend to enjoy him for some time to come, and I will not throw that away for a mere night's pleasure."

He then gestured, raising his voice slightly. "Here, shall we find a cab back to our hotel?" They made their goodbyes and set off.

CHAPTER 23
THE TIERGARTEN, LATER THAT NIGHT

When they got back toward the hotel, Alexander was trying to gather himself when Carillon said, "A postprandial walk in the Tiergarten? I could use some fresh air."

At Alexander's jerk of a nod, he leaned forward to say something muffled in German to the driver. It got a laugh and a nod, then the driver made a different turn. A few minutes later, he pulled up along an edge of the park and nodded at a particular spot.

"This is the magical area. Warded and such, with some quiet seats." Carillon hopped out and waited for Alexander to join him on the pavement. It was brisk out now with a breeze, but nothing too unpleasant with coats charmed for warmth.

They found a spot out in the open, well-lit by lampposts. They were well away from anywhere someone else might choose as a lover's lane or whatever the Berlin name for it was. They simultaneously checked for anyone listening with amulet and book, then nodded at each other.

"You are sure this is the best option?" Alexander spoke

first. Something in the evening had set all his nerves on edge, and it wasn't just the touch or the frankness of the sexual discussion.

"Still, yes. The good thing about an orgy is that people want to sleep it off in the morning. It will give us a window - if we do not overindulge ourselves - to get out without being closely observed."

"I don't suppose you have any potions for alertness?" Alexander had a couple of things along that might do.

Carillon shook his head. "They're not at all good for me, and my alchemist hasn't figured out a suitable alternative that works better than strong coffee. Which, at least, we should be able to get." He hesitated. "The supper brought up a number of points."

Alexander nodded, wanting to pace now, but that would draw attention they didn't need. "Where do we begin? With our plans?" He lifted a hand. "Moment. Tell me about their portal, the details, I mean?" It had been nagging at Alexander since Sepp had brought it up.

"Unusual, yes." Carillon picked up the actual question easily enough. Most of the portals on the Continent were for more general use. They were all Fatae made, through painstaking negotiation each time. Alexander had read most of those agreements at one point or another, because they were illuminating when the Council needed to approach the Fatae in Albion. Most of the portals were two, three, four hundred years old now, set in place long before the modern borders had begun to coalesce.

Having one at a private home, a relatively remote private home, that must have been some particular coup for the family. "A particular story?"

"Gerhard tells it best, but some signal aid to the Fatae during the Thirty Years War. They have a grand painting or two about the tale, but of course, not anywhere public. The portal was a gift."

"And does that imply the family can still muster that kind of magical aid in the current generation?" Alexander was thinking through the implications.

"These are fallen times, comparatively. But yes. Assume your trunk will be searched. Anything in a blood lock should be fine, at least as long as it merely looks like your own personal collection of drugs and medicines. Better, if there's something we can share, which I have and will bring out at an appropriate time."

"Of course you have something for that." Alexander ran his hand over his face, through his hair. "Why am I not surprised?"

Carillon grinned broadly. "I have, as you say, a pet alchemist. And a clever wife." He seemed damnably relaxed about this whole thing, though there was an edge to him, the more Alexander watched him closely. Going into battle, yes, but the way a man who'd been tried and tested did. Not foolishly, not brashly, but using every tool at his disposal.

As Alexander would. Did. There was something at least a little reassuring about that. "And our plans?"

"Arrive on Thursday. We'll see who else is there. Who knows, we might find out something for your fellows that would be of use. Or for my connections. Possibly both!" That was almost gleeful. "We can establish a desire for time on our own, both in whatever rooms they give us, and in a walk or ride or whatever the options are. I'd prefer a ride. It's faster, but they might want to send a groom with us, and that's no good." He shrugs. "There are many pieces of this where we will have to trust our instincts. Put our best foot forward."

Too many for Alexander's liking. But to be fair, he never had enough information for his tastes. "And your friend?"

Carillon glanced down to check his book again, and reassured, said quietly, "Lizzie will post a letter first thing tomorrow. It will get there Wednesday evening thanks to the portals, looking like an ordinary communication from my pet alchemist about some materia research. It will let my friend know we will be in the area, and arranging something that will enable brief communication if we're careful. From there, we coordinate a meeting, so you can figure out what is needed. And then likely another, to do the work."

"More risk to get away twice. Three times, if we need to scout the area."

"There's no hope for that, really. It's a large forest. While I know roughly where he'll be, I don't know what the protections are like." He glanced down at his book again, then kept his voice quiet. "How much of a guard there actually is. Or how competent. There probably is one, but my friend is not prepossessing as a risk as these things go. A man with a gun or a bit of ensnaring magic could manage on his own."

Alexander nodded again. "And the party, then." He barely repressed a sigh at it. He had done worse things since joining the Council. Rather a lot worse. And this was in a good cause, both the direct information Berthold could share, and other details that might come out with time and care.

Carillon hesitated for a moment. "May I ask a personal question?"

"Ha." It came out as a bark of a laugh. "You are presumed to be my lover. Surely personal questions are part and parcel of the expectation."

Carillon tilted his head, momentarily diverted. "One

may love the body, and never come near the heart." Alexander shivered, once, unable to repress it. That Carillon would home in on the heart, rather than the soul, as might have been just as likely in English. "And one may love the heart of a person, and have the body always chaste. Or love both, which I admit, is far preferable."

"Go on." It came out as almost a growl, but that did not apparently discourage Carillon from asking.

Carillon's tone next was barely present, the whisper of an owl about to take a mouse from the field. "How long has it been since someone touched you in kindness?"

Alexander couldn't stop himself from closing his eyes. "Beyond a common handshake, a ritual, my man, or a tailor? And not Isembard and Thesan?"

"Just so." There was an intensity there now to go with the whisper that pinned Alexander in place, back to that day in August 1917.

"Seventeen years, nine months, twelve days." It had been dark then, too. He closed his eyes hard against it, and against the memory of Perry leaning against him in an abandoned cottage. It had been comfortable, trusting, and a sense of belonging, despite the surroundings. A moment later, he felt Carillon's hand rest on his arm again, so delicately he could have shaken it off with a twitch.

"I am so sorry." Carillon's voice was pained now, not that Alexander could look at his face or look anywhere. He had only strength enough to sit and not flee madly into the dark. To feel the pressure of the hand on his arm. Carillon didn't move, didn't press further. He didn't make it worse, and it had been just as long since people didn't make it worse.

They sat like that for what felt like hours, but must have been only minutes. As Alexander managed to take a breath, then another slightly deeper, he fought himself back to at least a facade of normality. "Pardon."

"You have nothing to be sorry for." Now, that silken voice was sharp, but not at Alexander, not remotely at Alexander. It was if Carillon were bodily inserting himself between Alexander and the thorns of the world, making a space that allowed him at least to breathe. "Take more time, if you need."

Alexander shook his head. "Can't." If he let himself linger now, he'd lose his grip. That was eye-catching in a public park. It was dangerous, in this park and in this city. And it might destroy any chance of their plans coming to fruition.

That got a small grunt. "Stiff upper lip, then. Right." Beside him, Carillon let out a puff of breath. "I believe that Sepp has been cautioned against making advances. I wasn't sure of his tastes."

"I am an older man. Surely..." Alexander suddenly did not know how to finish that sentence.

"If I thought you would welcome it, I would list your virtues, apparent and hidden." At that, Alexander's eyes snapped open, to see Carillon raise his hand, now looking almost amused. "I won't. You won't have it, and we've already talked about how you get to have preferences, and have them respected as much as we can. But you are a good-looking man, eye-catching. Besides those other things."

Alexander shrugged and heard the tension in his neck crackle. He consciously took a breath or two to settle his magic and his body. "Should I anticipate an attempt? And what are his tastes, anyway?"

"In general, as well as specific?"

Alexander managed a small nod. It was necessary information, and it would let him sort himself out better while hearing it.

"I am taking this from observation, you understand? I might be wrong, though it's based on fragments of gossip, then and now. A fondness for drugs and drink, also charms to discourage a man saying no. He likes a bit of a struggle. Not outright violence, but persuasion. Talking his partner into things. Which is where matters might get tricky for you."

"You worked this out how?"

"The way he leaned forward, at your discomfort. There's a certain sort of man - and woman, I suspect it's to Anneliese's tastes to watch, too - who likes to see the walls come down. Done properly, I admit, it's a glorious thing. But they would rush." He flicked his fingers. "I would lock your door at night and check your food and drink. But you were going to do that, anyway. I will as well, of course. Unless circumstances require otherwise on the door. You have a range of charms at your disposal, should someone press in private?"

"Oh, of course. Some will attract more notice than others. I won't be able to tell until I get a feel for the warding."

"A pleasure to be working with a competent profession-al." When Alexander glanced over this time, that was almost vulpine. A fox raiding a hen house. Then he laughed. "I am teasing and not teasing, of course. Trying to get you to smile a little, truth be told."

Alexander wanted to grimace and grumble, but he saw the point. "I do think my showing nerves is not going to be a problem. And we know now how I react to teasing. Or..." He gestured feebly with his far left hand. "Though I am beginning to envy Thesan."

"For what reason? I can think of a number, actually, but I'm not sure which applies."

"She's left-handed. And also not a duellist. She can rest a hand on Isembard's left and not be in the way. We'll foul ourselves up, one or both of us, if we do the same."

"Ah, there you go, you're strategising again. I am relieved." Only then did Carillon lean back and relax. "Though quite true. I can rest my hand on your thigh or waist, depending on the seating. Subtle, mild, and doesn't block charm-casting. Though I suppose you're reasonably ambidextrous, where you can be?"

"I am properly trained. Whatever else I am, they made sure of that." Alexander was not so recovered as he wished to be. He recognised the slip as soon as it was out of his mouth.

If Carillon noticed - and surely he had, the man noticed near everything - he made no comment about it. Instead, he nodded once. "Anything else? It would do no good to catch cold before we arrive. And I admit, I could use a good scrub from some of the conversation at supper." Then, again, the flashing and quick, "May I be of any other help?"

Alexander shook his head. "A bath and a glass of something soothing. And a book." He could retreat into the sense of a book. Carillon understood that, too. Without further comment, they went to find the main road and a cab back to the hotel.

CHAPTER 24

ARRIVING AT A COUNTRY SCHLOSS ON
THURSDAY, MAY 16TH

Thursday morning, a car pulled up outside their hotel to gather up Carillon, Alexander, and their smaller trunks. Five minutes later, they pulled up and acquired a languid looking young man, rather wan, and a young woman with bobbed golden hair. They draped themselves against the seats after the briefest of introductions - Rudi and Lulu. Both were perhaps twenty-five at most, and they made Carillon feel tremendously old. He glanced at Alexander, who must feel more so, but Alexander smiled and nodded.

Five minutes after that, Lulu had determined that they knew none of the same people. Also that they were coming along at the particular invitation of Sepp and Annelise, and that neither man was going to say more about that. An air of mystery wouldn't hurt anything, and it was, in its way, the most honest response, if clearly also boring to her.

And ten minutes after that, they pulled up at a third hotel, which discharged a stereotypical American. He was also golden-haired, broad shouldered, carrying the sort of battered leather suitcase that suggested extensive travel.

Lulu took one look at him, and sprawled herself into Rudi's lap, letting the man take the other half of the seat.

He tipped his hat. "Guten Tag!" Very bright and cheerful, though his accent was curious, even in the bare few words.

Alexander inclined his head. "American?" He asked in English.

"Oh, sure. From Connecticut." He then considered Alexander's age. "Sir."

"Alexander Landry. English, obviously. This is Lord Geoffrey Carillon. We've been on an art-buying expedition, and Carillon knows our hosts from previous travels."

"Their parents rather better." Carillon could pick up his cues properly. "But we could use a bit of time somewhere more private, mmm?" He glanced at Alexander knowingly.

"Theodore Adams. Not the Massachusetts Adams, worse luck. Pleased to make your acquaintance, I'm sure." He glanced at Rudi and Lulu beside him. She wriggled her nails at him before going back to exploring Rudi's mouth. Clearly, they were not going to be conversational. Carillon took a good look at him. Well dressed, though by American standards rather than British or German ones. He was wearing good shoes with a surprisingly solid sole. More than he'd have expected from someone of modest resources, with that sort of hand-me-down suitcase and unexceptional tailoring.

"How do you know our hosts? Alexander's done some travel in America. Perhaps you know the same people?"

"It's a very large country, sir. Your lordship?" Theodore nodded at Alexander, apparently finding him easier to deal with.

"Herr will do fine, if you need a title here." It did double duty, honestly. "Most people call me Carillon, even my friends." Carillon could pull off every inch of the lord who didn't fuss about such things because he knew his place in the world.

Theodore nodded, focusing now on Alexander. "Where have you travelled, then?"

"New York City, a bit up to Boston. Philadelphia, the District of Columbia, Chicago. Cities, largely. Not much in the south, though I've had brief trips through. A memorable week or three in New Orleans at one point." Alexander considered, then added, "Matters of business, rather tedious except for the people involved."

"Art?" Theodore waved a hand. "I studied art history at Yale. You'll know Yale, of course."

"An excellent library, and also an art collection, yes." Alexander smiled at some memory there.

"The oldest university art museum in the western hemisphere, sir!" Theodore's eyes went bright. A reasonably active passion, then, whatever else had brought him to the Heinrichs' attention.

"Under the circumstances, Alexander, please." Alexander waved a hand. "Last I was there was some time ago. They were acquiring rather a lot of items from an excavation in Egypt." He didn't give any sign of what he thought about that. "And a rather charming watercolour, by William Henry Bishop. Better known as a novelist, but I admit I'm intrigued when people explore multiple art forms. Have you read any of his, Carillon? Theodore?"

Carillon murmured, "I believe only his travel book. But he was a Yale man, wasn't he?"

Alexander wound the conversation around, here and there, asking about what it had been like to attend Yale, before adding. "Carillon went up to Oxford, among his other virtues. But do you mind, I'm curious, where did you go to school before that? I spent a brief two years teaching, and of course we both went to Schola."

Carillon half-smiled. It was the first time he'd actually heard Alexander mention his time teaching. Theodore had a few questions about it. Was it as isolated as it sounded, being out on an island? Then Alexander said, "We have our secret societies, of course. That helps keep some of us busy. I was fortunate enough to be sponsored into one. It helped me make connections that have anchored the rest of my life."

That had a queer note there, nothing most people would notice. But Carillon was now increasingly attuned to the places where Alexander chose his words that precisely. Not friends, not brothers and sisters. And that choice of 'anchor' could be good, bad, or both at the same time.

Theodore lit up at that. "Oh, the same. I was at Exeter, you might know it? Not magical, of course, but my parents thought it would set me up well for the future. I went down to a man in the ville for tutoring while I was there." Alexander nodded. "But the time in the society house was... Well, after my initiation, that was an ordeal, of course, as it's supposed to be - some of the best. Talking freely with chaps, our own personal pursuits."

"Mind, I wasn't invited to any of the societies. Younger son, at the time, and I didn't show an interest in the things that might have led to an invite until later. What is it you say, a late bloomer?" Carillon inserted that as much for Alexander's benefit as anyone else. "Always rather wondered what people got up to. Pranks, I suppose, as well as more serious things?"

That, predictably, got a trio of increasingly disastrous stories. Alexander encouraged him along, telling a couple of stories of what it was like to deal with student pranks as a teacher. He didn't touch on any of the more notable ones Carillon knew about, even ones during the time Alexander had been a teacher at Schola. He got the sense Alexander was on the tail of something, but he had no idea what.

After nearly two hours, the driver pulled into a long drive, away from the main road. Ten minutes later, they were in front of the Schloss, a large and rather imposing stone building. They let Rudi and Lulu pile out first, in a spill of frothy frock, then Carillon, then Alexander, followed up by Theodore. A small line of liveried servants appeared to take the cases and trunks. Another led them up the steps to the front doors, and into a rather grand room, all gilt and silk.

Anneliese was lounging on a chaise longue, sipping delicately from a champagne glass. Her German was flowing. He suspected she'd been sipping for a while. "Darlings, you're here. We've two more cars coming quite soon, I hope. Do go wash up, the road dust gets everywhere. Now, do let one of the staff know if there's anything you need. If you want to be hardy and wander outside, that's quite fine. Just check for a map. There are some areas, down toward the nearest village, not entirely, well, certainly not our sort of people, wouldn't want to cause a bother."

Carillon bowed slightly and murmured, "Of course. Anneliese, you look lovely, naturally." She beamed at him and waved her hand. "Go sort yourselves out. Lulu, darling, you come right back down and tell me all the gossip after we left last night."

One of the maids showed them up the main stairs, turning left, and then down to a door at the end of the hallway. "Frau Heinrich wished you to have these rooms." She opened the door, revealing a solitary bed with a sitting area. "The bathing room, it is just through there, sirs."

A single bed. Well. Bother. Carillon didn't look at Alexander. He strode in and spun in place. Asking for more room wouldn't do. "Thank you, Fräulein?"

"My name is Helga, sir, if you need to ask for me." She bobbed. "I am to see to your needs." That added a dimple. "Though Frau Heinrich was most clear that you are not to be disturbed without knocking and waiting."

"Just so." Carillon nodded. "Could we have a carafe of drinking water and a glass or two? We are old men, and likely to be earlier to bed than the party, and earlier to rise, on the whole. May I ask the arrangement for breakfast?"

"There is a room for it downstairs, sir, or ask any of the staff to fetch what you like. The bell to ring is there." She indicated that cord, well away from anything they might pull accidentally.

"Very well." Carillon glanced over at Alexander, who just nodded. "I see our trunks. We would prefer to unpack for ourselves. The suits, for pressing, there?" He nodded at the frame, waiting for them. When Helga nodded again, he smiled. "We will be ready to go down in, mmm. Half an hour? Yes. Half an hour."

Helga bobbed and disappeared, and Alexander immediately pulled out his little amulet, as Carillon went for his book as soon as the door was closed. They both took several minutes to walk through the space. Large bed, at least, they wouldn't be crammed against each other, but there really wasn't any other furniture suitable for a passable bed. Just two easy chairs, and a table between them, looking out the window. Carillon was old enough to never want to sleep on the ground again, and he wouldn't make Alexander do so. The bathroom at least had its own bathtub, and the piping suggested plenty of hot water.

Once they'd both had a good look, Alexander went to

the wall by the door and pressed his hands against it, palms flat against the rather garish wallpaper. He closed his eyes, as if attuning, and focused entirely on it for a good three minutes. He was humming something faintly under his breath at the end, the theme of a Bach fugue. E-flat Minor, Carillon thought, not one of the ones he knew particularly well.

When he turned around, he brushed his hands together, the automatic gesture of any ritualist concluding his work, and then went to wash them in the bathroom sink. When he came out, he said, "I will need to check it regularly, but we are reasonably private as long as no one is in the walls." Which no one was. Carillon still had his book out.

"A corner room, at least." He nodded slightly at the other window. "And curtains on the bed."

"We surely don't have long. Ten minutes, at the outside?"

Carillon shook his head. "What's important here?"

"Keep an eye on the American. Whoever he is, he's - mmm. Not who he says he is. It might be nothing."

That made Carillon's eyebrows go up, impressed. "Oh?"

"Exeter doesn't have society houses. Andover, mind, does. Both court the sort of families who expect to go to Schola, but non-magical in the main. New England preparatory schools." He flicked his fingers. "And Andover's the more usual route to Yale, but that's less certain as a determination."

Carillon snorted. "You were busy. I could tell you were on to something, but not what. Me, I just found his shoes a tad - mm. The sort someone might wear if they needed to do a lot more walking than this party suggests."

"And I would not have thought of that." Alexander

nodded in turn. "Any chance he's connected to your... Seeing as he's American?"

That brought on a shiver, and Carillon couldn't repress it. The last thing he wanted in this moment was to wonder how long Madam A's reach was. "America is a big place." He said it more to convince himself than anything else.

When he looked at Alexander again, the older man had his head slightly tilted. "I was beginning to wonder what gave you pause. I'll have your back." It was a clear statement that whatever else, they were here together, in a strange and quite possibly more dangerous land than they had anticipated. And he was not alone with it, even if Alexander remained his thorny self.

"Appreciated." Carillon held up his hand, tapping the poison ring. "And we will be careful about our food and drink." Which was going to be a tremendous bother, but you did what you had to. Then he remembered. "You're in Dius Fidius, then?" He was fairly sure Alexander wasn't in Animus Mundi, the secret society that focused on ritual magic, from a few things he'd said - and not said.

Alexander nodded, though he turned away to see to unpacking his suits to be tended and set out shirts to be pressed. "I'm a bit surprised you weren't snatched up by someone."

"I didn't really settle into my interests until the end of third year. And I think no one knew what to do with me. Quite fair, it took me a while to figure myself out." Not as long as he put about, but long enough. "Shall we ring for help finding our way downstairs?"

"Once more unto the breach."

CHAPTER 25
THURSDAY AFTERNOON

Alexander had been at his share of country house parties, generally lurking on the edges. This was something like the Beckers, and nothing like it. Everything had an edge to it. Drink flowed freely, and people passed around little cases of pills and powders. And of course, everyone was all over each other, anytime anyone was sitting. He barely knew where to look and knew his blushes were a matter of comment. And compliment. Being shy about it was, apparently, as Carillon had said, something of a novelty. Especially in this circle.

Theodore had settled right in, amiably acquiring a bouncing girl on his lap, teasing her. His German wasn't bad, but it was obviously not entirely idiomatic. He kept pausing, to increasingly shrill laughter, to ask people to explain this phrase or that. He seemed entirely artless, in a way that Alexander was now quite wary of.

It did not actually turn into a proper orgy. Plenty of people removing part of their clothing, hands everywhere, and mouths. Carillon had settled next to him, his left hand behind Alexander's back, generally not quite touching. It was a constant nagging presence, especially when Carillon murmured in his ear some comment about who this person was or that. Little fragments of gossip, of how people were swapping partners, what tastes people seemed to share or differ on. Annoyingly, Carillon had a better gift for keeping track of who was who than Alexander did.

Finally, that purring voice got a bit louder. "Come along, Alexander. If you won't indulge me here..."

Alexander ducked his chin, flushed, and shifted to stand up. "Tomorrow," he said to the room. Anneliese was lounging back, a plump and half dressed woman spilling out of her shift in her lap. She flipped a hand, amused. Sepp was nowhere to be seen. As they made their way up the stairs, they could hear sounds from one of the other downstairs rooms that suggested someone was doing something a wall was not entirely designed for. Energetically.

Once they were back in their room, they took their time doing a thorough check. No one had added listening devices, no one appeared to be lurking in the walls. Alexander took a few proper minutes to renew the warding, certainly something he'd do any time they spent much time in this room. That, at least, would not be too unusual.

Any magical family knew people had their own preferences and sometimes requirements, through oath or affiliation. He had tucked the layers of his magic tidily behind the house wards. They were not up to Isembard's standards, or for that matter Alexander's own, but most people's weren't.

He padded into the bathroom to change into pyjamas and wash up. When he came out, Carillon had settled to the left of the bed, a book in one hand. "Curtains closed, charm light left on low?" It would mean if something did interrupt them in the middle of the night, they wouldn't need to fumble in the dark.

"Just so." Alexander pulled the third curtain closed as he got into bed and suddenly felt suffocated. On the other hand, it was rather essential no one realise they certainly didn't sleep like lovers. Even a nervous one.

"Again, I apologise if I kick. Or make noise. More likely make noise. Not much help for it." Carillon seemed very much in earnest.

Alexander shook his head. "The War?" He presumed it was. Carillon just nodded. "It doesn't usually get me like that." Alexander turned away to check the curtain. His War got him a dozen other ways, yes. But in his sleep, behind his own wards, his dreams weren't quite like that, even on the regular evenings they were bad. The sort of thing that made you wake drenched in sweat, afraid to make a sound, not the sort that meant you kicked or shouted or drew attention to yourself.

"If I bother you, elbow me. I'll do my best, but."

"But we aren't entirely responsible for our sleep. The same." Alexander reached for his own book. "Anything to discuss?"

"Nothing new. I set an alarm for half-eight. We can go for a walk after we've had breakfast. It should be quiet."

With that, Alexander picked up his book, and they both read quietly. Carillon tucked his book away before Alexander was entirely ready to sleep, facing toward the far window through the curtains, presenting his back to Alexander. Ten minutes later, Alexander took up the mirror of that position.

He woke sometime in the middle of the night, when the house was truly quiet. Something had woken him, but he wasn't sure what. There was the soft glow of the charm light above the bed, and Carillon had shifted onto his back, one hand up by his head. His pyjama top had opened in the night. Perhaps that restlessness was what had woken Alexander. Now, the glow of the light showed Carillon's chest and the edge of that scar. More than just the edge, the way he'd angled himself.

The knot of scar tissue looked quite deep, nestled in just at the joint, suggesting some injury to the bone beneath. A line of healed skin showed the bullet had hit and ricocheted, perhaps with the arm stretched out for some act of magic. One of the Triadic protection charms, perhaps, from the angle.

Alexander couldn't keep from looking. It seemed indecent to stare. Certainly, everyone else in this house would assume he was staring at the chest, the broad shoulders, the virtues that men had been declaiming about downstairs earlier. The muscles, certainly, were remarkably well-defined. Not quite what the classical sculptors had favoured, but certainly respectably attractive, if Alexander understood the aesthetic principles correctly.

No, it was the scar. It would be unfair to say that Carillon's question about a kind touch had reminded him. He thought about Perry every day. Not just his prayers in the morning, the proper incantations to keep Perry's name alive. It was all the other moments, wanting to discuss some new trick of warding, some charm, some book that Perry would have leapt on and delighted in. Bad puns that relied on fluency in three languages, certainly.

But that scar was - on Perry, the wound had been a hand's breadth to the left, an inch down. A tiny distance, all things considered, to leave such a hole in the world. It had taken his heart with it, amid the blood and the panic and the frantic rush to at least bring Perry's body home. Not to have him left. They'd managed it, but then Perry's parents had barred him from their land, from the family cemetery. He had nowhere to make proper offerings that would last.

His hand shuddered and clenched. It had been a long time since he'd felt like this. Seventeen years and six months, at least. There was a week there he didn't really remember for the blankness, not until the ferry landed at Dover and they were back in Albion, however briefly. When he'd noticed how shattered Isembard was. Worse, how Jim and Wally had been shepherding them both, like their world had cracked at the foundation. When Alexander had finally understood that he looked like a walking abomination, and even the walking was dubious.

Alexander thought he'd made himself strong enough, since. His people, his mother's people, they had a place for the antagonist challenging the world in a way the Romans never had, and that Albion ignored. He'd never claimed that, not out loud, but he'd known it in himself, in the way he made his own way in a foreign land.

Alexander had borrowed Set's strength as a cloak against the worst of the world. He'd tested himself, over and over, and come out on the other side. It didn't make up for that moment of being too far away to shield Perry. Of there being no way to staunch the blood fast enough, to bring Perry through into a world after the War with him. He wondered who Carillon had been protecting, if it had worked, and if so, how he'd managed it where Alexander had failed.

Alexander's hand clenched again, and he tried to make himself relax. He couldn't, he couldn't even make his fingers uncoil. He felt the jerk of one leg, and then Carillon was stirring. Not just stirring, coming awake as if there'd been an emergency. As if something were seriously wrong.

The man didn't move, but he was watching now. Those

bright, gleaming eyes were entirely focused on Alexander. Not that Alexander could meet them. His own wouldn't stay focused, his hand kept moving without permission. It was like something was bursting out, refusing to stay where he'd put it. There was a lightning flash in his head, of that horrible moment, seeing Perry die, only it wasn't Perry's face.

It was a gap. It was Carillon. In the oldest stories his mother had told him, it was the track of the uninvoked serpent, spat from the mouths of the gods. The flash was the unmaker, the destroyer of all that was. It stole the light and the warmth and all the sun held and left nothingness.

If that sniper had been a slightly better shot, he'd never have known this man. Never been baffled and irritated by him. He hated that confusion, hated the way this man who was everything he distrusted had made a place in his life. Despite himself, Alexander hadn't backed away. Hadn't taken a dozen chances to refuse or change his mind.

He knew himself to be a coward. To have failed. Set had stood against that destruction, Set had - for all the other tales about him - held back the unravelling of the world. Alexander had been too slow, too far away, too many other things. Perry had bled and died, unmended and unmendable, and that bright light had gone out of the world forever.

His hand hurt now, but still, Carillon didn't move. Not toward him, not away from him. He didn't reach for his book, or for the wand that lay on the dressing table. He didn't say anything, and Alexander couldn't. All his words had fled, somewhere far away. Alexander shuddered, caught in something, snared and tangled in a spider's web.

Everything about him was exposed. It was like he was back in the challenge at the Council Keep, when he was twenty-six and thought himself ready to take on the world. There, he had been stripped down, made vulnerable, and been shown something so vast he could only fall to his knees in awe.

Then, there had been a presence, gentle like feathers, but undeniably there, warm and easy to touch. Now, he was like a snake just shed his skin, everything too tender, too cold, far too exposed and raw. And now, he was too far from any such kindness, too far from that blessing presence of the land.

He didn't know how long they were like that. He certainly had no sense of time passing beyond the faint tick of the clock on the dresser that suggested it did. Or, alternately, that this were some unusually pragmatic hallucination. He still couldn't move, couldn't do anything but lie there and shiver.

Carillon's whisper cut through it. "May I cover you with a blanket?" He was leaning in slightly, a change in angle, still not touching, not moving. Alexander managed a jerk of his chin that might be read as a nod, rather than a denial. A moment later there was a blanket pulled up, carefully, with a charm on it for warmth as well. He caught the last words of the incantation.

Alexander whimpered despite himself. Despite showing that frailness. Carillon would discard him now, of course he would. This moment had hung over his head near all of his life. It was the point where the metal that made him had been overworked to brittleness and shattering uselessness.

Instead, there was that quiet again, a watchful stillness. He couldn't hide from it, it was the divine gaze from which no one escaped. He was laid bare, opened up, far worse than his Council challenge. He could only lie there, barely breathing, frozen. Warmer now he'd stopped shivering.

Whatever was frozen, it was not physical. Had not been physical. Except that he lived, perforce, in his body.

And that warmth had come from Carillon. Again. Who seemed to be there, still. Who had not moved, other than to adjust the blanket and the charm, then settled his hand back by his side. Alexander swallowed hard, then again. Finally, painstakingly, giving his every inch of willpower to it, he managed to open his fingers, one by one, until his hand pressed flat on the bed by his head.

"There." The voice was infinitely gentle. Like the voice he'd heard, what seemed like centuries ago, in the Council keep during his challenge. That warmth, too. Not the scorching sun of Egypt's summer, but the warmth of Albion that turned flowers to perfume. A particular warmth that drew people into company, whether it was outside for a picnic or curled up by a fireplace. "Good. Take your time."

Alexander had closed his eyes somewhere in there. He could listen to the voice. It wasn't asking him to do anything. It just wanted him to be. He wasn't sure he was able to be, never mind be anything, but he could lie here. He felt his breath slowly returning to something that faked normality, no longer sharp knife-edged gasps that left him dizzy.

CHAPTER 26
IN THE MIDDLE OF THE NIGHT

Carillon knew well enough what was needed right now. He'd had the gift of it, over and over, first from Benton and then from Lizzie. Without them, without the years of both of them making space, he'd have done this wrong, right off.

He'd have tried to touch, for one, a hand on the shoulder or arm, and he knew that would make things infinitely worse. Space, quiet, no demands, until Alexander showed some sign of being able to respond. Like one of the birds of prey - beware the talons, the beaks, the wings. Wait. And offer a rhythm of steady breathing that Alexander might eventually match.

So he waited. He only moved when Alexander could respond enough to the offer of the blanket, adding the warmth charm automatically. He did not like the sallowness beneath the brown of Alexander's skin in the dim light, and he certainly didn't care for the way the shivering was shaking his shoulders. As it slowed, then faded, Carillon finally relaxed minutely. This was not good, nothing that looked like this was good. But it was a more stable sort of problem.

It took at least another twenty minutes before Alexander made any further attempt to move beyond that hand. It must ache, likely his back or shoulders or hips, too, the way he was twisted on his side. And his back to the room, Carillon couldn't have stood it for that long.

Only once Alexander had shifted again, Carillon asked, "Water?" Alexander nodded, another of those little jerks, though more firmly a nod than a shudder this time. Carillon stood, taking his time, feeling the way his own hip had stiffened. He didn't want any sudden movements now.

He went to the carafe on the dresser, pouring a glass and bringing it back, then sitting on the bed, as Alexander pushed himself upright enough to drink. Fixed on Carillon's every movement, it seemed like, as if he were a threat.

"Here we go." Carillon repressed the urge to add 'not too much at once'. Treating Alexander like a first year at Schola who had no idea how to handle the aftermath of his own mind would also do no good. And it might shatter everything forever. "May I dry the sheets? Lend you a bit of vitality?"

The first question got a nod, but the second question got a disbelieving jerk of his chin. Carillon had expected that. Fortunately, tending to the sheets didn't require Alexander to move. Carillon pressed his hands against the cloth, willing them dry and warmed, as he'd once asked Benton to show him. It made no end of difference when camping. And there'd been that day when Benton was no good for anything after the snow leopard.

It drew another shudder out of Alexander, but the sort that made him take another sip. Then another, as if he were measuring them out by some song or verse in his head.

When he'd taken another two, he finally spoke, his voice cracking at first. "You would?"

"Of course." Carillon didn't know how to explain it. For one thing, they were likely to need to rely on Alexander's magic far more here. Carillon had expected all along he might need to lend his own magic. Perhaps not tonight, but he was, if not well-rested, at least well fed, and he had avoided the sort of magical work that drained him for weeks. Even better, he could still feel the fullness of the land magic and May Day. Much quieter now than right after the ritual, but it was still humming in him, contented and happy. "May I?"

Alexander looked at him, eyes wide and completely unshielded, then he nodded and offered the glass. Carillon set it aside on the table for the time being, and then held out both his hands, palms facing down. It was easier to let it flow, for all magic did not actually follow the constraints of gravity.

Slowly, cautiously, Alexander reached for a pillow and moved to half-sit. He set his own hands palms up on the pillow, as if he didn't trust himself to hold them up. Or steady. Probably both. Finally, he nodded, and Carillon moved to rest palm to palm. He could not get the line from Shakespeare out of his head, palm to palm, a holy palmers' kiss. Barely touching, not making Alexander take any of his weight or bear any more contact than was necessary.

Instead of lingering on that, he simply gave himself over to that humming warmth, letting his magic bubble up and flow freely. He could feel how Alexander soaked it in, like rain on dry land. It went on and on, but Carillon had it to spare. Alexander's fingers jerked long before Carillon would have stopped, but his skin looked much better, his breathing was easier, and he was actually managing to focus on Carillon's face. "Enough." The tone by itself forbade any questions, as if this were as fragile a thing as that shuddering panic had been.

"As you wish." Carillon didn't move his hands until Alexander nodded again, and then he rubbed them together briefly, with a breath of a kiss, sealing his magic. "Your glass?"

"Please." If they had to have this conversation in near monosyllables, it would take quite a while. As Carillon turned for the water, Alexander pushed himself to be half-sitting up in bed, the blankets pulled up to his chest. He took the glass, then glanced at the light.

"Dimmer?" Carillon adjusted it down, just enough to see the shadows of Alexander's face as it moved. He wondered, all of a sudden, if the dark might encourage a few more words, or if he'd just forced them quiet, but it was too late to do something else. He'd have to carry on.

The silence settled, much like the blanket. Carillon could hear the small sounds of the glass, see the flicker of light as Alexander moved, finally setting it aside. "My apologies."

"You were right. Less screaming." It wasn't a joke, but suddenly, Carillon felt he might shiver into his own fears. That wouldn't do. They'd have to do something that brought them into a different place. Together, at least in counterpoint, if they couldn't actually manage harmony.

Something in it had amused Alexander, enough for a fleeting quirk of his lips. "Still. I should not have..." He didn't finish that sentence, and probably couldn't. Carillon certainly never managed it when he was coming out of the worst of his nightmares.

"It was not something you chose." That slipped from Carillon's lips before he could reconsider it. "I will not ask.

You needn't worry about that. But is there anything else I can do to help?"

Alexander went still, the sort of still that might turn into a hundred different shapes. All the lethal, complex potentiality that the man had in his grasp, however weakly he held it at the moment. Then, shifting key and metre, Alexander shook his head. "Is there anything you recommend?"

"You have had water. If we rang for tea, it would be inadequate. We are men of standards, and all German tea is insufficient for men of Albion." As Carillon hoped, that raised another fleeting almost-smile. "I'd rather not break out the bottles I have. Keeping that for something else, and the aftertaste wouldn't help any. I'm sure you couldn't manage food. A wash, when you feel up to standing?"

"How can you be so calm about it?" That slipped out of Alexander's mouth, and from his expression, he hadn't intended to say it either.

Carillon shrugged. "The virtue of my house, of being an Owl," he said, "is that people expect logic from you, when they're paying attention. Two-thirds of the time, it's just working through the logic. You know where the loo is, you know your own resources. Might need a bit of reminding, I generally do when I've got in a state. There's plenty more water, if you want some of that. But I'm also sure you won't take a sleeping tablet, not right now. So we are limited to a few creature comforts. Or talking it out. And I'm clear you don't want that."

That got a grimace, an expression more like he'd come to expect from Alexander, who had a remarkably expressive face when he wasn't putting on a show. Admittedly, that seemed to be most of the time. "They insisted on putting me in Fox."

"And you think better of it now?"

Alexander's shoulder twitched. "I have for a long while. Dius Fidius, too." Of course, the two often went together. A secret society for those who thought they should dispense bounty like Jupiter Almus who nourishes all things. It would be one thing if they managed it, but they so rarely did. They didn't do a lot of harm, exactly, but they didn't do nearly as much good as they wanted to praise themselves for.

"Ah." What did one say in such a circumstance? Anything Carillon could think of, all the questions that came swimming to his head, they might shut this door against him forever. "That was my brother. Both parts, actually." That would not help, either. Carillon did not need that set of thoughts lurking uppermost in his mind whenever they attempted sleep again. "I will say that Owl has a certain expectation of ruthless honesty. With yourself, at least. Anything else produces incorrect suppositions. That's no good."

"Huh." Good. Now he'd got Alexander thinking about something. "I suppose that's true. Not just being swots, repeating what other people have thought."

"Goodness, no. Not if you're doing it properly. Of course, you have to start there, if you're new to a field or a topic. Building the vocabulary is a thing, and the foundation. As one does in ritual, of course, working from Allery's Twelve Principles, through to the geometric arrangements, and then on to more complex forms. Practising one's scales before attempting a simple song, and the song before the symphony."

Alexander snorted again, then reached for the glass. "One more, if you don't mind?"

Carillon smiled warmly, delighted that Alexander had

actually asked, instead of pressing forward and doing it himself. "Of course." He stood again, fetched the water, and when he came back sat again on the bed.

Alexander took the glass, drinking in several long sips. "Your magic is very warm."

"So I'm told. Especially going into summer." Carillon glanced down at his hands, turning his right over, palm up, then back. "I meant that. You may need every scrap. I can play my part with very little magic, though admittedly, I'd rather keep some reserves."

"You know how to measure out what's needed." That praise made Carillon look up, just as Alexander twisted, nominally to put the glass on the bedside table. Then he pushed himself more upright. "The loo is a good idea." He managed to get standing and take the first few steps without stumbling. Carillon focused on re-buttoning his pyjamas and rearranging the blankets for their mutual comfort, such as they might find.

By the time Alexander came back, he'd smoothed all his masks back in place. Carillon had, honestly, expected that. He did it himself. It would be hypocritical to blame Alexander for doing the same as he did. Those small glimpses, though, made him wonder how badly Alexander had been hurt, and how often. More to the point, he wondered who had had the power, the authority, the influence to push Alexander not only into Fox, but into Dius Fidius.

He had thought, initially, in as much as he had thought of the Council at all, that they all came from the sort of family who had influence, who used it like breathing. The same mould as Temple, or many other people he and Lizzie knew. The more he saw of Alexander, however, the more sure he was that whatever face he showed, the roots grew from very different soil.

He was working, though, from the briefest of hints and slips of the tongue. That comment, the other day, about 'them' not letting him do anything else. A few remarks today. Most of all, the shape of the panic, when Alexander could not do anything else, to choose anything. It had made him small, still, except for that dreadful shivering. Submissive, in all the most destructive ways, that might be a way to put it.

CHAPTER 27

FRIDAY MORNING

Alexander woke a hair before the alarm sounded. He could see light beyond the curtains, just enough time to gather himself before Carillon startled awake with the alarm. The man had ended up curled on his side on the bed, the way he'd started the night, as if nothing had happened in the middle of it.

Alexander immediately swung his legs out of the bed. "First go." It came out gruff, but that was how he felt, and there was no use trying to hide it. He hesitated only long enough to check the wards were still sound, and they were still not being overheard. Then he went to wash and make his morning ablutions.

As he'd expected, his head ached, several old scars burned, and the rest of him felt like he had run a marathon or two in the middle of winter. It would improve with a headache potion, a touch of salve, plenty of liquids, not too much coffee, and a bit of food. If he could convince his stomach to accept the idea. But it was one more weight on him, of how he had slipped and failed yet again. Nothing would fix that sense of being scraped thin, being made smaller.

When he came out, Carillon was perched on one of the chairs, standing with a nod, unreadable again. He disappeared into the bathing room, leaving time for Alexander to make his morning offerings. He poured a tiny amount of water into the cup he used on his travels and made the invocations. For Perry, and for his other dead, a list that took an increasingly long time in the morning.

He spoke the prayers to Perry last and aloud, but so quietly no one would hear. "Your name which was spoken by Ptah when he conceived you in his heart will resound for millions of years. It will not fade; it will not be forgotten; you and your spirit are pure and censed with the perfume of your brothers, the gods. The double gate of heaven is thrown open for you, that you may be numbered among the undying stars; you emerge in the daylight by the power of your heart; your offerings number in the thousands. As the Jackal you open your passage forth, as Ptah you hold the power of your name, as Osiris you shall not grow weary of heart a second time."

Twenty minutes later, they had both dressed, still in silence, and gone down to the breakfast room to eat. Carillon kept to mild conversation about this thing or that in the morning papers, all entirely non-political, sparing Alexander the challenge of focusing on the paper himself. He managed to make plausible sounds of interest, agreement, or question as appropriate. Blast the man for carrying on so smoothly.

Thirty minutes after that, they were out the door, with a map of the grounds, with the areas to avoid marked out. They set off on a path that would lead toward where they wanted, but that also suggested they were looking at a particular view, a bit of lake. Carillon did not break the silence until they were a good ten minutes from the house, and only after checking for listeners. "About another twenty to the lake. He's in a compound on the far side. He says he can go only so far from his laboratory and cottage. The name magic binds him."

"Are we meeting him today?" Alexander flicked an annoying bug off his shoulder with his fingers.

"Likely not, but we still need to get a sense of the land." Carillon's voice stayed even, but he glanced over at the movement.

Alexander grunted, feeling his shoulders finally ease up a little from the soreness. A good walk was, annoyingly, often quite helpful. "What's this river we're supposedly looking at like?"

"Your average small river. Grassy banks, some sheep or cows - let's say they were dots in the far field, both will do that. Very unscenic of them, but usefully vague." Carillon took a breath, as if he intended to go on, then shook his head minutely.

The silence was, in some ways, rather worse, because it left Alexander entirely alone with his thoughts. Carillon had done none of the things he expected last night. Alexander had expected coldness, dismissal, the undeniable bitter harvests of his failure. Perhaps there might have been a flurry of useless fuss, beforehand. Clearly Carillon thought himself a considerate man and lived up to that in his head the way Alexander lived up to his own impossible goals.

He hadn't expected the magic. Not the offer, and certainly not the way it felt. The warmth flowing into his hands, soaking in like oil on skin, carrying perfume and pleasure. Not simply water that cleansed and refreshed, but something that lasted longer.

The magic certainly lingered like scented oil. He could still feel it humming in his system, undeniably there. And Carillon had given it so freely, as if they were friends, comrades, not at odds about their very natures. Had the man forgotten all his quite reasonable distrust of the Council, for whatever list of excellent reasons he had?

Alexander had wanted to soak in it, to roll in it, like a puppy with a mud puddle. He'd had to stop, to pull away, as soon as he could bear to. He couldn't stand to feel the touch of the land like that. Not from Carillon. Not here, far from Albion. And not when the only reason it was offered was that he'd failed yet again. He'd been useless last night, and he was nearly useless today. He barely felt competent to walk through a path along a field, for all the gods' sakes.

Worst of all, though, he could not figure out what Carillon was up to. It was abundantly clear the man had a dozen plots going. To free his friend, his former lover, certainly. That was noble, and if the alchemist had the sort of information claimed, also patriotic and, better yet, actually helpful. But he also had other plots. The art was not just a cover - certainly not now, when they'd got two statues shipped off home.

Carillon had been careful to leave options for later, all along, Alexander had noticed. With their contacts in Vienna, with the Beckers and others in Berlin. And here, he was playing it with amusement at Alexander's shyness, leaving even the option for an orgy later dangling, just waiting to be taken up like the sacrificial apple.

It was not remotely normal. Neither was it ordinary, expected, typical, or entirely natural. It was, he had to grant, ruthlessly pragmatic, taking a long view, but Carillon didn't seem to skimp on it. Any of it. Including Alexander.

Which made Alexander wonder what uses he would be put to before this was done. There had to be more. There always were, even if he had to admit Carillon had given him the bare outline from the start. While he had sketched in more and more details in the process, that outline had been truthful, as far as it went. It did not explain anything, certainly not usefully.

In due course, which was to say, about another ten minutes, they arrived at a tree near the lake. It was reasonably large. Alexander pulled out his amulet, keeping an eye on things as Carillon rummaged in the fork of the tree, bringing out a tin. Into it, he placed a smaller tin and a folded wodge of paper, two or three sheets folded several times.

Just as Carillon turned back, Alexander frowned. "Hold still." This, at least, he could do something about. It was a matter of moments to cast a notice-me-not charm on both of them. It would hold well enough as long as they drew no attention to themselves by making a sound. At least as long as no one got too close. If someone did, well, they'd handle that as it came.

Carillon, beside him, shifted his weight slowly to hold his knees slightly bent. More comfortable for any length of time, more stable. Good, he knew how to do this kind of waiting game. That made things easier. They waited a good three minutes, nearly four, before Alexander saw a figure coming along the road.

He was not, blessing on blessing, apparently looking for this tree. Or any others. Instead, he was going down the path. As he came closer, there was a slight satisfied inhale from just behind Alexander's shoulder. It was Theodore, the American, and he was definitely heading down closer to the village.

They watched him recede into the distance. When he was well beyond hearing range, Alexander whispered, "How far to the village?"

"He should get turned back, mmm. Five minutes. Do we make a break for or wait?"

"Wait. We don't want him catching our backs." Alexander could not walk away, knowing someone might. Accordingly, they stood there, shifting position slightly while they could to ease their knees and hips and ankles. Despite himself, Alexander could feel Carillon's presence, steadily, right behind him. Another man would lean into that, magically, if not physically. He wanted to, and he knew he couldn't. It would go away, it would turn into bitter dust in his hands, or something venomous.

Fortunately, they did not have a long wait. Theodore reappeared, this time escorted by someone in something that might have been livery, or might have been a uniform trousers and shirt. Without the jacket, as if he'd been interrupted at some task. He kept guiding Theodore on up the road. They caught only a few sentences of Theodore going on. He had the rolling bumps of an American sure of his place in his world, that he'd just been out for a walk. It was a fascinating mode to compare and contrast to Carillon's confident lordling mode, but being used for the same ends.

Whoever was escorting him was having none of it, responding in tight German phrases that gave nothing away. "This way, sir. People value their privacy, sir. Please do not walk down this way again, sir."

"He'll have to come back, the guard." Carillon said, once they were well up the path. "Do we duck off now? If you don't mind a longer walk, we can edge round the lake here, off to the river, and then back. If we run into anyone, it shouldn't be suspicious, and it's where we said we'd be going anyway." He considered. "And whatever cows are out should be there for a bit. It's late enough in the morning."

"There are times I forget you are far more agriculturally minded than you look." Alexander nodded. "Carefully, but let's."

They walked up around the edge of the lake, and from there another twenty minutes at a reasonable clip. They could honestly say they'd seen the river, and it was an excellent small river. The cows were indeed scenic. Calming, even. It wasn't until they turned back that they saw anyone to speak of, a farmer coming out to work in one of the nearer fields. Carillon waved amiably.

Alexander hesitated. "Is this our best chance to talk? How long dare we take?"

It got a snort, something deeply amused, and Alexander couldn't figure out why. Carillon waved a hand. "I think so long as we turn up for luncheon, we're fine. There was a bench out by the smaller pond, wasn't there? Or a log. We could manage a log."

He headed in that direction without further discussion, a slight alteration of the heading. He must have the map firmly embedded in his head. Alexander thought he'd got most of the details sorted, but Carillon had an unerring sense of how far and which angle to take. He wondered, all of a sudden, how far any gifts from the land magic went, so far from home.

"Last night." Alexander began and then stalled. They had to talk about it, didn't they?

"I am rather angry at a lot of people right now. You are not one of them." Carillon said it, in the sort of tone Alexander would use about the idiocies of endless decisions during the War. Tightly repressed fury, knowing the outburst would do no one any good, but making his position crystal clear.

Alexander didn't even know where to start with that. Or how to go on, or end, for that matter, not that those were going to be relevant just yet.

CHAPTER 28
IN THE FOREST, BY A POND

Carillon glanced over at Alexander, who had gone still again. Oh, he was walking. They were almost up to a bench that would give them a grand view of the pond and both paths. But his face was near frozen, as if he thought anything might go wrong. Carillon gestured him to the bench and circled a good thirty feet around the bench, picking up, charming, and dropping pebbles to alert them if anyone came near. That done, he settled on the bench, bracing one ankle on his other knee.

Of course, then they sat in silence for a good five minutes before Carillon coughed. "We have a fair bit of time, but not so much as all that. Let us begin from first principles. I am angry, yes. Not at you." He did his best not to let that roaring fury bleed through. It wouldn't do any good here. Not yet, anyway.

Alexander's chin came up at that, the reaction of a man who was far more used to being teacher than student. Certainly by this point in his life. "Who?" Carillon would not let himself comment on the breathiness behind it, the uncertainty that was now lurking there.

"Those who should be your brothers and sisters. The others on the Council." He held up his hand. "I am not angry at Isembard or Thesan. I am beginning to realise they're the only people who've treated you with decency for at least a decade, nearer two?" He caught a shift of Alexander's eyes, the sort of thing even the best couldn't hide, especially when so battered by the world and uncentred. "Far more than two." He let Alexander hear his anger again, those last four words, and saw him draw back for a moment.

"I thought you harmless." Alexander's voice was quiet now, but it was the sound of a bird beginning to find her way with her falconer.

Carillon spread his hands as smoothly as he could. "You were supposed to think that. You and all the world." He half-closed his eyes, searching for how to put this in a way Alexander might hear. "You and I have seen dreadful things, and, I suspect, done worse." Alexander's eyelids opened a little wider at that.

"You were alone or near alone with yours." Making it clear that Carillon had his own dreadful things. "I began with one, and now I have a nest of trusted friends. You tease about my cryptographer, my alchemist, also my several analysts, my master of locks, my keeper of wards, my stable master, my tailor. My model in holding the land oaths well and in being the kind of father I want to be. But there they are. A garden, each individual, each making the whole stronger. Certainly, the menu is more varied."

As he'd hoped, that brought out a small snort. No comment, though, so Carillon went on. "What is your Council for, if you do not even lend each other your vitality? If my offering my magic was such a shock? They are who I am angry with. They have treated you abominably."

Carefully, as if Alexander were translating through half a dozen languages, he spoke again. "You are angry on my behalf?" As if it were a strange sentence. As if Carillon had proclaimed a great wyrm from myth was rising from the tiny pond before them, dripping fire and ice and acid.

"I am." Carillon left it at the two bare words.

Alexander shook his head, as if he could not make sense of it. Probably couldn't at all, Carillon knew. He'd just upended the roots of the world in an act of logic and decency and above all consistent application of the heart of magic. He wasn't sure which one was most challenging.

They sat like that for a good five minutes, before Alexander cleared his throat again. "How did you know what to do?"

"Just because you are used to terrible people does not mean I am obligated to be terrible. I do have standards." As he'd hoped, that brought that little quirk of the smile. The one he was looking to, like navigators looked to Polaris, to guide him through this dance of falconry he found himself in. "Benton. It all comes down to Benton."

"I have not met - him?" Alexander's voice hitched upwards at the end.

"Benton came into my service during the War, and I brought him out of the trenches with me. My valet, until my honeymoon, now my steward. If I am truly blessed, he will be keeping an eye on me to the end of my days. We've saved each other's lives dozens of times now, I think, but it's not just that. You know the weight of it, and there isn't a weight to what we are. There's a buoyancy. Benton. Lizzie. Other people since. He is, mind, furious that he is not here with us, but he is very honest and forthright, and ongoing deception is not his forte."

Carillon shrugged, the good shoulder. The bad was

uncomfortably twitchy. "But it is Benton who has shown me how to tend someone so caught by fear and the depths of his own mind. Or flown so far away he's not remotely attached to his body. He's done it for me, over and over again. I would shame his care if I hadn't paid attention."

"Your steward." Alexander tapped his fingers on his leg. "Not in your list of your people."

Carillon half-smiled. "It is a rather long list. You have heard only a fraction. Though the most important lights now, by and large."

"No Council?" In someone else, at some other time, that question might have seemed almost light. Here, it was sharp talons, barely skimming skin.

"No." Carillon considered. "I have reasons, as I said. I am considering telling you what they are." There. Lay it out. See if that, the temptation of that knowledge, did something useful. He went on. "I look around my life, and it is nothing I expected when I was in my twenties. And yet, there is nowhere I would rather be."

"And you look at me, and you pity me." Alexander's voice turned harsh at the end.

"I think you deserve much better. First, you are human, and I live in hope that we all deserve much better. But I see your loyalty. Your strength of feeling. It has carried you through so many years, on your own." He lifted a hand. "Whatever you and Isembard have, it is complex. It means a great deal to you both, and I am not foolish enough to try to put words to it. I don't know either of you remotely well enough. But aside from Isembard and Thesan, who do you spend time with?"

Alexander shrugged. "Books."

Carillon half-laughed. "Fair. A book knows what it is. Here, how's this? I pity people who do not even have books." As he hoped, that got another of those little uncertain smiles, and even better, a touch more relaxation in Alexander's shoulders.

"I do too." Alexander let out a long breath. "When I was a boy, unformed, when I could have become anything, they talked about putting me in Owl House. Not Fox. I looked at the notes, professors at Schola can, you know."

Carillon raised an eyebrow, shifting slightly to turn a bit more toward Alexander. He thought, now, the touch of openness would not startle too much. "But there you were in Fox. And Dius Fidius."

"You don't approve?" That, now, that was a proper question, probing and incisive.

Carillon shrugged. "I think they - someone, anyway - said they were doing you favours. I am not yet sure what they actually thought."

That hit like another shock. Good. Pacing them out was the right choice here, finding the metre, so that as each one hit, it began to build up something new. Alexander rubbed his face, but this time, as he brought his hand down, he did in fact mirror Carillon's posture, turning his shoulders to match. "Because everyone should want to be in Fox?"

"I have not seen your records, of course. But I have seen a number of evaluations of students, as part of the work around the entry exam standards." Carillon turned one of his palms up.

Alexander took the feint. "You were nearly as fierce about that as Thesan, which is saying a fair amount. Why?"

"Benton." Carillon had that answer. "And Pride. Rufus Pride is master of my stables now. He has magic strong enough to turn a bog to solid ground, sharp when he's given the opportunity. None of the schools would take him.

We've made up the lack now, but it nearly broke him. Wasted years, certainly."

Alexander chose the diversion, as if thinking about wasted years was too close to some edge. "What would you think the files might say of me, then?"

"Strong magic, obviously, and I suspect from an early age. Ferociously competent."

"You can't know that." Alexander pointed out.

"Whatever your service was in the War, no one made it through years of isolated, dangerous work who wasn't both incredibly competent and tremendously lucky. We will take your competence as read, even without the mystery of the Council challenge." Carillon had chosen 'mystery' deliberately. He was rewarded with another slight flare of Alexander's pupils. Another hit.

Alexander shrugged, looking away for a moment as he blinked. "Go on."

"I know only the barest outline of your family, in the usual public sources. My analysts are very good, but they can't find things that aren't written down."

That got an outright laugh. "And there is not so much of that, I suppose, not in any available record. My library, naturally."

"Over which I continue to wist." Carillon agreed. He got another laugh for it and a wave of Alexander's hand in acceptance. "You have done well for yourself. But they - whoever they are - set you to grow in a shape that has never quite suited. Why did you stay? Why did you come back?"

Carillon did not expect an answer, and he did not get one. Instead, Alexander swallowed. "This is not the time for that."

"No. But if you ever choose to trust me with the telling, I

- I am at your disposal in that matter. And I suspect a number of others." Carillon let that settle, not rushing it.

They sat in silence again for several minutes, though now more looking at each other than at the pond. Also, not-looking. Alexander wouldn't meet his eyes, as a rule, and Carillon did not push to do so. Other people might make a show of domination and power, and that was not his way for a number of reasons. Certainly not here and now.

After long enough to run through Tallis's motet "Spem in Alium" in his head, a good ten minutes, Carillon lifted his eyes, having made a decision. Alexander met them, then raised an eyebrow. Carillon spoke as evenly as he could, his voice soft. "In the dark hours of the night, early on February 3rd, 1922, I woke in a bed in Kenya, and knew my brother had died without warning."

"Yes?" Alexander's voice trembled, for just an instant. He was, of course, clever enough to know some of what was coming.

"Hesperidon and Silvia Warren, Livia and Garin Fortier, and two others from the Council were in attendance at a house party there. Only two had previously been guests." He did not say anything else. He did not need to.

CHAPTER 29
FRIDAY EVENING

Alexander had floated somehow through luncheon, through some attempts at amusements in the afternoon, into the evening. There had been an attempt to drug him, and he'd slipped the offending dish out of the way, muddled enough to make it unclear how much he'd eaten. He had more information now about Lord Geoffrey Carillon and his many faces, but it did not help at all. Even when the man told him things, it simply opened archways into an abyss of greater mystery.

He had taken Carillon's carefully chosen words to heart. Six of the Council - well, five then, but Silvia was Hesperidon's wife already and entangled in his plotting. All of them at a house party held by a Lord, and an unexpected death, suggested a number of things, none of them good.

If they had not killed Temple Carillon, they had as good as arranged matters so that the world fell out that way. It was the presence of Garin and particularly Livia that made that almost certain. They were not known for social pleasantries, either of them, or extended outings. Especially in each other's company.

Alexander himself had been far away in 1922. The treaty, in America, or rather the shadows of the treaty agreement, taking advantage of the people gathered in Washington. It was not a matter anyone would ever have trusted to the journals, nor to any letter. He had no idea what they might have decided. Or more importantly, why. And he couldn't find out, not until he could return to the Council keep and the records.

No wonder Carillon was so protective, so cautious, and so blasted incisive. He was right not to trust anything the Council touched. Even if, somehow, he was also furious at them on Alexander's own behalf. If one breathed wrong on that logic, it would explode.

The metaphor stuck with him through supper and into the more intimate amusements of the evening. In the early part of the evening, the topic turned briefly to politics. Of course, Alexander paid attention, and he was sure Carillon was as well. Even if Carillon was doing a remarkably good job of appearing to be relaxed, entirely at ease. He was sprawling back against the sofa at an angle that blocked off anyone from coming near them, without ever quite touching Alexander's body.

Any fool could tell that Germany was moving rapidly into a far more aggressive mode. There were rumours, even at this party, of some new announcement, beyond the orders for submarines and the declaration of rearmament, just since March. Alexander prided himself on not being a fool.

He did, however, keep a close eye on the American. Theodore seemed undaunted by his adventures that morning, but he also gave no hint that he'd seen Carillon or Alexander out and about in the same direction. He didn't shy from talking about the walk, going on about the vista, and how he'd wanted to see the river.

Carillon, after five minutes of this, said, "We went out along the river. Saw a bit of the lake, up to the river, the cows. Good brisk walk. I do enjoy a country walk."

It got someone asking where he was from. Of course, they didn't particularly know British geography, and Carillon was gloriously unspecific. "The family estate's in the south of England, fair bit of forest around." Which was, also, a suitable protection when in the midst of a country with dangerous rumblings. He added, "I prefer a tree to open land, mind."

Alexander wondered, suddenly, if that was for the same reasons he did. Trees gave cover. It was possible for a sniper to strike through them, but magnitudes more difficult. And the number of truly expert snipers in the world was actually finite. The number of people who could hit the broad side of a barn in a field with a gun or with magic was regrettably substantially larger.

He never quite found himself lost in thought, but he let himself be pulled along without directing the conversation. Finally, though, Carillon brushed his fingers down Alexander's arm, just once. "Come up to bed, Alexander. If you won't play down here, I have an idea."

It led to hoots and laughter from the others, and more than a few bits of teasing that relied heavily on sexual slang not in Alexander's useful vocabulary. He might have to bring himself to ask for a lesson from Carillon, who grinned at several pieces of it. He made a mock-show of teasing and keeping secrets, before he gestured at Alexander. "Come on, do."

Once they were securely back in their bedroom, behind the warding, Carillon shrugged out of his jacket and discarded it on the clothes press. "Business. Get comfortable?"

Alexander blinked at him. "What sort of business?"

"I've a message from Berthold. And I think from Lizzie. It's bloody annoying to determine the ping of magic in your shoe when you're trying to be a dissipated lordling, even if you are expecting it." He rummaged, pulling out two small sheafs of paper from a hidden slot in his trunk. "Yes." He cast some sort of charm on the paper - Alexander could feel that pulse of magic - before handing it over. "The other will be a few minutes."

While Carillon bent over a rather large book, scratching out words against a letter, Alexander looked at the note he had been handed. The man had the sort of handwriting he'd expect of a German. It was simultaneously crisp and a tad too fond of black-letter to be easily read, even when it wasn't trying to be obscure.

This, however, made arrangements for a meeting the following morning, so that Carillon's - some reference he couldn't make sense of - could examine the binding and see what he made of it. The letter had an air of the frantic to it, and Alexander spent more time contemplating the implications of the heavy impressions of the pen. He rather hoped no one paid close attention to the man's blotting paper or notepads.

Alexander glanced up, and Carillon was still scratching at his paper. He took another few minutes, then finally stretched. "Give me a minute, trying to solve one more piece." He stood, going into the bathroom, letting the water run over his hands. Alexander knew that trick, the way it anchored one in the body, or soothed, or unstuck something. Sometimes all three at once, if you were lucky.

Carillon came back out and made three more notes.

"You can read it if you like, but you'll need the translation." He offered the other pages, which were, in fact, a mass of referential comments about art. Some were actually about pieces they'd been discussing. Others were far outside anything they'd been paying attention to. Frescos in Siena, as compared to Assisi, for example, or early Roman sculpture. He looked up to find Carillon watching him.

"How much of this is Giles and how much is someone else?" Alexander wanted to figure out how you even went about deciphering it.

"The structure comes from Giles. The specifics of the implementation are mostly Lizzie. Not entirely." He waved a hand. "If you are very, very good, I will let you come talk to Giles sometime."

Alexander snorted. "That may be the oddest bribe anyone has tried on me yet. Though an excellent incentive, honestly." He waved the other letter. "Tomorrow morning. And he thinks evening, for the work. Full moon, of course. Scorpio still in the morning, to do the initial work, and launching into Sagittarius in the evening." He grimaced. "This is where I wish for an astronomer."

Carillon silently handed over something that had been tucked into his book. "Not Thesan, alas. Though if you and I continue to collaborate, I would be very interested in sounding out her willingness for some of this. My other option has irregular obligations and a different set of expertise."

"As an intellectual puzzle, or knowing what she's doing?" Alexander glanced up at that. He had no idea what either Thesan or Isembard might say to that.

"You know how I feel about people getting to express preferences. Knowing that's what they're doing." In someone else's mouth, that might have been scolding, in

Carillon's it was simply thoroughly amused. "Do you agree on the timing?"

The chart was neatly drawn. Spare, not fussing about with asteroids, just the seven principle planets and a handful of the fixed stars. "It's not ideal, but needs must." Besides, astrological timing was almost never uniformly ideal. It was instead a question of where you bent and bowed or kept a watchful eye.

He tapped his fingers, looking at the alignments. "That Saturn placement stands out, but the trine to Jupiter and Venus gives me some ideas for structuring the rite. Working against the challenge from the square to the Moon and Mercury. What's his nature?"

"Not nearly so mercurial as I. I'd look to the Mars placement. Not warlike, but seeking the competition, wanting to be first with an idea made real. He's never been purely theoretical, that's the good and bad of it."

Alexander nodded and grunted. "I can make this work. Assuming the binding is something I can manage, which I won't know until I meet him. I'll need a bit more time with it."

"Another walk, then. And tomorrow night, I will arrange to be quite distracting."

Something in Carillon's tone rang hollow, just the one word, 'quite'. "What should I know about that?"

Alexander could see Carillon making decisions here. The man was letting it show. He had to be. Alexander waited to see what he'd actually say. "Did you hear about the goldwasser? 1924, but I believe before you came back to Albion."

"I heard enough gossip to know I missed something significant, but I was - well. I'd taken some nasty curse damage, and they swept me into teaching as soon as I was upright. I didn't begin to catch up with specifics for months."

"A small group of those who thought themselves much more clever than they were had an idea for a new drug. It was shaped with shavings of gold from coins that had not been back to the dragons recently. All that travel, all that imbued magic, picked up as the coins danced through the world, far and wide. Turned out to be disastrous to the coin, to anyone who carried one, and the drink itself..." He shrugged. "Addictive. Compelling. Transporting."

Alexander frowned, furrowing his eyes. "You've tasted it." He considered the evidence before him. "More than once." The addictive did imply something. "And you have some here?"

Carillon lifted his hand. "Yes. Yes. No." He let out a breath. "Pet alchemist. He made me something akin, without the lethal aspects. I've four bottles with me, shaped as liqueur rather than wine. It should go quite a long way."

"But?" There was decidedly a counterpoint there, hovering unresolved.

"I don't know what it will do to me. No matter. I've done far worse things than be debauched in the service of the land." Carillon shrugged it off, and Alexander's eyes narrowed.

"If my preferences matter, so do yours." As a logical supposition, in the weeks of their ongoing arguments with each other, it was a sound starting places.

"Doing this work matters more." It was flat, deliberate. "Get Berthold free. His information. If I have a bad night or two because of it, it's worth it."

Alexander had no experience of that particular form of bad night. "It's never just one night. You know that as well as I do." He then held up his hand. "I am not arguing. We don't have time. We need our energy for other things." He did not like it, but he was not arguing. "What other references do you have? Let me see what I can pull together tonight."

Carillon nodded once, briskly, then went to his trunk. He handed over three slim but useful books to Alexander, then disappeared into the bathing room, ran a bath, and did not come out for an hour.

CHAPTER 30
SATURDAY

Carillon could feel the growing tension the next day. They had circled carefully to meet Berthold on the far side of the lake, where they were less likely to be seen either by his guards or by the American. Watching him size up Alexander, and watching Alexander make sense of Berthold, would, in less fraught circumstances, have been hilarious. They were rather like two cranky cats circling each other to claim territory, though in utterly different ways. And for reasons that might be at the opposite ends of the world.

As it was, Carillon spent his time keeping watch, to allow Alexander to work through the necessary diagnostic charms to figure out how he might undo the naming magic. Berthold took the poking and prodding with more or less good grace. He had, wonder of wonders, remembered to bring a copy of his notes with him. The originals, though he said he had duplicates in his lab in case anyone looked. As Alexander finished, he nodded once minutely to Carillon, and withdrew slightly to make notes.

"How do we arrange the aftermath if all things go well?" Carillon cleared his throat as he asked the question. Alexander had done as much as he was going to do today, and his eyes were half closed in thought already. "The ritual work tonight, while I keep them busy. Then tomorrow, we hope, we get you out?"

They had talked through it on the way to the meeting. Better to split up the name magic and the escape. Carillon handed over some of the sedatives, in the hope Berthold could add them to the food or drink for the guards tomorrow night. "And what will you say?"

Berthold repeated, like an amused schoolboy who knew his recitation. "I have a new idea. I will be in my lab for a few days, disturb me on pain of explosion. If you can arrange for signs of something happening - bad smells, lights, whatever - once I am gone, that might help."

"And you have a plan for where you are going." Alexander cut in a bit abruptly.

"I need a few hours clear, but yes. Borrow a horse, make for a train station they won't expect, get the first train out in the morning. Once I am to the ocean, I can get to - well."

"Albion, please." Carillon said it crisply. "We will come find you, otherwise. You know that's best." Not just an exchange for the resources of this project, but keeping Berthold safe in the longer term. Or as safe as any inventive alchemist was. They were a danger to themselves at the best of times.

"Keep the slip, write when you have a route, or if you have problems." He then handed over the last container. "Bite down on it until it comes apart. It acts within five seconds. If you can only swallow, it will act in a minute or two, that's less sure. Only if you must, don't hold it in your mouth, but it's safe to carry in your hand if you need. Don't let them catch you with it on you."

Berthold's eyes went wide. Then he nodded. "You have my papers. The samples." He patted his pockets and handed that over. Then he ducked his chin. "Tonight. I will tell them I am busy starting this afternoon."

Carillon glanced over at Alexander, who seemed to be doing maths in his head, but he nodded. "Tonight. Here. If you can, wear linen and wool, not silk or anything else. Bathe before you come in salt water, or at least wash your hands and feet and face thoroughly in it. Bring something with your current name on it. We will go from there. I hope to be here by nine, after dark, but if you need to take longer to get away cleanly, do that. I will take you back, after."

The necessities tended to, Alexander and Carillon walked back to the Schloss. "I have a set of papers for him. It's not the best work. We didn't have an entirely satisfactory example of the proper version, but it will do. Can you fill in whatever name is necessary? There's a photo that is sufficient, at least unless it gets close inspection."

Alexander raised an eyebrow. "You have a forger in your nest."

Carillon grinned and shrugged. "Not exactly for papers, but close enough for government work."

That afternoon, Alexander claimed a headache, and retreated to their room to do the finicky necessary ritual preparation work. When it came time to change for supper, Alexander was dressed in dark clothes, and he had his cloak hanging ready. "How do we get me out? The window?"

"Too likely to be noticed. There are those acrobats, over an extended supper. You may get annoyed with me, whatever you like, storm off, and say you're going off for a walk.

Grab your cloak and go. I am hoping the acrobats will be engaging for a bit, and then..." Carillon shrugged, and went to get the four bottles ready to be brought down. They glowed golden, looking like they ought to bring joy and light and illuminating bounty. He made himself touch them lightly, the way a lover would, rather than sharply. "You have everything you need?"

"I would rather have you there." Alexander said it hesitantly, as if he had wandered into a maze and did not know the way out.

"We need me to be distracting. We need you to do what must be done." Carillon brushed his hands. "Right. Let's to?"

Supper went as Carillon had expected, and then the music and the acrobats. In one of the early intervals, Alexander raised his voice. "You're not even paying any attention to me." Then he got shrill. "I was trying to tell you..."

"Now is not a time for talking, Alexander." Carillon's consonants came out clipped and sharp. "Leave it. Settle. Let me have a bit of fun." As Alexander jerked back, Carillon turned away. "If you don't want to play, go somewhere else. I want to have a good time tonight without worrying too much about your..." It was sharp, hard, and harder still to avoid saying a thing that might truly hurt. To keep his edges to things that Alexander didn't want to have in the first place.

He heard the huff and the raw and abyssal, "My lord." He didn't turn, he didn't look, and no, that was the hardest thing tonight. Hearing the footsteps go, and then one of the willing young men leaning over. "If your hands are free, mein Herr..."

Carillon grimaced before setting it all aside. "You are much more willing for pleasures, aren't you? If Alexander isn't, he can't have any." He ran a finger along the man's hand, teasing, as the acrobats started up again. By the time he heard a faint murmur, out in the hallway, the young man was half in his lap, enjoying watching and wriggling.

Half an hour later, without things having progressed too much further than that, the acrobats finished. Carillon caught the attention of one of the servants, asking them to bring out the bottles he had brought down for the evening. "A treat. Most rare, there are only a few dozen bottles left, even in Albion. You have your goldwasser, yes?" They all laughed. "This, though, this is charmed, enchanted. Enough to send strong men mad with longing, and bring women to weeping. All the distant places you have known and loved, all the people you might share them with."

"You have some?" One of the younger women arched a perfectly shaped eyebrow, lipsticked lips going wide in an O. "I heard about it, a little, a decade ago. More. I was very young, mein Herr." She tittered and giggled. She must, in fact, have been a schoolgirl at the time. "Please, may I?"

"A gift, for all here. Now mind, I do not have so very many bottles." Carillon waved a hand, and around went the little glasses and the golden liqueur. He let the sounds of the oohs and ahs roll over him, pacing himself. Once everyone had a glass, he lifted his own, and made the necessary toast, "To the journeys of our desires." And then, without hesitating, he threw back his head and drank the three swallows.

He'd not dared test this before they left. It wouldn't have helped, anyway. He felt the weight of it hit him. Not weight like rock, like a mountain nearly falling on him, like it had in the Tirol near thirty years ago. Not like a wave breaking over him. Like being pulled down in honey, pressure and sweetness and sensuousness.

The taste on his tongue wasn't sweet, though, certainly not cloying. It had a brightness to it, like it was made of light itself, radiating through everything it touched. He opened his mouth to sigh, and then he heard the sounds around him, whimpers and a moan.

His head spun. He could not make the room focus. He could feel the people around him, every time they moved, as if they were all connected, interconnected. Like bees in a hive buzz buzz buzzing away, dancing, radiant, always moving. But these weren't worker bees, not all these lovely people around him, all the curves and lines and arches of muscle. All the temptations he'd sought in earlier times.

It rolled over him, through him, in him. If someone had asked, he'd have shed all his clothes, if he could remember how. He could feel people brushing against him, bodies moving. There were the sounds. Oh, yes, he loved the sounds, this particular music made of people's pleasures. Everyone should be happy, everyone should have joy and delight. Everyone should have all the good things the gods bestowed on those they loved, all the gifts of the land.

Somewhere, far away inside the depths of his head, the part he had locked up tight before this began, he knew how dangerous this was. He drank not just the once, but twice more, ten swallows in total, to keep things going. He'd clung to that, knowing that was needed, for some reason he couldn't remember anymore. Just like he knew there was some reason to protect himself, that no longer seemed important. Only there was this prickling of his magic, just under the skin, that wouldn't rest. That wouldn't fade away into all the other delight.

Time passed, and he only knew it because positions

changed. This person had been rocking the seat beside him, intent on passion, that one had leaned their head back, moaning, making the arm of the chair vibrate. Cries of ecstasy rose and fell, like the most intricate of fugues, changing instrumentation every repetition. Now soprano, now alto, now deepest bass. He could feel a hand upon his leg, moving to undo trousers and shirt, purring something in German that almost made sense.

Then, a voice cut through, like a tenor's entrance over the orchestra, the sound you picked out before any other. He heard a footstep behind him, and another, someone still wearing shoes. "Oh, Geoffrey." That name, it cut through everything, it brought him back to himself for just a moment, enough that he could reach out a hand in that direction, wanting suddenly. Then, sharper, the voice said to someone else, with a rolling warning growl to it. "Mine. Go elsewhere."

Then there was an arm under his shoulder, a murmur to someone else, and another arm. "Our room." Something in that provoked a titter of amusement, through the room, and he couldn't place that either. Then he was lifted, braced between two strong arms and shoulders, and near carried up the stairs, down a hall that went on forever, and then dumped into bed.

He let himself fall, boneless, barely making sense of the sounds going away from him. The next thing he knew, it was as if there was some great quiet wall between him and the world. None of the other people were around now, none of their calls and cries and whimpers. It was quiet in his head, just him and the gold and the honey. Before had felt good, this felt splendid, and it made his breath catch with need.

Then there was someone there, again, a weight on the

bed. He wriggled, feeling like a kitten circling for the warmest spot, settling his head on something warm and solid. "Mmmmyes." It came out as a mumble. "All - all warm. Best. Here." It was suddenly urgent to him, welling up from his heart, that he made that clear. "Want."

CHAPTER 31
LATE SATURDAY NIGHT

Alexander went still. Carillon's head, Geoffrey's head, his head was there in Alexander's own lap, hair come loose. Alexander, for lack of anywhere else to sit, had settled with one foot tucked up under him. The other was stretched out, and Geoffrey had nestled with his head on Alexander's thigh. Whatever Alexander had expected to come back to, it wasn't this.

His own blood was still pulsing with the fire of complex, finicky magic, the way it always did when he was clever, sharper, better, brilliant. He could feel it, like the sparkle of the stars on a clear night, a beauty that took the breath away with its purity and perfection.

And then he'd come in, and someone was reaching for his - Geoffrey's - trousers. To undo them. To tease. And Alexander had known in that moment that if he let it happen, it would poison everything near it. Taint it. Spoil things forever. He'd never be able to look Geoffrey in the eye again. Somehow, Geoffrey.

In his lap, that golden head shifted. "Warm." The voice was insistent, but it didn't make sense. Geoffrey was giving off tremendous warmth. Physically, Alexander could see the faint sheen on his skin, even feel it, where he'd had an arm around Geoffrey's back. But it wasn't just the physical. Here was trust, here was vulnerability, here was openness.

Hesitantly, he moved to rest one hand on Geoffrey's shoulder. "Geoffrey." The eyelids fluttered at the name, and Alexander felt something new there. "What do you need? Water?"

That brought Geoffrey's eyes open, widely dilated, as much as Alexander had ever seen in someone, the black leaving only the faintest ring of stormy blue around the iris. Then, instead of using words like Alexander had vainly hoped for, he just nestled down again. "Safe." It came out as another mumble, rather than the man's usual articulate drawl.

Alexander wasn't sure if that was a question, a demand, or a statement. "My best wards." And damn the implications. No one downstairs in the party was in any state to investigate. There was always the question of the staff, but he'd do the same thing again, call all the magic swirling inside him to make space here. That would hold. He'd flung all the potential he'd stored up and not needed into that, a technique he'd honed once upon a time, with Isembard, in desperation.

It brought a contented sound, so perhaps the word had been a request for information after all. Alexander patted once, remembering all his lessons - the ones he had learned and the ones he had taught - about coming back to one's body after strenuous magic. Remembering where the body was, where the limits were, that was often a challenge. That brought another happy sound, not a laugh or a sigh, but something made of relaxation and comfort.

They sat like that for a good minute or two. It was some

time before Alexander even thought to count beats of his heart or ticks of the clock. Geoffrey did not seem to be in any great distress, not at the moment, anyway. But he had no idea what it would be like when the drink wore off. Geoffrey wriggled down and murmured something incoherent.

"What was that, please?" Alexander did his best to avoid his teaching voice, the one that could come out sharp and insistent. This was neither the time nor the place for that. Nor the person to do it to.

Whatever Geoffrey heard, it made him twist a little, making the lazy, easy smile more visible. "Never thought you'd let me."

"Pardon?" Alexander didn't even know how to parse that sentence. What it referred to. What Alexander would permit?

"Head. Lap. Safe. Warm. 's good. Best." Then Geoffrey's eyes closed again. He did that little disarming shift, still very much a cat, and went quiet again.

Alexander left his hand where it was, resting on that left shoulder. He thought of the scar, not so far from his thumb now. If it hurt less, in this moment, or more, or differently. His own calf was aching, but at least for him it was a known way, an old companion by now.

He had no idea how long they sat. Alexander thought, somewhere in there, that Geoffrey had fallen asleep. But whenever he tried to move, Geoffrey shifted with him. His left hand slipped away from his chest to fall and rest the back of his fingers against Alexander's other leg. He couldn't stop thinking about it, the gentleness of it, how fragile and lovely it was. Like holding a tiny baby, only not at all the same.

An infinite time later, not that Alexander could mark

time, beyond the fact it was not yet dawn, there was a shift again. It seemed as if strength was returning. Then, almost before Alexander could react, there was a shudder of the shoulders against his leg. The way Alexander knew far too well from the inside, two nights ago. He instantly tightened his hand, steadying.

"Easy, Geoffrey. We're in our room. Solid wards around us. Take a breath." It came out rushed, too rushed. That wasn't any good, but suddenly he was worrying he wouldn't be enough.

As if obeying, Geoffrey took a breath. "Good, another. There we go. And another." It took a good twenty, talking him through each one, before Alexander felt he could leave off that. That relaxation had fled now, though Geoffrey hadn't attempted to move at all. "The drink wearing off?"

It got Alexander a tiny nod, felt more against his thigh than anything else, before Geoffrey made a faint dissonant whimper.

"I'm right here. It went well. All you need do right now is rest." Again, he felt the irritated flick of a shoulder under his thumb before he had any other cue. He didn't want to risk a charm light, and despite the full moon, the light was uneven.

Alexander hoped it was enough. And for a minute or so, it seemed like it might be. Then there was another shudder, a catch in Geoffrey's breath, and a strange tension beneath his fingers. He lay like that, the way Alexander sometimes woke in the night, unable to move or speak. Just completely aware of everything around him and all the places his life had gone wrong.

It looked different from the outside. More than that, it felt different from the outside, the way the soft relaxation had turned into edges and resistance. He wanted to coax that ease back, and in all his travels, all the things he'd learned, he had no clue how. Alexander took a breath, and thought, both absurdly and sensibly, of what Thesan would do.

He'd seen her, with Isembard, with her children, with her students, with her family. He'd frankly envied her that ease of moving from person to person, her own personal, illuminating star, bringing each person into her orbit, and then passing on again. How she could talk to someone, and set them to smiling, even though she was, he knew, still uncertain in the more glittering social spaces. She shone one on one, the essential gravity that brought them together. He took his own breath, let it out, then twice more, girding himself for what was needed.

"Can you tell me what you feel, please?" He didn't move his hand, and after a moment, added a tiny shift of his thumb. He didn't dare stroke, he didn't know what that felt like in this moment, enough to be sure it was the right thing. But he could do the thing that reminded of the presence that was there already.

Geoffrey's breath stopped, then he let it out in a rush. He inhaled, the sort of gasp that lead to cries and screams in men with far less strength of will. "Aching. Heart aching. Not myself." There was an echo in his voice now Alexander could hear it better, made up of open fourths and fifths, the chasm of the harmonies of the late mediaeval period. Music that brought one to awe and too often to shame.

"What might help?" He wondered about listing things out - food, water, a wash - but he worried the list would turn into a deluge. Thesan would leave space here, and so would he. Patiently.

Geoffrey was silent for a long moment, several breaths. Then, slowly and carefully, choosing his words like he was picking a way across a minefield, he began to speak. "Every-thing was warm. And now. Colder." He swallowed, and then made slightly better sentences, but with a queer sepa-ration between his words, each one dropped in a row.

"I am - Lizzie has been there. Benton. My people. Been a long time since I felt like this and they were not...." His voice trailed off.

Alexander swallowed hard. "They love you." It came out like a prayer, like a blessing. Like he'd taken all the ritual from earlier tonight and condensed it down to one shim-mering drop of magic that transformed everything in its past.

There was another sharp shudder, a worrying one, like something in Geoffrey was going to crack open, and then another. Alexander could feel, far more than see, Geoffrey's hand clenching at the blankets. "I'm here. I'm not going anywhere. I won't leave you with it. My magic against the world, to give you the space and time you need."

Somewhere in his thrashing for the right word, the incantation that would make the spell, it worked. That terrible shiver eased, and then Geoffrey was deflating against his leg. Alexander thought that might be all anyone said for some time, but instead, Geoffrey spoke again. More evenly this time, though still with that space and caution.

"I almost died, my shoulder. The worst nights, I die again. Only I am the last. See everyone go first. The faces change. More of them, now. I feel it slipping through my fingers. And - Benton, his strength. Lizzie and her resilience." There was a quiver, now, but the quality of it had shifted. Modulated in key, from something ominous to something more simply aching.

"What happened?" There were dozens of things he wanted to ask Geoffrey, now he was talking. In this state,

Geoffrey might actually answer. He could not take advantage, and he knew it.

"Sniper. Tried to kill Benton. Could not have that." Geoffrey had, perhaps, forgotten how to make contractions, the way that came out. One would expect the metre of 'can't have that' in the assured drawl of a man who could have near anything he wanted.

"A protection charm, yes? One of the Triadic ones. Tricky to do in the moment." Alexander ventured moving his thumb again, and this time was rewarded with Geoffrey shifting slightly into the touch. Perhaps, just perhaps, he was not failing at this. "Are you a duellist?"

Something about that got an actual snort, like a horse settling. "No." The tone, though, that was promising. "Not compared to some." Geoffrey took a slower careful breath, then managed, "I feel horrendous."

"Physically? Emotionally? Magically? Ah, erm. Having done things you did not wish?" Alexander wasn't even sure how to ask that last one.

"First two. Mostly." Geoffrey moved his hand, stretching his fingers, but misjudging, so they brushed against Alexander's leg. Alexander was not entirely sure he trusted Geoffrey's judgement on much of anything at the moment.

"We should get you out of your clothes, washed up. A bit of water. Can you let me stand for a minute?"

Alexander's legs had both gone stiff, his left foot had nearly fallen asleep. He managed to avoid a comedy show by being careful about moving. First to bring Geoffrey a glass of water, then the pitcher and basin, and a towel to wash his hands and face. Finally, he cleared his throat. "Clothes?"

"Pyjamas. Only..." Geoffrey's voice trailed off. To be fair, Alexander knew that feeling, when even his hair hurt.

"I have seen men naked before. I am not some innocent maiden." He managed to get the proper amount of arch amusement into his tone, and Geoffrey looked up at him, with the light flickering in his eyes. "Here, let me get a good look at you with a light, may I?"

Geoffrey blinked at him, but nodded. Alexander called a charm light now, setting it where it would not glare. Geoffrey was flushed, the way someone might be after exertion, perhaps after the particular exertion that was sex. Not that he was going to ask about how much of the drink had had that flavour. His eyes were still dilated, but returning to normal, that was reassuring, and when Alexander reached for Geoffrey's wrist, his pulse was more or less even.

"What should I do?"

Alexander drew a long breath. "A bit more water, out of your clothes, and then rest. We'll see where we are in the morning." Geoffrey did each of those things, though Alexander had to help, more with balance as he wriggled out of his trousers and underthings than undoing them. Finally, he got Geoffrey tucked into bed, under the blankets, with a warming charm for good measure.

"Did I—" Geoffrey spoke in the darkness, then stopped, as if he wasn't sure he should go on.

"Did you what?" Alexander had settled on his side. He had been trying to convince himself it was to make his hip stop complaining. But he knew it was because he wanted to watch Geoffrey fall asleep when he did. Make sure all was well.

"Did I do good? Do it right?"

"Oh, oh, yes. Everything I could have hoped. It was ..."

Alexander wasn't sure good was the proper descriptor. "You were clever and brave, and it all came out right."

"Oh." That was a small soft sound, and then Geoffrey nestled into the blankets, shifting one hand toward the middle of the bed, between them. Alexander found himself reaching to rest his there, just barely touching, before he could stop himself. He lay there, listening to Geoffrey's breathing slow again, this time into true sleep, before he finally drifted off.

CHAPTER 32
SUNDAY MORNING

The first thing he knew in the morning was the way his head ached, but not his heart. His dreams had been baffling, rather like the tapestries at Ytene that ran from story to scene to reference without apparent rhyme or reason. And yet, there had been something reassuring in them. Not that he was back on the land he loved, but that he would be. That no matter how far he wandered, it would - she would - be waiting for him.

He stretched out a hand without opening his eyes, and brushed against another. His eyes flew open, and then he winced. Entirely too much light. Immediately, the hand covered his. "Headache?" It was as if he could feel the pulse there, soothing and reassuring like last night.

That was Alexander. It could only be Alexander. He took a breath, frowning. Alexander sounded different. The room sounded differently, honestly, even when there was no other sound, the space did. He managed a little nod. "Yes?"

"Everything went well last night. Let me get you a potion and some water." Alexander moved, and he let himself relax. It wasn't quite making himself, he felt like a sprawled foal, unable to get his legs under him. A minute or so later, the bed shifted again. "Headache potion, water. It's about ten." He could feel the potion bottle pressed into his hand. "One of mine. I don't want to risk your trunk."

"Please. Tap..." He moved his hand, tapping the rhythm, the dactyls of the opening of the Odyssey. "Top right corner. Panel will open." He felt Alexander tap them on his hand, and he nodded. The bed moved again, and in a minute, Alexander was back.

"Clever. Here you go." The right shape of vial was pressed into his hand, small enough to drain in a swallow or two. He knocked it back, and then let it flood his system. The headache abated, not entirely, but substantially, and he let himself fall onto his back as the rest of his body caught up. Once the room stopped spinning, he levered himself onto one elbow to find Alexander watching him from a foot away, sitting on the bed, one leg tucked up.

"Ge - may I?" There was a hesitance there, as Alexander held out the glass.

"You called me that last night. Geoffrey. Do you want to?" Even in his entirely decrepit state, with holes in his memory, he realised that the name was having an effect on him. Physically, that was, and he was glad the blankets were up around his waist. It wasn't just that only a few people used his first name. Lizzie, Pross. Ferry, if she were being pointed. He certainly didn't have that particular reaction to anyone but Lizzie, a desire for something far more physical than he had time or energy for this morning.

Alexander's mouth quirked. "If anyone remembers my coming in last night, they might comment on the change."

"As you prefer, then." Geoffrey managed a half-smile, feeling his way into the name inside his own head. "May take me a little. What - what happened?" More precisely, had he said some of the things he half-remembered, or were those just in his head or in his dreams. Alexander didn't seem angry or upset or have the tight-lipped self-restraint that came after an awkward pass.

"You should bathe, and we should go for a walk, if you can bear the outside. Geoffrey." The name sent another shiver through him, and not just the name, but that Alexander was taking charge now, seeing that things were sorted. "The house is still quiet, as far as I can tell. Need a hand to the bath?"

Geoffrey considered his options here. "My dressing gown? And if you'd go start the bath after that?" It would give him a moment to get decently covered. He rubbed his face as Alexander found the gown and ran the bath. By the time he came back, Geoffrey was standing - a bit shaky, but upright. "Could you ring for some food? Something gentle, an egg and toast? And whatever you want." He hesitated. "Or think I should have?"

That got a snort. "I'll wait to pull my wards until you're in the bath, all right? You need a bit of a buffer."

Once he was settled in mercifully hot water, Geoffrey called out, "Ready." He felt the warding shift, the way that quiet padding dropped away, leaving a brittle echo in its place. Impressive work, not that Geoffrey was at all surprised. Or if he was surprised, it was only that Alexander had had sufficient resources left after the naming ritual.

Twenty minutes later, he was bathed, dressed, and applying himself to a roll with honey and butter, two soft-boiled eggs, sliced meats and cheeses, as well as lashings of coffee. "We are the first ones awake, I gather." Alexander looked cheerful, almost manic with it, that edge of light-ning that suggested a particular reaction to the magical working.

"I'm up for a walk, so long as we are not too energetic for a bit. Down to the river again?" They found shoes and cloaks, and ten minutes later, they were well up the path.

"Do you need to get a look at the arrangement of the lab spaces?" Alexander asked it quietly. "For tonight?"

Geoffrey considered. "How much did you see last night, walking him back?"

"They have been relying on the name magic binding him to a radius - they don't guard the back nearly as well as they should. I couldn't see much last night, even with the moon. There are enough trees to cast shadows, but I think we might walk around the back of the lake and over that direction. I saw his lab, but not for any length of time."

They walked on in silence for a few minutes before Geoffrey cleared his throat. "Thank you for last night. I am not entirely sure what actually happened, but I know you —" Now he had no idea how to finish that sentence acceptably to Alexander. Surely that last part about telling Geoffrey he'd been clever and brave was some part of the wish-filled fantasy, the goldwasser.

Alexander's step hitched, and he turned to look. "You ended up with your head in my lap, but were otherwise quite considerate. I particularly appreciate the lack of mess. You make a very agreeable - whatever that is. You weren't just drunk. How much did you have?"

"Ten swallows." He waited a moment and heard the explosive curse beside him. "I suspect most of them had twice that. And didn't bring the good headache potions."

"And you're upright?" Alexander shook his head. "The English aren't supposed to have that kind of head for hard liquor."

"I," proclaimed Geoffrey, amused, "Have a pet alchemist. What's the point of having a pet alchemist if you can't create something to favour your constitution? Though I'm glad I didn't have to drink more." He had a point, and Alexander knew it, since he walked on in silence again until Geoffrey cleared his throat. "Tell me how brilliant you were last night?"

That got another hitch in Alexander's step, and a rueful laugh. "Exceedingly. For the record, there are perhaps two other people in Albion who might have sorted that, and neither of them could have done it near as quickly. Long and short of it, I renamed him, wrote it up in his papers, and I don't know the language for it in English. Or German. Anchored it in his souls." Plural clearly. "He's Bertram Hofler now."

"Bright raven." Geoffrey knew the meaning there. "That suits him rather nicely. Clever like a raven, inquisitive. And near enough his old name he'll answer to it."

"And no monogram will catch the eye, nor any time he uses his initials. Give me credit, Geoffrey, for knowing the basics of espionage." The tone there, easy amusement, friend teasing friend, made Geoffrey's heart sing. Whatever had happened last night hadn't spoiled Alexander's tolerance. If anything, matters were rather better.

"Walk me through the details, sometime when we're home, then. So I can appreciate at least some of it." He offered it almost casually, but he caught Alexander's nod, the tentativeness, out of the corner of his eye. "The lab?"

"Entrance from the back, if no one's watching too carefully. One large room, with an attached sleeping and sitting room, about twenty by twenty. I'd not want to sleep so close, but I suppose he doesn't have a choice. The existing gas pellets, for testing, are stored in the corner. We'll want to be careful not to trigger those unless we're on our way out. He thinks they're moderately stable, but..."

"But his idea of moderately stable and our idea of it are rather different." Geoffrey agreed. "What are our goals, then?"

"Make sure he's actually destroyed any copies of his notes. Including whatever's scratched into the blotting paper and notepads. I'd like to destroy the stores, but we'll need to see how to do that."

"And he's planning to get out this evening." Just as Geoffrey finished speaking, there was a movement up ahead. In unison, they ducked sideways behind a large tree near the lake. They saw Theodore coming along, walking down the path. He glanced from side to side, but more often back over his shoulder, as if he were rather more worried about someone coming up behind him.

Geoffrey frowned. "Was he there when you came in last night?"

Alexander shifted beside him, his breath coming warm against Geoffrey's cheek. "I was not exactly counting heads. Or other body parts. But - perhaps not. Bugger." It was an unlikely swear from him.

They watched him walk along, not taking particular precautions. Geoffrey noticed the way he left footprints in the softer ground at the side of the path and gestured. "Let's avoid complicating that. Do we need to see the lab, truly?"

"No. I'd rather plan." They waited a good twenty minutes before taking the long way back to the house, across the fields, pausing at the bench by the smaller pond.

"What resources do we think he actually has? Or skills?" Geoffrey settled, facing Alexander, and smiled as Alexander matched him almost instantly. Ankle on knee, hand on thigh, leaning in a little.

"Not as many skills as he should have. Which makes

our lives easier and harder." Alexander grimaced. "I do hate working around amateurs. They're so unpredictable. Have I said, actually, how much of a pleasure it is to be doing this with a fellow professional?"

Geoffrey laughed, feeling the delight bubble up. "Likewise, as I've said. We make a fine pair, I think. Complementary skills. I am glad you said yes." He wriggled his fingers. "Do we break into his rooms while he's busy? Is that too much effort? Does he want to get at Bertram himself? Actually, let me check." Geoffrey pulled out the half sheets of paper from his shirt pocket. "He said he felt someone snooping around. He'll be slipping out as soon as he can tonight. Do whatever we see fit. But he did manage to get something in the stew for the guards tonight."

"If it takes, that will be a help. Though you never know what cooking does to a sedative." Alexander raised a finger, amused. "Your pet alchemist is excellent. I envy him. But they are not above the laws of magic and chemistry, no matter how much they think they ought to be."

It made Geoffrey laugh. "All right. So we don't search Theodore's room. We need to figure out how we get out of the house tonight, what we bring with us, and - blast. American. He probably has a gun."

"The question is, is he any good with it? I don't get a strong sense he's in our league, magically. No sign of really solid warding. And I fancy I notice the strength of someone's magic, as well as anyone."

"It isn't just the strength, it's the training. But you know that too. Lizzie hasn't found out anything about him, but I'm not surprised, with only a couple of days. My nest of people does not extend far into America."

"Perhaps I can be some help there, in due course." Alexander shrugged. "Right. Getting out of the house."

They could not make a decision without more information at the moment, but it was worth the risk of going out the window once it was dark. Better if they could go out visibly, but it would take the right setting and excuse. Storming out to have an argument, something like that. Satisfied they'd done as much as they could, they went back to the house for an unsurprisingly solitary late luncheon.

CHAPTER 33
SUNDAY EVENING

Alexander repressed his desire to twitch again. It had been a rather subdued supper. Everyone, whether or not they admitted it, was still hungover. That was rather impressive, really, given the range of drugs and drinks he'd seen go by in the past few days. Or perhaps that was what was continuing the hangover.

No one seemed particularly upset about it, which was odd. The conversation over supper had been all about people comparing the places they'd seen in their visions and dreams. Everywhere from palm-tree dotted islands to the great palaces of Europe to Monte Carlo's tables of chance, and near everywhere in between. Certainly, he'd caught people not mentioning something that was on the tip of their tongue. But no one seemed resentful or cranky. More tired and lost inside their own heads.

He had certainly snuck into places in worse conditions. The weather was even cooperative for a wonder, a haze that obscured things, without yesterday afternoon's drizzle. He was keeping an eye on Geoffrey, who seemed to be largely recovered. Both had various supplies tucked about their persons, with rather more in their cloaks.

As they'd planned, Alexander pushed away. "You keep asking, Geoffrey, and I just - I just don't know what to say. I'm going for a walk." Geoffrey let him go, but pouting and grumpy about it, letting that show.

Alexander wanted to tell him not to overplay it, but it wasn't as if he could say anything. He heard the laughter start up behind him, and Geoffrey waving it off. "If he doesn't come back in a bit, I'll go find him, remind him of the benefits of a good time."

Thirty minutes later, Geoffrey strolled up to where he was waiting, in a copse of trees near the turn around the lake. "Bertram got away an hour ago. They're being languid back at the Schloss. The wine and drugs are flowing. I don't think anyone will notice how long we're gone."

"Theodore?"

"Still there when I left. Sepp was having some fun with him." Geoffrey shrugged slightly. "He didn't seem to mind, so I'm taking that as 'exhausting the person who might notice his absence and then following on.' Which means we should be timely."

"Quite." Alexander sketched a bow. "Shall we?"

They made it to the back of the little village simply enough, and into the lab. It was barely a cluster of houses, perhaps for gamekeepers in some former life. Once in the laboratory, they were confronted with rather more than they'd wanted. No one had been nearby, or even visible in the little cluster of houses.

Alexander started off by casting a charm that would muffle any sound. "Not so sure as yours, but it will do if no one's listening in the windows." Which were, thankfully, covered by both shutters and curtains, blocking any light outside. "And the door's locked."

"Left or right?" Geoffrey glanced around.

"I'll take the left." Alexander had seen the desk there, and he intended to clear the paper at a start. Twenty minutes later, they met at the far end of the room. "His rooms." Alexander held up a hand.

"Let me, you were eyeing the lab bench. I'm decent with materia, I suspect you're better." Geoffrey went off without waiting for an answer. Alexander eyed the workbench, frowning, and then grimacing.

By the time Geoffrey came back, he had nudged one wooden casket, exceedingly carefully, out of the row of cabinetry. "Do you know what that is? Don't wake it." The label was clear enough. Mandragora. But it wasn't the label that worried him, it was the sullen pulse of magic he could feel, like a budding infection. A sleeping wrongness, a broken scar ready to spread through the world.

Geoffrey blinked, then winced. "He didn't tell us everything, did he?" He waved a hand. "We can't leave that. What do you think they're doing with it?"

"Not having my research library to hand, and working from memory..." Alexander sucked in a breath. "An alraune. Currently sessile, with luck."

"It is neither screaming nor walking." Geoffrey agreed. Seeing as how it was made from a mandrake root, it could potentially do either or both.

"Fire." Alexander let out a breath. "It's the only way." He looked up. His heart was pounding now, the gut-wrenching drumbeat that he'd felt pulse through him in the worst times.

It wasn't just the alraune itself. He knew what they needed to do. He knew he could do it, if he were only permitted. Alexander could call the lightning and fire to his hands, and burn it all up, loose all Set's destructiveness on this creation of Isfet. The alraune was wrongness given form, and he could not let it linger. He could feel the magic already rising in his blood, burning with that fire and heat.

Some part of him had to try to explain. But Geoffrey wouldn't understand. No one had ever understood. He'd felt this way a handful of times before, and each time, he'd been told that he must set that instinct aside, and do as proper magicians of Albion did. When the Fortiers had first taken an interest. His first week at Schola. After his brother's death and his mother's, when he'd wanted to rage at the world and break free of every expectation, and had done neither. After Perry had gone home for the last time, and he couldn't follow.

The handful of times he had tried to explain to Hesperidon, Alexander had been shut down. He'd been sent away, like a rabid dog might be, until he brought himself grudgingly to heel. This was worse than all of those together. Those had been trivial matters, in comparison. He didn't know if he had the words, if he could form them and bring his tongue to shape them, but he had to try.

"We have to destroy this, you understand?" Alexander clenched his hands, feeling the way his fingers cramped, the way his muscles had started to twitch. He was talking too fast, but he couldn't stop. "I don't know whether they're intending to make a preparation for a gas that would let men walk through fire. One that would send all of ours to a dead sleep, then a sleep of death. Or whether the goal is a thousand thousand soldiers of such might that nothing can stand against them. Whichever it is, it cannot come to pass."

"Are you..." Geoffrey didn't finish the sentence. Instead,

he looked at it. It was admittedly a small casket, but Alexander could feel the weight of it, like a black hole or a star so dense it pulled everything toward it, unbalancing everything. It was too much, too strong. It overpowered everything that might be good in the world.

When Alexander could focus again, Geoffrey was speaking, thinking out loud. He'd missed at least a few words, possibly more. "Our goal was to get in and get out. Without attracting too much attention. For our own sakes as well as the larger goals." He was going through it carefully, and Alexander loved and hated his caution in equal measure. Now was a moment for action, for cutting away the reaching excess.

Alexander forced himself to simple words. "Do you have orders against a commotion? Direct orders?" He felt himself start to stutter on the last words. His control was slipping and he clenched his hands harder, riding the pain of it to keep his mind clear. Alexander honestly wasn't sure exactly who had guided this mission beyond Geoffrey himself. Someone in the Ministry, but perhaps they had just approved it, and not fiddled with the means.

Geoffrey slowly shook his head. "Not directly. Strong, mm, encouragement." Geoffrey was looking him up and down, steadily, as if he didn't realise he was on the edge of a chasm, that Alexander was only barely in control. "You really need this." It wasn't a question.

Alexander couldn't do anything but nod. This needed to be stopped, that he could do that, that if he couldn't stop this one thing, it might shatter him, for good. That it was something about his nature, his name, his blood, that was being snagged and torn, every moment he wasn't making this better.

Even if he'd had the words, he wasn't sure he could

have used them. Every time he came close to a sentence in his head, it blew apart in hearing Geoffrey call it sentimental or slight or not enough. All the things he'd heard from other people. Instead, Geoffrey let out a long breath. "What would you do if I said yes to your plan? How would you do it?"

Alexander made himself pause, he refused to give way to the torrent of ideas that wanted to pour out of him. He sucked in a quick breath, begging the fire in his blood to hold back just a little longer. He didn't want to hurt Geoffrey, not if there were any other chance, but he could feel it pressing, rising and cresting like the Nile about to flood.

Instead, he laid it out as clearly as he could, barely trusting any of it would do any good. "Fire. Multiple fires. A time charm, ideally, to give us time to get to Berlin, or further away. I assume Bertram has some history of locking himself in for several days? A long fuse. We could set something to go if someone forced the door."

"There were four days of food in his sitting room, on neat little trays. That part of his plan seems to have worked." Geoffrey rubbed his face. "Someone might check on him. Or there's the problem of Theodore. It wouldn't do for an explosion that doesn't actually destroy. In this case. We can't take it away with us."

"No." That was flat and sharp. "I daren't move it. Never mind take it inside the Schloss's wards. Either they'd alert someone, or it would wake the alraune. Probably both."

"Let's not," Geoffrey agreed. Alexander tried not to fidget or shake out his hands, but he didn't dare do that. The magic was far too close to the skin now, the movement might make it flare loose. Then he tried not to pace and was slightly more successful.

Geoffrey didn't rush, Alexander wouldn't force him.

Couldn't force him. If he was taking his time, he had reason. But he could feel the magic beating at him. Not just from the alraune itself, but from the thread of his mother's magic that ran through his veins. Whatever they meant it for, whatever it was dreaming of, was a perversion of the heart in a way far worse than death, even death by gas.

At least he could only feel the one. Alraunes, from what he remembered, true alraunes, were quite rare. It was even possible, remotely, that Bertram truly hadn't known what he had. He'd mentioned some supplies being brought in in the past few weeks, for a later project that he hadn't looked at yet. Once he was done with his current gasses.

Finally, Geoffrey's eyes opened fully. "I'll need at least half an hour. Maybe twice that. Neither of us cares for Theodore, right?" Something in Geoffrey's matter-of-factness gave Alexander breathing space at last. The fire was still there, the burning need, but Geoffrey was there, and steady, his own face suggesting he was running down a dozen plans of his own now.

Alexander closed his eyes for a long moment. "You'll let me?"

"I'll help you." The words came softly, but they rang in Alexander's head like the clang of a great bell. When he could get his eyes open again, Geoffrey was standing square on both feet, ready to move.

When he saw Alexander focus again, he patted his cloak, then ducked a hand into one pocket, pulling out a modest flat tin of white powder, then another. "Hand me, mm. That strip of wood." Something off a crate, supple enough to bend, light and only about three inches wide, and perhaps a foot long.

"Do you routinely carry - is that Plaster of Paris?" Alexander then realised there was a question. "Theodore has been sloppy. I don't particularly wish him dead, but if you're planning to implicate him enough to scare him off, be my guest." He felt scattered, confused, but there was a way forward. Somehow. Miraculously. He didn't have to deny himself, and he would think about that later, all of what it meant.

Geoffrey gave him a flashing smile. "All the best-prepared spies have their secrets. Quite handy, and not just for this. Not bad for key moulds, either. In a pinch." He nodded. "I'll be careful. You check for any further notes, and do whatever you need for your charms and enchantments. Can you aim for it to go off on, hmm. Tomorrow mid-afternoon, if not disturbed?"

"Under a day? Yes." Alexander hesitated. "Take care."

That got another amused grin. "Always." Then he pulled his cloak tight around him, cast his own notice-me-not, and slipped out the door, taking wood and plaster and whatever else he was carrying with him.

It left Alexander to do his part. His heart had stopped pounding, and he set up points that would burn hot and pure. He fed all his fury and his rage into them, half a dozen bundles of herbs and magic that would go off like bombs.

Once he could think more clearly again, he set to work on the more delicate work, figuring out how to discourage anyone from trying the doors. He set tripwire charms if they forced them, and anchored the chronological magics in something that would last long enough. Rummaging in the sitting room turned up sufficient walnuts that he could charm and roll into the corners. They'd anchor the charm in case someone opened the door, a thin thread did for part of the trigger, he'd have to set the last bit as they left. He'd centred the fires in six places, linked to feed each other, with the largest formed around the alraune, with plenty of fuel to burn.

He did another check of the room, coming across one more pile of notes stashed half-behind the desk, as if they'd fallen. He rolled those into a deep pocket in his own cloak. They'd need to read those later.

By the time Geoffrey slipped through the door again, just a hint of a brush of magic to alert him, everything was almost ready. He was carrying two plaster footprints. "Has your work gone well? I've inserted several prints around the back, carefully avoiding any impressions from the plaster." They were, in fact, rather neatly trimmed.

"You've never taken up ceramics? You have a tidy hand." Alexander glanced over his shoulder, able to talk like an ordinary person again. "Can you take some of these? Additional samples, quite inert as far as I can tell, unless they're prepared. I found more notes."

They made the last arrangements in near silence, handing over this tool or that stone. Finally, Alexander nodded, and they pulled the door closed behind them. He set the last trigger not across the space between the door and the frame, but tucked into the space between them, so that if the door opened, the whole place would go up.

Easing their way back up halfway around the lake, even with notice-me-not charms, took a good hour. Then Geoffrey stopped. "Damn and blast. We can't trust him not to go poking his nose where it's dangerous. Can you manage a night out?"

Alexander saw the problem immediately. Though, in truth, he still felt like a feral animal, not fit for company or putting on a civilised face. A night among the trees, as a hunter, would suit him well. "He's likely to approach from the road or this path." Two of them, two paths. Keeping watch was not the problem, but the discipline to keep it up until sometime past dawn would be an effort tonight. "Hard on you?" He offered that cautiously, to get a glimmer of a smile.

"I've done worse. Not recently, but... " Geoffrey shrugged. "We can come back in daylight. And we were leaving in the morning, anyway. We can sleep, well. Later."

Alexander nodded. "If you need—" He didn't even know how to finish that. It wasn't like they could come to the other's aid. "What will you do if you see Theodore?"

"I was just thinking to scare him off. Footsteps, noises of guards. If he takes the hint, nothing worse. If he doesn't, I suppose send him to sleep, if I can."

That left rather messy loose ends, but Alexander nodded. "Same." He made a slight bow. "Let me go round the other side. Spare you that much of the walking."

Geoffrey nodded. "Meet you at the bench at an hour after sunrise."

Alexander sketched a not-quite-bow. As he walked, keeping an eye out for errant Americans, local guards, unreliable alchemists who should be well out of the way, and the usual complications of a stroll at midnight, he couldn't help thinking about the whole mess. He'd been truly angry, upset, no matter how much he'd held it back. And Geoffrey had just accepted that.

More than that, he'd helped. Unstintingly. He'd had excellent reason to tell Alexander no. And instead, he'd put all his cleverness to making something new, something necessary, work. Alexander did not know what to do with that, not remotely. And a good seven or eight hours to stew on it wasn't going to help at all.

CHAPTER 34

A TRAIN WEST ON MONDAY, MAY 20TH

By the time they made it onto the train to Brussels, Geoffrey was nearly asleep on his feet. He'd kept awake all night and had cast the charms to sound like heavy-footed guards twice. He thought only one had been Theodore, but it was hard to tell.

Then they'd had to make their way back to the Schloss, pack their belongings, and join a chattering crew on a ride back to Berlin. They stopped at their hotel for their larger trunks, making a comment about his wife needing him back at home, alas. Without much conversation, they bought tickets for the next train that would get them promptly out of Germany just before noon. Neither of them dared risk the portals. There was too much magic surrounding them that might raise suspicion. And it would be far too easy to trace where they went.

It was only once they made it into their compartment that Geoffrey could begin to relax. The porter had tucked their trunks under the seat, and Alexander glowered at anyone who seemed to consider joining them. Somewhere in the first twenty minutes, Geoffrey fell asleep, his face pressed against the glass of the window like a schoolboy coming home from an outing.

He didn't wake until rather later in the afternoon, coming into twilight. He blinked slowly, frowning and trying to get his bearings. Alexander shifted - he was barely an inch or two away, reading a newspaper. "We're twenty minutes from Brussels. Do you mind going on to Paris? This train is continuing."

It was entirely too soon after waking up for that to make sense. "Paris?"

"I'd like to pick up something from my bank vault in the morning. And - we should talk. A hotel, somewhere that will bring supper up." Alexander was now all civilised contained politeness, as if some switch had flipped since last night in the laboratory.

Geoffrey rubbed his face. Again. "Yes?" It seemed the only possible answer. "Is there anything to eat?" He had nuts or something somewhere in his cloak. He was suddenly ravenous, and it would be another hour or two to any kind of real supper.

Silently, Alexander handed over bread and cheese. They bumped along the rails in silence into Brussels, which at least gave Geoffrey enough time to write to Lizzie. He got across the barest sketch of everything that had happened since Sunday afternoon and his last note. She had been concerned, of course, about the fake goldwasser, and he had done his best to explain that Alexander had kept him safe, in all the ways, including several dozen he hadn't expected.

Their revised codebook was still not precisely adequate to the situation, it turned out. But her note back had suggested she had the gist of it, and they could sort out the rest when he came home.

Whenever Geoffrey opened his mouth, Alexander shook his head and went back to his paper. Though he did at least hand over a section of it when Geoffrey got bored looking out the window at darkness.

It wasn't as if he could spend the time looking at Alexander, who looked as worn as Geoffrey still felt, all faded and smudged and bruised. Geoffrey wondered if any part of Alexander also felt healed and mended like he did, under the battering they'd both taken. Alexander had been in full fury Sunday night, in a way that should have terrified him.

It had, and it hadn't. He'd known, though, that whatever Alexander wanted that much - he was not a man who showed his wants - needed to happen. He trusted Alexander had good cause, and the only issue had been arranging matters with a certain plausible deniability and no link back to them. Fire was very effective that way.

An hour after their arrival in Paris, they had a hotel in one of the magical streets near the Bibliotheque de Magie, a simple but well-appointed suite. They'd each had a quick wash, against the coal and soot of the train travel, and the staff had brought up a hearty meal. As soon as they were alone, Alexander had, without consultation, set up those wards that made everything quiet and far away. They'd finished eating, and were down to the last glass of wine each, enough to pad against the strain of the day.

Finally, Geoffrey cleared his throat. "A pleasure."

Alexander's chin came up, and he opened his mouth, then closed it. "I don't know how to have this conversation."

It made Geoffrey smile, the sort of smile that threatened to crack his cheeks. "I don't want to have it with anyone else, so we'll have to muddle through together." He added.

"Not that we did nearly as much muddling as most would these past few days. It really has been a pleasure working with you."

There was a silence, a leading silence, that wanted the bass line to fall away and the upper voices to resolve, not be left hanging. He went on, wanting to be absolutely clear. "Not just the work at hand. You are - will you come and stay with us for a bit?"

Alexander's eyes widened. "Why?"

Geoffrey closed his eyes, trying to figure out what to say here. That he remembered his head on Alexander's leg, the way it felt secure. That he could finally let down all his guard. The way they worked together, like how he and Lizzie were, but also different. Of course it was, Alexander had his own particular skills. The hints he'd got, of Alexander's reactions to the land magic. Alexander had said, himself, that Geoffrey knew his oaths and loyalties, those included the land, if in a very different form than his own link with Ytene and the New Forest. Geoffrey wanted to share that warmth, and perhaps now, this prickly, proud bird of a man might give him that much of a chance.

"It's been a long time since you worked closely with someone else. The War?" Geoffrey hesitated. "Can you tell me about Peredur?"

Whatever Alexander had expected, it wasn't that. Geoffrey both regretted and rejoiced in the shock of it hitting him. Geoffrey knew that expression from the inside, well enough, the feeling of scrambling to rearrange the premises of your world when something changed under your feet. He added, "The date did rather stick in my head. It was the day ..." He gestured at his shoulder.

"Oh." Alexander's voice was hollow. He stood, pushing

up from the chair to stare out the window. "I can't tell you here. Not now."

"Come stay."

Alexander turned around, looking over his shoulder, now suspicious. "Why?"

"I don't know the half of it. But I don't think you should go back to your excellent library and your solitary life. Not just yet, anyway. We need to talk, more than we've time for tonight. When we can sort through the past days and weeks. Will you?"

"Your wife?" Alexander's voice pitched upwards.

"Would be delighted. She's already said so, and before I asked, for the record." Geoffrey shrugged. "And I gather the redoubtable Mrs Mudthon has been trying new dishes you might like."

"There are things I need to do first." Finally, Alexander turned back, though with his arms crossed in front of him, protective and defensive.

"So long as you'll come as soon as you can." Geoffrey hesitated. There was a great deal he wanted to say now, and it wasn't time yet. About how he'd started thinking of himself, somehow, as Geoffrey. About how he was yearning far more for his own land than he had on previous trips. If anything, it was strongest with Alexander standing there, unsure of his place. "May I ask a question?"

"Another one?" Alexander grimaced, then said, "Your room, perhaps? You should get comfortable."

"Me? You're the one where the shadows under your eyes could be wells. You didn't sleep at all on the train, did you?" The teasing made Alexander snort. "My room. It has a better comfortable chair."

Five minutes later, Geoffrey had removed his shoes, donned a dressing gown, and had settled into bed. It did, in fact, feel very good to have something soft and steady beneath him. "I am not nearly as young as I was." Neither was Alexander, who was, in fact, meaningfully older. But Geoffrey would not tease about that.

"And you had the harder road, Saturday." Alexander's voice got cautious. "I did not overstep?"

"Good grief, no. You—" Geoffrey faltered for a moment, not sure how it would come out. "I felt safe with you. Safe as houses. I just knew I was. And you did all the ritual work, and the set-up in the lab."

"Do you think there's any way for us to know what happened?"

"Chances are decent I might hear. It would come by mail, though. Most of that lot don't have journals. The German ones aren't nearly as reliable as ours. Tomorrow, perhaps the day after, if Friedrich or someone else passes on gossip. If we're lucky. Or perhaps one of my Ministry contacts might hear."

Alexander nodded, tucking that away. "You were going to ask something?"

The fact he'd brought it up made Geoffrey smile and sip his wine. "You were away from Albion for a long time. So was I. I am beginning to think they weren't for such different reasons."

There was the briefest hesitation before Alexander said, "You first."

Geoffrey had half-expected that, and he'd been trying to find words for the last few hours. "Temple was our father's heir. He'd been sworn to it since I could remember. I never expected to inherit, or if I did, when I was well into my, I don't know, seventies. Eighties. Old age. He preferred our house in Cumbria, our parents did too, once we were grown up. But it's always been Ytene that had my heart." He shrugged. "If I couldn't have her, I didn't much want to be in Albion. That's what I've come to think."

Something in that made Alexander grunt, the sound Geoffrey had been suppressing every time Alexander used his forename. It wasn't just arousal, nor purely physical, but it was something viscerally moving, in the deep ways, the ones that reshaped the world as they went.

"More things I can't talk about right now. Not here. But." Alexander swallowed. "I was born in Albion. I think I've always loved her. More after..." His voice trailed off.

"When you're ready." Geoffrey said it as gently as he could. "Though I am very curious, I will restrain myself. From teasing, as well."

That, as he'd hoped, got another of those amused smiles. "I am told I am excellent at not explaining myself until I'm ready. To give you fair warning."

"I had noticed that about you, yes." Geoffrey shrugged. "Is that why you travelled? Like me? You couldn't love her - Albion, the land - the way you wanted or needed? And it was easier to be away and yearning than there and unable to?"

Alexander grunted again, this time more in thought. "More or less. I went - near mad, the last years of the War." He jerked one shoulder, making it clear that was part of what he wasn't talking about here. "Gods know how I made it through. And then I wrote to the Council, told them to send whatever business they had elsewhere my way. I didn't come back until I had to."

"You mentioned a nasty curse." Geoffrey wondered now how bad it had been, besides 'tremendously'.

"It took me the better part of a year to properly recover. Another year to rebuild my stamina to where I could tolerate it. Teaching all the time, and that is not nearly as restful as most people think."

"I have gathered not, from some of the stories we hear from Isembard and Thesan. And then you—" Geoffrey let that lead in.

"If I'd stayed another year at Schola, I'd never have left. Or they'd have yanked me away, sent me somewhere, and it was better to lose it on my own terms. So I thought at the time." He shrugged. "It's complicated. All of it. It always has been. I'm well used to that."

"How did you come to Albion? In the beginning?"

"In my mother's womb, as all the best stories begin." That was another moment of amusement. "My father had a connection to the Fortiers. They took my brother in, Phillip." Geoffrey noticed those were both names that would do well in Arabic, in French, in English, and he wondered suddenly how deliberate that was.

"Mother couldn't go back to Egypt. And Phillip did well. He died saving Isembard's father's life, or so they've told me, repeatedly." Not that he'd ever gesture at his own doubts about what had happened there. "I was just finishing school. Mother died the next year, and I was on my own. They felt guilty, I think, some in that set. Arranged an apprenticeship, but then I had to pay it back."

"Challenging for the Council?" Geoffrey wasn't sure how to nudge at that as delicately as it needed.

"I am considering telling you a bit about that." Alexander's voice now was measured and thoughtful.

It flung Geoffrey back to their discussion by the pond. He inclined his head. "As you choose, of course. Your preferences, above all."

That won him a smile. "You do insist on that." Alexander let out a long, slow breath. "Let me get what I need from the bank in the morning. We can take the portal together. I have some business to tend to, a day or two, but - I will come to Ytene if you and your lady wife will have me."

Geoffrey nodded. "Good." Just the one word. It was enough. More than enough.

With that, Alexander stood. "Sleep. It's been a tremendously long day."

Geoffrey wanted to ask him to stay, now they were used to sharing a bed. But he knew this man would need time to come to that idea, if he ever did again. Now was not the moment.

CHAPTER 35
YTENE ON TUESDAY, MAY 21ST

"Geoffrey." She was trying the name out. It had a different feel to it, now that he'd told Lizzie. What it did in his head, that Alexander had used it. He'd told her badly. He didn't have words for any of it.

"Are you jealous?" Geoffrey was curled on their bed, head in her lap, looking up at her. She had gracefully managed the rush of the children wanting to welcome him home. He had spent the afternoon out in the garden with them, sitting on a blanket. He'd watched them run back and forth with toys and leaves and snails and other things to show him, pressing his hands against the ground whenever he could.

They had shared all the ordinary moments of tea and supper. He had read a chapter from the latest story book, baffling because he did not know this one, and they were halfway through. Silently, insistently, Lizzie had taken him by the hand and led him back to their rooms.

"Surprised." Lizzie's hand shifted to pull the hair back from his face. That was her thinking voice, where she did not yet have enough information to commit to anything more specific. He knew it well, and it was one of the things he loved about her. She did not judge in advance of the information. "Tell me about it, from the beginning of this trip."

Geoffrey nodded, half-closing his eyes. He wanted to watch her, the little reactions, but he could feel most of them through his fingers, and he was still terribly tired and worn. Complicated about it, too. His initial descriptions of Sepp and Anneliese amused, at least. "They are a certain type, aren't they?"

"Hanging on to the world that is rapidly passing." Geoffrey shook his head. "I have no idea what their elders will make of the whole thing."

"We will come back to the unexpected explosion in due course." Lizzie's hand brushed his forehead. "So, there you, and - tell me about this American."

"Looked like an American. Sounded like an American. Brash. Bold. Very visible."

"That is indeed rather like the assumption of an American." She tapped his hair with one finger.

"Alexander was sure he was lying about his background. A tiny detail, something most men would have no idea about. Even fewer women. Even more so than, oh, assuming the societies at Schola were also at Dunwich. But I am fairly sure that whatever else he is, he is also an American."

"Which has her own, yes. I see the point." Lizzie frowned. "And then you kept seeing him."

"And his rather distinctive footprints. And no, I don't think he was the obvious partner of a pair. We do know our work, both of us. He came alone, spent no particular time with anyone else, other than Sepp."

Lizzie nodded. "Who, logically, is in a different class. Did you have any other theories?"

"The one I already mentioned, or rather, that was Alexander's question. Whether Madam A. had sent him. But he seemed to take no particular interest in me, beyond the natural flow of the party. Less in Alexander." Geoffrey wasn't sure what he thought about that, actually.

Alexander, even without whatever Geoffrey's own personal interests were, was eye-catching. He had a sense of presence beyond the more visible details that set him apart in Germany's favoured classes. At the very least, a competent spy should have been curious about what Alexander was up to.

Lizzie nodded. "I don't have much yet, beyond what I told you earlier. That there are some reports of an explosion in the right area, source and cause undetermined. I should have more in a day or two. Or Vivian will. She's got a better network in Germany, some of her cousins."

"Mostly, I would be exceedingly reassured to know for certain that the whole place went to ashes. Alexander made very sure, as much as we could, but you know as well as I that any little thing might go wrong." He coughed. "Bertram?"

"Duly taken in by the Ministry last night, off the ferry. Cephus was going to go have a lengthy chat with him tomorrow. Probably the rest of the week. He's a tad cranky about that. We'll have to make it up to him."

"Cranky." Geoffrey rolled that around in his mouth. "Alexander has been cranky."

That made Lizzie make a noise deep in her chest, a suppressed laugh. "You do have it bad."

Geoffrey blinked up at her, confused.

She ran a finger down his cheek, then cupped it in her

palm. "Had you noticed you have been pining, my dear subtlety?"

"I was - um." He flushed. "It seems very rude of me. I've been away from you for weeks. Churlish. Being a cad. Like..."

"Hush. You're nothing like Leander was. For one thing, you have been very good about telling me things as they unfold. As for the rest, I'm still working through what I think about it. I'm not angry with you."

That phrasing, mind, made him laugh hard enough he had to lift himself to breathe. After he explained, he added, plaintively, "I do have it bad."

Lizzie petted his hair. "And he let you touch him. More to the point, he got you out of an awful situation and took the kind of care of you I would have. So, really, I would be churlish if I were angry at him. No anger for me."

"You're teasing, domina." He blinked up at her. "I am for logic. You are for creative solutions to problems in the moment."

"And we learn from each other, you. Or I hope we have. Otherwise, we're going to have problems. With our children, if nothing else. Edmund is - well. Last week's adventures here can wait. But he's got all your brains and all my desire to figure out how things work, and all of both our desire to explore. We're going to need a more adventurous and capable groom to go out with him. With a solid set of magical skills. And likely a different tutor."

"I'll talk to Rufus about the groom." He let out a long breath. "How worried has Benton been?" He was going to circle back to Alexander, and what Alexander had done to the inside of his head, he promised himself that.

"Exceedingly, but you knew he would be. He always is.

Though setting him on hiring a suitable tutor would soak up some of the excess."

He'd have to get the full story out of one of them soon. "I could have used him on this, honestly. Having a third would have made things easier. And as it turned out, we didn't have to flee the German countryside in the middle of the night."

"But he does have trouble with that kind of party. And he'd have been glaring at Alexander all the time, which seems rather a lot to manage."

Geoffrey snorted. "Quite. And if you'd been there, we'd not have got that particular invite, I suspect." He spread his hands, then nestled in a little. "You're truly not angry with anyone?"

"With Bertram, for not being honest. But that's not any of your doing. I do gather - bear in mind, this was only the initial report this morning - that he only got the alraune within the past fortnight or so. Well after you'd put the plan in place. He must have been terrified you'd call it off."

"We might have, if we'd known. And it's not an easy thing to discuss in code."

"I have plans to talk about more thorough codes with Giles, Monday fortnight. He's working on another project next week."

"And I have presented you with other complications this week." That, Geoffrey was a bit apologetic about.

Lizzie snorted, more amused. "Is that what you worry about? We can't host a massive house party here, and we don't want to." They had the house in Cumbria for that, if they needed it. "But there's the suite just above this one, lovely view of the garden, quite private and quiet. All ready for him." It was the best of the guest suites, most often used for the eldest son and his wife in other times, or the most honoured visitor. "The pillows are fluffed, the woodwork is freshly dusted and polished. The drinks cabinet is stocked, and I've laid out a few tempting titles to read on the desk."

"You do think of everything, domina." He let out a long breath. "I feel safe with him." He hadn't quite meant to say it that way, but it was true, and she needed to hear it.

Her fingers paused in his hair, then resumed. "That is rather obvious, Geoffrey, love." She paused, choosing her next words carefully. "Tell me about the goldwasser, then? How was it alike? How was it different?"

"Except for the hangover and the legal implications, Cephus could make a fortune. While you're drunk on it ..." His shoulder twitched. "Euphoric, entrancing. I got lost in my own head, but not in a bad way, the ways that get tangled. I don't think most of the others did, either. Not like, oh, opium, or some potions can. Where it goes sour if everything's not just right. Not like the original in the sense of that pull to travel, but also not as destructive to one's magic."

"Less pain?" Lizzie's other hand dropped to brush against his shoulder.

"I wasn't in a state to notice? Which tells you enough, really." Geoffrey caught her nod. "I was drifting along. There were people having sex near me, I knew that. I could hear them, feel the furniture move. Someone was reaching for me, and I heard this voice calling me Geoffrey. It was..." He stopped.

"Take your time." That was an actual order, and it made his mouth quirk up.

"I trusted his order. His sharpness." Geoffrey swallowed hard. "He was very possessive, in the moment. He even used words about it. Well. 'Mine'."

"Goodness." Lizzie sounded amused, at least, and Geoffrey opened one eye to find her own dancing with it, before he closed both of his again, snuggling into her lap.

"He got me up to bed, with one of the staff, and next thing I knew, he's set incredible wards. Everything was quiet. Knowing nothing was getting through that. My head's in his lap, and he let me, and it just - I felt safe."

"What I give you, my dear subtlety..." Lizzie spoke quietly. "I give you many things. I know that, we know that, you don't need to convince me at the moment. But I can't make you feel safe like that. I'm never going to be able to. Those are not my skills. It's not our past, and if it's our future, we have some problems coming."

That was her problem-solving in action. As much as Alexander commented on his logic, Geoffrey leaned on that gift of hers. She had a knack for seeing a way to move forward, where he might get stuck in the pure articulation of the premise. "And?"

"Oh, love. I want you to feel safe. The way you make me feel safe and whole. I'd be an awful person, never mind an awful wife, if I wanted you to be smaller and worse off just to make me feel more secure."

"Best of women and best of wives and lovers." He let out a long sigh, truly relaxing now, rubbing his cheek against her fingers. Then, softer, he added, "He took care of me in the morning. Far more gently than I expected. And the rest of that day, and then Monday on the train."

"He told you to do things, didn't he?" Again, that burst of amusement. "I didn't know you'd trust anyone else to do that. Good. I'm glad."

Geoffrey blinked up at her. "Truly?" He needed to hear it again.

"Geoffrey, love, he sorted out something inside your head I've not been able to touch. He made you feel safe. I want all those things for you. I don't need to be the only one who can give them." She hesitated, then added. "And about the land?"

"The land?" That made him press up now, remembering how he'd been sitting for much of the afternoon.

"You were rather insistent about it." Lizzie gestured, mimicking the gesture.

"He loves the land. Like I do? Differently than I do? I don't quite know, he wouldn't talk about it. When he comes. If he comes. I hope he comes?"

"If he does not accept our invitation, you know where he lives. And where else he might be. We can have a campaign of insistent presence until he gives in."

That made him throw back his head and laugh. "Now I wonder what you'd come up with. Opera galas, we've done that."

"Tea shops. Bookstores. Getting an invitation out to the bohort at Schola. His stationer. I could probably find out which colourman he favours. He's the sort to go direct to the maker for his inks."

Geoffrey grinned and then shifted to settle a hand across her body. "Enough talking?"

"For the moment." Lizzie agreed. She didn't need to ask him to demonstrate his affection and love and trust, but it was certainly all he wanted in the moment.

CHAPTER 36
THE COUNCIL KEEP ON WEDNESDAY, MAY 22ND

B y the time Alexander got back to Trellech, it was far too late to go to the Council Keep and look at the records he wanted. He made a few perfunctory notes in his journal, letting Cyrus know that he'd returned, he'd be working on a report. Settled into his private library, he found himself sitting in front of the fire all of Tuesday afternoon and evening. He'd lost track of time for hours at once, rolling the signet ring back and forth in his fingers.

Even once he hung it on a chain and slipped it around his neck, he couldn't make his thoughts settle. When they arrived in Paris, he had been expecting they would part ways. He might see the Carillons at this gathering or that, across the room. And then Geoffrey had insisted he visit. At Ytene, where Geoffrey's wife was. By the time he turned up, if he turned up, he could assume she knew the details of what had happened. Most of them, anyway.

He began to see why it might be easier to have a marriage like Garin and Livia - or even like Silvia and Hesperidon had been. Mutual interests, but rather different lives. The negotiations between the relevant parties seemed time-consuming, and as likely to tie one in knots as smooth the way.

The next day, he still hadn't decided what to do about that. His man had set up a freshly packed suitcase at his request. But when it came down to it, Alexander simply took his satchel, adding his ritual case to it as he went. He expected to be out at the Council Keep at least through the weekly meeting, if not supper afterwards, postponing any further trip until Thursday. Perhaps Friday, or never.

That done, Alexander threaded his way through the morning traffic in Portal Square, stepping through to the Council Keep with little difficulty. It was still early in the day, barely half-nine, and most of the others didn't care to get up early. Or if they did, they didn't want to see other people. He left his satchel in his office, bringing his personal notebook and a fresh supply of pencils off with him.

He began, like any sensible researcher, with the most obvious source, the minutes from the Council meetings. He knew the date of Temple's death, February 2nd, 1922. But whatever had caused it had roots further back. The question was how far. Was this a matter of weeks or months or even years?

He hesitated then, pausing to check the records on what Temple had done in the War. They kept duplicate copies here, both as a secondary archive in case of some disaster in Trellech, and because they so often needed to check some detail. It was both quicker and far more private to have their own set.

At first, the record seemed much like other men's. Temple had been in Fox House, as Geoffrey had said, and in Dius Fidius, though from what Alexander remembered there, he'd been unremarkable. A man of power, prestige, and position, who did not stand out among others of his kind. Not that Alexander had paid much attention to that once he was out of school, beyond the yearly formalities.

Temple had been adequate enough at Ritual, though nowhere near the top of his class. Nowhere near Alexander's peer, certainly. And he'd done a fair bit more with Materia and Incantation. He wished, suddenly, for access to the Schola records, but he couldn't get at those without being very obvious about it.

And he couldn't bear scrutiny on this. Not right now. Probably not ever.

The War record wasn't what he'd expected. It wasn't so unusual that Temple, as his father's Heir but already in his 40s, hadn't gone into the trenches or near the front. Not when his younger brother was already there. It had taken a good year or two into the War for them to realise that particular problem, mind. But he had gone into some arm of research and design for the Ministry.

He flipped further into the slim file. The journals, of course, it made sense. He'd seen Geoffrey's book, Geoffrey had said it was a family magic, of course Temple would have had some knowledge of it. With those magical skills, he could have been quite useful in developing the journals that allowed one to write to others and get an immediate reply. They were a fragile lever in wartime, and they had not had many copies until the end of the War, but every bit counted. And more to the point, it made communication such as they relied on now vastly smoother.

Beyond that, though, there was not much detail. He glanced along the other rows of files, and no, most of them were much thicker. This was a bare twenty sheets, perhaps thirty. No details on what Temple Carillon had actually worked on, nor was there much about who he'd worked on it with.

He slipped the file back into place and went back to the Council minutes. More or less at random, he picked a file out of June 1921, and found a reference to an earlier discussion, and then an earlier one, tracing back to 1917. The few threads there were slender. And the Council meetings were erratic, too, into 1920.

He and several others had been on the Continent, fighting or supporting it. Livia, sometimes, for one. Others had been buried deep in their work. They'd been in the alchemical labs, doing the ritual work to preserve Albion's magic, handling logistics support, or coordinating with the Ministry and a dozen other arms of government, magical and otherwise.

Meeting by meeting, he skimmed through, making notes in his personal shorthand in his notebook. When he got to March 1920, the discussions about the land magic got more involved. He knew that they'd begun to worry about it, seriously worry about it, by then.

War was always hell on people. But, if anything, it was even worse for the land. Even a war that had never directly touched Albion's soil, not the same way it had in France and Belgium and Germany, all the way across the continent. If it wasn't an actual battle, it was the poisons from gas and explosives. It was their using and their making, getting into the soil and the air and the water, and back into the land. It was the deaths, and all the ways that shook the land magic.

Then all those men had come back, and no few women, with their magic shaken up and bruised, the edges chipped off. That memory made him pause, and go to flip through the records again. After a moment's hesitation, he pulled Geoffrey's file, feeling like he was peeking at something he had no right to. Even though these files were public enough for the asking, for anyone with a more than casual curiosity.

He thumbed through quickly, looking to see if there was a first name that went with Benton. He then added the appropriate "Benton, Thomas" to the pile, and one that read, "Pride, Rufus." After a moment's consideration, he found Lizzie Penhallow's file - now Geoffrey's wife, Lady Carillon - and added that.

What they told him wasn't a surprise either. It gave him something of a sketch of Geoffrey's War. The time in the trenches, as he had said, then Benton being assigned as his soldier-servant. In 1916, a few months before the S.S. Sussex went down in the Channel - he pulled that file as well - Geoffrey had been pulled out for Intelligence Corps work.

Someone had recognised his facility with languages, his skills at ritual magic, and his extensive experience adventuring. That had carried on after the war. That trip to Tibet and one in Europe in the 1920s were both Intelligence tasks, whatever else Geoffrey had also been up to. They weren't described that way, but he knew how to read the hints in the file.

Flicking through the report on the Sussex gave him the names of Geoffrey's parents. They had the sort of file that also suggested Intelligence work, though more as couriers than anything else. Perhaps also the kind of people who could host sensitive guests of the Ministry at a remote country house, a sort of prison away from home.

Alexander went back to the other files. Thomas Benton had remained in Geoffrey's service, he knew that, but his record trailed off after the War. No one paid much attention to men of that class, even though they really ought. Rufus Pride had been one of four brothers, the only one to come out of the War alive. His magical scores were, in fact, very strong. There was a notation that it had likely saved his life and those of a dozen or so people near him during a trench collapse. He wondered for a moment if the man knew at all.

Lizzie Carillon's file suggested she'd been a ferocious administrative aide at one of the hospitals that did triage of those coming back from the Continent. He remembered Master Groton, who'd run the place, made enemies like breathing in pursuit of his goals. That wouldn't have been much help afterwards, and administration didn't give one a sense of someone's actual skills without a lot more details. Details he did not have.

He returned the files, tucking them in so no one would realise what he'd been looking at. Automatically, as he always did, before adding the brush of a charm that would erase his magical signature. He went back to the meeting minutes. He'd only got into later 1920 when he heard a knock at the end of the shelf, a good five feet from the table he'd claimed.

Cyrus stood there, dressed as he often did these days for a day of office work, in magical robes rather than a suit. "I noticed you were here." He nodded at the records. "I didn't expect to see you today." He'd brushed his dark hair back, knotted a ribbon around it, very pragmatic, but Alexander could see more silver there than even a few months ago.

"We've the meeting this afternoon. I don't have a report yet, mind."

It was a challenge to authority, the kind he had made routinely to Hesperidon, seeing how far he could push today, and how rigid the response was. Where Hesperidon would have ignored it, or sharply corrected him, Cyrus glanced again at the materials on the table. "That's not directly for your report, is it?"

"Related. A matter I got curious about."

"1920. 21. 22." Cyrus counted them off. "Anything in particular?"

Alexander leaned back, willing himself not to let anything show. He did nothing so crassly obvious as crossing his arms, all the little gestures that shouted as loudly as a toddler having a tantrum. But the rigidity of his shoulders was probably enough. Cyrus wasn't stupid. Neither was he as willfully stubborn as Hesperidon could be. He noticed things. Annoyingly often, in fact.

"I was around for most of that. A trip here or there, but short. I could fill you in, most likely, faster than reading the files."

Which would mean Alexander would have to explain why he was curious. Only, there were plenty of things that didn't make it into the files. And of all the Council, Cyrus might actually have an answer. He and Mabyn had done a tremendous amount of research about the land magics, the way the War had warped things, back seven or so years ago now.

The question was whether he dared risk it. Every other time he'd thought that he could trust something like this, it had bitten him, sunk nasty sharp fangs into his ankle and dragged him further under.

Cyrus just watched him for a moment. "Look. Come down to my office. I can make some excellent tea. You look like you've had a time of it. It would be a help to get a precis of your adventures, even without the report, so I know how much time we'll need in the meeting. Do you want to shelve things, or bring them with?"

Alexander grimaced. Cyrus had his own set of minutes in his office. "Let me shelve." That way, he could make sure no one else would catch him out. "Tea. Certainly. As you wish."

Cyrus nodded, and didn't press. Rather notably didn't press. "If you aren't there in five minutes, I'll come find you."

Now, that was more what he expected.

"Ten. Let me wash up, too."

CHAPTER 37
WEDNESDAY ON MAY 22ND

Eleven minutes later, Alexander was settled in Cyrus's office. He'd completely redone it since taking over as head of the Council at Hesperidon's death five years ago. It was all hearty green leather, polished wood, and various small artefacts and art from his wide travels. A statue from India sat here, a series of American books there, examples of minerals were tucked along on the shelves.

Alexander had barely crossed the threshold a dozen times in those years. He had not known how to bridge the gap between the man who had - he thought - been his friend, and the man who now had the power of life and death over him. Who might at any moment turn out like everyone else who had valued Alexander only for what he could manage to do, that nobody else could.

This most recent adventure would not help that, either. It was just going to get him more of the same. He'd be sent away from Albion to do something no one else was good for or that no one else would risk. Cyrus might regret it, but he'd do it anyway, and in some ways the regret was harder to take than the ruthless and dispassionate pragmatism of his predecessor.

Cyrus set the teapot down after pouring for both of them, leaning back in the smooth leather chair. "Your German trip?"

"Resolved. I have quite a few details to pass along, things I heard or noticed. The particular threat in question is no longer a problem." Alexander realised how that likely sounded. "We got the alchemist out, and his notes." He didn't go into the rest of it, not yet. He hadn't had confirmation that the explosion had done anything.

"Good is not quite the word, is it? But I am glad you are back - it seems to have been rather an excursion. You look like you could sleep for a week, if you could bear to. And there are a few matters where I'd appreciate your thoughts. Not this week. Next or the one after."

Of course there were. Cyrus kept having those. Though he did in fact listen to Alexander's thoughts on whatever matter was involved, Alexander had to spend endless amounts of energy couching them in an acceptable format.

"What brought up the older records, then? Something you discovered in the process?" He waved a hand at the neatly bound rows on his own shelves.

Alexander shook his head. "I got curious about something —" No, he couldn't do that, not here. The name, the way the name rang in his head, would give him away. "Carillon said. Do you know much about the family?"

There was a moment there where Cyrus went still, then visibly did some maths and came to a realisation. "What does he know about his brother? Do you know?"

Blast the man. That was the trouble with everyone on the Council actually being competent in their own way. It was hard to get things past people. Alexander should have known better than to even bring it up. He began to stand, wanting to be anywhere else again.

"Please. Sit. Give me a minute. That's an unfair question." Cyrus held out his hand. "Give me ten minutes of your time to lay it out."

If he didn't know better, Alexander would have thought Cyrus was guilty. Felt guilty. Guilt was not a luxury any of them got to have. He sat back down. "Ten minutes."

Cyrus took a full minute of that time to gather his thoughts. "You weren't around at all, of course. And much of this, we argued back and forth between us, whoever was at each meeting. Some of it's in the minutes, a lot of it isn't, because we kept going over the same ground, again and again. It drove me up a wall, teeth-grindingly awful. People being stubborn for all the wrong reasons, all our pet follies."

He was trying to be friendly, and it rubbed Alexander the wrong way. However, that was, in fact, useful information, tidily presented. "And?"

"We've talked a great deal about the damage the trenches did. Not to everyone - Lord Carillon is one of the exceptions, for reasons we don't properly understand. He's never wanted to talk to anyone on the Council about it. For, honestly, sensible reasons."

Alexander wondered what Cyrus would do if he mentioned that eager invitation to spend time at Ytene. And then, if Carillon would tell him why the War hadn't shattered his landsense. If he'd be willing. What he'd want from Alexander for the knowledge. If Alexander would tell anyone else, even if he learned the secret.

"You can take that as read. I do actually read everyone else's reports. Including yours. Yours are quite readable, mind." Alexander flicked his fingers once, then folded his hands in his lap.

That made Cyrus smile, the way he used to, before he became Head. Alexander wasn't sure what to do with it. He still wasn't, but he nodded once, and Cyrus went on. "There were, of course, various offices doing War work. Research. The journals, for one, but a number of other things too."

"As there are now." Though they had just derailed some of that research, hopefully permanently.

"Quite." That was dryly amused. "Temple Carillon, by then Lord Carillon, was heavily involved in the research behind the journals. But then he was part of other projects. They kept very little in the way of notes, but something about it, it poisoned the land sense. Or - no, that's a wrong word. Blighted it might be better. Mabyn prefers blight." And Mabyn was far better with plants than either of them.

Alexander considered that information. "To a degree that the Council had to take an interest in?"

"Had to and did. We didn't rush to judgement." Cyrus leaned forward, suddenly earnest. "What you'll find in the minutes, the private ones, are a dozen large arguments and several dozen smaller ones, about what to do. How to do it. Three different people tried to approach Temple and two others for more information. They tried to lure him back to Ytene. None of it worked."

"Did you, perhaps, try talking about it using the small, simple words?"

Cyrus spread his hands. "That part, I was away for. Small simple words were not Hesperidon's gift. We all know that. But they said they tried. And Temple was unyielding. He ignored Ytene, except for the barest of the land rites. There was something wild, unmoored about him. Like someone in the last stages of a great illness, dancing madly because he saw death coming, one way or another."

"And so they - you? - killed him." Alexander hated himself for the faltering on the pronoun.

"They." Cyrus grimaced. "The hope was to poison him. To induce something like a heart attack and make him have to go back to Ytene. I gather there's a healing well, there, a decently useful one." Most places had healing wells. The question was what they healed. "Even just getting him back on the land might have been enough. If he couldn't live on it, they hoped he'd at least die on it."

Alexander grimaced. "They botched it." Multiple times, from the sound of it, in the worst ways possible. Not that he would risk saying that. Even granted that it was tricky to wound someone enough they could retreat somewhere else.

"They did." Cyrus didn't duck that. "Not how I'd do the thing. Or ask for it to be done. And I don't have any idea why Delphina died. They wouldn't explain, so we can assume that was an error somehow. On the other hand, you know who was there, yes?"

Alexander nodded. "Not a set of people who'd take guidance lightly. Even if Hesperidon hadn't had his hands deep in it. How much did Silvia know?"

"At the time? Not a lot. Now? The whole story. She talked to Mabyn about it when she found out the specifics. And to her husband, after that, I believe."

Alexander snorted. To be fair, that was the sensible way around. Mabyn would have given her a better answer, more or less. A more useful one, anyway. He then rubbed his face. "Thank you for the summary. It's most helpful."

"What does our current Lord Carillon know? Is he going to make trouble?"

That was the question, wasn't it. Alexander closed his eyes. "I believe he knows what happened and has for a long time. The bones of it. What he doesn't know is why." If Geoffrey had been inclined to make trouble, he could have done so long since, and perhaps Cyrus had the wits to know it.

"And he has chosen a very different road. Ytene's flourishing. You've seen it yourself now, yes?" Alexander nodded, not daring to risk a larger comment there. "He does his part, unstintingly." Cyrus half-closed his eyes. "I trust your judgement in what you tell him. Mind, I couldn't stop you if I wanted, so let's be clear I'm refusing to make you go around me."

"Both masters of ritual language." It would be a trick for Cyrus to bind him if he didn't want to be bound by an oath. They had different approaches, but near enough equal skill there.

When Alexander looked up, Cyrus was smiling. "Besides. I don't want to. I do trust your judgement, Alexander, and your skills, and I'm glad of them. May I say that?"

That offer made Alexander almost shiver. It was like Geoffrey's offered warmth, or his unstinting agreement in the laboratory, only this was something else. Older, deeper. Every time before Cyrus had said something of the kind, Alexander had turned away. This time, he didn't hold out a hand, he couldn't quite. But he didn't turn, he didn't back off. "Thank you. For the trust. I..." Then he wasn't sure what to add.

Cyrus spread his hands. "Go somewhere else, Alexander. We weren't expecting you back yet. You don't need to be at the meeting this afternoon. If you get out in the next hour or two, no one will know you were here today. A report at next week's meeting would be welcome, on whatever you feel we should know. Let me know how much time you need to present."

Alexander swallowed. It was a gift he didn't know what to do with. Not just the offer, that was actually logical enough. He was raw and uncertain enough to be difficult just for the sake of his nerves. After a moment, he offered a cautious gesture of something he didn't know how to name. "I had a discussion about that approach to Demera's Third you might be interested in, sometime. The elemental variation, of course."

Cyrus's eyes lit up. "Oh, that would be grand. We must find an hour or two. Perhaps even supper some night?" Another offer, a more personal one.

This time, Alexander couldn't deny that perhaps he might want that too. He'd missed those conversations with Cyrus, and the more so after the ones he'd had with Geoffrey about ritual theory, during their travels. "Perhaps. We'll see. I'll get my notes together." He then stood. "Thank you. For the honesty. I'll have my journal if anything comes up."

"We'll try not to, for a bit. Do get some sleep or at least some rest." Alexander didn't dignify that with a further answer. He stopped by his own far smaller office, picked up his satchel. He stood there for five minutes before writing a note to the Carillons and getting confirmation he was welcome to arrive that afternoon. Alexander followed it with one to his man to meet him with his suitcase.

Then he spent ninety minutes in the library, confirming what Cyrus had told him. Everything matched up with the notes, even the parts that weren't actually in the notes. Alexander slipped out of the Council keep before he ran into anyone else.

At three in the afternoon, precisely as he'd arranged, he stepped out of the portal into the courtyard at Ytene. Rather surprisingly, the man who met him was not Geoffrey, and it wasn't a footman.

Instead, it was a man, slightly shorter than Geoffrey, in a decent but undistinguished suit. His eyes were a sharper, brighter blue than Geoffrey's and his nose had a lump, as if it had been broken and badly set. "Magister." Not Council Member, not sir. "Lord Carillon asked me to meet you. May the footman take your case? I am his lordship's steward, Thomas Benton."

The man looked him up and down, and Alexander had a distinct sense of being measured and found wanting. Or at least, that this man was withholding judgement. There was a footman lurking just behind, in proper livery. Then Benton offered his hand, formally.

Alexander shook it. "Geoffrey has sung your praises. I am glad to meet you." Something in that comment - more than one thing - made the man's eyes widen, but then he nodded. Alexander set down his case for the footman to take.

"His lordship is in the forest garden. This way, sir." Benton led him through the formal garden that was closest to the house, through an arch at the back. They came out into a garden that seemed as much made of trees and shaped bushes as formal plantings.

Geoffrey was lying back on a blanket on a mossy hillock, sun dappling through the trees across his body. One hand was out, like that night that had caught Alexander's attention. A book was closed near his other hand. Benton, beside him, cleared his throat from ten feet away, and added, "Your guest, your lordship."

Geoffrey stretched and sat up. "Grand, Benton. Alexander!" There was delight and joy in Geoffrey's voice. "Be welcome to my lands and all they hold."

It was the most far-reaching of the ritual welcomes, the one used only for the closest trusted allies. And Geoffrey was making it here, with a witness. He had forgotten - again, somehow - that Geoffrey was himself a master of ritual language. This was no accident, no chance slip.

He meant it. And all its implications.

CHAPTER 38
YTENE ON WEDNESDAY AFTERNOON

Geoffrey propped himself up on one elbow, delighted in the shift of Alexander's expressions. At least ten of them, some far too fast for him to label properly. Behind him, Benton's face was also a picture, the slightly raised eyebrows of 'you are in a mood, sir.' Whatever Alexander had said on the way here, though, Benton was not disapproving. Too much, anyway.

A moment later, Benton nodded, saying that he'd got what he wanted. "Supper, sir?"

"Supper. Thank you, Benton. If you'd tell Lizzie on your way by?"

"Of course, sir." That was amused now. As if Benton would forget.

By the time Benton was back through the archway to the formal garden, Geoffrey had got up. Alexander was looking him up and down. "You can't mean that."

"Have I ever said anything to you I didn't mean?" Even under duress, actually.

Alexander went still, then shook his head. Geoffrey left the blanket. Nanny would be out with the children in a few minutes. He looked Alexander up and down, thoughtfully. "You didn't sleep well last night, did you?"

"Cyrus made some comment about that." Alexander shrugged. "It doesn't matter."

It did matter, even if convincing Alexander of this point was an ongoing challenge. Geoffrey felt better that someone else had said something. Instead of pressing on that point directly, he held his hands out, palms down. "May I? Will you permit? Please?" He couldn't stop the eagerness bubbling out now. He didn't want to scare Alexander off, but he was here, at home, and he knew it showed in everything he did.

Alexander looked at him, hesitating. Geoffrey felt vastly better than he had yesterday, echoed by both his mirror and Lizzie's eyes. Being back on his own land, coming into full summer, made him feel like he was blooming. More than he'd expected, actually.

Neither of them moved for a good thirty seconds. Then he felt Alexander's palms lift against his. As soon as they touched, Geoffrey sent a brief evocation of praise and adoration to the land beneath his feet, to the water in his blood, and let it flow.

He'd done this hundreds of times before. It was like what he felt with Lizzie, during the rites, only an entirely different flavour. There was electricity between their skin, the charge of the oncoming thunderstorm. There was a blessing in it, the cool healing of the well. Most of all, most complicated and most welcome, there was that rise of pure arousal and pleasure and desire, climbing his body and making his heart pound.

Alexander nearly staggered back with the rush of vitality, but he didn't pull away and he didn't try to stop it prematurely. Just the one foot, bracing himself, his eyes closed, his shoulders moving from rigid and up by his ears into something far more at ease. The shadows under his eyes and the slight sallowness faded. All the signs of deep fatigue lifted, as if he'd just come from a delightful stroll and a restorative meal.

When his eyes opened, Alexander swallowed. "You're sure."

"About a great many things, yes. At the moment, that this is the land I love, and she loves me, and we welcome you." Which was an entirely different statement, drawing on all the dance of the land magic he had come to know. He felt Alexander's fingers half close against his palms before they dropped away. He wondered how dazed Alexander was now, what that had felt like to him. His eyes were a little unfocused, his breathing still uneven.

"Come along. I'll walk you up to your rooms. A little to talk about before supper, and give you a chance to settle in." They had not specified how long Alexander might stay, mind, and that would depend a lot on how the next few hours went.

As they came through the doors from the garden, Lizzie looked up, then stood. Geoffrey immediately went over and kissed her. "Domina, Alexander is trying to decide what I mean about things. Again." He caught Alexander's brief reaction to that particular title, as he'd intended.

"Don't you mean still?" She beamed at him. "You are truly welcome, for as long as you wish. Please, do let me or any of the staff know if there's anything you need or prefer for your comfort. Or, of course, your well-being. And you are welcome to add whatever charms for privacy or warding you see fit."

Geoffrey slipped an arm around her waist, kissing her cheek. She had learned to rise to the particular etiquette of these moments, but most of their closer friends had been his before he met her. She rarely got to be the one to make this kind of offer. And few of those stayed the night, not here.

Alexander inclined his head, still visibly uncertain - to Geoffrey's eyes, at least - of his footing. "La - Lizzie." He swallowed. "Geoffrey is rather insistent about some things, isn't he?"

It made her laugh, the honest, joyous laugh that made Geoffrey sure she was fine with this, truly fine. Whatever this was going to turn out to be, anyway. "Only with those he likes best. But yes, he is." She waved a hand. "Love, I'll be down here for another few minutes, then I was going to stop at Ferry's and check in, back before supper."

Alexander would likely read it as the ordinary sort of coordination of any married couple, but Geoffrey nodded. Here, it was laying out her particular plans. "We'll be up in the guest suite. This way, Alexander, do? The drinks cabinet up there is fully stocked." They went up the stairs in silence, down the hall, until Geoffrey opened the door.

Alexander took in the suite of rooms with a long, slow look around. "You don't do the thing halfway, do you?" Someone would have unpacked his case already. He set his satchel down on the desk in the corner of the sitting room. "Who normally uses this?"

"Our most honoured and welcome guest, at the moment." He gestured. "Explore the drinks cabinet, pour yourself something you like? I have a bit more news from Germany, as an apéritif of the intellectual sort?"

Alexander went to the drinks cabinet, turned to raise an eyebrow at Geoffrey. It was, admittedly, perhaps a tad excessively stocked, everything he'd seen Alexander prefer. Once they both had glasses of brandy in hand, Alexander settled in the chair across from Geoffrey's. "Germany, then."

"There was, in fact, a massive explosion. As we had intended, and you thoroughly arranged at some cost - don't think I didn't see those last two charms. It took them a full day to put it out, the entire place went to ash. I gather there were some injuries, but none likely to be directly fatal." Whether anyone would succumb to elements of gas or potions or whatever else was in the air was less certain. But there had been more rain and wind. They could hope it was all contained or dispersed, as appropriate.

Alexander let out a massive sigh of relief and lifted his glass in a mute toast. They both drank, and Geoffrey added, "We're still working on more about Theodore, but we are fairly certain he left Germany under his own power. We'll need to see if he pops up again anywhere. I've alerted our Ministry folks, and my Intelligence contacts." He'd have to report to Lap in the coming days, but that much he'd passed along immediately.

"Appreciated. I'm curious what you hear, of course." It was a gesture at further contact, which Alexander then added to. "I - there's rather a lot to ask about. But I should start by saying I would be pleased to welcome you to my libraries, at some point. Repay the favour."

Geoffrey arched an eyebrow. "Share the knowledge. We are, I think, somewhere beyond counting favours between us. Certainly I would consider it so."

Alexander went still at that, then closed his eyes. "Why am I here? And what—" He swallowed. "I do not understand you. Or your wife. Or, or you said there were things we weren't discussing yet."

"Is that where you wish to start? With my preferences in the more personal matters?"

He watched Alexander weigh it, visibly. There were so many places they might begin a conversation, but this was a fine one. Geoffrey could lay out the basics of it in the time they had before supper and give Alexander plenty to chew on. Then Alexander nodded. "I do not know where to start, what to ask, mind. I am a novice at the subtleties."

Geoffrey settled back, propping his ankle on his knee comfortably. "Where shall I begin?"

"You calling your wife 'domina'. I know my Latin, of course, but I cannot decide if it has implications. You suggested, in Berlin, that your preferences were not solely those you were presumed to have. Socially speaking."

"The pillow books are elsewhere. A proper lecture on the topic might do better with illustrations." Geoffrey said it lightly, but was pleased to see Alexander's faint blush. "As I keep saying, I will do nothing without your permission, tell me if the teasing is too much." Alexander waved a hand, not arguing. "I am, as you may have noticed, more than a bit of a hedonist, given my head."

That, and the dry way Geoffrey put it, made Alexander laugh and almost swallow his brandy the wrong way. When he recovered, he gestured slightly with the glass. "I had observed, yes."

"The trick is, there are precious few people I actually trust to have proper care, if I give myself over entirely to that pleasure. All the erotic charms in the world - and I know quite a selection - and that's a thing they don't begin to touch. I trust Lizzie. I had two other lovers, decades ago, where I would give myself over to their..." He hesitated, trying to find a wording that would make sense to Alexander, then settled on it. "Letting someone else lead the ritual, trusting that they will do it to your standards in all the ways."

That got a rather glorious grimace. "I am terrible at that." Alexander admitted it ruefully. "Bar those things where the leader is set out by custom. The Council magics. It's one of the things that the head does, q.e.d. the head is in charge."

"Even if they're not primarily a ritualist?" Geoffrey was intrigued now, but the way Alexander's eyes widened, he suspected no one had dared question that point. "Don't feel you need answer that right now, please. Or ever. I do not know your precise oaths. Do not press against them on account of my curiosity."

Alexander tipped his glass slightly. "And otherwise, you prefer to be the one in charge?" he asked. "With, um. Friedrich, and Bertram, and Antonio, and whomever else?"

"Mmhmm. If Sepp had taken an interest, we'd have had to sort that out. We'd probably have settled on something where it was more equitable. Hands and enchantments, rather than those positions and passions that suggest more submission. Mind, there is a trick to being the one in charge of the pleasure one is being given by an active partner."

"That, I am quite sure you have a mastery in." The teasing, hearing the teasing back, made Geoffrey glow with pleasure. He hadn't expected it. When he met Alexander's eyes, they were both grinning broadly. This, oh, this is what he'd dreamed of, and hadn't been sure they would find. Alexander's relaxing and trusting this far. That he could ask and know he would be taken seriously, that his gaps in knowledge wouldn't be mocked or made light of.

"Lizzie may talk your ear off on that matter when she realises you've spotted it. She does not have many outlets for that specific complaint." Then he waved a hand. "If you would like to learn more about the range of possibilities, simply so you have filled the intellectual gap in your knowledge, I am delighted to oblige. Lend you books, discuss. I have not nearly as much shame as I probably ought."

Alexander nodded slowly, taking a minute to think. Geoffrey gave him the time. There was no rush. When Alexander spoke, though, it wasn't what he had expected at all. "I said I was considering telling you something about my challenge." The Council challenge. There was only one thing he'd speak of that way. Geoffrey tried not to imitate a retriever ready to charge for a fallen bird, but he admitted he was doing a poor job of hiding his interest.

"We don't talk about our challenges. Even with each other. Almost never, anyway. Pardon my fumbles." Alexander took a sip from his glass and forged on. "When it came to it, in the midst, the pinnacle of the challenge, there was the land, in all her glory. Aset, I thought first, the way my mother's stories told, cloaked in feathers, her magic spreading and touching everything. Queen of life, mother of magic, she of the beautiful throne." He slipped into another language, then, not Arabic, Geoffrey knew enough of that to at least recognise it, before he shook his head and returned to the conversation.

"The lady who dwells in Albion, under whose cloak I serve, must be her sister. And she is the one I love. She who is the land." Alexander looked up, searchingly now. "I've never told anyone else."

Geoffrey let out the breath he'd been holding as Alexander talked. He set his glass aside, standing and stepping before he came to rest on one knee beside Alexander's chair. "Most people don't understand." A moment later, Alexander had taken his hand. He could feel the racing pulse. "Of course you love her. I love her. We are sensible men who know what we see."

Alexander shuddered, and then he was laughing and

squeezing Geoffrey's hand, a great eagle-owl or a golden eagle launching from the arm in the pure delight of flight. That rolled on and on for minutes, both of them needing to pause and catch their breaths. When it finally stilled and the room was quiet again, Geoffrey grinned up at him. "We understand loving the land here."

"I - I have more to say about that. Later? After supper? I need..." Alexander gestured faintly. "May I have a little time?"

"Of course." Geoffrey glanced over at the clock on the desk. "Someone will come show you down to the dining room in forty-five minutes or so. Make free with the books, or anything here, or ring if you need something else." He added, because honesty mattered here. "I will be reading to the children. You'll hear the gong."

Alexander squeezed his hand awkwardly one more time, and then let it go. "I like that you insist on time with them. And you were away a long time. Thank you."

Geoffrey got up, triumphant, for all that standing up from sore knees was difficult to do triumphantly. When he glanced over his shoulder as he opened the door, Alexander was indeed browsing the books Lizzie had laid out, all intended to intrigue him. Good. Far better than simply good.

CHAPTER 39
WEDNESDAY AT SUPPERTIME

Alexander had intended to spend the time he was on his own exploring the space. How people hosted told him a great deal about them - and about their expectations for him. He glanced at the books on the table, spotting two he'd been meaning to read. And there was an older treatise on ritual theory he and Geoffrey had been discussing idly in Berlin. The other two books he didn't know, but they seemed intriguing.

Instead, he sat down in the chair and frowned. He could feel the land magic humming through him. If Geoffrey felt this all the time, even most of the time, how did he get anything done? It must be quieter in winter, of course, but it would be like birds relentlessly singing the dawn up at this time of year. He kept closing his eyes, losing track of time, just feeling it flood him. Feel her touch him, if he permitted himself the image.

The knock on the door startled him, almost enough he was in a defensive stance before he remembered better. He rearranged his legs into something far more civilised and called out. "Come in?"

After that comment, he had not expected Geoffrey, but perhaps Benton, the housekeeper, or a maid or footman. Instead, there was Lizzie, smiling warmly at him. "May I have a word before we go down?"

There wasn't an edge to her, where there might be in so many women of his acquaintance. She was secure in where she was and what she was doing. He gestured. "Please?" She closed the door behind her and came to settle on the chair.

"I hope you are making yourself comfortable?" She glanced at the desk, and must have realised he'd looked at the books, because she was beaming when she looked back. "I realise this must be strange to you, in a dozen ways."

"Oh, I am well up into the scores, at least." Alexander could at least reply to that with good grace.

"I know you and Geoffrey have a great deal to talk about, and I've an idea about some of it, and not yet about other parts, I'm sure. In large part because neither of you are sure about a number of things yet." She wriggled her fingers. "Geoffrey is logic, and I am the one who makes sense of the pieces and fits them together into a working device, as it were. There is still a lot of mist and obscurity in the mix. If you were a map, there would be plentiful labels saying 'here be dragons'."

"Now, there's truth." Alexander felt himself smiling. He barely knew this woman, other than the ways you knew an analyst through their work. But she was exceedingly competent at that. And while she did not have quite the same hum to her of the land magic as Geoffrey did, she wore it like a glow.

"He feels safe with you, in a way I can't give him. I never fought. I don't have those skills." She came right out with it, clear and unrelenting. "And I want him to have that, if he can. So, I do hope you'll stay and talk, and figure out whatever you want to be to each other going forward. Now you are past this initial set of expeditions. Friends. Allies. I don't know what else."

It was earnest, and, Alexander realised, it was truth. He looked away, toward the window, while he gathered his thoughts. When he turned back, she was waiting patiently. "I have some things I need to tell him tonight. I don't know what that will change."

She didn't fuss over what it was - not that he'd have told her before he told Geoffrey. Only the nod, followed by "I'll have my journal, if you need me for anything. And you and he, take all the time necessary." When Alexander opened his mouth to point out Geoffrey had only been back for a night, she lifted her hand. "We will sort ourselves out, thank you. I'm fine." Then she stood. "Supper? Benton and Cassie - his wife - are joining us, as they usually do when we are en famille."

The supper that followed was unlike any Alexander had been to in a long time. Well, outside of Thesan's, on an occasional snatched visit over the holidays to her family in Cumbria. Cassie turned out to be an incredibly in-demand dressmaker in Trellech, whose professional name he'd heard praised by a number of people, including Thesan. Here, at supper, she was teasing and laughing, alternating between stories about her recent apprentices, someone Benton was mentoring, and a bit of Trellech news.

Benton had unbent a bit through the conversation. If anything, he was keeping an even closer eye on Geoffrey than Lizzie was, at his end of the table. She, on the other hand, considered that entirely normal, and spent her time coaxing him into telling a few stories of their shared travels. Geoffrey, after a few minutes of this, cleared his throat. "I was thinking about the snow leopard a few nights ago, Benton."

Cassie got the sort of delighted grin of someone who knew the tale, but loved hearing it told, and Geoffrey added to Alexander, "That first night at the Heinrichs." Which made him wonder why that misery had brought the tale to mind.

It involved, apparently, being up in the Tibetan plateau for reasons unmentioned, and being stalked by something, always feeling watched. They had made camp in a cave with a storm lurking on the horizon. Benton had gone out with one of their guides to find whatever bits of fuel or food they could to keep them for a few days.

The guide had screamed and fled, leaving Benton staring at a very large snow leopard. Then she had turned around, stalking off well up the mountain, demanding he follow with twitches of her tail and rumbling growls. He'd scrambled and climbed after her, a good mile or two across the landscape, terrified he'd lose the way back.

Finally, he came to a crevasse, and found a little one had fallen down. The cub had been unable to get a purchase on the smooth ice and stone. There wasn't enough room for the mother to boost the cub onto solid ground again. It had taken near all his magic to get the cub out, safely, without scratches or bruises or a further fall. After an hour, he'd managed it, then staggered back to the camp, feeling the leopard pacing him all the way.

"The next morning, we found a dead ibex just outside the cave. It kept us fed until the weather cleared. It almost made up for the cold." Benton shrugged at the end of the tale.

"It did convince me that learning how to heat up a bed properly on my own was worth doing, mind." Geoffrey added as they finished off their meal. Benton and Cassie took their leave, and then Lizzie split off to the library as Geoffrey walked Alexander upstairs.

Alexander settled on the sofa, likely looking as uncomfortable as he felt. It had been building up in him that Geoffrey might well turn him out for what he'd learned from Cyrus. It was against all the laws of hospitality, and that sort of miasma spread, as the Greeks had it. His mother's people had seen things somewhat differently, but that didn't hold weight right now.

Geoffrey settled on the other end, ankle on knee, as he so often seemed to do now, in soft house slippers. "Benton is reserving judgement, but pleasantly surprised, for the record." Which had been Alexander's rough translation.

"There's a man whose sun you are." As he said it, Alexander almost regretted it, but Geoffrey seemed to bloom with it rather than become defensive.

"I don't know who I'd be without him. Dead, certainly, several times over. Steady as a rock, pragmatic to the core, and always anticipating." Geoffrey leaned back, and then added, equally conversationally. "You don't want to tell me something, do you?"

"You, Geoffrey, are annoyingly perceptive. I can't get anything past you." Alexander swallowed. "Drinks, first. Brandy?" Geoffrey nodded, and Alexander went to pour them glasses. "If you wish me to leave when I've told you this, I will. You can send my case on after."

As he came back, Geoffrey raised an eyebrow. "Something you have learned recently." He said. "Or realised. Since Paris."

"Since Paris." Alexander handed a glass over and sat down, waiting until Geoffrey had set his own down safely on the table. "May I tell you what I know about your brother's death?"

He had been thinking of how to phrase that for the last few hours, woven in and out of the other conversations. He watched Geoffrey's eyes widen, the way his jaw moved, then the single decisive nod.

"He was killed by the order and the hands of the Council." Alexander ran through what he'd found out. Not just what Cyrus had told him, but a precis of the rest of the discussion. The neglect of the land and her magic, that wild awfulness that had seemed to possess Temple Carillon toward the end. That something had gone wrong, he hadn't found out what yet, and that part he might never, given who was involved. What they'd been trying for.

Geoffrey breathed out. "They wanted him to die here." Then, there was a long, low string of something in Latin. It was too fast and too soft and too fierce for Alexander to catch more than a fleeting word here or there. The sort of rush that suggested it was a prayer long repeated, the ones you could do at speed in full fury.

When Geoffrey fell quiet, Alexander waited, took a breath, and then said, "I swear to you that if I had been here, it would have been done competently. You would never have known. It would not have been that shambles." He had to be honest about it, even if Geoffrey chose to hate him for that truth. Nothing else would do.

That made Geoffrey's mouth open, close, his eyes following, giving himself over entirely for a moment. He made himself entirely vulnerable, his magic as well. Alexander could have done anything. He reached cautiously, brushing Geoffrey's hand with one finger, only to have his hand snatched and held.

"What do you think of what they did?" Geoffrey's voice was all talons now, tearing the world apart.

"The land loves you. You love her. And." This was the terrifying part, the truth that had to be said. "I don't know why, but Temple didn't. She didn't. And you know that. For all it was awful, you tend and love her as she needs." It was the only logical answer, and he had to trust that instinct, the one Geoffrey had shown again and again. He had to answer to the mirror that Geoffrey made for him.

All of a sudden, Geoffrey deflated, collapsing. Alexander hesitated for only a moment before moving on the sofa, and offering his shoulder. Geoffrey had slept there, on the train, though he might not have realised it. But it was still a jolt to have that much contact. He could hear the ragged breathing and feel the way Geoffrey's pulse was pounding in his hand.

"She loves me." Just those three words, a bare whisper. "You - he."

Alexander swallowed. "If you permit, I will lend my every skill to finding out why. What brought him to that."

There was a little catch of Geoffrey's breath, then a long one out, as Geoffrey relaxed against him. "Oh. Yes. Please." Then, as if he were rearranging the foundation of his world, he inhaled and lifted his head. "When did you find out?"

Alexander felt a roar of relief through him, a burgeoning need for something he had no idea how to name. But here he was, and Geoffrey did not hate him for his part in any of this. He had offered his help, and had it welcomed. It made him shiver and close his own eyes.

"I went to the Council Keep this morning." He hesitated, then added. "Cyrus told me some of it. I confirmed it in the notes. Garin might tell me something, if I ask just right. And bring him some distracting alchemical challenges."

"It doesn't press on your oaths to tell me?" Geoffrey looked suddenly worried at that.

It made Alexander laugh, almost sliding into hysterics. "Cyrus told me I could. Told me he wouldn't stop me. Comes to the same thing." Then, he did have to pause and catch his breath, leaning a bit against Geoffrey now, so they were mutually holding each other up.

CHAPTER 40
WEDNESDAY EVENING

Geoffrey's mind was whirling. He had, honestly, never expected to have an actual answer to what happened to his brother. Even this much was an incredible gift. To know that he hadn't been wrong.

There were still endless questions. What had been so horrible that they thought this was an acceptable option. What in magic's green earth they thought it would help. Most of all, what had broken Temple's love for the land. Geoffrey was sure it had been there once, even if it had been nothing like what his own had grown to. What had he missed, while he was away, or not paying attention, that left his brother dead?

But Alexander had told him. Told him, despite fearing it would change whatever they had. It made Geoffrey close his eyes again and lean, because here was Alexander, willing to be leaned on. They were both quiet for some time before Alexander spoke, dropping a single pebble into a still pool. "You're not angry at me?"

The echo of the words in the wood made Geoffrey smile

and squeeze the hand still somehow in his. "Very angry at them. Not at all angry at you. You had no idea at all."

"Not the sort of thing one writes down, except in the exceedingly private Council minutes." Alexander let out a huff of breath. "I had no idea. And now I have no idea how much else I missed, how much no one else told me."

"Rather a lot, I suspect." It was the truth, and Geoffrey would offer the truth every chance he got. It would do neither of them any good to duck it. He hesitated, though, before asking the next question. "You asked Cyrus?"

Alexander nodded. "Do you know him? More than socially in passing?"

"A couple of days on a ship to Port Said in, mmm. 1912. We spent it being very polite at each other." He considers. "Another ritualist, though. Which means you either enjoy his company or argue with him all the time. Possibly both in alternation."

That comment made Alexander laugh loudly, and settle, excellent. "Both in alternation. I used to consider him a friend. Then he took over as Head and I've not known what to do with that. Today was different, perhaps. I do think he was honest with me about what he knew. He was around for the discussions, but not directly involved in the, erm. Act."

Geoffrey nodded. "You are very lonely there, aren't you?" Then he held up his hand, not opening his eyes. He could feel the stiffness and thorns returning. "I'm not pressing about that, not today." Besides, he had other difficult things he wanted to ask about, and that one could wait.

Alexander subsided, and Geoffrey let them just be quiet with each other. Birds settling in the mews, who had been well fed and better tended. Once Alexander's breathing was even again, he asked, keeping his voice gentle, "Will you tell me a bit about Perry?"

There was a catch, tension in the shoulder under his head, all the breath going still. Then Alexander coughed once. "What do you know?"

"The sketch that is in public pages. The obituary. The way it dances around your name." Lizzie had got hold of it first. "Not nearly enough to understand the ways you've been alone with it." That got a shudder against his shoulder. "May I offer you my arm? Or would you prefer to move somewhere more comfortable?"

"Somewhere dark? The bedroom. I don't think I can do this in the light, not to start." Alexander was gathering himself to do this, though. Geoffrey could hear the determination in his voice now. Like it was a great pool of water building up, finally ready to burst in full flood. The Nile rising, indomitable.

They reclaimed their glasses and retreated to the bedroom. Geoffrey paused to rearrange the pillows, checked there was enough room on the side table for their glasses. Then he went to find a headache potion and a carafe of water and an extra glass. He suspected that might be welcome in due course. By the time he returned, Alexander had changed into a dressing gown and settled with his back against the pillows at the head of the bed. He raised an eyebrow at the supplies.

"Best to be prepared. Consider it the plaster of Paris of the moment."

As he'd hoped, that got a smile, even if it were a tad shaky. Geoffrey went and dimmed the lights, leaving only a charm light illuminating the room, along with the now waning moon. He toed off his shoes, settling on the bed, not quite touching. Of course, with the break in the middle, the moment had changed.

Alexander knew it too. "Did you - you must have lost people in the War." Everyone had, at least everyone who had fought.

"Out of my years in the tutoring house, only two of the boys are still alive. One, beside me." Geoffrey let out a long breath. "I'd have to go count the numbers out of my year at Schola." He leaned back. "Plenty of people I knew, but I was the sort, then, who was friendly with a lot of people, and not close with many. Several at the Academy. Giles, later on. Others, through particular interests. But I was travelling after my apprenticeship, and we drifted apart. I felt responsible, though. Especially in the trenches. So many awful, baffling orders, and so little I could do to improve anything."

"That is the War I didn't know." Alexander's voice had gone smooth again, that sign that he was repressing a dozen emotions. "We were a select group. Izzy - Isembard, as he prefers now. Perry. Jim and Wally. They both made it through, though Jim's foot will never be the same."

Geoffrey nodded. He had some sense of the ways the War weighed on Isembard, not that they'd ever discussed it, beyond a few mentions. Isembard had a few other veterans he spent time with, when he could, and that seemed a kindness. Especially for a man who lived with the unpredictable variety of young men and women who didn't realise how their pranks might affect someone with a soldier's nightmares and reflexes.

"And you knew the Fortiers. Complicatedly."

Alexander barked a half-laugh at that. "To be fair, I do

not think I am capable of doing a thing simply. But I owed them repayment for the gifts of my apprenticeship. They wanted my skills. The mysteries of my mother's magic, not that they paid much attention to the doing."

Geoffrey nodded slowly. "What did that mean, in practice?"

"I was more or less a tutor to Garin, then to Isembard, whenever they were home, once they went to tutoring school. I didn't mind it much. Garin is clever, though he saves all his curiosity for Alchemy, such as it is. Izzy ..."

He fell into the old nickname. "Izzy needed to understand how things fit together. It's been a wonder, seeing him find himself at Schola. He always had that gift that's at the core of the Protective magics, seeing what might go wrong so you can mitigate it or avoid it. It took him a long time to grow into it, though. After the War. He might have done it far faster, with a different tutor."

Geoffrey nodded. "He very much looks to you, though. We've not discussed it in detail. I am not so much in his trust as to ask that sort of thing, and I know it. But I have got the impression he is always thinking of Schola's well-being. Not the way I think of Ytene, but not as different as it looks at first glance."

"Just so. He is not lord to that land, but he is very much her champion and defender." Geoffrey made a small sound of things clicking together. That made sense. He wondered, suddenly, what Schola's land was like, if you got to know her. If it was a her, there was no reason it had to be. Though Alexander had said so. Before he could wander down that path of thought, Alexander went on.

"Perry and Izzy had been friends from tutoring school, but it wasn't until they came home for holidays from Schola that - Perry was around a lot. He was a changeling in his family, his magic nothing like theirs. They saw he had potential, but had no idea what to do with it."

That happened, sometimes, and the sensible families found people who could nurture that. Geoffrey had given the matter some thought already, not just for Edmund but for Merry and Rosie. Whatever their talents led them to, he wanted them to have the best guidance he could find. He'd learned that from Richard and Alysoun, even more than from his own parents.

Alexander went on, shifting to lean more on the pillows. "I trained him up, with Izzy. No one minded too much. They drove each other to learn more, more avidly and quickly. And of course, if you're teaching the martial and protective magics, it's far better to have a partner to work with besides the teacher."

"That is a tidy bit of logic, to get you a thing you wanted. And that Isembard also wanted."

He could see the crooked smile as he glanced over at Alexander. "Just so. And Perry was brilliant. Not the way his family wanted, but truly gifted. Able to take a dozen threads of different stars, time, space, wild magic, the most formal structured ritual, and weave them together. He never met a piece of knowledge he didn't want to collect."

"Like you." Geoffrey said it softly, and then felt Alexander nod.

"After some arguing and persuasion, they thought I could prepare him for the Council trials. We didn't care about that, we just wanted to explore all the possibilities, the things magic could do when you stopped making assumptions."

Geoffrey was caught by that phrasing. "For what purpose?"

There was a long silence, and for a moment, Geoffrey

wondered if he had gone too far, pressed too much. Alexander went on, more softly. "There is a sort of destruction and chaos necessary to bring a better future. I wondered, we wondered, what that might look like."

"If it were applied to all the staid order of the Council, of the Great Families. The way we have codified and labelled magic down to the smallest twitch over the centuries." Geoffrey considered the evidence he had. "Not anarchy, but beginning from first principles?"

"Just so." Alexander went still again, as if waiting for judgement.

"It does explain how your explosion was an act of perfection, considering." It had been, too. As far as their admittedly limited sources had discovered, it had taken out only the laboratory and Bertram's rooms, not the buildings around it. "Perry was your apprentice. More than just an apprentice?"

"We'd talked about my adopting him formally. Ritually. Continuing my line of the family magics, which I never thought I'd be able to do. Even if we told no one else. But then there was the War."

Alexander pressed on, as if he knew that pausing would mean bottling this up forever. "When the War started, I knew we could do more useful work, do something meaningful, if we weren't in the trenches. It took half a year, but in the spring of 1915, we had our five. Izzy for warding and protection, Jim for enchantment, Wally for Materia, Perry for ritual magic and duelling, though all of us were competent with the last within three months. And me to plan things out and coordinate."

"And that went well for a while?" Geoffrey could do the maths on the dates. They'd had a two-year run or so.

"With increasingly difficult assignments, but we rose to

the challenge." Alexander rubbed his face with his hand. "They tossed coins for it, Perry and Izzy. Who went which way. And I was up and behind a farmhouse. I saw Perry fall, and I saw the sniper getting away, and ..." He let out a long breath, and then he was twisting, not quite reaching for Geoffrey.

Geoffrey shifted his arm, not caring a whit for the way it wrenched his bad shoulder. A moment later, there was Alexander, curled up, as if needing every wall against the world that Geoffrey could offer. He took a breath, and willed the warding stronger. He could do it that way because his family's blood was in the mortar of these walls, and a few drops of his own. He sensed the wards rising, felt Alexander give out against his chest, and just held on.

Alexander didn't sob, he didn't cry, not exactly. But he shivered, fit to split apart. It was an utter destruction that left nothing but wreckage behind, a few fragile shards of beloved things to mourn. All Geoffrey could do was be steady, make sure the ground beneath would be there when all the dust and fog and chaos came to rest.

A long time later, Alexander mumbled, without moving. Then he tried again. "I don't remember anything until Dover. Not really. Izzy might."

Geoffrey nodded. "I have gaps in my head, too. For far less reason." They terrified him, as this must terrify Alexander, and perhaps knowing they both did would be a comfort. He took a breath, not rushing this. "You said you went mad after that. What did that look like?"

Alexander swallowed, a shudder that almost pulled him away from Geoffrey's side. "They wouldn't have me at the funeral. Wouldn't let me visit the grave. Haven't. There's..." He fumbled at something, a chain around his neck, buried under his shirt. "This, my vault, Tuesday."

That was enough for Geoffrey to piece it together. A signet ring, he couldn't make out the shape carved into it, not the way Alexander was clutching at it. "Perry's?"

"I gave it to him. He was wearing it when, I mean. It was my promise he was my heir."

Geoffrey sucked in his breath, the dawning horror that this was all Alexander had been permitted besides his memories. Then he had to ask. "What memorial would you give him, if you could?"

"It should be a tomb, for a thousand thousand years. His name in diamond that will not wear away, that will last forever." Alexander made a pained gasping noise. "Can't. Couldn't. They—" His voice broke off.

"The name, remembered. Him, remembered." Geoffrey shifted his arm a little to offer more support, ignoring the stretch of the scars. "Beyond you, beyond Isembard. Generations."

There was a tiny nod against his chest. Then, softer and more uncertain. "You - your shoulder. A few inches, and that was Perry."

"I was very lucky. And he wasn't aiming at me, not to start." Geoffrey kept his voice quiet, but matter-of-fact. "If it bothers you to see, I'll make sure you never do." He had got careless about it, the last decade, when Lizzie knew, and wasn't distressed.

Alexander lifted his head at that, peered at him, then realised how he was settled. He moved, something that changed the angle of it, and Geoffrey let out a little sigh of relief. He'd have to talk to Lizzie about the Judsons. Possibly Isembard, too, and see what small leverage there might be. Other things, as well, but that would take more planning.

For now, he leaned his weight back against the pillows.

"Will you tell me about what Perry loved? All the things you taught him?"

Slowly, hesitantly, Alexander allowed himself to talk. Piece by piece, beginning with their earliest lessons, he laid out what he saw, what he'd delighted in, all the ways Perry had challenged him.

CHAPTER 41
SEVERAL DAYS LATER, ON SATURDAY

Alexander felt he had fallen into some sort of pastoral fantasy, but an exceedingly effective one. Something out of Elgar, or perhaps Vaughan Williams. He had kept Geoffrey up well into the middle of the night on Wednesday talking about Perry, letting it pour out of him as it hadn't for nearly two decades. When he'd finally fallen asleep, completely drained, he had known Geoffrey was there, keeping an eye on him.

The next three days had been full of country comforts and steady work. They had spent plenty of time tending to their respective reports about their activities in Austria and Germany, as well as the more suppositional analysis of what might happen next on a number of fronts.

It was novel for Alexander, working in parallel. He and Geoffrey, along with Lizzie - and twice Benton - would swap ideas back and forth. They'd debate about wording and the best approach to get those reading the report to do the desired thing with all it contained.

But there were also frequent moments of simple pleasure. Geoffrey was indeed a hedonist, and he built those moments of delight into every part of his life. It was not the sybaritic luxury of a wealthy man, pleasure for the show of it, but the joy of a man who loved the physical world. Excellent food and drink punctuated pleasant walks in Geoffrey's immediate demesne lands and rides through the forest on delightful well-trained mounts. Geoffrey preferred a particularly clever black mare and had loaned Alexander a sturdy chestnut gelding who had the most comfortable gaits.

Geoffrey did not press for contact, but he made Alexander constantly aware of his presence. Rather to Alexander's bafflement, he found those touches welcome. There was a hand to get up, a shoulder against his while reading from the same text, an arm or leg brushing as Geoffrey moved around.

They'd spent the evenings up in the library or Alexander's rooms, often on the sofa together, heads bent over a book, or twice in the workroom. They'd explored different approaches to ritual techniques, checking each other's form and movements. Near every moment of it, except perhaps the reports, was calculated to be a pleasure to Alexander.

Now, on Saturday afternoon, they were lounging on a blanket under the same tree where Geoffrey had welcomed him. "Your wife had a word on Wednesday. She was..." Alexander didn't know how to finish that sentence.

"Surely she was sufficiently clear?" Geoffrey stretched lazily.

"Yes. No. Both?" Alexander grimaced. "You undermine my words, Geoffrey." He pushed himself up on one arm, considering. "Why am I here? Why are you making me so welcome?" He had his guesses, from those few words after he'd got Geoffrey up to their shared room. But he was at a point where he needed to hear how Geoffrey named it.

"When I came back from Vienna, I was lying with my head in Lizzie's lap, as we do. She asked me what I thought of you. When I told her your virtues, she asked if you were a tenor or baritone." Geoffrey blinked up at him, agreeably, but with that focused attention he brought to what mattered most. "I realised you are exactly the sort of man I fancy. Not, of course, that you are obliged in any way by that. I believe we've established by now I will do nothing you do not agree to. That is not your preference."

Alexander nodded. They were indeed clear on that. More to the point, he couldn't imagine Geoffrey wanting to do something he didn't wish, and that was an entirely novel sort of feeling.

"But I do want you as a friend. An ally. Someone to talk with half the night. Decidedly on my side against the world, when that is called for." Geoffrey waved a hand. "And you are delightful company. All sorts of new stories. I am, mind, thinking about how to introduce you to my other friends and nest of experts."

Alexander grimaced. "I'm here." It wasn't at all adequate and he knew it. "I don't know what to call what we are in English. But I don't want to stop."

As he'd rather expected, Geoffrey pounced on that. He could almost see the wriggle and shift, as a cat did. "In some other language, then?"

"Among my mother's people." He had to feel this out. He'd barely talked about it with her beyond the purely cosmological. It was the sort of conversation impossible to have with his mother, at least, if not most mothers. "We have many gods. Thousands. So many names and stories. You know a little about Set, perhaps, and Horus?"

"More about Horus." Geoffrey was paying close attention now. "Given the falcons."

"Of course you would. We call him Heru, more often. We have the idea of multiple souls. And the concept of what in my mother's mother's mother's endless mother's tongue is bawy." He pronounced it carefully. "The twin souls, the souls that are about manifestation, being effective in the world. That it is Heru and Set, two faces." He gestured. "You, as Heru, seeing as you are a ruling lord, drawing your power from the land and from your community. And, as you say, the falcons."

Geoffrey inclined his head, slowly. "And you fighting to tear down all those assumptions that do not serve. Chaos in motion, the chaos that is needed."

Alexander shivered, to be seen so clearly that way. It was the part of himself he had repressed for so long, because it was utterly dangerous to everyone who held power over him. "Just so. Roman myth has nothing like it. Greek only barely does. Dionysus comes closest, I think."

"And we are so very wanting to be Roman, aren't we? Especially the Great Families. That being rather the point." Geoffrey nodded, then asked, more deliberately, "What does that mean to you?"

"May I give you a name?" Alexander offered it hesitantly, only to see laughter bubbling out, visible in Geoffrey's face before the sound followed. It was delighted laughter that pulled Alexander along with it, despite his confusion.

"You already have." Geoffrey held up a hand. "I'll tell you in a moment. Yes, you may. As many names as you wish to bestow. You are a master of naming magics. I would be a fool to deny such gifts."

That, oh, that hit home. At the same time, he began wondering how many epithets he could dredge up for Horus, and which ones might apply to Geoffrey in which mood. He suspected Lizzie would find it deeply amusing, and he wanted that too. Golden, of many-coloured plumage, lord of the sky, of the two horizons. He had not yet seen Geoffrey as the distant one, but he supposed it was possible. That could wait. For now, he said, "Nekheny. It means falcon. Simple enough, yes?"

Geoffrey let himself fall back on the blanket, sprawling again, just grinning. As foolishly ecstatic as he had been after the false goldwasser, the pleasure shining out of him like Horus holding the sun. Then he rolled onto his side again. "Any time you wish." He then let out a long breath. "You gave me back my forename."

Alexander blinked at that. "I did?"

"I told you, I did not think of myself as anything but Carillon. For - well. Sometime in the first year of the War to a week ago. I lost my name somewhere that night, and then you called me Geoffrey. Now, inside my head, it's there. Comfortable again. Not just when Lizzie uses it."

Alexander reached out a hand hesitantly. "How does that feel?" He had not meant that, though of course he'd had all the naming magics much to mind at the time, far closer to the surface.

"Glorious. Um. Physically, erotically, as well as all the other ways. Just to be entirely clear. Though that isn't any of yours to bother with unless you actually choose. I enjoy it, mind. The spark of it."

"Geoffrey." Alexander couldn't resist. "Nekheny. Golden One." He let his hand rest on Geoffrey's and felt the shiver at the touch. "Even though I have no desire to reciprocate that way? I told you, it is only the land that..." He shrugged. More things there was so little language for.

"I will pine decorously and chivalrously for whatever small touch and sign of favour you wish to bestow, so long as it amuses both of us. If you change your mind about what else you permit, for whatever reason, including simple curiosity, you have but to say the word. It is enough to know you know what you do to me. To be honest about it, not hide it."

"You are, mmm. Very full of the land, right now. And your lady wife, as well." Not that Alexander was at all prepared to talk at the moment about the feelings he had, the idea of the lord of the land carrying that magic in physical form. He glanced around, taking in the burgeoning bounty of the season, then said, "Cyrus is very curious why, how the land responds to you so well. I won't tell him, not unless you give permission. But you are a puzzle, of the sort that is actually in our remit."

"Ah." Geoffrey let himself settle onto his back, pulling his free hand to rest behind his head. "We're almost sure it has to do with my shoulder. I came back to recuperate. I'd been able to get a portal. We went to Hawk's Breath, the Cumbria house, and my brother...."

He shrugged, then winced slightly. "Was having a house party. Middle of the War. I don't know why, but I couldn't bear to stay. So we came on here. By that night, the infection had set in, and I lost the next few days to it. There's the healing spring, we rode by it yesterday. I begged Benton to get water and use it to wash the wound, for me to drink. He boiled it and cooled it first, but he humoured me. Between that and the Healer he got out, I turned the corner, but it was a - he won't talk about it."

"You came here." Alexander considered that. Far easier than contemplating this bright, fierce lion of a man dying of a slow burning infection.

"One of my friends, one of my treasured analysts, thinks that it not only saved my life, it saved my landsense, which had got badly shaken in the trenches. And I didn't go back there, of course. The rest of my War was other things." Geoffrey hesitated. "I've come to think my nearly dying might have been necessary, too. I couldn't stop whatever happened. I couldn't wall it out."

"Walling out water is rarely an easy choice. The timing might have mattered too. In some traditions, Lammastide is a time for sacrifice." Alexander brushed his thumb over Geoffrey's hand, careful now. "Benton took superb care of you."

"As I keep saying, if I am lucky, he will to the end of our days. See, I am already experienced in complicated relation-ships that no one understands. We've muddled along, far better than fine, for going on twenty years now."

Alexander snorted. "It reassures a bit, yes."

"As to Cyrus, mmm. I am not entirely unwilling to talk to those you trust on the Council about it when you ask. I also know that, at the moment, you are not sure you trust any of them. We can continue to discuss, as things develop. I am, however, far more willing to talk to any Lord or Lady of the land, or any Heir. Any of those who have lost their landsense. I'm glad to see if I can suggest anything that might be of help to them."

It was a very precise sort of offer, but it was far more generous than the Council deserved. Cyrus, at least, would have the sense to know it. Alexander couldn't argue with that comment about his lack of trust, either, seeing as it was entirely true. "Thank you." He then shook his head. "I am still getting my head around being on the land, you know."

That made Geoffrey squeeze his hand, once. "I had an idea, but only if it will actually help. And it is something that must be to your standards in every way. I have some thoughts about the Judsons, but would it be any help to have some place you could honour Perry? Somewhere..." Geoffrey hesitated. "Trellech changes, and that's your home, isn't it?"

"Not a place for an endless memorial, that will outlast all of us." Alexander had thought about it. But he knew how often the walls were moved and the gardens reshaped, as people bought and sold the houses. He didn't even properly own the land his townhouse stood on, he just had a century's lease.

"I have land. It's been in the family centuries and centuries, back to the Domesday Book. There is every reason to hope, now, that will continue. Would you ... " There was a hint here, of where that distance might appear, if this went wrong. Alexander realised that whatever the question, whatever his answer, he would have to be gentle and careful. "May we make space for a memorial here, in whatever form you feel is proper? Where you can know it will continue? I know Perry had no ties here."

Alexander sucked in his breath, then he couldn't breathe at all, all the air had rushed away. He'd never even thought to seek this. Isembard would never have thought of it in Essex. And even that land might go back to some other part of the family in time, who would not understand.

But here, he could trust the stories would be told, generation to generation, as long as there was anyone to hear. He'd seen and touched the tapestries, the twelfth-century carvings, the stonework outside the library. A dozen dozen pieces, nurtured through long stretches of time and scores of conflicts. Protected and honoured.

"Oh. Yes. Please. I can't." Before he completely lost every scrap of self-control, Geoffrey sat up, getting an arm around him, and let him just be with it. He didn't rush the thoughts of what a memorial stele should be, what it must include. They sat there, quiet and together, until the gong went to change for supper. By then, he was recovered enough to let the stories they shared roll over him and include him.

EPILOGUE
YTENE, LATE JULY

Alexander came through the portal and handed his bag to the footman who was waiting there. "Will you let Geoffrey know I'll be in the garden until it's time?"

He got a nod in reply, but he was quite sure Geoffrey already knew that. For one thing, he was about ten minutes early. For another, he was entirely aware that Geoffrey was choreographing something. Alexander had some guesses about what, but no idea about the specifics, and it made him twitch.

He had spent the last two months watching Geoffrey. And Lizzie. He'd been out at Ytene at least two nights a week. His obligations elsewhere meant he spent the others in his home in Trellech or in some passing room elsewhere in Albion. Whenever he turned up, they were delighted to see him, and it wasn't as if they weren't also busy.

Alexander had tried to get a sense of who else they were close to. The Summer Solstice festivities should have helped. But as far as he could tell, Geoffrey was on good terms with everyone who liked horses, which included a vast percentage of the population. And Lizzie had shifted from conversation to conversation with a smile and a deftness that was like a fast clipper flying with the wind behind her. Together, they were fascinating to watch, but not at all informative.

He hadn't known how to talk to Thesan and Isembard about any of it, and he was going to have to do that soon. He'd seen them both looking at him, now they were recovered from the tail of the school year.

They hadn't asked, mind, but he had the sense they were holding off for reasons of their own. That couldn't last forever. Probably not even a fortnight longer, unless he avoided them entirely, and they'd notice that too, and be hurt. Besides, he didn't want to.

He took the turn into the garden. Their plans for the memorial stele were moving along well, in the sense that they had actually selected a stonemason to work with. But they were still at the sketches stage, with Alexander trying to figure out how to handle the texts. Also, how to make the translations elegant, because there should also be translations.

He could, at least, go and stand where it would go, in a sheltered corner of the garden, facing the small pond, and catch his breath. It had been a busy morning, with three fiddly conversations, and now here he was for an afternoon with people who had every reason to be cautious with him.

He'd been standing there for six minutes when Geoffrey appeared, striding freely through the garden. "All the children are off at - well, one of our guests. Well out of the way for the nonce. Staying over, actually, so no one has to rush. A great treat for them."

Alexander inclined his head. That suggested some details, but not so usefully as all that. Plenty of people had children near enough the same age. "Nekheny. You're not going to give me any hints, are you?"

"We might easily have invited double the number, but we thought better a good conversation without having so many we'd split off. We can do that, certainly, but by choice, not sheer volume, mm? We've food, drink, amusements, books to read when anyone needs a break. All the civilised comforts."

"I am not running away. You note that, yes?" Alexander sucked in his breath. "I have done much more challenging things."

"You have. And you do not know any of these people well, unless I am very much mistaken, but they are favourably inclined." Geoffrey offered a hand. "I have vouched for you."

"When you put it like that." Alexander took a breath. "Lead on, Long-Striding One."

"That is a new name!" Geoffrey had been delightedly collecting epithets. It was useful indeed that Heru had a great many. They walked side by side, up to the doors that opened from the library to the garden. Inside, Alexander found seven unexpected people settled in chairs and sofas, with Benton standing between what was presumably his own chair and Lizzie's. They'd left the sofa open, presumably for him and Geoffrey.

He knew six of the guests by sight, but two only barely, and one not at all. Geoffrey gestured him into a seat, where a glass of his favourite brandy was already waiting. "Lord Richard and Lady Alysoun Edgarton. Gabriel and Rathna Edgarton. Giles, you know. His wife Kate, Captain in the

Guard. We have Richard to thank for that, in part. And Elizabeth Mason, there." Geoffrey added, "We'll be getting Rufus for supper, along with Ferry. He's still out in the stables, of course. Hungry horses wait for no man." And Ferry, Rufus's wife, had her own work as well, though that implied that she was included more for fondness than for plotting.

He took in Lord Richard and Lady Alysoun first. He had been two years behind Alexander in Fox House at Schola, and far better suited for it. She was enough younger they hadn't overlapped, but he'd heard comments about her parties. She had a gift for keeping things running smoothly, no matter what happened, with a generous determination to do the thing properly.

"And who are these people to you, then, Geoffrey?" He heard the little murmur of his use of the name, but Geoffrey just smiled, before Alexander added, "Many-Dappled One, you are plotting. Still." The good humour in his voice got the others to laugh.

"I am breathing, so yes." Geoffrey settled back, eyes half-closed. "We are lacking my alchemist, he still doesn't want to meet you. Also my master of locks. That is my valet, for the record, he's upstairs. Rufus, obviously. Master Osric, my tailor of choice, does not generally leave his shop. But we have here my keeper of wards. That is Kate." She was not in Guard uniform, but she wore something that might well have been cut from the same fabric in a dark green to complement deep auburn hair. "I would like, for the record, to get Kate and Isembard chatting in a gathering such as this, sooner rather than later."

Alexander inclined his head. The implications for that, that more warding would be needed, well. They had all heard further rumblings out of Germany, and they all expected there were many more to come. And then the desire to include Isembard hit him. Geoffrey was making space for the two people Alexander most often turned to, without question. Where Alexander had spent the past months ducking spending time in private with them.

"Giles, of course, you have met properly." Giles nodded from his chair next to his wife. He had, in fact, been quite welcoming. He had promised Geoffrey and Alexander a suitably wide-ranging code for their purposes, no matter what might come up, though it would take time to construct. Alexander had vastly enjoyed the conversation, and how Giles kept everything straight even as the conversation wandered to and fro.

"My forger of choice is Elizabeth Mason." That was a dark-haired woman at least some years older than he was, with skin about as brown as Alexander's own, though her features suggested something out of the Malay States or perhaps parts of China. "Mason is a Penelope, theoretically semi-retired by now, but no one can stop her working." She nodded, and Alexander considered she might be the most dubious of the group.

"Photography is, I admit, not one of my better arts. I get distracted. My manuscripts, however, pass himself's quality standards." She flicked her fingers at Geoffrey, amused at something, and he beamed at her before he went on.

"Gabe is, besides being his father's heir, also a Penelope. Rathna is, of course, a Portal Keeper." Alexander inclined his head at both of them. He had seen them at various events this summer, though never with the more aristocratic crowd that Alexander might have expected.

Gabe leaned back, as if sitting in an ordinary chair were tedious. His wife had that serenity of someone who knew the mysteries of space and time, quite like Thesan. He looked very much the match to his parents, like he should be gracing the cover of some illustrated magazine, the perfect young nobleman. Rathna, for her part, was wearing a day dress not unlike Lizzie's, but in a vibrant burgundy that made her brown skin glow with health and vitality.

Alexander inclined his head. "Pleased to make your better acquaintance. Magistra Edgarton. Thesan speaks highly of your skills and knowledge, which, of course, means I am intrigued."

That got a laugh from her, suddenly relaxed. "Rathna, please. We are fairly informal, as a whole, though you take your chances with Gabe's parents." That was said with clear affection, which Alexander could at least make some sense of. "I was, as I expect you've sorted, the one who did the charts for your ritual work."

Gabe nodded once. He opened his mouth, and his wife raised one eyebrow, and he subsided. For the moment, at least.

"And then Richard and Alysoun. Alysoun is the first of the most excellent analysts I have collected, with Giles, Kate, and Lizzie, as well. And Gabe for untangling things. And Richard..." Alexander caught the slight hitch in Geoffrey's voice. "What I said then is true. Richard has been my model of what it means to hold the land oaths, and in being the kind of father I want to be."

Lord Richard waved a hand, but he looked rather pleased at that comment. "We will have to have you out to Veritas. Our lands are as well loved, but a different feel to it, which is only to be expected." Alexander knew he was a magistrate and a captain in the Guard, and he had never heard anything remotely dubious about the man.

It was at that point that Gabe spoke, rather like a pot

suddenly boiling over, with Rathna looking deeply amused beside him. "You duel, of course?"

Alexander had not precisely expected that, or at least not from Gabe. "I know Lord Richard's skill, at least by reputation. FitzAlan told stories of that duel in, what was it, 1906? Privately, of course. I was abroad at the time. I didn't hear the early discussion."

"Richard, please. Or we'll be forever about saying anything." Richard then grimaced slightly. "A difficult situation, though also, as it turns out, a meaningful one. Two of the others not here are my own apprentice master, now actually retired, Magni Torham, and—" there was a tiny hesitation here. "His partner in many things, Gil Oxley. We thought they might be a tad too much today, but Gil would very much like to discuss a few household ritual magics with you. Something about a monograph from three years ago?"

"I would be delighted." Alexander had, to be honest, thrown it together because of three different Council problems, in the hopes that it might find fertile ground somewhere. It was all about how attention to the materials of a home affected the protections that took most surely. Then the implications of how Richard had chosen to phrase that caught up with him. "As Geoffrey has said to me, being a hypocrite seems to be a quick road to self-hatred all round."

He glanced at Geoffrey, he was explaining himself badly, but there his other half was, the truth of the bawy. "As I said, Alexander and I are content with what we are becoming to each other, and that is not what Gil and Magni have, but what is?"

It made Lizzie laugh, at least wrinkling up her nose. Across from her, Lady Alysoun opened her mouth, and the others all fell quiet. "Before Gabe explodes - so messy, and rather harder on books than is entirely called for - we would be glad to offer our duelling salle, when you visit. With whatever forms you prefer."

Gabe laughed, entirely at ease. "Mama teases. Often. Fair warning. But I do find it's a good way to get to know someone. And to learn a few things, and oh, that is a fine day."

Mason rolled her eyes, visibly amused. "They would not allow him to apprentice to me formally. Something about blowing up too many workrooms. Though if you wish to risk him there, that's also a fine way to get to know each other."

Alexander spread his hands. "I know when my skills are over-matched. I appreciate your work, a great deal, and the innovations involved, but I can't possibly hold my own with them. If you have some matter of ritual magic, however, I am glad to place my knowledge at your disposal." Before Gabe could break in, he added, "And yes, I would be pleased to duel at some agreeable time and terms. My reflexes are, mind, tuned for fighting, not for show."

The introductions done, he glanced at Geoffrey, but Geoffrey was nodding at Alysoun. She shifted slightly in her seat - it was only then Alexander noticed a cane along her leg. "We have been talking, for nearly fifteen years, about the Council. We know there are things you can't tell us, and things you don't want to tell us, and certainly some things are both. But to be plain, we hope that somehow, we might better understand what the Council is trying to do. And whether we wish to lend more active and deliberate support to that."

Alexander raised an eyebrow. That was indeed quite direct. She went on after a moment. "This is not, shall we say, how we expected to get a connection where we could even have this conversation. But Geoffrey is a man of excellent judgement, and he is significantly less impulsive than Gabe. And there is a great deal that baffles us. Not to the good of the land."

"I - yes." He couldn't argue with any of that. "Geoffrey, I don't know what you've shared about our time in Germany?"

"The outline of the results, of course, and some of the specifics, though more with my alchemist than anyone here, beyond the larger political implications. More due to lack of time than anything, with the various summer obligations, it's been our first chance to get together properly as a group."

Alexander nodded, contemplating where to begin. "I have been talking slightly more to Cyrus. Now head of the Council, and rather different in approach than Hesperidon Warren was. I am, I admit, only beginning to get a good sense for what that means in practise. Where he might be open to discussions that were shut down before, at least in private."

Richard leaned forward. "You must have a list."

"Oh, a very long list. Where do I even begin?" Alexander looked over at Geoffrey to find Lizzie had taken his hand. "We have talked a fair bit about the landsense, about those who lost it in the War. Let us begin there?"

A murmur of agreement went around, and Alexander settled into what promised to be a far different sort of conversation than he usually got on the topic. As it went on, as they asked insightful questions. As they trusted his experience of it, even though he was not landed himself, he found himself beginning to relax properly, to stop guarding himself so tightly.

Certainly just as informative as his coming duels would be.

~

CONTINUE READING for the included epilogue novella, *Intimacies of the Seasons*. It follows Alexander and Geoffrey through the next year of seasons and changes.

AUTHOR'S NOTES for both books follow the novella.

INTIMACIES OF THE
SEASONS

LAMMASTIDE

Alexander returned to Ytene on Saturday afternoon, after a complicated round of social invitations and obligations over Lammas. What sleep he'd got the previous night had been wedged between a tedious dinner party that had run annoyingly late and a morning observation. That had started at dawn, not an hour he particularly favoured, for a bit of Council business. He'd been checking that the ritual of making amends for a young idiot who thought summoning the Fatae was a good idea had gone over well.

Attempting, in his case, of course. But he'd done it in a way that had required a finicky bit of ritual magic the previous morning to set right.

He nodded at the footman at the door. "Would you let them know I'm back?"

The footman cleared his throat. "Lady Carillon is in the library, sir. She asked if you'd stop in there first." That was baffling, but easy enough to agree to. Alexander handed off his bag, sure by now someone would whisk it up to his rooms. His. They'd made that abundantly clear in the past month.

Alexander knocked on the door frame of the library. Lizzie was at one of the large desks, books spread out, but he knew the look of someone who was not actually working. "Bad time?"

She grimaced - let him see it - and Alexander was suddenly quite worried. "Come in, close the door?"

He did. "Something's wrong." Not a question. "Is Geoffrey..." They'd have told him differently if there'd been some injury. Horse, falcon, all the ordinary and extraordinary risks of farm life and ritual magic and whatever else Geoffrey got it into his head to do in a day.

"Nothing - look, it's nothing we haven't sorted before. Just. Sit? Please?" Lizzie gestured at the chair on the other side of the desk. He noted, of course, that she hadn't said everything was fine. She wasn't lying to him, at least. That was, in its own awful way, reassuring.

He sat. No point in drawing this out. Lizzie drew in a breath. "Geoffrey has these moments. Not often, these days. It's been nearly three years since the last bad one." She let it out with a sharper precision "That lasted more than a day." Alexander was suddenly quite sure she could give the precise count.

"What sort of moments?" Alexander could think of a dozen things, several dozen, that men like they were didn't let show unless things were exceedingly awful. Not even then, if they could help it.

"He goes away, in his head, somewhere very far off. Where nothing here can touch him. The perfect gentleman, the lord of middle age, amiable and not at all a threat to anyone else." She looked up. "All the things he lets the world see, none of what we see."

Alexander appreciated being included there, but he frowned. "Something happened to cause it?"

"He won't say. Not to me. Not to Benton, who has vastly more experience working through this with him. And who does not shy from a touch of appropriate guilt when it's a lever that will move the world."

That phrase also amused, somewhere off in the far reaches of his mind. The rest was spinning, trying to figure out what to ask next. "What does he do when he's like this?"

"Something like - oh, he will eat and sleep and be pleasant. I know a great many women whose husbands have their Wars catch them in rage or shame, or even utter inability to do anything. Geoffrey's not like that?" She was, clearly, grateful. "But it. Well. Would you see if you can shake anything loose? Even what happened, which would be a step toward doing anything about it."

Alexander hesitated. "Are you sure I'm not treading on toes?" He was new here in this place, whatever he was to Geoffrey. New to Lizzie's trust, and Benton's, though the more he'd seen of both of them, the more he wanted them to trust him.

"I am asking you. Also, if you can actually do something, that would be a kindness. Bad nightmares, the last two nights." The nights Alexander had been gone, though surely that wasn't the cause. Besides, it wasn't as if Geoffrey shared his bed.

"Where is he?"

Lizzie glanced up. "Our rooms. I'll give you time. Better not to try and get him to move. He said he was going to see about napping, but of course I don't believe he actually is."

Alexander considered. "I have my journal handy. I can write if there's anything that would be useful." He had both done this sort of thing before if not remotely recently. And he had never done anything like this at all. "If at least one of us doesn't reappear by supper, send reinforcements?"

That drew a weak smile. "That will do." Then she stood and came around to kiss his cheek. "Thank you, Alexander." Before he could figure out what to do with that, she took a step, turned over her shoulder, and added one more comment. "I'll be out in the gardens for a few minutes. Journal handy." She waved it and then disappeared out into the hallway.

It left Alexander feeling like he was sneaking to the edge of the bannister, to look down at some adult party down-stairs. That sense that everything was on display, no one was hiding anything, and yet he was seeing something he wasn't entirely supposed to see.

Instead, he took a breath and made his way up to the first floor, down to the rooms he knew were Geoffrey and Lizzie's, the Lord's suite. He knocked on the door and heard a muffled. "Come." That was not someone who had remotely been asleep, no.

Alexander came in, first to the private sitting room, closing the door behind him. Geoffrey was not visibly in evidence, so he pitched his voice to carry. "Geoffrey? Alexander."

That had a longer pause, then a less muffled, "Bedroom. On the left."

Alexander came through into a room that was made of the New Forest. Rather literally, he expected, there was a great deal of woodwork visible, much of it carved into bas reliefs of the Forest or various fauna and flora. Various shades of green and brown, with gold and muted grey for accent. In the centre was a vast fourposter bed. It had certainly seen births, deaths, and everything in between, and it was even larger than the ones they had shared while in Germany. Geoffrey was sprawled out on his stomach more or less in the middle, head turned toward the door.

Alexander hesitated for only a moment, and then said, "I gather your proper epithet at the moment is Distant One. May I come over?"

As he'd hoped, that got a small sound of something - he couldn't tell if it was frustration or amusement or annoyance, precisely. But it was a response. That was a good enough start. And then there was the hand lifting, gesturing at the side of the bed. Like and unlike that bed in Germany.

Alexander promptly came to settle there - plenty of space. This was Geoffrey's side of the bed, clearly, with his pocket watch and a few other bits and bobs. Geoffrey was rather in the middle of it, a book off to the left, and his journal not far beyond that. He looked, frankly, like he'd been to hell and back. It wasn't exactly shadows under his eyes, but all the glowing bloom that had been there since they returned at the end of May had shattered.

Geoffrey closed his eyes, as if he couldn't bear to look at anything. Or say anything, as the silence went on and on. A minute, three, then five. After Alexander started counting the way the clock ticked over.

Only once the clock had chimed the quarter hour, another three minutes later, did Alexander venture to say anything. "May I touch you? My hand on yours?"

That got a shrug and a mumble. "As you choose." Which was not properly in keeping with Geoffrey's views on preferences, but it was agreement. If in that rather well-spaced precision Alexander had heard after the false goldwasser, when everything came crashing down.

Alexander considered his options, then removed his

shoes to settle with his back to the headboard, his hand reaching to cover Geoffrey's. A touch they'd done before, one he felt he had sufficiently mastered the basics of. Geoffrey closed his eyes again, but Alexander fancied his breath settled a little.

More importantly, he could feel the pulse under his fingers. Not so much the heartbeat, but the way his magic felt, how it had snarled up around something. He just waited. There was nothing good that would come by pushing, not right now.

It was a delicate tracery of a ritual that was needed. The kind that needed to be done by breath and hope and putting himself in the right place at exactly the right moment. All of that demanded patience. Putting the goal first, not selfish concerns. Certainly not ego. So he waited, just feeling the occasional twitch under his fingers. Finally, quietly, he heard. "Distant One. Fair. Lizzie?"

"Out in the garden for a bit. She sent me up, of course."

The 'of course' - or perhaps the absolute way Alexander had put it, the underlying bedrock - made Geoffrey peer at him, sideways.

"I would not have dared, otherwise." Alexander contemplated how to put the next part. "She said neither she nor Benton had got things to budge."

That made Geoffrey snort louder, then turn his head away, half-burying it in the edge of the pillow.

"Hey. Something new, then. New and old?" He was guessing, now, but there had been a wingbeat of tension, at the idea this was new. And a shiver, brief but so obvious from how they sat, at the second option.

Alexander considered the evidence before him, running through it three times in his head to make sure he wasn't missing anything. He had time, he would take that time. He knew Geoffrey and Lizzie had had their own obligations, a gathering on the first, a harvest faire on the second. Plenty of chances for someone to say something troublesome. On the other hand, if it had been an older wound, Geoffrey would have reacted differently. Or Lizzie, Benton, or both would have hit on the useful thing to say before this.

"Something Thursday night, then. And about the Council or about me, in some way." Again, the flinch. This time Alexander felt as Geoffrey's fingers clutched at the sheets beneath. Then that careful nod, still not turning back.

"It's almost certainly nothing I haven't heard before." That much was true. He didn't know all the gossip out there about what he was, but he knew the outline.

Geoffrey let out a beleaguered sigh. "I do not care for it." That sharp precision, quieter this time.

"I can make my guesses. Something about my role on the Council. What people think it is, at least." There was another shiver, and Alexander knew he'd hit close enough. He hesitated, then shifted his hand to rest on the back of Geoffrey's shoulder blade. "Will you tell me? Please? I can't tell you the truth until I know what they said."

That got Geoffrey turning his head back toward Alexander. "You would tell me?"

Alexander shrugged. "Not the details of some specific issues. We do have oaths about confidentiality. But as much as I can, yes. Whether what you heard is truth or lie, or the percentage. It's probably a percentage. The things that are all lies don't sting and ache as much as the gossip that has a seed of truth." He let his thumb shift slightly. "Besides. I can see why Lizzie and Benton are worried, if you're like this. I don't care for it either."

That got a grunt. "You are relentless."

"One of my better qualities. It's certainly kept me alive a few times." Alexander kept his voice lighter, but they were getting into depths now, and he was not at all sure how to navigate them.

Geoffrey shifted then onto his side, making space for Alexander to do the same, facing him. Not eye to eye, but enough they could, in fact, look at each other without straining. If they chose. "The party, on Friday. The - the way they talked."

"Who was there? At the Asquiths, yes?"

"The senior Asquiths, all three children and their spouses, two cousins and theirs, the local magistrate and his wife, and three other couples I never quite placed. The Asquiths are distant cousins of mine. They were hoping they might end up in line for Ytene. Or at least some of the other family estates."

"Surely there are a few people in the way? Not just your children."

"Some people have bigger hopes than they should." Geoffrey was working around to it, Alexander could tell, and he didn't get in the way with another comment. "We were having drinks after dinner. They still send the ladies off. Cigars, too. All very much a show. And someone - one of the next generation. Rewan, I think. He said something about how he had heard Prosper Harelton had been stirring up trouble."

Then he paused. Alexander resisted the desire to guffaw. It wouldn't help, not right now. "Go on? I can tell you about what Prosper's been up to in a moment. The outline, anyway."

Geoffrey ducked his chin. "That Smythe-Clive was too soft." His voice shifted tone, clearly mimicking the pitch of the conversation. Nasal, more than a bit drunk, not nearly careful enough. "That Hesperidon would have had Livia Fortier or Landry out there to give him a talking to in a minute, if you know what I mean?" The last part had a particularly nasty note to it.

Alexander shifted, reaching to brush Geoffrey's hand again, more awkwardly in this position. "A seed of truth, a lot of lies in there. At least in this case." He coughed. "And I know that's not enough. Moment. Thinking how to talk this through as sensibly as we can, when you're all tangled up with it, and I won't take my anger out on you."

Geoffrey shivered hard at that, contracting slightly. Alexander winced. "Right here. Going to tell you the truth. Swear to it on the Silence, if that helps."

"Tell me?" Geoffrey's voice was tiny now.

"Prosper? Young idiot, yes. The sort of young idiot where I'd be sent off like a hunting dog after him? No." Alexander kept his voice as matter of fact as he could. "Finicky bit of ritual work, apologising for his idiocy. Much easier to do yesterday. I spent this morning checking that the offerings were acceptable. Not exactly routine, it's the sort of thing we do a couple of times in a bad year? Cyrus is glad to let me go do the finicky bits."

Geoffrey cracked an eye open. "And you like that part?"

"I enjoy a finicky ritual, or had you not realised this about me yet? A lot of the propitiation rituals are satisfying, really. You know quick enough if they've done what you meant."

That got a little more of a movement, a half-amused snort. "Fair. Can you tell me anything about that? Ritually?"

"In a bit." Alexander let his hand shift, his thumb petting. "As your reward for talking through the rest of it." It was taking a risk. They'd talked around the issues of power in a relationship, and he wasn't entirely sure how Geoffrey would take it.

There was a long silence, and then a sigh. "You will out-stubborn me, won't you?" His tone was slightly less distant now, though there was still a note of strain.

"I am fairly sure I can do so. With Lizzie and Benton's aid." Alexander considered his choices. "You want to know what I've done. You can't bear to ask, but you want to know. I can tell. Before I tell you that, the outline, the range. Tell me what you knew of me, from the gossip, before you approached me."

"Everyone knows you're dangerous." That came out quick enough. "I wanted, at the gala, to get you wrong-footed, so you'd listen to me for long enough. Get in under your defences. Not so much you would treat me as a threat."

"How did you set that up, anyway? Getting me alone? Are you sure you don't duel?"

That made Geoffrey actually smile. "Lizzie. Though we had four more ideas for getting you somewhere I could have a word. Public for my safety, enough quiet for the question. I was glad not to have to lurk by your preferred stationer. Not in winter, anyway."

Alexander shook his head. "Other people would send a note." He lifted his free hand. "And I'd have ignored it, or perhaps sent back a polite non-reply. I know, I know." He then nudged the more delicate part again. "What did you know of me, then?"

Geoffrey hesitated. "That you were the Council's war dog. Sent off to attack whomever they said. You and Livia Fortier, though other names that come up here and there."

Alexander could hear something else lurking. "And?"

"But." Geoffrey made that adjustment clear. "I knew

you hadn't had anything to do with Temple. Not directly, and maybe not even known. As, it turns out, you hadn't."

"And you keep saying you don't duel." Alexander chuckled softly. It made Geoffrey peer at him, then nestle a little closer on the bed, and Alexander shifted to offer an arm. Awkwardly, this wasn't something he'd done before, but he wanted to be able to feel more of how Geoffrey reacted. And he'd do near anything to encourage something other than that isolated raw distance. "So you could approach me. Besides needing my touch with name magic." They'd talked through the actual details of that three weeks ago now, and Geoffrey had been gloriously appreciative of the skill involved.

"Just so." Geoffrey let out a long breath and closed his eyes. "Gossip. About how they send you out to bring people to heel. Regularly. Killing people who..." He shuddered at that, and Alexander immediately tugged him closer.

"Here. None of that. You're letting all your logic slip. I know it's - it can't not be personal. But that, your brother, that was nearly three years of on-again off-again discussion. None of them liked it. Every two years, three, there's something that needs that set of skills. Not death, even, all the time, but sincere threats, making it clear what will happen if someone presses. Far more often, they've sent me off to get something from a house or a safe or plant something. Or get evidence that can go to the Guard. Not entirely aboveboard, but..." But sometimes necessary.

Geoffrey burrowed against him a little. "And?"

"And I do that. I have the skills for it. Not everyone does, even on the Council. I do it competently. I can't abide people mucking around with dangerous things. But I'd rather get sent off to be diplomatic and do the ritual language right." He encouraged Geoffrey a bit more against his shoulder, feeling how it was to have a weight on his casting hand. "The last time I killed someone..." He actually had to count. "Besides that explosion, where I hope we didn't. Four years ago?"

Geoffrey grimaced, but nodded. "Six years for me. And that was raw bad luck."

"And see, sometimes that's a thing. But you don't get the gossip about it. I do. Because that's all people think I'm there for." He hesitated, then went on. "Cyrus talked with me about it. A fortnight ago. The news gets worse and worse out of Germany. Neither of us have illusions about what might be needed. And Italy's no better. About what I'm willing for, what I'd rather not."

"What did you say?" That brought Geoffrey properly out of the depths. Alexander had hoped it would.

"We talked it through. That I'd prefer the ritual work, but he can't leave Albion often. Certainly, he shouldn't. He'd been the other person doing most of the travel until he became Head. And the Head needs to be in Albion, or able to get back within hours, which really means France or Ireland or a few other places. If there's another war, that's going to get harder, too, much more risky. I made it clear I will if it's needed, but not for every random bit of distant travel." He swallowed. "I don't want to be gone that long. Not now. The logic I offered was that we need more people who can do it, too."

Geoffrey must have caught the tone in his voice, because he looked up, met Alexander's eyes, and then settled a bit more thoroughly in his arms, body against body. Reassuringly present. "Gave you a reason to be around." That sounded very contented.

"We've got a couple of people who are willing to do some of it. And with the journals, it's easier than it used to be. We can check the formal language, for example, wherever they are, without waiting ages for the post. And before I reward you with a bit of ritual theory and practice..." Geoffrey snorted at that in amusement, then sobered as Alexander went on.

"Logic, here again. Think about it. If we killed everyone who annoyed the Council, or who did something foolish, all the people we're rumoured to have taken down. Well, we'd run out of magical folk in Albion within a generation or two. Certainly, you'd hear a lot more about sudden unexpected deaths."

Alexander hoped that rather bloody logic would be a help. "The question isn't when we do something questionable, for most anyone who actually uses their magic to do more substantial things. It's what we're doing it for, and who it's hurting. That's a matter for ethics and whatever religion you might have and your gods and your immediate community. Not necessarily Council."

That gave Geoffrey quite a lot to chew on, a proper puzzle for the Owl in him. Alexander gave him a few minutes. "Let me tell you the bit of ritual I was doing, then we can go downstairs and you can demonstrate to Lizzie and Benton that you're on the mend? It's sunny out, a bit of time under the tree you like?" Which Alexander was growing to like very much too, honestly.

Geoffrey nodded, then added impishly. "Tell me a story?" for all the world like he was seven or eight.

"Prosper has got himself in trouble in the past. Not for a couple of years, admittedly, but he will have ideas. This time, he had come up with a whole new magical technique, half bodged together from something he read in a book. Utter rubbish, of course. It's not that the Fatae are always ones for precision, but they do tend to ignore incomprehensible babble."

That occupied them comfortably for the next thirty minutes. Both what Prosper had got up to and what Alexander had done to mend the gaps in the local land magic as a result. As well as making the proper apologies.

AUTUMN

YTENE, OCTOBER 5TH

Alexander got back to Ytene on the afternoon of the 5th. Geoffrey came sweeping out of the library as the footman was taking his bag. "Tell, tell!" He was like a schoolboy again, all light and amusement. "The library? I have drinks waiting. You did say you were on the way."

They went in together, companionably. Alexander took the glass Geoffrey was holding out, settling in the chair that had somehow reliably become his. "Shall I wait for Lizzie?"

"She said no, she has a do. Some sort of tea, philanthropic, but I can't remember if it's the Domestic Arts Utilitarian Reform Society, the Hespasia Morris Artists of Old, or the Reminiscent Veterans Society. She expects the aftermath to have her out into the evening. She may stay in town."

"I'd ask if those were really the names, but I know better." Alexander shook her head. "She'll need a drink when she's done with that."

"Oh, she's got a plot on, or at least she's hoping to.

You'll hear all about it tomorrow, I'm sure, especially if she got the bit she was after." Geoffrey waved a hand. "Your supper with Cyrus. Tell, please."

"You're being demanding, Geoffrey. My." Alexander lifted his glass, drawing out the moment. Then he relented. "I flatfooted him half a dozen times. He got me to laugh twice. Before we settled into the work of the evening, as it turned out."

Geoffrey leaned forward, his elbow on the arm of the chair, chin in his hand. Someone could take a photograph and caption it 'Lord at his pleasure' and be entirely right. But the casual viewer would assume the man was looking at a beautiful woman or some other mild and pleasant vice. Whatever Alexander was on his own, or to Geoffrey, mild was not the word.

"I'm fairly sure he was startled from when I met him at the door, mind. I had on my at home robes. He's seen them a few times, but not often, and not for years." Unlike Geoffrey, who had encouraged them on Alexander's stays when other things weren't better suited to their plans. They were also decidedly more comfortable for lounging, or long stints in the library, mind.

"And you set up in the library?" Geoffrey had helped him work out the plans. Alexander had wanted every bit of Geoffrey's ability to set a civilised and successful ambush. Both plan and result were much the better for working in tandem.

"Yes. It worked quite well. We've eaten there before. The dining room is a little ridiculous for two."

"You should turn it into an annex to the library. It's not as if you ever host dinner parties there. And you could use the shelf space. Even with the charms." Geoffrey waved a hand. "I'm thinking about the downstairs parlour."

"What does Lizzie say?" Alexander was distracted by the prospects of that discussion.

"That it depends how much of the shelf space she can claim for herself. Our negotiations are ongoing, I believe is the proper phrase." Alexander suspected that they were laying a string of bets, counting up the wins and losses, as Thesan and Isembard often did about such matters. He was fairly certain Lizzie would get what she wanted, for half a dozen reasons. "Go on. She'll want to be around for that banter, save it for later."

"As you wish, Dweller in his House." Alexander bowed his head, relaxed enough to smile at his own pun. "So we settle down to eat, I set out the soup, pour the wine. He asks if my man did the cooking, and I told him not this time." He snorted. "Mind, he was much of the way through his soup before he asked about poison."

"Not seriously?" The thing with Geoffrey was that those two words did a lot of work. He was, to Alexander's ear, asking whether Cyrus had reason to worry, and whether Cyrus was that foolish, as well as what Alexander thought about his usual line of precautions.

"I told him he's too trusting, but of course, I take my hospitality seriously, and my oaths on it. Which I'd done in proper form, of course."

"Are you even able to do it in improper form? I would think you'd shiver into dust, like one of the Fatae tales about a portal gone wrong." Geoffrey waved a hand. "Please don't demonstrate."

"Besides, if I did, you wouldn't get the rest of the story." Alexander leaned back. "It took him a bit to actually ask, of course. The pork was perfection, and the vegetables. Mrs Mudthon is a treasure, as I know you know, but I'll give her my particular compliments as soon as it's convenient to her."

Geoffrey grinned. "She must have her due praise, yes. And she was a trifle nervous about the balance of the gravy, always tricky to get right for stasis."

"It didn't come out too salty at all, though she certainly used a fine wine in it." The salt did sometimes have an odd interaction with the stasis charms, especially in transport. "I know I unnerved him. He spent quite a bit of time looking at me, before he finally settled into listening a bit to the land."

"Did he say as much?" Geoffrey leaned forward again, tapping his fingers, as he did when he was thinking particularly hard.

"No, but I know what it looks like on you. And I know what it ought to look like in him, enough. To give Cyrus credit, he has been doing that, regularly, and it shows. It helps, I mean."

"Quite." Geoffrey waved a hand. "So what happened?"

"I quote: 'You have come into a new, different relationship with the land. With the magic.' I had to laugh, of course. And I pointed out, not long after, that he had as well." Alexander let that settle.

"Which is the crux of it." Geoffrey nodded, and only now confirmed. "It did end well?"

"It did. Had you worried? I wrote as soon as Cyrus left." Alexander had, because they'd been so much help with all the arrangements.

"I pride myself on my interpretation of subtle information, but 'Supper excellent, more later.' is not, for the record, particularly informative about any details. Except perhaps the quality of the cooking, but we already knew that." Geoffrey tsked, far more in amusement than anything. "And yes, I could have asked, but that would spoil you telling me all of it now."

"And you do like to hear me tell you things." That touched on a tender spot, one Alexander didn't know how to navigate properly, so he forged on. "In a nutshell, he apologised, as much as he could for something he had no direct hand in. For Hesperidon, and how I was treated. How he didn't realise some of it until he became head, and for ritual reasons, I'm fairly sure. We touched on it, but he's still working out what he can talk about."

"A geas, or something else?" Trust Geoffrey to snatch onto the key of it.

"Due and appropriate caution. I got a bit of a sense of how much he tells Mabyn, and he told me. Well, he talks to her far more. Obviously. They share a bed. But he was forthright with me, as far as that went." Alexander had tested it, magically, as far as he could in that setting. But his wards were tuned to pick up most common kinds of prevarication. Cyrus had been honest, all the places he could be.

He skimmed over the specifics here. Cyrus certainly had some guesses about how much Geoffrey was now in Alexander's confidence, and vice versa. But trust was not transitive. If it were, much of Alexander's work in the world would disappear in a puff of logic. And besides, some things truly were Council business.

After a moment, he decided where to take this next. "He has a sense of things as head that he didn't before. We talked a bit about why him, not someone else. About what Hesperidon's approach had been, though I expect we'll be coming back to that and cursing it in places for a good while. Not that he didn't also do some necessary things, much as I'd rather not admit that."

"Hesperidon..." Geoffrey got the name out and then stalled.

"Cyrus said it straight out. Hesperidon treated me appallingly, even if he'd had reason for some of it. Making me into his war dog or continuing the making that had already begun. Cyrus is determined to do better. By me, in particular, insomuch as he can."

Alexander hesitated, thinking about how to explain this. "I asked him what it looked like, and - no plan survives more than a few moments with reality. But he'd thought about it, thoroughly and properly. Cyrus was in earnest about it. He was entirely willing to listen to me, to hear me, and that went a long way." He looked up. "Because I'd had it from you, I could. I could tell him enough."

Geoffrey nearly lit up at that. "It's a splendid gift, listening properly. I learned from Lizzie, and from Benton."

"You give them all the credit." Alexander shook his head. "And I'm still not sure how much is fondness and how much is truth."

"I'm sure I can't tell either." Geoffrey waved a hand. "Both, gloriously both. Anything else I should know, then?"

This was where it came a point. "I'd like your eye on it, yours and Lizzie's. And Benton's and Cassie's too, actually. He's convinced, and he's right, that we need to encourage challenges from a far wider range of people. People not so far up in their intellect that they forget about the ground beneath their feet, as he put it. Rufus and Ferry might have ideas, too."

"That's a big change, to take it so far. It's been ages since there was anyone not from Schola." Then Geoffrey got a wicked grin. "Set Thesan and her parents on that one, and you'll have a tidy list of competent people, often overlooked, on your desk inside a fortnight."

The idea was simultaneously terrifying and delightful. "I'll do that. Though not in term time, if we can avoid it, and we probably have time. Setting her and Mabyn and a few others on how to help people prepare, though, that's a pedagogical complexity that needs tending."

"We shall make a list when you explain all this to Lizzie." Geoffrey nodded. "Did he - did he treat you well, with it?"

"He did. Enough that I asked about vitality, about sharing, both ways. He does, but only with Mabyn, his sister, his daughter. In private, he mentioned that later. I told him how furious you'd been." This made Alexander hesitate. "Was that all right?"

It earned him a toothy grin, all sudden predator. "Oh, yes. Much better that he knows. What did he make of it?"

Alexander spread his hands. "He wants to know what we could be if we were better. That's when I told him about the food, where it came from. What had changed, how it had changed. The echoes of it, even if he can't see the thing itself in all its detail, because I haven't laid it out for him. And I won't, not unless you give me permission." Alexander twitched a shoulder. "It was a good beginning. I think he'll see it though."

"You're hopeful." Geoffrey's voice had gone soft now.

"For the first time in a long time, yes." Then the breath went out in a rush. "May we go look at undemanding horses or falcons or some such for a little?"

"Of course. Though the falcons are always demanding."

"Bawy." It was acknowledgement and claim and understanding.

WINTER

It wasn't until after New Year's that Alexander made it back to Ytene. Part of that was the Council obligations. Of course he wouldn't ask Geoffrey to come closer to that tangle of glitter and sharp edges than was required by the land magic obligations. Geoffrey had made his bow and formal report on the day before Solstice, as he had done every year since 1922. Geoffrey and Lizzie had disappeared promptly after as soon as they'd made the briefest nod to the social side.

Alexander, of course, had obligations. And complexities. He was working out how to come back to those. Geoffrey would need to know about it. Want to know about it, which was itself a complexity. To be fair, Alexander had had pleasures too. The simple joys of a family Christmas with Thesan's immediate family, full of the sort of delight that became contagious, children's toys and oranges and illusion tales.

It was nothing like his own childhood, and yet he still

soaked it in every time. This year, he'd spent the Boxing Day afternoon with Geoffrey and Lizzie and their children and household. Boxing Day was the more general feast of the estate. That had been a grand time as well, though he was still feeling his way through the dynamics.

It was there that Geoffrey had drawn him aside. Explained he'd made arrangements for something Alexander had thought he'd never have. Without - blast him - giving any hint of how much it had taken to arrange, so Alexander couldn't even weigh the gift appropriately.

Now, though, he could spend a week at Ytene in the winter quiet. Well, unless some Council business was unusually demanding. And of course, it was not as if the rumblings from Germany or Italy, or half a dozen other places had got quieter.

"His lordship is finishing a meeting, sir." That was the exceedingly precise footman, Adams. "He thought perhaps a quarter hour longer."

"If you'd let him know I'm in my rooms once he has time?" This was not a conversation for a public space, even one in this house. "He'll know what I want to talk about that wants a bit of quiet, if this afternoon isn't convenient. I'll have my journal."

"Sir." The footman nodded, and Alexander went up to what now felt like his rooms. He had clothes here, tended to by Geoffrey's own valet. He had brought several books related to ongoing research. Alexander could occupy himself for quite some time.

In the end, it was only twenty minutes. Geoffrey knocked, the particular knock that made Alexander grimace every time, the distinctive beats of the Fifth symphony. Not that it wasn't apropos. "Come."

Geoffrey's head appeared round the door. "I come with drinks and snacks. That particular conversation now?"

"Better than having it looming?" Alexander gestured, and Geoffrey came in, followed by a maid with a tea tray and a bottle of well-aged wine. There were times it was infuriatingly tricky to keep up with Geoffrey's wits, and yet it brought delightful things. Often both in the same paragraph, if not the same sentence.

Once they were settled with the biscuits and the wine and the little tea sandwiches, Geoffrey lifted his glass. "To love and memory."

Alexander didn't hesitate, repeating the toast softly, then drinking a sip. Then he slowed down to savour it. "The wine?"

Geoffrey made a slight gesture at a bow. "The 1870 Margaux."

"My birth year." Which meant the wine was getting on.

"An excellent year, actually, a superb vintage. Papa laid down quite a few cases. There were all the worries about phylloxera, quite understandably. Icy frosts made for a low yield in the harvest, but a scorching summer made the grapes particularly sweet." He lifted his glass. "Suitable, for a man of certain extremes, to share the year. And, like you, it has aged exceptionally well."

Alexander's mouth quirked up at the corner. "You're not at all sure what I'm going to say about your plotting, are you?" He could tell Geoffrey was nervous, he was getting vastly better at spotting the small tells. A twitch of a finger here, one specific note in his voice. Nothing others would pay attention to, other than Lizzie and Benton. Possibly Thesan, the way she'd been watching at some of the gatherings this autumn.

"Well, no." Geoffrey considered. "You're amused. You

didn't turn up furious on the twenty-eighth. But I wasn't going to pry. And besides, you had other places to be for a bit."

That had been true, and it was sensible, done that way. Isembard and Thesan had only well-scheduled moments of leisure, on a timetable they didn't control. And it had, in that moment, been better to be with Isembard, and all they shared.

Alexander nodded. "I am - you have made me speech-less, Geoffrey. So you are aware." That got a glowing beam. Alexander snorted. "Golden One, indeed. You are entirely smug. Tell me how clever you were, then."

Another man might have pressed for a trade in informa-tion there, but Geoffrey was not that man. He settled into the couch, not pressing to lean next to Alexander, though it would come to that in due course, they both knew. "Half a dozen plots. Lizzie helped. Benton, once, and also Rufus."

"Rufus?" Alexander blinked at that. "Oh, wait. I heard something about the Judsons having a difficult horse, didn't I?"

"Who they would very much like to keep in their stud farm, yes, but not if he keeps kicking the stalls down." Geof-frey considered. "I called in several favours, but I'd have spent them all if needed. It helped." That wasn't a question. Something about it shone in Alexander, then.

Alexander took another sip from the incredible wine, and then set it aside, carefully. "Tell me what you know, what you see? I have some language for what I feel, but I don't know - I can't tell, what it's like from the outside."

"The Judsons..." Geoffrey's voice trailed off. "If I am ever so lost in my hurt I'm like that, a decade later, please, do something. Whatever is needed. And they have fixed on you, as the cause. Isembard, less so, but they knew him very differently. They still think of him as an eager schoolfriend, charming and well-mannered."

"Which is not wrong, but is not the man of today, no." Alexander ran his hand through his hair. "They were civil to him. They didn't acknowledge me."

Geoffrey shifted, resting a hand on Alexander's. "Better than it could be. Still awful."

"Quite." That came out dry enough to be a desert.

"That is part of what we were working on at summer solstice, Lizzie and I. When you were rather puzzled by what we were up to. Don't think I didn't notice you paying attention."

"Dweller among the falcons." Sharp-eyed and quick as Geoffrey was, that was an epithet Alexander found himself using often. "Whose favours did you call on?"

"Richard, for an introduction. Alysoun exerted herself socially. If you feel you need to repay any of these small affections, it was hardest on her. She had a bad week, after. Not her favourite people, and she does hate the social obligations that require uncomfortable chairs and tight shoes at the same time."

Alexander nods. "I will make suitable amends, then." He let out a puff of breath. "And then you arranged that we could go there, pour libations, at least. Say whatever prayers I saw fit, so long as they did not linger."

"Not nearly enough, I know. Your magics, Alexander, the family ones, they're meant to last. And I couldn't give you that. They don't understand, their traditions are made of incense and ash. It all goes to the sky, nothing left."

Alexander shook his head. "I do not blame you for that. I'd - I've said the prayers every day. I'm sure even the days I don't remember, until we came back to Dover, I must have. Isembard remembers me saying something incessantly, but languages - especially that set - have never been his gift."

Geoffrey hesitated, making a decision on which way he'd arc. "And now?" He wasn't pressing for what it was like in that moment. What it had been like standing there in front of Perry's very English gravestone, the sort that bore absolutely nothing real of who Perry had been. All rote phrases, and a scarce few words. 'Beloved son, gone too soon'. More than too many got, but not saying anything that held together properly.

"They never knew him. They knew what they wanted him to be, but not him. And I can't say I knew him, either. Or rather, I did, and I didn't, and that was a lot of the joy of it. Figuring things out together, watching him learn who he was. Who he could be."

Geoffrey shifted again, moving so Alexander could rest a hand on his knee, covered immediately by Geoffrey's hand. "Did it help?" There was a definite quaver there.

"It did." Alexander let out a long breath. "It is not the memorial he should have. His name's up in the Council garden, but that's just the name. Cyrus is thinking about how we might better tell the stories of our own, who've died. Not just in the War."

"Huh." That had made Geoffrey sit up and take notice. Interesting. "That's a whole different ritual form."

"Know who we're living for. And who we might die for. Or with." Alexander shook his head. "Ugh, that's a morbid thought. Not today. And there will be the stele here, when it's done, and knowing that was also a great gift. That there will be a place that writes out enough of who he was."

"What - what did Isembard think?"

"He'd been at the funeral, though they didn't have the

stone yet, of course. But he hadn't been back. It did him good. It did him more good to see that I got the chance."

Geoffrey nodded, considering that. "He cares about you a great deal. Even if I'm quite clear that talking about some of that is a trick."

Alexander rubbed his face with his free hand. "I have no idea what he thinks about all this." He gestured at the rooms and the books and Geoffrey beside him. "Things we don't talk about. Or not yet, anyway. For one thing, he hasn't asked."

"You have trained him, Alexander, that asking does not get clear answers."

"The better to surprise him with, yes?" Alexander reached for his wine again. He would enjoy every last drop of that. When he glanced beside him, Geoffrey was looking at him with something that wasn't a puppy's adoration, but had something of that quality. "You were exceedingly clever, Geoffrey, and I am quite sure you know it."

"I like to hear it very much." Geoffrey beamed back at him. "That's the problem with not letting it show most of the time. Almost no one appreciates my skills."

"You may be quite sure I intend to continue appreciating them for some time to come." Alexander paused. "It isn't your cleverness I have come to care for. It's your kindness. The way you grant and share space."

"Even if I have been known to hog the blankets." There was the outright teasing. Last time Alexander was here overnight, before Solstice, they'd ended up curled up on Alexander's bed, talking through a bit of politics, until they both fell asleep.

"You do. But I don't particularly mind. I've certainly had far worse places to sleep." Alexander shrugged. "Do you have plans for the next few days? I have my usual Wednesday, but I'm somewhat at loose ends until then."

"There are always the mews." Geoffrey was irrepressible there. "And I've got training to do. The covered ring is a gift, this time of year. We don't have to do it in the mud. But you like watching."

"Who is it, the grey mare?" Who was exceptionally clever, and he suspected Geoffrey had ideas about what to do with her.

"Mm hmm. And the chestnut, we're thinking she'll be a suitable next mount for Edmund." Who, at nine and a half, should have something more energetic than an older pony. "But she needs a bit more training first to learn her manners." They settled into an agreeable conversation about which parts of that plan might best be scheduled, and Alexander mentioned a few of the things he was reading up on.

It wasn't until nearly supper that Geoffrey spoke about the grave again. "You asked me how you are. You seem more mended. Less edged about it. You used to be like the sphinx, largely whole but battered. And now, it's as if you've been smoothed out. No longer jagged, lasting through the time, more sure of coming out the other side. Does that make sense?"

"I suppose it does." Alexander hadn't known what he expected from the grave. Certainly he hadn't expected words of comfort, or anything obvious to change. "I dreamt of him that night. So did Isembard, he said. A kind dream. Not the nightmares we both have about that last day. Not being quick enough. But Perry, laughing and teasing, the magic lapping at him, eager for his attention."

He didn't remember the dream exactly. It had faded as soon as he woke, and the magic of dreams was not remotely his usual line of magic. It was one of the skills of his mother's side that he'd never had a gift for. "Like it opened a door and left the key in my hand."

"That will do very well, then." Geoffrey leaned over and kissed his cheek. "Supper and some music in the library. And then I can come back up with you and we can wrangle over that translation for a bit before bed."

That was a very fine evening indeed.

VERNAL EQUINOX

Alexander came out of the portal to find Geoffrey waiting for him, bouncing lightly on his toes. "Come see!" Something about him was boyish, a pure delight in the world that had not been squashed.

Alexander handed his bag off to the footman and shook his head. "You are impossible."

"Entirely possible. I exist, q.e.d. I am possible. That's first year Trivium. First month, even." Geoffrey led the way, one of the winding paths back behind the cultivated parts of the garden, not quite skipping.

Alexander shook his head. He had not intended to come out this close to the equinox, but Thesan and Isembard were at Arundel for the day with Garin and Livia, and he - well. He missed Geoffrey. Besides whatever surprise awaited.

Geoffrey didn't quite reach for his hand, and he wasn't quite doing laps around Alexander, waiting for him to catch up. But it was a near thing. "You're very eager."

That got another bounce on his toes. "Do you trust me? To blindfold you and lead you along?"

Alexander stopped dead, blinking. "Out here?"

"I promise you'll be safe. We're not far now. A twist of the path."

Alexander sighed. "You're going to be miserable if I say no, aren't you?"

It wasn't that Geoffrey pouted. He had more sense. But he would have expectations, usually about some gift of pleasure that only Alexander could provide, or Lizzie or Benton or sometimes Rufus. And it was terribly hard to deny him. Especially since he never pressed about it, just lit up his hopeful enjoyment to perfection, drawing Alexander back to the question over and over again.

He let out a long, slow breath, considering. "You promise." It wasn't a question, so much as making sure all of Alexander's mind heard it properly.

Geoffrey turned around, taking both of his hands and squeezing. "I promise."

"All right. You realise I've not let someone do this since my own training." And now, it brought back the memories of that, the quiver of uncertainty of it.

"Ah." Geoffrey hesitated. "I would trust you to keep your eyes closed, if you'd prefer."

Wasn't that just like Geoffrey? Letting him choose. He shook his head. "The blindfold. Just - be aware." His voice cracked on the last part.

Geoffrey shifted to kiss his cheek and then pulled a very long silk square out of an inside pocket. He had, indeed, come prepared. Once it was folded over properly, Geoffrey arranged it, checked. "All good?"

"Smoothly tied, and I can't see a thing." Alexander

couldn't, either. Geoffrey had practice at this, and the blindfold itself was almost comfortable.

"Here we go." Alexander had expected that Geoffrey would take both his hands, that this would be awkward and ungainly, but of course not. He'd seen Geoffrey guide Giles often enough, when neither Kate nor the guide dog was available or suitable. One hand on Geoffrey's arm, tucked in above his elbow, and Alexander could feel quite easily as Geoffrey moved forward.

They went on, perhaps two hundred feet, with an occasional comment about a stone or a softer bit of ground, until they stepped up on a small wooden something. A bridge, perhaps. Ten steps along it, then Geoffrey said. "Keep your eyes closed until I say, if you would? You've about two feet to either side, and a bit of a drop, so don't move yet."

"As you wish." A moment later, the knot was untied, the scarf removed from his head.

Then Geoffrey took his hand again. "Open your eyes, do."

What Alexander saw was a blanket of colour. A sparkling, twinkling white, from the trees around this meadow. Only a meadow because the leaves of the larger trees were not yet unfurled from the early buds. The ground, though, the ground shimmered with something that made him think of the aurora Thesan had shown him, on three nights. Only instead of shades of green or red, this was a vibrant blue-purple. Not the royal red-purple of Fox House, but something far gentler and a balm for the soul.

"Hester's Blackthorn, and the Celestial Bluebells." Geoffrey's voice almost surprised him. He'd been so lost in the shades of colour and beauty visible from everywhere he looked. "They usually don't bloom together. This year, though." He sounded like it was all his doing, and also like it was a great miracle.

Alexander let out a long whistle. "This is..." Then he asked, "The others have seen it?"

"Everyone who lives here. I was thinking we might invite Thesan and Isembard, the Edgartons, and whoever else can shake free for the afternoon tomorrow?"

Alexander was looking around, the way the green contrasted against the shimmers of the blackthorn. "Your alchemist?"

"Already been." Geoffrey gestured at the far corner, where some branches had been carefully harvested. "And now deep in his laboratory, I'm sure."

That made Alexander laugh. "Well. This is." He shook his head. "It's pure, somehow, isn't it? Untouched."

"You can't - they don't yield to agriculture. Even ordinary bluebells don't really, you can encourage them, but you can't make them."

"Isn't that like most plants?" Not, admittedly, Alexander's best field, though he was better on their uses.

Geoffrey snorted and slipped his arm through Alexander's. "Worth the blindfold?"

"Oh, yes. Though if we're bringing them out the same way, let me take Isembard."

"He's still not sure what to make of me, then?" Geoffrey was not offended, that much was clear.

Alexander shook his head. "It's not that. He's still not got past my talking about Perry. Or that I'm happy. How I'm happy. He's glad I'm happy. He's actually been very articulate about that, considering? But the reality of it is more wide-ranging than he's sorted out yet."

"And Thesan?" Geoffrey's question was entirely reasonable, especially in context, but as soon as Alexander heard it, he started laughing and couldn't stop.

Eventually, Geoffrey shifted to thump him on the back. "Breathe. I am not explaining how you were felled by a two word question, not to anyone."

That made Alexander chuckle. "Well." He let out a breath. "Saves me figuring out how to bring it up. So they get off to Essex for hols, and of course, I go up. I could tell Thesan had been chewing on something. It's not like she tries to hide it from me."

"Or from Isembard." Geoffrey agreed. "But she hadn't told him what it was?"

"Not in this case, no. I expect she might eventually, but she needs more observational data." Alexander waved a hand. "Do you want to know, or don't you?"

"Oh, I always want to know." That had a decided purr to it. Geoffrey might want to give gifts to people, of all sorts, but he also loved those tidbits of information, the rare ones.

Alexander considered. "So. Isembard's down in the salle for a couple of hours - ongoing training for a couple of his current students, when no one had to worry about the class timetable. And we're in the library."

"As you often are, it's a fine library. Homey." Geoffrey approved of libraries being loved. As did Alexander, really. Besides the other virtues of a library, the books and stores of knowledge.

"Thesan gave me tea, and then she made sure I was not currently drinking the tea. And what she asked was, 'You know he's in love with you, right?' No antecedent. Not that she needed one."

"My. Goodness." After those two words, Geoffrey broke into warm laughter, delighted. "I didn't think..."

"That she'd ask straight out? Oh, it gets better." Alexander shook his head.

"What did you say to that? I am, naturally, absurdly curious." Geoffrey's eyes were gleaming now, rather like sharp-eyed Athena's must have.

"I'm aware." Alexander let that settle. "That's what I said. My tone, I admit, might have been a tad less than stoic."

"You are excellent at negotiation and diplomacy, and at making your comments quite neutral." Geoffrey gave credit where credit was certainly due. "But this was Thesan."

"And she's got under my defences from nearly the first day we met." Alexander shook his head, thinking back on that. "She doesn't let it drop, of course. Next she says, 'So you haven't talked about it?'"

"Because, all the ways you are known to be, you wouldn't. You might not be cruel and toy with my affections, but we certainly wouldn't talk about it. Sensibly." Geoffrey snorted, rightfully confident in that part. As if Alexander could. He might yet be able to walk away, though he honestly didn't give himself good odds on succeeding there. But toy in cruelty? No. Never.

"Except, of course, that she has had an impact on me, and Lizzie has on you and various other people. And so, in fact, we do talk, even if we do not always bother to spell it all out." Alexander considered. "We left it at my amused repetition of her name, and she is, at least for the moment, satisfied enough."

Geoffrey looked out at the sea of purple, then at the shimmering white, as if he were letting it blanket him. "And so now you're thinking about what you tell them. When you tell them."

Alexander let out a long breath. "Yes. Because it is them.

She might not talk to Isembard about suspicions. Especially while he's still working through his own feelings in other directions. But once she knows? She won't keep secrets from him, and she shouldn't. She hasn't been bent and broken like we have, and may she never be."

Geoffrey nodded. "Let me think a little about it. Can you stay for supper?"

"If you don't mind having me." There was a momentary flash of something in Geoffrey's eyes that made Alexander blink. "Perhaps a conversation, in private. After supper, no sense in wasting the afternoon and these blooms."

They spent the afternoon amiably exploring the pathways and the other spring plantings, circling back for Geoffrey to check on the healing well. Supper was, as always, a delight, with some of the early plants coming in. Once they were well fed, Geoffrey came upstairs with him. They settled, as they had rather a lot in the past few months, on the bed, where they could lean and talk more comfortably.

"You had something to talk about, in specific?" Geoffrey was positively lounging, and Alexander savoured the moment. He had guesses about what might happen next, and it deserved time to unfurl properly.

"It has to do with seeing you over the course of a year. Seeing you on your land, in particular." Alexander waved a hand. "Wrong possessive, I know, but we don't have a full enough range of grammar in English, do we? The way things are between the land and you."

"And?" Geoffrey looked at him, head cocked to one side now. "It has been a year, though, yes. And a smattering of days."

It made Alexander laugh. "Yes. That too." He swallowed hard. "Again, I don't have the language for this. And I've certainly never talked about it with anyone else." He could feel Geoffrey's quivering attentiveness, the way it was utterly flattering. Also, not that Alexander would ever say this out loud, a bit terrifying. All that raw power focused on him. Alexander was beginning to understand much more thoroughly why other people thought him intense.

"Go on?"

"I said that I've never had any attraction, nothing remotely like what men talk about, to anyone other than the lady of the land. Whatever shape she takes."

"Yes?" Geoffrey was pacing himself. Alexander could hear that. Oh, he was being so cautious.

"Seeing you come into the spring, I - you mentioned, more than once, you would be glad to indulge my curiosity. And I might, perhaps, be." Alexander let out a puff of breath. "Be interested. At least in the discussion."

"Oh." Then Geoffrey lit up. "Oh!" Alexander could see the various permutations whirring through his head. He had to assume Geoffrey had given some thought to the matter. He'd made the offer out in the open, twice. Once to make it, once to be clear he'd meant it. But he'd let it drop after that, leaving it entirely up to Alexander. "Do you want me to fetch some books?"

"The books might be a help." Alexander rubbed his face. "I don't even entirely know what to ask. I had the usual sort of not sufficiently informative lecture from my brother. And of course, one hears all manner of things."

"And just as in ritual work or duelling, people do exaggerate their wands." Geoffrey grinned. "Back in a couple. Books will help, at least, illustrating the range of possibilities. You needn't do anything at all, of course. Even look at them. But I would like to be prepared."

When Alexander nodded, Geoffrey paused just long enough to lean forward and kiss his cheek, as if he had been given a delightful gift, just in the asking. Alexander watched him go, letting the sense of the magic wash over him again.

There was decidedly something about spring in the air. He'd had - well. Not the sort of response he gathered was routine for other men. But far more than he had felt in the past, about anything other than the lady he'd seen in his Council trials. He could feel it bubbling through Geoffrey, much more so than even a fortnight ago.

And it wouldn't do any harm to have a more educated mind. If nothing else, he could be sure that Geoffrey's explanations, whatever they were, would be fair-minded and expansive.

It took some time for Geoffrey to come back. A good twenty minutes, but he brought over four books, then went back out. He came back with another bottle of wine and a few other things he deposited on a chair that Alexander couldn't see. "There. Get comfortable, somewhere we can set these out. I brought the copies, rather than the originals, which are beautiful things, but a bit delicate to handle." He spread out the books. "A mix of styles and, mmm, areas of interest. Do you want to look through first, or would you rather I talk?"

"Oh, I think I'd rather hear your thoughts directly." Alexander managed to make that into a bit of a purr himself, and was rewarded by Geoffrey lighting up with delight. Well, lighting up more. He was decidedly a Golden One now, fit to rival the noonday summer sun.

"You might have trouble getting me to stop." But Geoffrey settled with the books in easy reach. "There are a number of things that men can do together, but the - well. The land magics do come back to a certain amount of symbolic references around one object going into another.

Swords and sheaths, swords and lakes, men into hidden places under the ground." He flipped his hand over.

"I know the ritual theory and symbolism, yes. But making it personal, that's something different, isn't it?

"Well, yes. For one thing, it's not just about your preferences, or about the other person's, it's about finding a place in between." Geoffrey contemplated. "Mind, I have fairly wide-ranging tastes, and with you, well. Wider than most others. It gives some scope. May I ask what you are interested in, broadly speaking?"

Alexander hesitated. He could lay it out here and now, or he could duck it forever. And he was coming to realise that if he did that, he would feel the loss. Not the notional sex itself. That was still for him, somewhat beside the point. But the intimacy of this conversation, of whatever might follow.

"You. The land magic. The way you're tangled up in the land magic." He ran his hand over his face. "Is that offensive? It feels like it ought to be."

"You have been entirely clear, Alexander, of your feelings and preferences. To be wanted for my land magic, in any sort of physical sense, is rather more than I expected you might be interested in. And, well. It is part of me, isn't it? It's not like I could set it aside if we wanted to. Especially in spring. Spring makes me lusty."

"Lusty, is it? And what does that mean?"

"Well, largely, it means that Lizzie and I schedule at least an hour of time each day when we're both free and likely to be awake to tend to matters. From, oh, about now to summer solstice. Not that we are, well, like rabbits, necessarily?"

Alexander raised his eyebrow at that. "You protest too much, Geoffrey. Like an untried youth."

Geoffrey blushed charmingly. "Age does slow one down a tad. Though honestly I prefer it to my youth, erotically speaking. But it's much easier to have the time set aside, and then curl up and do something else, than have to try to scrabble for our mutual satisfaction. Eagerness is one thing, scrabbling for the fastest possible encounter is undignified. Most of the time."

"That is rather more about your private life with Lizzie than I was asking, for the record." Alexander rubbed the bridge of his nose. "And what - what does that mean if we were to, I don't know. Talk through options, and then perhaps make some time to explore them?"

"I'd suggest just after Beltane for that. When I am most in the lady's sway, as it were, and particularly eager to join in anything that brings that pleasure. There are the rituals, and - well. We're taking the usual sort of precautions to avoid more children. Lizzie's at the age where it's a bit more risk, and we are entirely happy with our three. But there is something, when it comes to May Day itself, and the flourishing of the land, in a pair that is at least notionally open to procreation."

Somehow, the diversion into ritual implications made the whole thing easier, rather than ridiculous to discuss. "So, you at the height of the - um. Flourishing." There was no way around the innuendo inherent in the conversation, though.

"That next day, the second or third? The second's a Saturday, plenty of time without rushing?"

"We haven't even decided we're doing anything yet." Alexander held up his hands. "I don't, this is." He shook his head. "We are flipping back and forth between the intellectual and physical, the theoretical and the sensual, and I am no longer sure where my footing is."

"Here, then, let me make this easier and harder." The gleam in Geoffrey's eyes made his intention with that wordplay clear. "I cannot think of anything in the realm of sex you might want to do with me that I would decline out of hand. There are a few matters we might discuss for safety, but I don't think you're inclined to them right off, anyway."

"You would - I mean." Alexander wasn't sure how to continue.

"If you are in this for the land magic, then, logically, I am the land, and you are the ..." Geoffrey snorted, waving his fingers idly. "Oh, goodness, it does sound like a rather bad novel, doesn't it? Not a rampaging knight. I'm sure you could rampage if you wanted to, but it doesn't go with your mode this season of life at all." He stretched out, arching with amusement.

"You don't mind that?" Alexander wasn't sure how to ask what he was asking.

"First, there are quite a few ways to have pleasure, and we can discuss those in a minute. But yes, to be entirely straightforward about it, if you wished to be the one inside me, I would be delighted. It has been some time, there's some preparation to do. Quite pleasant, on several fronts."

"I do not believe you." Alexander rubbed his face again. "You're certain."

"Certain that I would like very much to explore whatever touches you might permit, to show you all the pleasure I can, to let you find what you desire? Oh, yes. The form that takes matters a great deal less to me."

Alexander swallowed. "What - I must trust, I think, to your experience here. How would you want to begin?" His voice did not tremble at the last few words, but it was only through sheer raw stubbornness that he managed it.

"Well. First, I know an extensive range of charms suitable for pleasure in bed. Pleasure in other places, too, but bed is both traditional and comfortable. Warmth, sensation, trailing arousal in the wake of my fingers, all sorts of things. You can take the books with you, see if anything strikes your fancy. Several of them are fantastic for knots in the shoulders, or along the spine, too. Or there's that spot on your hip you favour."

Alexander grunted. He could feel that one now, a knob of tenderness that ebbed and flowed and never fully went away. Something aggravated a long time ago that hadn't quite settled. "You suggest a massage, then?"

"A fine way to get comfortable with touch. Though I had - I do like to kiss. A number of men don't, especially not for a fleeting engagement."

"My cheek. I'd noticed."

Geoffrey snorted. "Mouths are different. Whether you care for it or not, that's another question. But there's an intimacy to mouths. Right up close. No hiding."

"I cannot decide if that makes it more intriguing or more terrifying." Alexander shifted, blinking at Geoffrey several times.

"How is this, then?" Geoffrey rearranged on the bed. "May we try a kiss or two now? You are welcome to touch me wherever you like. We both know I'm perfectly capable of tending to my own needs as things come up." He waited a beat. "Pun entirely intended."

"You are - as you said, quite possible. You are a ridiculous flirt when you think you can get away with it. That's what you are."

"Only with the best people." Geoffrey shifted then, shrugging out of his smoking jacket, leaving him in shirtsleeves and trousers. It was, Alexander admitted to himself, an aesthetically pleasing sort of show, in a particularly masculine mode. Once Geoffrey was stretched out again, he considered. "Will you let me guide things for the moment? For the sake of both our noses?"

The tone there made Alexander snort. "Can't have both of us going around with bruises. That would worry Thesan and Isembard quite a lot." He nodded.

Geoffrey didn't rush. He moved as deliberately as he did in any ritual, any time in the workroom. It had been that, Alexander realised, that had made him interested in trying this, as well as the land magic. Or rather, the land magic was why he was interested, but the dance Geoffrey made of his movements made him feel this had any chance of working. A man who moved like Geoffrey did among the ritual tools and tables, the diagrams on the floor or wall, he'd do the same when it was a finger or hand or leg in play.

Or mouths. While he'd been thinking, Geoffrey had shifted closer, enough that Alexander could feel the warmth of another body against his legs, not quite touching, but almost. And then there was Geoffrey's hand on his shoulder, steadying, and the tilt of his head and lips pressed against his.

At first, it did nothing for him. It was not unpleasant, no more than a brush on his cheek or hair were as signs of affection and connection. A thing he would gladly do if it made Geoffrey happy, but where he'd probably choose those other things himself.

Only then he could feel a pressure there, a tongue against the line of his lips where they met. It was a kind of yielding that was, yes, absurdly intimate. Both the thing itself, and the implications, for other parts of the body. That intimacy, that intrigued him. He could feel a slight hum, the one he'd come to associate with the land magic. Still quiet and subtle, it was still early in the growing season.

He opened his mouth to it, and then it was something like a dance, forward and retreat, Geoffrey clearly encouraging him to explore it. Back and forth they went, several times, before Geoffrey pulled back, his eyes gleaming now. "More?"

"I thought you said you didn't duel?" It had a feel of that, somehow, the interchanges and the way the rhythms of it felt, how his response depended on what came before. He realised how much of the experience other people left out - well, he'd always known the crude comments he'd heard were leaving out whole libraries of experience.

Geoffrey laughed. "It can be a duel, but - mmm. That's an advanced lesson." Then he caught something in Alexander's eyes. There was a soft grunt, the sort Alexander had learned to translate accurately as Geoffrey being caught by some physical aspect of his desire. They were still not touching, other than a hand on Alexander's shoulder, but after a moment, Alexander shifted his hand to rest cautiously on Geoffrey's rib cage.

"Oh, yes." That was a drawn-out sigh, then Geoffrey flushed. "I, before you do anything else, you - I am finding this decidedly arousing. To be clear. You needn't do anything about that, but if you move, it's going to be obvious."

That, well. It wasn't like it hadn't happened with Geoffrey before. Only this time, the way they were, the things they were talking about, Alexander considered. If he asked, he knew Geoffrey would excuse himself in due course. He'd disappear to the bathing room, and come out a few minutes later, flushed and tousled.

"If I were to touch you, would you like that?" It was a

foolish question. He knew what the answer was going to be. "Dweller in his house, can you tell me what you are thinking?"

Geoffrey was nearly overthrown. His head went back, arching beautifully. Any sensible Renaissance artist would have painted this, a fully grown man at his pleasure, surrounded by his dreams, rather than younger men made of muscles and little sense. It wasn't just Geoffrey arching in pleasure; it was how he let himself roll into it, let Alexander see that, before he could find words for it. "Your hand on me. Pressing, just - pressure. If I could have anything right now."

It was such a small thing, and it was a thing that Alexander felt he could, in fact, do. It did not ask for skill or subtlety, or for dexterity. Good thing, too. He was not sure how eagerly they would come to his call right now. Something in Geoffrey's expression overthrew him, as well. As if they were both caught in some realm made purely of magic. Somewhere where being honest was possible, where they did not have to reach for everything now, because there would be a later.

He wanted to linger here forever. To remember what it felt like when wanting things was safer. He suspected Geoffrey felt much the same, if for different reasons. Then he remembered to speak. "Then I shall." He swallowed. "Another kiss, please."

Geoffrey's chin snapped back. "Oh. Oh, yes." He leaned, making the angles work, but then he waited, letting Alexander shift his head to close the distance. This time, it wasn't Alexander yielding to that clever tongue, but exploring himself. His hand felt like it was in the wrong place. He thought about moving it between them, but then all his instincts, such as they were, wanted to tangle fingers in Geoffrey's hair.

As he did that, as he felt the curve of skull and the silk of hair, he shifted his lower body. Not far, but it didn't need to be far. Hip near enough against hip, thigh touching thigh, and it drove Geoffrey to a moan. Loud, pantingly eager, against the kiss. Alexander pursued that, wanting that reaction above anything else. Wanting to know what happened if he did this thing, or that thing.

They played with it, Alexander pressing and relaxing. Pausing here and there to let them both breathe before they fell back into it. It couldn't have been terribly long, in absolute terms. He felt Geoffrey's hips hitch against his once, then again, and dropped his hand down, to cup a hip not his own. That broke the kiss long enough to get a torrent of begging, "Please, your hand, there, oh, if you would."

So careful, even in this moment, when he was quivering with need. Alexander sucked in another breath before leaning into the kiss again and letting his hand fall between them. It was awkward, of course. All the angles were things he'd learned to avoid in all his years teaching ritual and duelling. But then, there was Geoffrey's body, the feel of his desire and need.

Alexander managed to twist his wrist, and then Geoffrey was rolling against his palm, hips driving against his touch. It lasted only a half-dozen arcing jerks. Geoffrey pulled his mouth back, hand tightening on Alexander's shoulder, and shouted his pleasure, a bellow of resonance that echoed in the room. Alexander could feel how his body shuddered, how the gasps shook his chest, how he gave himself entirely over to the moment. And, of course, a slight but obvious spreading warm dampness through his clothing.

And that, oh. That was power, that was connection. That was the moment he'd chased since his challenge. Not remotely the same, but far closer than he'd come in decades.

Geoffrey whimpered once, as he began to settle, burrowing in against Alexander's chest without asking. Not that he needed to. This part they had done enough that Alexander felt comfortable with it. It was only then that Alexander realised what his own body was telling him. That something in that had had just a bit of arousal to it for him, as well. Nothing so direct or active or loud as Geoffrey, not remotely. But something.

The magic, it must be, that hum of the land magic, which he could feel far more now. Something in the moment.

It took a good five minutes for Geoffrey to stir, but he made no attempt to pull away at first. It was only when he'd gathered himself that Geoffrey shifted enough to look at Alexander. "I—"

"Hush." Alexander shifted his hand to brush his thumb against Geoffrey's cheek. "Yes. The second. Yes. I don't know - I don't know what I'll be up for. Pun intended. But I am glad to explore."

Geoffrey blinked, and then kissed him, this time fast and delighted, before he pulled back to flop more on his back. The bad shoulder must have been bothering him. He'd been leaning on it for quite a while. "You mean it." It wasn't a question, it wasn't the kind of thing they made into questions. "I should wash up. And then we can look at the books, and you can ask questions. Now. Later. Whatever you like."

It was, admittedly, a delight to see all of that pleasure bubbling over. "You are a hedonist." Alexander shook his head. "Go do what you need, and yes. Books. Show me your extensive learning, please."

Geoffrey laughed, and then moved to sit, then stand, unselfconscious. "Back in a few."

Alexander watched him go. He was, as he had often been this past year, unsure what he'd got into. But the last year had taught him, if anything, that his willingness to trust would be rewarded. Here, if nowhere else.

LATE SPRING

THESAN AND ISEMBARD'S ROOMS, APRIL

In the space between equinox and May Day, Alexander found himself paying close attention to a whole language of interaction he'd previously brushed over. He was, of course, well-attuned to the various social graces and weapons, both local and foreign. But now he found himself drawn to how people showed affection.

He was sure, almost immediately, that Geoffrey and Lizzie had been restraining themselves, when it came to those signs of affection around him. After that conversation in his rooms, with the pillow books and explanations, and the fumbling explorations, they let him see more. Casual brushes of fingers, kisses, an abundance of physical affection that seemed stereotypically un-English.

He'd had a couple of rounds more with Geoffrey, nothing more than they had already done, other than getting the breadth of the charms for touch and pleasure. Warmth, as Geoffrey had said, the kind of warmth that lingered and infused everything and made it better, mostly.

A fortnight later, he'd been up in Thesan and Isembard's rooms after a bohort match. Isembard was reading stories, and Thesan had been puttering in their small kitchen, putting together a tray. When she brought it out and set it down, she straightened. "You were watching us more closely than usual this afternoon. And at supper."

Alexander hadn't meant to let it show. "Was I?"

"I don't think anyone else noticed." Thesan settled in her usual spot on the smaller sofa. She picked up her bottle of cider, gesturing for him to take his cup of coffee and whatever other treats he liked.

"Even Isembard?" Alexander had to grin at that.

"Take it up with him yourself. In a few." However, Thesan looked very pleased at something, and Alexander was suddenly sure they'd made some sort of bet about it. Or something related. And she had just won. She usually did win, mind, the fun of it was apparently in seeing how her bets played out.

"I was thinking about how you are in public. The, um. Signs of affection?"

"Were you?" That had a thoughtful sound to it. "Not your usual sort of topic, Alexander."

He shrugged. "I was thinking about Geoffrey and Lizzie - I can't tell if their current mood is the springtime or something else."

"Well, not just the springtime, or we'd see something else out of Garin and Livia." Thesan wrinkled her nose. "Though, all right, I think it's partly the spring in the case under consideration." She shrugged. "At home, yes, not out in the world?"

"Yes. Though they do show more affection there than most. I was thinking it rather un-English."

That made Thesan throw her head back and laugh.

"Your assumptions about class are catching up with you, Alexander. Take your average working-class family, and there's a certain amount of honest wenchery to be had. Of course people aren't nearly so affectionate when it's an arranged match for the sake of the family holdings, or a slim choice among the few approved peers and near-equals. Why Garin and Livia aren't happy. Well, one of a number of reasons."

Alexander was curious what she'd put on that list, but not right now. "And you and Isembard?"

That made her laugh again, amused and including him in it. "Two reasons. We live among a horde of young people, with their own passions and desires and a lot of very impulsive potential decisions hovering just under the surface. There's a line to being a model for how a loving relationship can look. Certainly, a fair number of them desperately need it. To see that it's a possible thing in the world."

Alexander inclined his head. "I certainly didn't grow up with one. And - well. Neither did Garin and Isembard, though their parents were at least the pleasantly distant sort rather than actively battling."

"Where I grew up with parents who still adore each other. They can't think of a better night than being curled up, one of them reading aloud, the other doing something with their hands. To be fair, that describes Dilly and Seth and Golshan, too."

Isembard came back in at that point, snagging a bottle of cider for himself and settling with a sigh, one arm immediately curling around Thesan's shoulders. "And you would too, except there are stars in the night. What are we talking about?"

"Shows of affection. I was pointing out the challenge of students. And how they need a model of appropriate restraint, at least in the classrooms and public spaces of the..." She paused as a charm sound like a bell went off. "My turn."

She was pulling on her teaching robe with its full sleeves as she went out the door. Alexander looked after her. "How often does that happen?"

"It's spring. About every three nights? We take it in turns to roust out whichever pair has got it in their heads that the astronomy platform would be a fine place for whatever they want to get up to in private. The third years are particularly, well, something this year. Eventually, they'll get a clue. Or I'll put the proportionate fear of something into them during physical training class. You want to wait for her to come back?"

Alexander did, and so they passed the next five minutes until Thesan came back in talking about the match and the potential gifts of the players.

"Certain people are getting reported to their Heads of House, that's the second time they've tried since we got back." She gave the names, not anyone Alexander knew, or particularly their families. "Did you keep going?"

"We got off onto bohort, of course. What was your other point?"

"Much the same as I made about families in general, your first year here. That I know people's histories well enough to know what would be unkind. Pross and Ibis are also very happily matched, of course, and long may we all be so. But Borea misses her husband. There's a couple of awkwardly ended romances for other people. And of course, it's only in the last five years or so that our junior librarian has given Isembard the time of day. Or me."

Isembard rubbed his face. "I'd apologise again, only..."

"That's not the point." Thesan twisted to kiss his cheek

as he put his hand down. "We talked it through, quite explicitly. By which I mean I laid out what I thought would suit. Isembard asked for three modifications, and we've kept up with it ever since."

"I was, of course, trusting to her greater tactical sense of the school and knowledge of individual histories." Isembard said, amused. "When you have an expert on hand, take their advice. First rule of most magic."

Alexander snorted, since he'd been the one to teach that to Isembard, once upon a time. "Fair, fair. So you are more relaxed here, or with Pross and Ibis, as near enough matched peers. And more restrained other places."

"Also, why we carefully rotate who we sit with at meals. At least a meal together every day, of course, plus whatever other time we carve out, but also at least one meal a day where we're talking to other people." Lunch, usually, since the supper table arrangements tended to run more formally, and Thesan never made it downstairs for breakfast.

"What brought on the topic, Alexander?"

As he was trying to figure out how to answer it, Thesan said, cheerfully opaque, "Springtime."

THE GREENING OF THE YEAR

YTENE, MAY 2ND

On the second of May, Alexander turned up at Ytene just before luncheon, as requested. The Carillons had had their obligations to the land and village yesterday, which included Geoffrey thoroughly bedding his wife, as well. And while Alexander would have been welcome for some of that, he'd felt like it was too much, as if he'd give something away.

He handed his case over to the footman and went first to the garden. The stele would be ready later this summer, and they planned to install it on the anniversary. It seemed as good a day as any. He had no idea what Perry would have made of his life now, no idea what Perry's life would have looked like. It seemed a distant world, now, to think about.

As he came into the manor, Geoffrey was waiting, pulling him into a tight embrace. "Lunch, a walk, and whatever pleases you? I've a few new books, just came in from the sales."

The afternoon was delightful - the weather seemed to bend to their desires. The walk turned into a stint training the falcons, with Lizzie along as well, afternoon rounds with the stable. Then Alexander had been shooed off to have whatever sort of bath he wanted.

Someone - Geoffrey, presumably - had added several new bottles of bath oils to his bathing room. One was far more French, one more Egyptian thick with spices, and one made of English flowers with a leavening of heather and pine. He sniffed the first two, but the third one was right. It was made for his life, not the ones his parents had wanted, or anyone else.

The supper was delectable, but Alexander did not pay it due attention, he was sure. Everything felt anticipatory. He found himself weighing every small movement differently. It was foolish, and yet at the same time, entirely logical. He'd felt much the same in some of his apprenticeship, before going into a new ritual. Certainly, before his challenge for the Council.

Finally, they were upstairs in his rooms. Someone had slipped in while they were finishing the meal and dimmed the lights to a warm gentle glow. They'd adjusted the temperature charms to something pleasant on bare skin, and left a covered tray in the bedroom, as well as a bottle of some sort of wine.

Alexander looked around and couldn't repress a shiver. Geoffrey's hand was immediately on his back, between his shoulder blades. "I will stop, any time you say. You are the one in control here. Whatever we get up to."

"And you like that." Alexander half-turned. "You think it's a good idea."

They'd talked, the past five weeks, about what they

might both enjoy. He'd been competent to coax Geoffrey's preferences from him. Or rather, once they'd got started, they'd flooded out, as if Geoffrey had been waiting to speak them. How Geoffrey wanted to watch his face, and to be watched. The ways that might work, man with man. Their options, if Alexander wanted to attempt penetration. What they might do instead, if that didn't seem likely. Geoffrey had, in a way that made Alexander flustered, explained how to tell what was needed.

And of course, they'd talked about what supplies might be useful. Geoffrey kissed his cheek now, and went to a panel by the bed, tapping it in that distinctive da-da-da-dum pattern, releasing a hidden cabinet door. He removed a bottle, the lubricant they'd discussed, as well as a folded pile of clothes. "For those things you wish to keep entirely private between us. It will only open to you or to me, at least once you attune to it."

"Do you think of absolutely everything?" Alexander was deeply amused now.

"It is a challenge that suits my talents, don't you think? Do you want to slip into something more, shall we say, adaptable? Dressing gown?" Geoffrey's own was lying over the end of the bed, on the other side from Alexander's.

"Who set up things in here?" Who else knew? That was the question.

"Benton. Who else would I trust with something this important? Or, well, Lizzie might have, but she was down at supper." And Benton had slipped away for some task, unspecified, while they were enjoying the after-dinner drinks on the terrace.

"Point underlined. You do think of everything."

Geoffrey turned to him, head tilted. "Why wouldn't I,

when it's for you?" He gestured. "Staring at the dressing gowns won't change anything."

Alexander snorted and picked his dressing gown up. Before he could decide what to do about changing, Geoffrey snagged his and strode off to the bathroom with a cheerful. "Back in a moment."

He had a plan. Well, being Geoffrey, he likely had ten plans and a series of themes and variations prepared for each. It wasn't as if Alexander could fault his planning ability. His part was to change into the dressing gown, leaving it belted, his clothes folded over the clothes press for someone to deal with in the morning.

Geoffrey came out, cheerfully clad in draping silk. It was a dressing gown Alexander hadn't seen yet, a green patterned with growing vines, trimmed in a tawny brown, the less common of the Owl colours. "Is that new for the occasion?"

"Oh, yes. Something to remember the day by." Geoffrey pivoted, bowed, and then came to take Alexander's hand. "Come be comfortable, at least. We won't rush. I have plenty of distractions."

He did, too. They settled in, facing each other, with Geoffrey leaning on his right shoulder. Alexander had been right about that, the first night, that it had been more uncomfortable than Geoffrey had admitted in the moment. Two minutes in, they were having a rousing conversation about a book they'd both been reading, and both wanted to deconstruct from different perspectives. Ten minutes after that, Alexander's hand was resting on Geoffrey's, feeling the beat of the magic.

Five minutes further on, Geoffrey came to the end of a comment, then looked up through his eyelashes. "You can feel it, can't you? All of that desire bubbling up? In me, at least."

His cheeks were a little flushed, as if this had been a particular kind of foreplay. Alexander couldn't quite venture to glance and see if there was a more direct reaction, but he could lean in, kissing. He'd learned the angles well enough. Their lips met and Geoffrey let out one of those sighs.

When Alexander pulled back, he arched an eyebrow. "Does it always hum in you like that? Last year, how has it been a year?"

"Less so when I'm somewhere else. But - yes. It's there, like a river. The magic doing what she will, whether I am paying attention or not. You, though." His mouth was open, breathy, as if Geoffrey were giving himself more over to the moment with every beat of his heart. "Having all your attention fixed on me? I suspect if you wanted you could bring me to shouts of pleasure with your voice alone. Exceptionally fine voice, mind, and you know how to use it brilliantly. Mostly, though, that it's yours. That you find me worth your attention."

Alexander blinked at that. It was not a sentiment he'd expected, for all Geoffrey - and Lizzie, for that matter - had made it clear they delighted in his company. Not something he was used to hearing, certainly not spoken aloud, for all he knew Thesan and Isembard held the same sentiment. Not many others, though he'd enjoyed more suppers with Cyrus and Mabyn, and sometimes others of their closer circles, in the past year. It was still uneven ground, though, the sort of cliff face he expected to crumble under his feet at any moment.

Geoffrey shifted under his hand. "Got lost in your own head, then?" His voice was gentle now, the one he used for birds and horses. He never talked down to them, like some people did, certainly never yelled. "Come back here, Lord of the Oasis."

It was not something he'd expected to hear from Geoffrey's lips, one of Set's epithets. His eyes widened, and then he found Geoffrey grinning at him. "Both of us know how to use a library. Though I will beg your instruction on the implications of various of the others. I am not entirely sure which apply, especially when some refer to virility and some decidedly do not." Geoffrey shifted his hand to cup Alexander's cheek. "Which means learning more of you, as well. How you are."

Alexander let out a long, slow breath, feeling it almost turn into a whistle. "How, then, Golden One?"

"It is the land magic you love in me most. No, let me put that better." Geoffrey shifted, beginning to stretch out on his back now. "You love me in many ways, as I love you. But in the moment, we are interested in our shared lady, how the brush of her magic is in my blood, all the flourishing potential waiting to unfurl." He reached down to stroke himself, the dressing gown still nominally covering him. "Skin to skin, touching, rocking. See how that goes, and what you wish to explore."

He reached his hand back, then, to check he could reach the lubricant on the side table, and then brought his fingers back to touch Alexander's arm. "Will you?"

Alexander let out a breath. He didn't know what he felt in the moment, except that he wanted to go forward, not halt or go backward. That this was, in its way, an oasis, a space outside the ordinary, where more primary matters ruled. Water. Magic. Life. Everything else could be set aside. When he nodded once, Geoffrey beamed at him, entirely sunny, and then shrugged out of the dressing gown, leaving an expanse of pale skin spread out against the darker bedcover.

Alexander pushed himself upright, then after a brief hesitation, loosened the belt of his own dressing gown and stretched out against Geoffrey's side. He couldn't quite remove it, nor could he face something far more explicit about all their skin touching, not yet. But he pushed up on one elbow, watching and considering the man beside him. Bar the scars, a few bumps that suggested a broken bone or two in younger days, the man was in fine physical condition. In an aesthetic sense. He set his hand, palm over Geoffrey's heart, fingers not quite touching the edge of the scar tissue.

He fancied he could feel the heartbeat. Certainly he could feel the rise and fall of Geoffrey's chest, little uneven breaths. When he met Geoffrey's eyes, he could see the openness, the way he wasn't quite panting, but he had given himself over utterly to the sensations now.

"I could do anything." Alexander felt it out. "You'd let me."

"Oh, yes." Geoffrey let out a slow sigh, like he was melting. "You don't mind looking at me?"

"Mind is not the word. Are you actually vain?" Alexander hadn't quite considered that possibility before, but as Geoffrey's eyes crinkled up, he was sure he'd hit on it. "You are."

"I value my mind a great deal. But there is something in 'mens sana in corpore sano'. Not all the awful muscular Christianity that I gather was quite a thing for the more ardently Victorian of the country, and our American cousins." The non-magical community, then. "But the Greeks and Romans had that right. I think better when I am active physically. And the riding does do fine things to a man's body."

Alexander snorted, but he let his hand wander down that chest, then across to cup the hip, angling to avoid more energetically masculine parts, for the moment. "Riding. Walking. Falconry. Whatever you get up to in other bedrooms than this. I'm fairly sure you must swim, when you get the chance. You have the shoulders for it."

Geoffrey shifted one in a little arch of movement that was half vanity and half amusement. "Do you like them?"

"It is your shoulder, so yes. It is also an aesthetically pleasing shoulder, but I do not necessarily wish to touch those." Alexander sucked in a breath, and then let his eyes and his hand shift, moving to brush against arousal. "And this."

That brought a far less subtle response, a groan and an arch of hips, quickly moderated so they didn't rise off the bed. "Tease." Geoffrey's voice was entirely amused. "Please. Tease more, if you'd like. Explore. Whatever you wish. Be welcome to my lands and all they hold. Be welcome to me, and all I hold."

The double emphasis made Alexander swallow hard, his fingers closing against sensitive skin, though not around Geoffrey's shaft, then opening again as he looked to meet Geoffrey's gaze. "You shouldn't. You don't know what I'll do."

"Nothing I don't want." His certainty was absolute, and nothing Alexander could think of to say seemed likely to shake it. They held there, neither of them doing more than breathing shallowly, before Geoffrey moved one of his legs. "Come embrace me, do. Stretch out against me, rock, feel the magic through my skin, explore all the ways you want to."

It wasn't begging; it wasn't pleading. It was laying out a

path, like a climb to one of the ancient tors, even the long climb up the mountain path to Dinas Emrys itself. One began, one climbed, one became more in the process.

Alexander nodded once, fumbling to rearrange. All his grace seemed to have deserted him, but finally he was above Geoffrey, bracing on one elbow to spare the younger man his weight. Geoffrey had bent up one knee, making space for Alexander's hips and body, putting them so close. Alexander could feel that desire, the way Geoffrey wanted to move and wasn't, the same way he could feel the breath and the magic that were pulling them onward together.

"Kiss me. Know me. Move against me, however you wish. I will follow your lead." Geoffrey was purring now, entirely sure of himself, and that confidence did more to move Alexander than anything else could have. He shifted the angle of his arm, then bent to kiss. It began slow and gentle, but it didn't stay that way.

Geoffrey held back, as long as he could, but Alexander could feel his hips rocking, the way Geoffrey was pressing up against him, a counterpoint to the kiss. Bass line and melody, with the hands forming the inner harmonies between the two. All warmth and timbre, not sterile purity, the sounds of violas and oboes, horns and timpani.

Alexander got lost in it. Every time he thought he might surface, something pulled him in again. It was only the sixth or seventh time that Alexander managed to get his eyes open. He watched the utter bliss on Geoffrey's face, realising Geoffrey was tremblingly close to a climax. If this were a ritual, and it was a ritual, wasn't it, the release was needed to build to something else.

He managed, somehow, to get a hand up to cup Geoffrey's cheek, to growl one command. "Show me." For a timeless breath, he didn't think Geoffrey had heard, was sure it wouldn't be enough, and then Geoffrey shattered beneath him. He rocked up, head thrown back, utterly given over to the pleasure like any Maenad in the wilderness. Alexander could feel the urgent jerks of his hips, three, five times, and then the explosion of liquid and need and heat between them.

Alexander saw flashes of the magic, sparks of verdant green and the lighter shoots of spring and new buds. Sparkles of blue, of gold, like the magic was flinging itself, the sort of thing he'd seen in only a handful of rituals. He wanted to gather it up, to dance among it, to hold it forever. He knew - all his training and long experience told him - that letting it flow, riding through it, was the only way.

It was only as Geoffrey was beginning to catch his breath, to focus again, that Alexander realised that somehow, somewhere in there, he'd become hard as well. Eager. He could feel the blood rushing to his own desire, and he had no idea what to do with it. Oh, intellectually, certainly, but it was now an entirely different question.

Geoffrey's hand moved to press against his back. "Will you fill me?" Again, it wasn't a plea, it wasn't Geoffrey as a supplicant. Certainly not submissive or passive, what ridiculous words for someone in this moment. For a fleeting second, Alexander couldn't help but think of all the spaces in ritual that gestured at this and failed to encompass the mystery of it. He nodded, his chin jerking, and then Geoffrey was stretching his arm back, reaching for the oil.

Perhaps he'd turned some magic to that, as well, because the bottle didn't spill, didn't tumble. Geoffrey was pouring it into his hand, as much as would fill, then adding. "Show me. Let me feel you."

He knew what to do, and his mind felt split now, the way one part of him still took each step like it was an element of the ritual. The things one did so the next piece would go well. Precaution, preparation, prayer. He stroked the slickness onto himself, shifting to do so, and as he moved, Geoffrey rearranged, both knees bent on either side of him now.

The new position, he'd done nothing quite like it before, knees bent so he might find his mark, but unable to look directly. For one thing, he wanted to watch Geoffrey's face too much, for all he was shy of Geoffrey seeing his own. A moment later, there was a hand brushing against his wrist, a murmured "May I?" When Alexander nodded once, Geoffrey's hand was guiding him, an absurdly intimate touch. It felt good, but not with the same urgency Geoffrey had shown.

Then, he was pressed against heat, intimately touching, feeling where he was supposed to be. Geoffrey managed a breathy, "Please." the first time he'd asked, the first time he'd begged, making his own want clear. Alexander closed his eyes for a moment, long enough for one breath, then he fixed himself on watching Geoffrey's face and began to press in.

No one's description had been remotely sufficient. Heat and tightness, certainly, but no one had found words for the quality of it, the way it could not be denied. This man, here, beneath him, was permitting this, making it possible. Giving of himself in a way that could have shattered them both. Would, perhaps. He rocked back and forth, finding more depth, almost slipping out, over and over again. It was like the rolling piano of one of the great sonatas of Chopin, feeling the thrumming in his body and his magic.

Then, almost without realising it, he was fully inside. Geoffrey moaned openly, loudly, the kind of sound that changed the world around him. His hand had fallen to his stomach, the other fisted on the bed beside him. Then those stormy blue eyes focused on Alexander again, and he was breathing in rolling sighs. "Oh, oh, yes."

It was a different kind of pleasure than before. Different for Geoffrey, in so many ways, Alexander could tell that much. Different for him, as well, as he began tentatively to begin to roll his hips, and pull back. A dozen shifts, and he began to have a sense of how far he could move. Geoffrey's legs came up around his hips, knees brushing against skin, then claiming him.

This was beauty. This was the deep magics. This was his blood beating in his ears, and the fugue of Geoffrey's sighs and moans, repeating and changing, developing as they moved together, as Alexander found a pace he could keep to.

Most of all, it was the bloom of the land magic. How he could touch it, now. How he was one with it, in a way that he hadn't felt except during his Council trial. It felt churlish, for a moment, to think of that when there was a living man here, but then the green magic swirled up and pulled him down. He knew, in a way he could not argue with, that it was neither one nor the other, but all of those things, tangled together. That this was as transcendent an experience for Geoffrey as it was for him.

It lasted forever, and it lasted no time at all. Alexander could feel his thrusts speeding up, reaching ever onwards, the way that the green magic unfurled and unfurled through the early summer. How the light was endless, how the waters nourished everything from deep aquifers below and rain above. How the world opened, and everything was possible.

Then he could feel everything building, a herd of galloping horses, a rushing onwards he could not - did not wish to - slow and stop. Geoffrey was made of gasps and whimpers, full of pleasure, his skin drenched with sweat. His own shaft pressed hard against Alexander's stomach, the slickness making it slide. Geoffrey's thighs pulled him close and tight, refusing to let him retreat too far, just that endless depth and warmth.

Then Geoffrey tightened around him, a quiver at first, then a series of clenches that drew shouts out of him and drove Alexander to a last urgent flurry, hips driving and seeking. He felt it overtake him, a rush of blood and magic and trust, as he exploded inside Geoffrey's body, grunting each time his body's demands drove him to more.

When the last of it finally let them collapse, Alexander whimpered against Geoffrey's shoulder. One arm went around him, a leg lowered, then another, and then there was another arm, letting him weep and shiver and mourn what had just slipped away. They lay like that until Alexander's heat had turned to clamminess, until his hip reminded him of old aches, until he was too shy to move or look.

Lips brushed against his hair. "Rest. Be." Being understood nearly brought him to tears again, but he burrowed his head against that warm and steady shoulder for at least a minute or two.

Finally, he managed, "You?"

"Utterly splendid." The warmth in that voice, the total contentment of it, made Alexander lift his head. Geoffrey was, in truth, glowing now. His hair, his skin, his eyes, all held the illumination of the most potent rituals, though it was fading slowly as Alexander watched. Geoffrey lifted his now free hand to peer at the skin, then brushed Alexander's shoulder. "You too."

It was true, there was gold there when he lifted his own

hand, and the warmth of copper. Living metal, sun-kissed, vitality and strength and shining blessings. He met Geoffrey's eyes again, unsure what to do now.

"Blanket, please. Let us rest. Talking later." As Alexander managed that much, some of it through sheer force of magic and will to get a corner of the cloth in his grip, Geoffrey snuggled in against him. "Warm. Best."

SUMMER SOLSTICE

YTENE, JUNE 25TH

In the end, Alexander had been given plenty of time to think. In the middle of May, Cyrus had sent him on a three-week tour to America. Near a week each way by sea, and five days of a portal trip each evening, crossing the eastern seaboard. The goal was to get a new set of more secure magical journals into various necessary hands. The people from the West Coast had, thankfully, come to meet him at the largest of the gatherings on a magical estate just outside of Baltimore.

It was not difficult work, and it was in fact the sort of Council work that Alexander liked almost best. Figuring out how to talk people round to what made sense, what would make things easier in the rapidly approaching future.

And he'd had a chance to shore up some personal connections, spread the reach of their nest of experts a little further into America. A couple of quiet conversations, passing along a bound book that would allow ready private communication. The small things that nagged at him that might mean something bigger later.

But the travel meant he had time to sort out his feelings about what they'd done. He wrote to Geoffrey and to Lizzie every day, little humorous sketches of his travels and his meetings, the various regional meals. He wrote less often to Thesan and Isembard. That was more that they were also busy with the end of term and he knew they'd both fret about replying promptly. When they did write, it was with snippets of the latest and largely harmless student antics.

He did not get back to Albion until five days before Solstice eve. It was a near thing, too. He'd almost missed the *Citrine*'s departure. Every bit of those five days was filled with what he'd been planning and hoping for.

Solstice eve found him up in the top of the Keep, the room kept for the trials. It wasn't forbidden to be up there, outside of when the enchantments were set for a challenge. People just didn't. It was scrupulously and eerily clean, even in the corners. Alexander had set up a padded pallet to rest on, a table he could use from the floor, and a small shrine.

Not those things he offered at home, but simple ones. An oil lamp, a pitcher of clear water and three bowls to pour it into. Fresh flowers, cut from Ytene's gardens that morning without seeing anyone other than the gardener. A bottle of excellent wine, and more water to sustain him, as well as cider from Thesan's home.

When he'd told Cyrus what he'd intended, the broadest outline of it, Cyrus had offered to make bread. That meant there was a single gorgeous loaf to offer and three smaller rolls for him to eat, with cheese and mustard and crisp pickled cucumbers. A dozen things, from people who cared for him, as well as books and paper he hoped he'd not need to keep him occupied.

As twilight felt, he lit the oil lamps and the candles, setting them carefully on the stonework. He placed himself in the centre of the room, to quiet his mind and just be in the space. He hadn't known what he'd expected. He'd honestly tried not to have expectations.

He didn't exactly have answers when dawn came, but he had drifted through the night. Not sleeping, not awake, not here in this room, not elsewhere. Somewhere in the middle of all of those. There were rolling images of the land in his mind, places he knew were glowingly tended, then those that needed attention. Some he recognised, others he sketched, a few he heard their names, as if hearing a conversation just behind him, over his left shoulder. Always the left, and he was sure there was some reason for that.

Lady Herrick, she'd been doing a fine job with the land, after her husband's death, as regent for their son. He got a flash of something about Lord Knapton, in the southern half of the New Forest. Nothing that was a necessity now, but some faint worry.

More than that, though, he felt a flicker in his mind of several of the newest to take over the land magic. Over in Trellech, Pelson was doing well. His magic came through clear and strong, despite all the worries there had been about him from less open-minded sources. But Lord Masters was, well, anything but masterful. His tie to it was a thin thread, near to snapping. Alexander would need to confirm that, some way, and then pass it along to someone. Mabyn, maybe, or no. He was the type to do badly with an older woman.

And there was Lady Irving, who'd inherited rather younger than expected, and he wondered if she were being bullied about by someone in her extended family. He'd definitely have to mention that to Mabyn. And possibly Rhoda or Silvia.

Ytene, now, that was shining. He didn't think it was just his personal connection there, but there was a shimmer to it, a glow. The ruddy good health and abundance, he could see that in several other spots. Kent, near Veritas, that wasn't a surprise either. Arundel didn't have that shine, but he hadn't expected it would. Garin was competent but not passionate, and he was sure now that made a larger difference than they'd realised. Lady Martin-Baddock was doing well by her land, though. That was starting to have the same shimmer, after near a decade of hard work to repair things.

He wouldn't assume the truth of it, not yet. He would check, or get others he trusted to do so. But he thought that was a gift. It wasn't the transcendence of the second of May, and it wasn't meant to be. This was something deeper and heavier, like a map on thick parchment rolling out before him. No, more like the tapestries at Ytene, where they'd been tended and restored, as the land was tended and restored, the new threads woven expertly with the older ones.

He made his offerings, closing his eyes briefly when he bowed his head in prayer. When Alexander looked up again, the offerings were gone, leaving a clean plate and empty cups and bowls, except for a single white Gallica rose, sitting on the plate. Not surprising, given that was Richard III's own badge, he who had established the Council. But much easier to tend and admittedly more subtle than a white boar.

The formalities, the next day, were much as he'd expected. Cyrus and Mabyn led the patterns in the dancing, as they always did. Alexander had asked Thesan to partner him, as they'd done a number of times now. It spared him the more complex negotiations with one of the unattached women on the Council about status and rank, and besides, they always had more men than women. Thesan didn't fuss at him, she did her part with competence, and she followed his lead unstintingly when it came to the ritual magics.

Two days later, on the twenty-third, his world had pivoted again. He knew he needed to talk to Geoffrey about it, but it took him five more days to even begin to grasp what had happened. How Cyrus had given him permission to remake the world, to reform what was hollow and let it soar again. How Cyrus had followed his lead, trusted him, as simply and complexly as Geoffrey had.

Alexander could not have done that work two years ago. To be honest, he probably couldn't have done it a year ago. Not until this most recent May. He couldn't have done what was needed, or what he was made for.

And so, finally, he made his way out to Ytene on the Sunday, when the last of the Midsummer Fair was wrapping up. He knew Geoffrey and Lizzie had obligations there, and weren't expected back until just before supper. Alexander stretched out for a nap on the chaise in his sitting room, glad to be somewhere where the land was happy and glowing and also settled.

Over supper, they caught up on the easier topics, flitting from local gossip to the bits of Alexander's trip he hadn't bothered to write about. It flowed smoothly, and Lizzie was particularly sparkling about a handful of her own plots. She had a wicked humour about people's foibles, including her own. Cassie had chimed in, with a few details about the clothes and the people she'd made them for. It felt good to be back among them, the way he was easily included.

After they finished eating, Lizzie kissed his cheek and excused herself to catch up on her own reading. The implication was very much that she didn't particularly expect Geoffrey to join her at any point that night, but she did it very deftly.

Geoffrey walked him back up to his rooms. It wasn't until they were inside with the door closed behind them, that Alexander turned to him. "Are you shy all of a sudden?" The sense of it had been building through supper. It wasn't any one thing, or obvious. It was the way Geoffrey had watched him for a moment longer than usual, then glanced away. Or the way he'd shifted, uncertain, finding his place in the conversation over and over again, as if he were distracted. Only not by something other than Alexander. Something about Alexander himself.

Geoffrey blinked, then nodded crisply just once. "Yes." Just that one word, then, more cautious, "You?"

"Changed. By May, and by things since." Alexander took pity on him. "Come, let's get comfortable. This will be a bit in the telling."

"This, whatever it is, before your trip?" Ah, there it was. Geoffrey was feeling out the priorities.

It took only a moment's consideration. "Yes." Alexander was sure of it. They'd work backward, this time, rather than forward. He wasn't going to tell Geoffrey all the details, but enough of the outline. What it meant, what had been possible, that was what Geoffrey needed to know.

They settled on the bed on their sides, in shirtsleeves with their ties discarded with their jackets. Geoffrey was leaning on his good arm, Alexander had a beginning. "You know that I went up to the challenge chamber on Solstice eve, of course. That went well. It was timeless. It helped."

"But that was not the whole of it." Geoffrey had shifted to rest his hand lightly on Alexander's wrist, as if he could read volumes through his fingers.

"No. Two days after solstice, I went up again. With Cyrus. I asked him." Alexander swallowed hard. "He let me be Set's hands in the world." He watched Geoffrey, to see how much of that made sense to him, and he could hear the inhale, see the way his eyes widened.

Then, amused and fascinated, Geoffrey said, "The Keep is still standing, yes? I'd have heard."

"Oh, yes. Better than ever, in fact." Alexander shook his head, still in awe. "I - it's not mine to tell. It's mine in trust. You don't mind." It was a statement, not a question, but he still had to check.

Geoffrey was quick to shake his head. "Not at all. I understand your commitments, and how deep they run. And I respect them. But whatever you can tell me, I will gladly listen."

Alexander nodded, and settled a little more on the pillow, relaxing now they were in the meat of it. "It was like filling up all the empty spaces, all the spots no one had tended, for years. Decades. Centuries, maybe. Time didn't make much sense for a bit in there."

"And now it's better." Geoffrey seemed certain of this.

Alexander exhaled. "Better. And I am better." He looked up, then said, "Cyrus let me, with all that means. He didn't know what I was going to do, but he trusted me to do what was needed, and gave it his all." Alexander swallowed hard. "I couldn't have done that before May. Before the year before that. I couldn't have gone forward. I would have been certain it was a trap or trick, one more way for him to gain power over me."

There was a silence, just Geoffrey's fingers slipping into his, delicately as he turned the pages of his rarest books. "And you could." Soft, breathy, full of the same wonder that Alexander had felt then, and since.

The thing to do was nod and shift to kiss Geoffrey gently, to make clear the way Alexander treasured what he'd been given, and so unstintingly. And what it meant, even if he was still getting his head around that. After a span of time, Alexander didn't bother counting, when both of them had settled, he cleared his throat. "Working back from that. My trip."

"I was a tad worried for a little. I was certain I was still fully in your affection, but the journal wasn't the place to talk about many things. Much as I - both Lizzie and I - enjoyed the stories you told. And she - well, she said as much at supper - delighted in the fact you included her."

"Of course I would." Here again Thesan and Isembard had been a model for what decent people who cared about other people did. Though gods only knew how Isembard had learned it. "Mother was very clear about manners." He said it, a little teasingly, for all it was true, then softened. "But also, I enjoy Lizzie's good humour. I certainly do not want her annoyed at me. For my sake, as well as hers."

That got a laugh. "Well. True enough." Geoffrey tilted his head. "You have some further things to say? About how we go forward?"

"First, how long were you actually drunk on the magic? It was a trifle hard to tell." That had been rather on his mind the last few days, because he was certain he'd be drunk on his own for a good few weeks, at least.

Geoffrey laughed, and that eased things. "Enough to

need to be so cautious? A fortnight. A month before it fully faded, as Lizzie counts it. Or as fully as it was going to. Now it's just summer, and that is also glorious and intoxicating in all the good ways." He did not actually twirl in place, but he might as well have. "Go on, do."

"My thoughts on the journey, then. And then a conversation I had with Thesan, just before Solstice. That has, um, bearing on you."

"My." That had a little arch of amusement in it, Geoffrey relaxing into the new topic properly. "Do I dare ask? The journey and your thoughts, I suppose, first. They are more directly of interest to me, I suspect."

Alexander chuckled. They'd get to that misconception in due course. "I had quite a lot of time on both legs of the voyage. The other passengers were not very much to my conversational taste." Three widows who clearly thought Alexander would be a grand catch, even if he were reputed to be dangerous. Two people on the trip out and four on the trip back, who he'd had previous Council dealings with, telling them off and saving them from themselves. None recently, but it made an impression.

And then the usual range of drinkers and gamblers and people made more of damaging wit than sustaining and interesting thought. All of whom could do as they wished, but that didn't mean Alexander had to be around them while they did it. His patience had been fraying, the past year and more, in watching people refuse to admit to what was hovering in the none to distant future.

"May Day, the second. It was..." No, he didn't have words for it again.

Geoffrey waited through the silence that followed, then cleared his throat. "May I say something, and see where it gets us?"

"Go on, then." Alexander inhaled, taking his time, suddenly worried. Worry breaking through the bliss of his recent magic, like sun through clouds.

"Have you noticed how the land is flourishing? More than usual. You will have to trust my judgement and Lizzie's, but you saw last year. This is more. More fluidly, more freely, more abundantly. There's already talk about the local farms taking the top prizes at the harvest faire. Largest marrow, best canning, all that sort of thing. A sweetness, where there should be sweet, a resilience where that's needed. A spark to it all, like bees humming and dancing over their honey."

"And you think..." Alexander couldn't quite finish that sentence. "I had noticed something, but I wasn't sure if it was my bias in the way."

"I would, I admit, very much like to repeat the process next May, at least. If you are willing. I'm quite sure it won't work if you're not, even beside the fact that I'm not willing if you're not willing." Geoffrey blinked up at him, shy again now.

That logic made Alexander snort, relax, and lean back. "It changed the stars around us. And something deep in me, but I am. I remain myself. I can appreciate the thing, without wanting it. Does that make sense? Except in a very occasional circumstance."

"Well, rearranging the stars - besides being unkind to the astronomers of our mutual affection - is rather exhausting, isn't it? I might be up for more than once in a season, but perhaps not so many as all that, even if you were inclined. So we seem remarkably well matched, if for different reasons."

"And you take all that burgeoning springtime lust to your marriage bed."

Geoffrey spread his hands. "Well, yes. That being an entirely suitable place for it, and Lizzie does have certain expectations." He tilted his head. "Do you know that Jewish law dictates that a husband has obligations about his wife's sexual satisfaction? She thinks it entirely sensible."

Alexander rubbed his face. "I did, yes, but how on earth did we end up here." He swallowed. "So you don't mind that - it's not that I'm interested in you, that way?"

"Give me a moment." Geoffrey considered, closing his eyes to focus, taking his time. Alexander appreciated that about him. Too many fools rushed in, when rushing wasn't actually required. From the first, he'd appreciated Geoffrey's mastery of time. When he spoke again, Geoffrey was quiet, that deep intensity entirely present now. "There aren't names for any of this, are there? I mean, even in the poorly constructed polyglot mess we've got as it is. May I lay out what I understand?"

Alexander nodded slowly. Whatever Geoffrey said would be informative. Probably not so uncomfortable he'd want to flee.

"So, then." Geoffrey stretched out on his side. "You had a childhood that did not grant you near as much affection as you should have had. Care, yes, attention to your skills, yes. Better than many children, in a number of ways. Then you were brought into a knot of families for whom affection is, shall we say, generally among the least of their virtues."

Alexander thought of the suppers with the elder Fortiers and their associates, and grunted in mixed amusement and memory. "Just so."

Geoffrey nodded once. "And then you were in the Council, and they - most of them, anyway - wanted to make you more like them. In ways that comforted them. Where you, my other soul, are made for afflicting the comfortable."

"It is a danger to leave you alone with research materials. For the record." Alexander shook his head, but he was amused now. "You are also accurate. As you know."

"I will not lie to you, either." Geoffrey shrugged. "I don't know how much of your preferences - or how they run in different directions than most people - are a result of all that. It doesn't matter, and there's certainly no reason to make it into an intellectual parlour game. What matters to me is that you have those things you will welcome. Besides treasuring your company, I do enjoy giving you things. I hope there are some places where I may let my affection show, beyond discussions of books and archaic ritual forms, and whatever else I might think of along those lines."

"Those are quite welcome, yes." Alexander let out a long breath. "And I do - the leaning and all that. The casual touch. I didn't think I'd find it comfortable, but I missed it, out on the ocean."

"Well, then. See, there we are. And if you would be interested in bedding me again next May to assist in ongoing well-documented magical research," Geoffrey grinned suddenly, "Well, I would be quite pleased. Even if it's not exactly a properly controlled experiment design."

"The scientists of our acquaintance would at least be amused. If we told them. Well. Thesan and the Penelopes, anyway. I'm not sure about your alchemist."

"He - oh, I hadn't told you? He and Bertram are getting on like a house on fire. Usually not actually literally, thankfully. Bertram moved into his digs last month rather than just staying over half the time. I have not dreamed of inquiring about their bedroom arrangements, but they're both doing well and coming up with dozens of new things on the regular. Very much making our efforts to get Bertram loose of value to those who have these little requests of me."

Alexander laughed. "You'd not mentioned, no. Well." He let out a long breath. "So you do not mind that - while, yes, very occasional sex might be a thing I am willing for, it is not a thing I am ever likely to seek out. Desire of my own accord, that way. Or, I don't know. The ways other people apparently have relationships. Anniversaries and what."

"Besides, we missed ours. You were on a ship, I'm fairly sure. Whichever day we actually count from, there being several options. With Lizzie, I do in fact count each of them, and with you, I had not, except as an intellectual amusement."

Alexander thought about asking how Geoffrey was counting, and then decided against it, at least for the moment. He shifted to settle more comfortably on his back. Now this particular bit of conversation was sorted, Geoffrey stretched out himself on his side, wriggling his fingers. "May I?"

"Yes." Admittedly, he liked Geoffrey asking every time. Not just for the obvious reasons, but because it meant he got to choose to say yes to it, every time. Alexander was, at this point, sure that was just as deliberate as the way Geoffrey trained his falcons. Once the hand was settled on his chest, there was a slight tap. "Yes, I know. I said two things."

"Thesan." Mind like a steel trap, for all Geoffrey often made it appear not to have one. Alexander smiled. Which had been, honestly, why he'd said it when he did, so Geoffrey would hold him to speaking about it.

"As you said? I hope there's not a problem?" Geoffrey was suddenly very much in earnest.

Alexander snorted. "Well. Not a problem for you. Not a

problem for her. I am less sure about me. Though it does raise the question of - I should tell them something." He went on. "She has figured out there is something between us. I mentioned her brother. I suppose it makes it easier to spot when people do not match up in the expected duets."

"We are rather something about the *Marriage of Figaro*, that whole bit about the number of voices you can have going at once, and still make sense." Geoffrey agreed. "And her brother lives with his wife, and another man, you said. Very happily."

"Yes." Alexander smiled. "They are quite welcoming, too. They host holiday suppers. Ones I actually want to be at, which is quite the trick." He then shrugged. "Anyway. Just before I left, Isembard was doing his patrols, and she and I were having a drink in their sitting room. She made it clear that she'd sorted that you and I feel a serious sort of way about each other, whatever label we might or might not put on that. The question was - well. Two questions."

"Presumably one is about what Isembard might know."

"Yes." Alexander laughed at the memory. "The other is - well. The other is about her being of Horse House, and better sorted there than I was to Fox. But also having two mentors, people she deeply loved and trusted, down to her core, who were both truly Foxes."

"My." Geoffrey leaned in. "How does that come out, then?"

"Thesan sat there, mild as could be, and pointed out that her current question was whether she told me straight out what she'd explained to Isembard, or whether she held out for a proper trade from me."

Geoffrey blinked, then he started laughing, collapsing until he was shaking against Alexander's shoulder. Alexander couldn't get an arm around him, so he reached over to pat that golden hair, but he agreed with the sentiment. After a rather long stint of laughter fading and beginning again, Geoffrey finally managed, "What did she do? What did you do?"

"Like sensible people, I agreed to give her a full and proper explanation of something to be determined at some later date. So long as it did not conflict with my other oaths. At which point she laid out what she'd told Isembard. He apparently spent the better part of a month bringing it up every time he had a chance, sorting through it. Probably best I was gone."

"And?" Geoffrey peered up.

"She noted he is still rather baffled by the wholly unfamiliar landscape he's found himself in with regard to me. Very happy, just still mapping it out, as she put it. Proper star charts aren't made in a day, to quote."

That made Geoffrey laugh again. Alexander felt, honestly, that the 'still drunk on land magic' still applied. "And you are comfortable with that?"

"I need to talk to Isembard about it, now they're done with term. That's my project for next week. Figuring out how and where, at least, even if we don't manage the actual discussion. I didn't explain our May revels, mind. Just that you and I are firmly entangled, now."

"You know you're welcome to bring him out here. Chat, we can amuse Thesan, or you know, just let her loose in the library. And then he can see us together, in that mode, after. If that would help."

Alexander contemplated. "Honestly, it might. The feel of the land would be a help, I'm sure. He's by far more attuned to Schola, especially these days, but he has a good native sense for it. Thank you."

"Let us consult Lizzie and various others tomorrow

morning about good dates on our end. Though I don't think we have anything immutable in our diaries for the fortnight. I wasn't sure when you'd be back, among other reasons."

"Also, it is summer, and you wish to lounge around soaking it in." Alexander ventured the teasing and watched Geoffrey light up at it. Not quite actually, but near enough. His praise, he was finding, could bring that near the surface very quickly. "You do like it when I approve of you, don't you?"

Geoffrey let his eyes close, entirely trusting now. "You tell me the truth. You have high standards. If I have met them..." He shrugged his free shoulder. "It is very good to hear that." The last came down to a bare whisper.

Alexander shifted just enough to press his lips to Geoffrey's hair. "It is also good to be heard. To have your welcome in all its forms."

〜

Read on for the author's notes for both *Best Foot Forward* and *Intimacies of the Seasons*.

Reviews are a tremendous help to authors, and I deeply appreciate reviews wherever you got the book, on Good-Reads, or recommendations shared on social media.

My newsletter is the best place to hear about upcoming books, including a novella focusing on Alexander in America in 1938, out in the spring of 2023 called *Nocturnal Quarry*. (And I'm not done with either Alexander or Geoffrey yet!) Read on for more about them and about upcoming books.

Author's Notes

Thank you so much for joining me on this trip from Albion to Austria to Germany, and into an entirely different period of history. *Best Foot Forward* is the first of a seven book series exploring World War 2, the land magic, and the many kinds of relationships we have in our lives. Keep an eye on my website or sign up for my newsletter (https://www.celialake.com/newsletter/) for all the details of new and upcoming releases!

My particular thanks to my editor, friend, and other half of my brain, Kiya Nicoll. This book comes from a comment Kiya made while editing *Eclipse* (in chapter 14), saying: "I now sort of want the buddy cop story in which Alexander and Carillon team up to utterly destroy a munitions smuggler." Every one of my early readers for *Eclipse* agreed. I'm so glad I figured out how to write something that has that spirit. Even if a number of details are not quite the same!

Also, an additional thanks to Maren Richter, who kindly provided some corrections to the German in these pages. Much appreciated!

A number of the characters in this book appear in my other books (and will likely continue to appear). My authorial wiki at bit.ly/celia-lake-wiki has the most up to date information. Geoffrey Carillon is thus far introduced in *Ancient Trust* (1922, when he inherits the title from his brother, available via my newsletter), has his romance with Lizzie in *Goblin Fruit*, marries her in *On The Bias*. Alexander is a secondary character in *Eclipse*.

This book references a tremendous amount of music, thanks to Alexander and Geoffrey both having a long-standing passion for it. Albion (and the magical community) of course have their own composers. For example, Alexander references Reticelle and the Illusionist school of composers in chapter 1. However, for most of the book, it's the non-magical composers who matter.

There's also a story about the music in this book. I started music lessons when I was very small, and continued them up through a music major in college (focused on theory and composition, though at various points I've sung, and played piano, flute, bassoon, and folk harp). My last semester in college, however, I had a completely destructive class. It was supposed to be a conducting class, but instead, much of our grade depended on repertoire and "drop the needle" tests, where we'd have to identify a given piece we'd studied from 15 seconds of music from anywhere in the work, and give the title, movement, key, instrumentation, and other details.

We had three Beethoven symphonies on every exam as well as eight or so other pieces, so I spent a lot of that semester in 1998 (which was after portable CD players, but before any kind of streaming music access) walking around going "It's the third movement of Beethoven something, but I have no clue which one." It destroyed my ability to listen to most classical music for decades (aka between 1750 and 1900 or so, in Western Europe).

Somehow, Alexander and Geoffrey dragged me back into listening to it - into being able to listen to it - in a way I never expected.

And so, I put together a playlist of the music referenced in the book, chapter by chapter. You can find it on my website at https://www.celialake.com/music-of-best-foot-forward/. There are also links from the book page for Best Foot Forward on my website at celialake.com, as well as my authorial wiki at bit.ly/celia-lake-wiki.

That quite long post includes explanations of the pieces and their implications or why they were chosen. The two particular concerts Alexander and Carillon attend in Vienna and Berlin are both actual performances with some complex and fascinating history behind them. Other pieces reference composers of the day, particular styles of music, or give you a glimpse at the intricate insides of Carillon's head.

Normally, I listen to instrumental music that sets a mood when writing, but once I started writing *Best Foot Forward*, I'd listen to whatever segment of the playlist was relevant to what I was writing or editing. So for this book, you can listen to exactly what I was listening to! Check out the music post for all the details about specific pieces, though I'll mention a couple of the concerts here as well.

∾

With the music sorted, let me work through the book in chronological sequence. It's really the only way to keep anything in order here.

Chapter 1 : The book opens with a gala fundraising performance at the Trellech Opera House, the main large orchestral and choral performance space in Trellech, the largest magical city of Albion. Lizzie and Carillon deliberately lured Alexander by means of music, including a piece they had reason to suspect he'd find intriguing, **Hector Berlioz's *Les Troyens***, an epic French opera completed in 1863, but only performed in full for the first time at the 1890 performance that Alexander attended. Luise Reuss-Belce was a famous soprano of the period who sang Cassandre's role in that performance, and had recently retired in 1933 after a long career first as a singer and then as a voice teacher and opera director.

Chapter 2 : My background research for this book included reading up on the state of research into **gasses and chemical warfare** in the 1930s. Not at all cheerful reading! I found *A Higher Form of Killing: The Secret History of Chemical and Biological Warfare* by Robert Harris and Jeremy Paxman particularly helpful in putting a lot of different pieces into context. Especially helpful was learning that in the 1920s and 1930s, British and German research in these fields was rather more advanced than American research.

Chapter 3: Carillon references **Debussy's** music, and the way it uses different scales and tonal centers, including pentatonic scales, whole tone scales, and modes not commonly used in classical music of the period.

Chapter 4: I loved the chance to revisit some other **characters**. Alysoun and Richard have their romance in *Pastiche*, while Gabe and Rathna find theirs in *The Fossil Door*. Kate and Giles meet and fall in love in *Wards of the Roses*. Giles' guide dog is quite new to him - they only started being introduced in English-speaking countries in the early 1930s.

Chapter 6 : Carillon has spent a pleasant season in Vienna in the past, including a delightful interlude with an operatic soprano. ***Der Rosenkavelier*** had the advantage of being recent enough, first performed in 1911, that he'd not seen it on his extended stay in the city on his nominal Grand Tour in 1908. (While Carillon tended to prefer men for dalliance, the women he spent time with before Lizzie tended to be musicians dedicated to their art.)

The concert that **Bruno Walter** conducts is from March 10th, 1935. Comments on the playing style of the orchestra and Walter's conducting come from various reviews of the orchestra and online bios of Walter himself.

I couldn't resist a brief reference to **Roderick Sterling-Wise** here. The other artists are largely real people, but you can learn more about Sterling-Wise and his art in *Fool's Gold*.

Chapter 7 : First, setting any of this in Vienna is a nod to my maternal grandparents, who were living in a flat in Vienna in 1935. They'd been married about 9 months when the book takes place, and my mother was born in late 1936.

Naturally, I couldn't set a book in Vienna and not spend a little time in the **Prater**. It is one of the city's great parks, originally a hunting park for the emperor, then a public park with amusements ranging from cafes to performances to carnival rides. The **Ferris wheel** there is magnificent, and indeed built by Englishmen. Obviously, the perfect place for an entirely private conversation.

Alexander and Carillon both agree that **Dufay's *Nuper rosarum flores*** is a gem. It was written for the consecration of the duomo of Florence, and for many years it was thought to represent the architecture of the building in the structure of the music. (More recent research had looked at this and said, approximately, "Can you people even count?" because the numbers don't add up.)

Chapter 9 : Starting around 1846 (and the discovery of Neptune), there were a lot of theories about a **Planet X,** out beyond Neptune's orbit. X in this case stands for "unknown", not the Roman numeral ten. Pluto was discovered in 1930, and people thought it might be the Planet X. These days, Pluto is not considered a planet, and we still wonder about some massive planet out around the Kuiper Belt that affects orbits of objects we can see, even if we can't see that planet itself.

For a discussion of the **Schola houses** and how they play out for people, see *Eclipse* for more. In brief, Alexander was sorted into Fox, and as Carillon says late in the book, it might have been meant as a favour, but that doesn't mean it was. Alexander, by innate preference, is much better suited for Owl, or arguably for Seal. (Seal is the most liminal of the houses, and the one that tends to get people who don't fit societal assumptions in some ways).

Chapter 10 : I was delighted both to find historical records of the **weather in Berlin** in 1935, and that the weather was as awful as I wanted it to be for narrative purposes. Namely, several weeks of rain with bits of hail and downpour and other misery, keeping Alexander and Carillon indoors and around other people.

The **Berlin Zoo** is as described, thanks to surviving detailed maps. The "human zoo" was also an unfortunate reality, mostly made up of imported individuals from Africa and other far away countries put on display. The comment Carillon makes about a polar bear living in the Tower of London and being taken to fish in the Thames is entirely true. (And one of these days, I hope to write something that makes more of the history of the Tower of London menagerie.)

The music post linked earlier has more detail on the famous **Furtwängler concert on April 25th**, a particular political statement where Furtwängler agreed to conduct, and the German government wanted to make a point. He was in fact called back on stage seventeen times. In a later concert that spring, there's quite some chaos when he arranges to be unable to shake Hitler's hand (or to salute).

Chapter 11 : **Goethe, Shiller, and Schubert** are some of the foremost German creative minds of the 18th and 19th centuries. A nod, here without getting in too deep.

Chapter 12 : Having gone to a concert featuring Beethoven's Sixth and Fifth symphonies, played in that order, it's a natural starting point for the discussion here. And, as it turns out, the Fifth provides an excellent metaphor for the rest of that scene.

Chapter 14 : In the return to England, we have a bit of joyous expansive music (Mozart's **Jupiter symphony**, the 41st). Carillon got to know **Hippolyta FitzRanulf** in *Ancient*

Trust (a free novella, sign up for my newsletter to get a copy). She also appears in *In The Cards*.

Chapter 15 : Excavations in **Memphis** (the city in Egypt, once a capital city) had been done by the University of Pennsylvania. Memphis, like all Egyptian cities, had particular gods that it honoured above others, but the gods vary city to city. The Memphite Triad is Ptah, a crafting god, as well as Sehkmet and either Nefertem or the deified mortal Imhotep as their child. You can see more of Ibis in *Magician's Hoard* and *Chasing Legends.*

Chapter 16 : I have known for a very long time that Carillon had trained and hunted with **an eagle-owl** (Theodora), and had to give up flying her after the injury to his shoulder during the Great War. But I had not, exactly, articulated bits of this to myself until Kiya and I were chatting in February of 2022 as I was writing this. It honestly hadn't occurred to Kiya that I hadn't entirely twigged to the fact that Carillon kept walking into hunting parties carrying an eagle-owl, rubbing everyone's noses in the fact he's sorted into Owl House and not Fox House (as most people of his background are likely to be). Over and over. Repeatedly.

Brains are very odd things, is what I'm saying here. And so I had to give the joke and the resulting 'rolling on the floor laughing now' moment to Alexander.

Anyway, by the time of *Best Foot Forward* he has retired the **merlin** he began flying in 1922, named Helena, and now flies another merlin named for an empress, Hildegard. (In this case, named for one of Charlemagne's wives.) Merlins are absolutely tiny birds, and as noted, they are often considered a lady's bird.

Lady Juliana Berners is as described. Her Boke of St

Albans was published in 1486, just after the Pact and also in the very early days of the printing press, making it of interest to Alexander and Carillon for a variety of reasons. She also wrote what is considered to be the first work on fly fishing. (According to a friend, quite useful for the purpose, if you adapt for modern materials and restrictions on feathers from migratory birds.)

Chapter 17 : **Richard Haliburton** was a famous adventurer, widely considered to be gay - and certainly quite libertine and scandalous. Carillon's comments about not being a hypocrite in the nursery are rather telling about his and Lizzie's priorities as parents.

Enid Nesbit is a famous author of children's books that intertwine ordinary childhood adventures with magic.

Oxford University is of course itself. One of these days, I will write a book focusing on the Academy, the magical college tucked in among Oxford's many colleges. Those from Albion are part of one of the known colleges, but are part of additional tutorials in the Academy, attend lectures, and so on. (Giles Lefton is part of the Academy, from the teaching and research side, at this point in his life.)

Why Exeter College? It was my father's college - he did his Master's degree at Oxford, though not his BA or PhD. However, when I was looking for Exeter's reputation when Carillon was there (in the very early 1900s), I was delighted to discover it was the perfect fit. As mentioned later, Exeter undergraduates had a reputation for doing their work but also having an active life outside of academics. Perfect for scooting off to do some ritual magic or alchemy or what have you.

Chapter 18 : **The Scottish Play** is of course a reference to Shakespeare's *Macbeth*, called that by people who are a tad superstitious about that play's reputation. (And by most actors.) Carillon spends enough time moving in non-magical circles to have internalised that one.

The state of **laws about homosexuality in Germany** at this point is very much in flux in the spring of 1935. Up until the Nazis took power in 1933, gay communities and networks were flourishing in Germany, particularly in bigger cities. (And Berlin, in particular.) There was significant research on various related topics, and a significant number of fairly public organisations, social groups, and cultural events. Starting in 1933, Germany began to prosecute homosexual behaviour (and particularly gay men) under Paragraph 175, the part of the German criminal code that banned sexual relations between men.

This began ramping up even more after the arrest and execution of Ernst Röhm and others in June of 1934. This was partly about politics and power - Hitler saw Röhm as a threat. But it was also a chance for the more homophobic wing of the Nazi party to act. In late 1934 there were increasing arrests in gay bars and other gathering spots in Berlin and Munich, and by early 1935, 80 percent of the prisoners in concentration camps were there for alleged homosexuality. In June of 1935 (just after Alexander and Geoffrey leave Berlin), Paragraph 175 was amended to include two men looking at each other with lust or desire, or even fairly innocent physical conduct in some cases.

Chapter 19 : **Neu Venedig** or "New Venice" is a series of canals southeast of Berlin, designed as a spot for recreation and getting away from the city. The canals are more or less as described in the text, a network that sprawls out, with periodic docks.

Chapter 24 : This is me being incredibly geeky about a truly obscure bit of history. Phillips Academy **Andover** and Phillips Academy **Exeter** are two of the earliest boarding (private, in the US sense) schools in the United States. In fact, they predate the United States, since Andover was founded in 1778 and Exeter in 1781, both before the end of the American Revolutionary War in 1783. (They were founded by cousins, hence the similarity in names.)

Andover did indeed have secret societies beginning in the 1870s, complete with their own society houses. They continued up into the 1940s, when secret societies were banned first at Exeter and other peer schools, and then at Andover. (Exeter's societies never had their own houses, though.) The physical houses were later given over to other uses for the school.

Chapter 25 : One of the fascinating pieces about this book is looking at the different context Alexander comes from. In **Egyptian theology**, Set is a necessary part of the world, challenging the established order and destroying what is no longer working so it can be rebuilt. **The uninvoked serpent** Alexander references is the ultimate face of evil, threatening the ordered cosmos at its most fundamental level, eater of souls. He is sometimes called Apep or Apophis, and depicted as a serpent or sometimes crocodile.

Chapter 26 : The line about "Like one of the birds of prey - **beware the talons, the beaks, the wings.**" comes out of a video from a wildlife rehab vet that was circulating on Twitter as I was writing this. The vet is putting an owl coming out of anaesthesia (with plaster casts on its legs and talons) in a cage. He casually comments that you want to avoid the dangerous parts of the bird, the beak, the wings, the talons. On watching it, Kiya and I both went "So, well, the whole bird?" and started laughing a lot.

The line about "hand to hand is **holy palmers' kiss**" comes from Shakespeare's *Romeo and Juliet*, early in the play.

Chapter 27 : Kiya designed the **prayers Alexander says for Perry** for me, based on various sources. The ancient Egyptians believed that keeping the name alive mattered a great deal, and so prayers and monuments are key parts of both funeral practices, and day to day religious life.

Chapter 28 : The **wyrm** dripping fire and ice is a reference to one of the Norse creation myths, and quite suitable for their current geographical location.

You can learn more about **Rufus** in *Outcrossing*. He comes into his own under Carillon's wings, and he appears briefly in *Old As The Hills*, the second full-length novel in the Land Mysteries series (out in May of 2023).

The **Thomas Tallis motet *Spem in alium*** is written for 40 voices, and is a very complex piece. The details of Carillon **inheriting** that he refers to here are found in *Ancient Trust*.

Chapter 29 : Alexander mentions being in **Washington**, he was there for the Washington Naval Treaty. You can see more of his connections and adventures in the United States in the next book in the series, *Nocturnal Quarry*, a novella set in 1938. (It will be out in early 2023.)

This is also where we get into some obscure **astrolog-**

ical magical theory, also reflected in the chart on the cover. Both Carillon and Alexander are working on a theory of planetary influences, framing the structure of the ritual that's being planned to take advantage of the magical energies of the moment, and of the focus - Berthold, in this case.

The cover shows the chart as it was for that evening. (Keep an eye on my blog for more about the covers for this series.) Saturn is associated with limitations and boundaries, so useful for releasing Berthold from what binds him. Mars, as Carillon notes, is often very competitive if not outright aggressive. These are considered the two malefic or harsher planets in astrology, while Jupiter and Venus are benefics or blessings (so anchoring a rite that draws on those relationships might be helpful) especially when they're in the angle called a trine. A square, in astrological terms, is a challenging aspect but one that can also be illuminating about what's going on in a situation.

Carillon's investigation of the **goldwasser** - and his romance with Lizzie - are in *Goblin Fruit.*

Chapter 32 : **Alraunes** are just one piece of the **mandrake** lore. Mandrakes - as you may know from other fantasy works - are thought to scream when you pull them out of the ground. There's a lot of traditions about someone stuffing cotton wool in their ears, tying a dog to the mandrake, and luring the dog to pull the mandrake out. (This is not healthy for the dog.)

Because mandrakes are often shaped more or less like a person - head, two arms, two legs - they were often associated magically with all sorts of things. I drew on existing lore about alraunes in particular, which were thought to amplify magic to an extreme. The comments Alexander makes about what a skilled alchemist could do with one are in keeping with the lore. (A gas that would let people walk through fire, put an entire stretch of army to sleep or deeath, or hundreds of thousands of super soldiers who were impossible to injure or defeat.) Fortunately, alraunes and mandrakes suitable for that kind of magic are exceedingly rare.

Chapter 38 : **Aset** - also called Isis - is often depicted wearing a cloak of feathers. She is the queen of life and mother of magic, as Alexander says, with many images of her magic sweeping out from her and blessing the land.

Chapter 41 : My endless thanks to Kiya for Egyptian religious consulting throughout this book. **Horus and Set** have a tremendously complicated relationship throughout Egyptian myth and story. Sometimes they are very much allies, sometimes they are very much opposed. However, there is an understanding of the need for Set's difference, for the way he stands outside the structure and sees where it is weak or needs attention, that isn't present in nearly the same way in the Roman myth that Albion's upper classes favour in particular. Future books and stories will be getting into this a bit more (*Nocturnal Quarry* among them.)

Bawy is the name of the god formed when these two gods combine into one. It's a concept that goes badly into English, but is all about the way the two in this particular pairing are each other's souls, each other's mirrors, and how that makes many magics possible.

If you're curious about that **house party** when Geoffrey was injured, it is part of *Bound for Perdition*, out in February 2023.

〜

INTIMACIES OF THE SEASONS

I started writing Intimacies of the Seasons expecting it was going to be an extra that goes out to the mailing list. I didn't get very far in before I was certain it had to be part of the book itself, an extended epilogue following Alexander and Geoffrey through the next year of their lives.

(There are additional extras for *Best Foot Forward* though! Sign up for my newsletter to get them. I'll be sharing them over the winter as we move from 2022 into 2023, and they'll be available thereafter. They include Thesan and Isembard's side of the puzzle, as well as Benton deciding what he thinks about Alexander and his lordship's choices in the matter.)

Epithets are a common method of referring to the Egyptian gods or netjeru. Names have an incredible amount of power and magic in ancient Egypt, and using multiple epithets is a way to best describe the aspects of the deity you are addressing. Alexander takes great delight in the various epithets for Horus he applies to Geoffrey, and Geoffrey gets his own back eventually.

Dweller in his House is, in fact, referring not to Horus or to Set, but to Hetheru or Hathor, whose name literally means "House of Horus." She embodies joy, feminine love, and motherhood - though also sometimes very protectively. Obviously, it applies here to Lizzie, rather than Geoffrey.

1870 was in fact a particularly notable year for wines. It has to do with both a tremendous challenge and then weather blessing and challenging the wine. The challenge was phylloxera, insects that eat the roots and leaves, killing the vines. They were first discovered in the Rhone region in the 1860s, and by 1870 had destroyed about three-quarters of Europe's vines. The weather was a mixed blessing. An icy frost led to low yields, but the summer had very hot conditions, allowing the grapes to fully ripen.

Lady Martin-Baddock is the same person as Nora Martin from *The Hare and the Oak*. (She chose to add the familial surname to her own when she took on the title.)

Made for afflicting the comfortable is a perfect description of Alexander, and it comes from an old saying, "comfort the afflicted, afflict the comfortable". It has its origins in a humour piece (quite critical of the press) by Finley Peter Dunne in 1902, but it was picked up by newspapers as a goal in the following years.

The Marriage of Figaro is the root of an old set of apocryphal comments - seen in the Peter Shaffer script for *Amadeus* - about having too many notes. The counter-argument, however, is that opera has space for many voices at once, without automatically becoming cacophony.

Thank you again for joining me on this trip through Alexander and Geoffrey's lives. Again, if you'd like to read their earlier adventures, the current books about them include *Ancient Trust* (Carillon inherits the title in 1922, a novella available via my newsletter), *Goblin Fruit* (Carillon and Lizzie's romance in 1924), *On The Bias* (Benton and Cassie's romance, with Carillon and Lizzie as secondary characters, in 1925), and *Eclipse* (Alexander as a secondary character, in the 1924-1925 school year at Schola).

My authorial wiki (bit.ly/celia-lake-wiki) has pages, timelines, and maps that connect characters, places, and events in various ways. Please let me know if there's additional information that would be helpful to you.

Finally, let me leave you with a bit of a teaser about what's coming next! The Land Mysteries series has five novels and two novellas. The next book is a novella featuring Alexander in America in 1938, *Nocturnal Quarry*. It will be out in early 2023. The next novel, featuring Gabe and Rathna (previously seen in *The Fossil Door)* is set in 1939 and 1940. It's called *Old As The Hills* and will be out in May of 2023.

The first book in the Mysterious Arts series, *Bound for Perdition*, set in 1917, will be out in February of 2023, and it features Temple Carillon as a secondary character (with a brief appearance by Geoffrey). This series is exploring various art forms and magic during the Great War and into the 1920s.

The newsletter (https://www.celialake.com/newsletter/) and my social media accounts will have all the details about new and upcoming releases, and I hope to see you one of those places! Until then, happiest of reading to you.

Also by Celia Lake

The Land Mysteries Series

Best Foot Forward

Nocturnal Quarry

The Mysterious Charm Series

Outcrossing

Goblin Fruit

Magician's Hoard

Wards of the Roses

In The Cards

On The Bias

Seven Sisters

The Mysterious Powers Series

Carry On

The Fossil Door

Eclipse

Fool's Gold

The Hare and the Oak

Point By Point

Mistress of Birds

Charms of Albion

Pastiche

Sailor's Jewel

Other stories

Complementary

Winter's Charms (a novella collection)

Learn more about the world of Albion and future books at my website, celialake.com. Additional information linking characters, places, and timelines is available at bit.ly/celia-lake-wiki

Sign up for my newsletter to be the first to hear about future books and learn about fascinating bits of research. Happy reading!